MERMAID
MOON

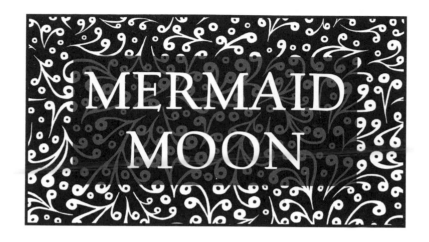

MERMAID MOON

SUSANN COKAL

CANDLEWICK PRESS

For Leslie Hayes

◆

This is a work of fiction. Names, characters, places, and incidents
are either products of the author's imagination or,
if real, are used fictitiously.

First edition 2020

Library of Congress Catalog Card Number pending
ISBN 978-1-5362-0959-4

19 20 21 22 23 24 DGF 10 9 8 7 6 5 4 3 2 1

Printed in Foshan City, Guangdong, China

This book was typeset in Centaur.

Candlewick Press
99 Dover Street
Somerville, Massachusetts 02144

visit us at www.candlewick.com

FSC
www.fsc.org

MIX
From responsible
sources
FSC® C124807

Fire leaves no history;
Air ever forgets;
Water washes away;
Land holds on too long;
Time is the measure of all.
                —*The Mermaids*

The moon lowers herself to draw the tide.

When she knew her time had come, she slipped from the quiet of her father's house to make her way down to the docks.

It wasn't easy. The pains came fast and hard, even at the start. In the light of a half-made moon, she stumbled in the familiar ruts and puddles of the path she'd raced down many times before. Each pain was an ember blazing from her belly to the tips of her fingers and toes; pain blinded her and stole her breath. Only force of will kept her on her feet and stealing toward the waterfront, the one place she knew — or hoped — she'd be safe.

Her body was ripping apart. She was being drawn and quartered like the worst kind of criminal, a thief or a murderer whose limbs were tied to four different horses and the horses then spurred in different directions. Blood sport. Something to think about as she both gasped for breath and tried to keep silent, because the worst thing she could do now would be to make a sound loud enough to wake her neighbors. If things were as bad as she thought they might be, the villagers would come after her with torches and sharp-tipped hoes. Her parents, grudgingly kind as they had been to this point, would lead the charge.

Stars swaddled the sky while she sweated through her linen chemise and into her coarse wool dress. She fixed her eyes on that half pie of moon as her knees buckled under an especially terrible pang. She clutched her belly and pushed herself against the streaky wall of a butcher shop. It held her up as she smothered a groan. The butcher and his family slept above the shop; she shouldn't wake them.

The smell of her blood mixed with ripe meat was nauseous.

Pain is thirsty work, even in a cool month when green things are just beginning to take on summer hues. She wished for a barrel full of rainwater but instead found a pebble to pop into her mouth, and she sucked to draw the water from inside her own body.

In all her eighteen years she had never felt so alone as tonight, under the thick white stars. But soon she wouldn't be alone anymore. Soon she would have a baby.

A large — another rending pain — an enormous baby.

And that was about all she knew. She knew it was coming, yes, and she knew what she'd done to make it, and she knew she had to get down to the water fast because—because—because that was the only place she could birth this baby safely.

This would be a special baby. No one in memory had given life to a baby such as this. No one had dared.

By the time she reached the narrow strip of sand that was the only beach in this country of cliffs and caves, she was exhausted, crawling on hands and knees. Not easy to do with her belly heaving and her skirts, soaked with birthing waters, tied up beneath her arms. But she had no choice. This was where she had to be.

The tide was slowly swelling to meet the half-moon. The sharp blade of it was cutting her open and drawing her tides, too, as it sank gracefully toward the horizon.

Would her lover meet her here? Would he bring sisters and aunts and cousins to help, as he'd promised he'd try? His people had unusually keen hearing, but she had done her best to make no sound at all. They might find her by smell, though; she smelled like an animal, sweaty and afraid. And of course he'd warned that the women of his clan might not come. They disapproved of what he and she had done as much as her own people would, *if* they knew—and she was determined they wouldn't.

The sand was cool against her palms and knees and shins. It felt like comfort. She let herself sink onto one side and press her temple against that yielding damp, breathe deep of the clean wet air. The *lap-lap* of the bay's rising little waves was soothing, too; even the stars seemed gentle and kind, floating behind wispy drifts of cloud, now that she'd reached the place that was her entire plan.

She lay there, let the pain and the elements take her while she prayed. *Holy Virgin, Empress of the Seas, have pity on a sinner* . . . And: *Bjarl, my love, please find me.*

He did find her. First a wet head bobbed out among the waves — it could have been a seal. She didn't even notice it at first, but then came the steady plash of water as he propelled his powerful body along. He was flicking and steering in a way that both fascinated and revolted — revolted because it might mark this baby, too, and what would she do then?

She moaned. It did not give as much release as she wanted, but it was all she could allow herself.

Soon Bjarl's arms were around her, and the chilly skin of his chest was propping up her head. He had humped his way onto the sand where they used to make love. His hands somehow raised her knees and shifted them apart, though in a way very different from their old giddy nights. It was a position at once awkward and reassuring; in arranging her this way, Bjarl seemed expert, as if someone had trained him for precisely this moment. Maybe he was taught by a woman of his people — which might mean the women would not come to help at all.

She realized that Bjarl was pulling her from the sand into the shallows. The little kidney-shaped bay's salt water bathed her most fevered parts, stinging where they were already starting to tear but otherwise soothing with coolness.

"It won't be long," he promised, pressing his lips to her brow. "Our babies come quickly."

She wished he'd tell her that he loved her.

"I love you," he said, as if he could hear her thoughts. She believed him. His people, the *marreminder*, claimed not to set much store by love, he had explained, because it was not something they could eat or hoard, and in their long, long lives they usually outgrew all emotion. But if Bjarl said he loved her, then surely he did.

She gasped out a few sounds to let him know she loved him too, and then she growled, because for a moment the pain became stronger than love.

In a lull she heard others surfacing, nearly silent splashes followed by snorts to clear waterlogged breathing passages in nose and neck. She heard palms digging into sand, bodies scraping over it. The women of his *flok* were here after all.

An old creature of vaguely female outline propped herself between her legs and studied them with the keen eye of one who sees in the dark. She slid her fingers inside (*pain*), feeling for the baby's head.

"All as it should be," she assured the parents-in-waiting.

A cloud drifted away from the half-moon, and a shaft of light revealed that old woman's face—horrible, cracked, snaggle-toothed, and moldy—leering over her.

She recoiled and closed her eyes.

"*Shh*, beloved, the old one has powers," Bjarl said.

The hideous crone cackled as if deliberately to frighten the poor girl, who had known nothing but her own village until the day she looked into the water and saw Bjarl looking back at her.

"Call me a witch," said the crone, "if it comforts ye."

The word was not a comfort, but she trusted in Bjarl's choice of helpers. At this moment in her short, violent life, she had no one else — certainly no one who had shown her kindness.

The younger women set to work on her belly, rubbing it gently and singing to it in their trilling voices. One pair of hands circled her temples in a way that lifted much of her pain; another rubbed her scalp in a way that would have been pleasurable if not for the pain elsewhere; and of course Bjarl's arms remained around her.

Oddly enough, at this moment, she felt more loved than at any other in her life.

"Tell me how we fell," she whispered, delirious with suffering but still hoping he would understand her. "How we fell in love."

She knew he was smiling; she felt his beard against her cheek, shedding water that sprinkled her neck with droplets.

"You were crouching on a rock," he said, "and scrubbing linens against it. You were crying because your mother had been cruel to you that day. And I'd been fishing nearby when I felt your tears dropping into the waves, and I thought I'd never tasted anything so sweet. I swam up and looked at you through the waterskin, and you looked down and saw me. You were so astonished, you fell off the rock and into my arms."

In spite of the pain, she smiled. It was her favorite story, and Bjarl told it a little differently each time she asked. The one part that remained constant was this: *They fell in love.*

"That afternoon I gave you a sea star and asked you to be mine," Bjarl finished, so quiet she was almost certain his women could not hear him.

More cold water splashed against her split legs and mounded belly, even her face, from the old one's hands. She was glad for the cold. She looked up again, blinking, and admired the iciness of stars and moon, forever fixed in the blue bowl of sky. Sometimes, in the months when the sun never set, the moon was visible along with it, waxing and waning according to its own wishes. Sometimes it shimmered in yellow-green streaks of light that (though familiar) seemed to promise some life beyond the one lived on this hardscrabble island.

"It's time to push," said the old woman, spreading the girl's legs wide, as if to pull her apart like a chicken.

The wavelets *hiss-hissed* as they receded down the sand. It was a pleasant sound.

Bracing herself against Bjarl's strong chest, surrounded by his people, she pushed.

Now, at last, she let herself scream as loudly as she wanted.

She screamed both pain and love.

Chapter 1

To the list of events I never intended, it is time to add this: the first of the so-called miracles that have made these Dark Islands famous on land and sea.

The miracle, as these people have named it, begins with my first step on a pebbly shore; it ends in a wall of flowers stained red. In one form or another, it becomes the stuff of song and legend and even, I'm told, an entry in the books written by monks and illustrated in paints made of ground stone and gold and beetle shells, to be kept among other such objects in a place called Rome.

My own people sing of it, naturally. Their songs focus on my bravery and cunning, but the truth is that I wasn't brave or cunning at all—just lucky or unlucky, depending on how you view the events that followed.

This is how the songs go. I don't need to point out that I never sing them myself.

Sanna the Lonely, Sanna the Meek —
She who was first to set foot on the land —
In the midst of their feast,
In savory and sweet,
Her body sang out the elements:
Air and earth and fire and time
Dyed themselves red in her blood.
Sanna the Clever, Sanna the Wise;
Sanna both Never and Always.

I don't like what they call me, but who is ever entirely happy with a name given by others? And in any event, my names are not the worst exaggeration. The story grows and blooms as it passes each pair of lips, and soon the singers will have me slaying an empire and taking its wealth for my own.

I intend to narrate everything here exactly as it happened.

anna

When I first come to the Thirty-Seven Dark Islands near the northernmost reach of our known world, what I imagine, what I intend, is finding my mother. She was just a girl when she made me, and she must be a woman now; but blood calls to blood, and though I was taken from her at birth—in a place my people don't remember because the witch of our *flok* worked a magic of forgetting—still there must be something, *must* be, in me to spark recognition from her.

I think my mother and I will recognize each other, all at once and completely, on first sight. I have my father's yellow hair and pale green eyes, with something of him in the point of my nose, but the rest of me (I believe) must be hers. She and her people will know me by my high cheekbones, sharp chin, and wide mouth, and they'll rejoice to find the baby was not lost; then some missing, broken part of myself will be found and fixed.

That doesn't happen.

As I approach the castle where my quest truly begins, the ground rolls and twists. My legs tangle in the soft blue skirts of the dress I'm wearing, the overgown I chose from a chest that obviously once belonged to a fine woman. I also took a white veil and a silver diadem for my head.

I anticipated this awkwardness—*getting my land legs*, Sjældent calls it, and it happened each time I practiced on solid ground. In a way I'm still practicing now, as I have a few islets to cross after the pebbly beach where I landed myself. Sometimes there's no bridge from one islet to the other, but I don't need to jump and don't trust my legs to do it. I find it's easy to wade, skirts hiked to my knees. But all of this is tiring, and I'm soon winded from effort.

I ache in unaccustomed places. With each step, I wonder if I should turn back or perhaps wait for another day, as my destination seems all but impossible to reach.

"Go to the castle," said Sjældent, the oldest of the *flok* but still not considered an elder, one with the duty to govern, because she is so strange. She is the witch who taught me my magic and also, on the day of my birth, made everyone forget.

"What castle?" I asked, because I'd never seen one from where we liked to float just beyond the bay's waters; also, I'd learned from our travels that the word *castle*, or something like it, is used to describe all manner of landish buildings.

Sjældent (squinting, as she always does to make things a little clearer through the white fog over her eyes) explained what a castle is here: "A many-chambered place where people live with weapons and treasures. This one grows out of a big rock farthest to these islands' west, and it's the only one in the whole miserable place. Ye won't be able *not* to find it, if ye follow the wind."

"And my mother will be there?"

Sjældent cackled, one of those coughing laughs that she thinks are so unsettling to the rest of us — because they are. For her they're as natural as a burp to a child just learning to hold her breath underwater. My father says that when one is finally as old and ugly as Sjældent, a laugh commands a kind of respect.

And fear. Most of our people fear the old witch, and for better reason than her laugh.

"Ye'll find something," she said to me that day. She rarely answers questions directly. "Ye'll find the whole landish *flok* gathered in one place. A woman who can help ye. And something to bring back here. To me."

It would be easy to become irritated with Sjældent, if I didn't need her so much. I've grown used to her during the suns and moons of my apprenticeship. So I asked her then, "Will the something be my mother?" I also thought, who better to help me than the woman herself?

She cackled again, ending with words children use for

taunting one another: "That, my girl, is for me to know and ye to find out."

"I suppose I will find out," I said, calm as could be, "and then we'll both know, won't we?"

She liked that. "Not so meek as when I found ye," she said smugly.

I said, "I'm the one who came to you," and then dived off the rock and deep under the seaskin, to show her that I might leave just as easily.

Arriving in the Dark Islands, as this place is called, took far more effort than a dive; it required nearly a year of training and chanting, trying and failing, breaking my pride over and over. And now that I'm here, my whole body stings and soars and throbs at once.

Excitement. Hope. Fear. Magic. So many questions perhaps to be answered . . . One big question, rather. And a single, secret name that Sjældent conjured for me to tuck in my heart, far (for now) from my lips.

I can tell the castle is close when I emerge from a place covered in so many trees that I know to call it *forest.* I smell fire, and sweetness, and meat cooking, and people massed together. When I leave the trees, there it is — a great pile of rocks rising from the sea at a place where the currents are strong and the waves beat a spray as high as I stand. A castle, in fact, so much a part of the rock that it seems to *be* the rock and is not easily seen from the sea.

So close, now, but how my feet ache! First there's a bridge

to cross over a freshwater channel, then a wide island shaped like a bowl with a well-trodden ridge down the center.

To keep steady, I count each step I manage without a stumble or a stubbed toe. One, two, five, and then I start counting again. It will take a while longer to learn, this walking over rocky earth.

The ridge is bounded on either side with a garden where plants grow in arithmetic patches and straight lines, which landish people find a useful way to organize nature and thus control their element, because they are anxious folk who cannot accept that there's no such condition as control. I sniff at the various rows and recognize some things I've tasted before, berries and small fruits for which we've traded with friendly peoples, but I've never seen them actually growing from the earth before. The wind blows their leaves the way the tide pushes and pulls at the weeds undersea, but both more gently and more fast.

On that wind, I catch the unmistakable odor of bodies together: landish bodies, moist with landish sweat. And the sounds of landish voices, speaking and exclaiming, and at least a hundred pairs of jaws at work.

I also smell pleasure, which adds a sweetness to the cloud of their scent. It carries easily on the wind and has a tangible substance, like a kind of web that might tangle me up.

I won't let my step falter. I push myself, willfully, a last dozen paces over the green-bowl island and across a wood-beamed bridge caked with mud, then finally — a *big* push — into the castle itself.

Cool. Stone. Crusty with salt from the sea. I can draw strength from that.

"Surely you can manage ten more steps," I say out loud and sternly, for the benefit of my feet. They feel as if someone has smashed them with hammers and set them on fire, which is not too far from what they've endured today.

I limp under a series of archways, and then I see them: the landish folk. There are many more here than belong to my own clan and *flok*, and they are sitting on broken trees arranged within a big five-sided hollow of stone, with so many shining objects around them that my eyes are dazzled. I smell them fully, and hear them—all at once, overwhelming with sensation, as if smell and sound are always tangible things (to us, they are) and batter my body like waves.

"How are you going to bear them?" my age-mates asked when they heard of my plan. Especially Addra, who is flame-haired and dark-eyed and the most beautiful of all, forever admiring the reflection of her face and breasts in a rock pool—though she has the tongue of a dead clam, as Sjældent likes to say, and must rely on her beauty, not her singing, to win her way in the world.

Whenever the subject of my quest arose, Addra shuddered exquisitely, completely disdaining the people from whom, after all, we take much of what makes our lives feel so joyous.

"Their smell," she said, and she counted landish flaws on her fingers, where the webbing is as delicate and pink as her nails: "Their awful, raspy voices and their breath that reeks of corpses; the taste—"

"She's not going to *taste* them," my loyal cousin La put in. "Are you, Sanna?"

Of course not.

"To be fair," Pippa the Strong said once, to shut Addra up (Pippa is practically an elder by virtue of strength, and she finds Addra as irritating and unimportant as a sand flea), "you think that the landish reek of corpses because by the time you keep your promise to kiss them, they've died."

And that is true, too. Addra's face, if not her voice, has lured many a sailor to his death.

But in many other respects, Addra was speaking the truth. Landish breath, especially when so many are gathered together, *does* reek of the dead, and it's enough to make my knees weak now, even as my mouth waters with a mix of hunger and revulsion. The landish *flok* has been feasting on landish animals, their earthy meat choked in smoke from a fire and stuffed with plants from the dirt, then drowned in sauces made from other things that grow in the ground. If only they ate a raw fish once in a while, they wouldn't smell so bad.

As I step toward them, I get another sensation, that which we call the *Down-Below-Deep*. I feel as if I'm moving below the sea's striae of buoyancy, so far down it takes days first to swim and then to sink to the bottom. Anyone who reaches that place risks being held by the weight of water until it crushes her to death.

I am almost afraid enough to turn back, but I don't. I am sworn to the quest. And anyway, my poor new feet can't walk to the water again, and my grip on my magic is weak; I might not be able to change.

So I take a deep breath, and then the last few steps into sun and the edge of the crowd.

In the sunshine, on the walls, grow dazzling white landish flowers. They are one source (but not the only source) of that sweet aroma of pleasure. Above the people's heads on the westernmost wall, in a nook where no flowers grow, stands a lady in a yellow gown and a veil to match, lips bumpy and pink, face also bumpy but bluish white. Not a real lady, I see very soon, but one of those figures that imitate the real. The landish like them for reasons we don't quite understand; perhaps the false figures make them feel less alone. This one has arms outstretched at her sides and is missing some fingers. Her flaking lips smile as if to welcome me home.

She makes me happy deep down, for reasons I can't explain.

But happiness here is a danger.

Seeing her, I fall. In front of all those staring landish people, I tumble. Into the flowers that cling to the walls, into branches that tear at me. They rip my fine blue dress apart, right down to my tender new skin.

I feel blood leaking from me—tiny drops, little red pearls—and I hear it hiss and sizzle in the air.

• Chapter 3 •

A feast of virtues and sins.

It falls on a warm, windy day in late summer, this Feast of the Virgin's Assumption. When they wake at dawn to the toll of the church bell, the farmers who haven't yet finished their harvest are of one mind, and that mind is on crops.

Wheat. Rye. Oats. Hay. The people stretch and shove each other out of bed, thinking of the ordinary things that they and their animals will eat in the lean, dark months that are coming, when most of their work will be done by touch as the moon passes in and out of her phases and the sun appears rarely if at all.

Turnips. Beets. Parsnips. Apples. A very few pears. Preserves of summer berries stored in clay jars. And ropes of onion and garlic, the poor man's (and woman's, and child's) staple flavoring. Salted fish kept in stinking, briny barrels.

This will be their fare, if they are lucky.

Except today: Today is for a feast. They can eat whatever they want, as much as they want, on a holy day that coincides with harvest — the single day of the year that Baroness Thyrla opens her gate and unlocks her larders, ordering her cooks to do their best for the town. It's the day she welcomes the islanders to carry Our Lady of the Sea into the courtyard and set her in a niche, the day when she shares her own stores. And there will be plenty of the exotic goods brought in by ships that dock at her private harbor and never venture into the much larger Dark Moon Bay, on the shores of which these good people raise their crops and their children but almost never their hopes, because the land is rocky and very far north.

Father Abel says that August 15 should be devoted to all things Holy Mother. The day marks the Virgin's earthly dormition or death, and her body's rise up into heaven on a crescent moon lifted by angels' wings, But who can really be blamed if, as the lone church bell rings tinnily over the islands, thoughts of delicacies to be eaten mingle with the Blessed Mother?

Like all good things, the bounty from the Baroness's kitchen must be earned. So the townspeople assemble (stomachs growling) in the church nave to pray with Father Abel. The elderly priest leads the ceremony in a language they don't understand; they know only that it is holy. *"Shh,"* a dozen mothers hiss to their fidgety children, perhaps with a knock on the head. "Look at the Virgin. Think of your virtues and sins." They guess that's what Abel is running on about in his inscrutable Latin.

And who wouldn't want to gaze at Our Lady? She is the

town's pride — except that pride is a sin, too, so it's best to say they simply love it. Her. The statue.

No one knows how old Our Lady of the Sea is or who made her, but they do agree that at one time she was carved out of wood, a great piece as big as a living woman. She is somehow larger than a real woman, though, and more beautiful, with her lips parted and her arms spread to welcome good men and sinners alike into eternal forgiveness.

It is an honor to perform her annual cleaning and freshening of paint, preparing for the trip to the castle. The most skilled men in town (a town of very limited skill, it is true) vie for the honor of passing a cloth over her white face, stroking a new layer of yellow paint onto her robe and veil.

The years have not been kind to Our Lady of the Sea. Salt air and freezing temperatures corrode and shrink her paint, so her surface has become bubbly and uneven; her face and dress flake away at the touch. Also, in all the well-meant repainting, her eyes have migrated, such that the left one sits a thumb's width above the right.

Sheep's urine, that's what makes the yellow paint. Other towns might pay through the teeth for blue stone mined far to the south and east, to grind into the color the Church Fathers have unofficially associated with Mary. But in this town of fishers and farmers who struggle to pull a living out of the rock, a little urine is no dishonor. They use it to strengthen the wool of their clothes, to paint their houses, to fertilize certain plants in their gardens; there's no corner of the islands in which a body can take a breath and not smell waste. The church, just now, as the day warms up, reeks like a baby's napkin, and nobody minds a bit.

At last, Father Abel begins a drawn-out, singsongy *A-a-a-a-a-a-m-e-en.*

As the final note dies into the church walls, six sturdy men approach Our Lady of the Sea. They lift her from her pedestal and onto a bier already decorated with late-summer flowers. Girls of the town (all virgins themselves, skinny and mouse-haired under their caps) heap more asters and daisies and stalks of grain at the statue's ankles.

Father Abel opens the church's big door, and the sturdy men carry the bier into the light, to loop around the church and westward through its garden of graves, on to the series of Islets that skip like stones to the sunset.

Now, walking, the girls and boys sing songs about the Virgin. She may look even shabbier in the bright outdoors, but she is theirs, and today she will gain them access to the castle. Their songs give her glory.

Steadily, singing, the villagers follow their Virgin up slope and down gully, over bridges, past fields fed by freshwater springs, through woods and over an island shaped like a bowl, where greens and vegetables and other sallets are grown for the castle. Then to the castle itself, squatting dark and gray and jagged on the last bit of rock that could be called an island. This rock is so big that it is said the builders needed no mortar to fashion the four towers and countless rooms; the castle was almost entirely carved out of bedrock, with additional rubble from the ballast in the ships that traveled far to bring riches back to Baroness Thyrla and her family (she must have had family at some time, though no one remembers them now). The castle has five sides and is widest to the north, where a towerless corner juts like a ship's prow into the sea — or, as mothers tell naughty children, like a blade-thin door for the dragon who lives in the rock below to burst through at the Baroness's command.

Preceded by Father Abel and the Virgin, the villagers pass the guards stationed at the castle gate with halberds erect. Then (still singing) they enter the five-sided courtyard and circle its rose-clad walls to set the precious statue in a niche at the far western end. She nestles into a gap among the roses that spring white as salt from the vine that runs all around the yard and that is also older than memory, perhaps as old as the rock. Feeding the castle's bees, who dance over the white blossoms before sinking inside to drink.

With the statue in place, the people find benches to sit on, at tables laden with their particular favorite treats. They see young pig and venison, honey cakes and spiced ale, fried squash blossoms and pies of unknown but no doubt delightful contents. Thyrla has had three of her cows butchered, and an exaltation of larks has come to ground in the center of each table, dressed in a fragrant sauce.

The people exchange covert smiles. When children squeal with excitement, they are hushed quickly, as is Old Olla, who greets friends too loudly (she's gone peculiar, living with the bees) with an "Oh, it's you!"

They remain standing while the Baroness and her

seventeen-year-old son, Peder—both lavishly dressed, even regally so, in cloth of gold and ropes of jewels that set off their bright hair and silver-gray eyes—enter the yard and assume their places on the dais, where only the Virgin statue and Father Abel are allowed to join them. Even young Peder's paid companion, a boy of the village named Tomas, sits among the commoners on this day, with his widowed mother, known as Inger Elder, and his sisters and brothers.

As one body, the villagers bow so low they could lick their own shoes. So low they smell little of the food and much of the roses, which are lightly and pleasantly sweet.

"Please, good people, do stand," says the Baroness in her imperious manner. She keeps herself so beautifully adorned that her mix of gold and silver hair (tending more toward silver now) has become the feminine ideal. She is so forceful, so sure of herself, that she would be magnificent even if she were covered in warts. As it is, she wears a patch over her right eye that would have disfigured a lesser woman but on her is another ornament, a triangle of white silk delicately embroidered with the outline of an eye closed in a wink.

No one has ever seen beneath that patch.

"Stand," this marvelous woman invites them again. "And then sit."

"*Eat!*" her son interjects. "Drink! Eat and drink until your bellies burst!"

"We give thanks for the Lord's bounty," Father Abel

says humbly, facing Thyrla and her son. "We give thanks for the Blessed Virgin and for the fruit of her womb, Jesus."

He holds a Bible in trembling, knotty hands. Tradition dictates that he must stand as others begin the meal; he will read to the crowd what little the Bible says about the Virgin Mary, followed by pages of old writing about how her Son's life reflects well upon hers. Only when Mary's tale is thoroughly explored, and a good bit of Jesus's, can he share in the feast.

"Begin!" Thyrla commands them, her people, as she waves her white hands.

Father Abel opens the cover of his precious book.

The townspeople have been invited three times now, so they are ready to eat. And to make each bite a prayer. They reach for their favorite morsels, shaking with the hunger that will finally be satisfied.

Everything seems ready and right.

But they are not prepared—because never once has it happened before—to see a stranger crashing into the yard. Tall, blue, a blur. She *really* crashes, perhaps tripped by one of the dogs that twine around legs looking for scraps. Stumbles and falls into the vine that holds the wall together.

What happens next puts a stop to the prayers and the pleasure. Food drops from mouths to the ground, where animals eat it.

The white roses are turning red.

• Chapter 4 •

It sounds like a sigh.

In the silence, they hear the change. It sounds like a sigh—as if flowers are relieved to become what they've wished to be all along, or as if the dragon inside the rock has turned over in his sleep.

Maybe it's just the wind from the sea. But for one moment, there's not so much as the call of a gull to distract anyone from what's happening on the walls.

The tide of red washes through the flowers of the ancient vine that has suckled on the courtyard stone as long as anyone can remember. The flowers, too, have never changed in memory, but everyone who sees them now somehow knows that they will always be red hereafter.

While the people watch, they're tickled with an unfamiliar feeling. It wells up within them like their own blood, but it's even stronger than that and much more foreign.

It's bliss.

The roses are pouring forth a deeper scent, one that plunges to the bottom of the belly. It is the best scent, and the red is the most beautiful color, any of these poor people have known in their lives.

And the cause of it all — that stranger, the pale-haired, blue-robed girl — now lies in the rose vine's embrace, with thorns in her skin, her own blood glittering richer than Baroness Thyrla's jewels. Richer even than the red of the roses.

The people break out both laughing and weeping. When at last they can speak, they cry, "Miracle!"

They rush toward the stranger, knocking benches and tables on end. They want to, *need* to lay their hands on the miracle, get her blood on their fingertips, taste the salty wine of it. They lick the drops away while the lavish feast from the Baroness's kitchens grows cold and flavorless on the tables and the roses bloom and bloom and bloom.

Even Father Abel joins the rush; even Peder, the boy who has grown up with so much pleasure that he thinks any fresh brush with it is his due. Only Baroness Thyrla hangs back, watching her people descend like brown beetles on the once-bright, highly irregular, lavishly dressed intruder.

Only the Baroness, that is, and Our Lady of the Sea, the wooden statue presiding over the feast. The edges of her niche mark the last place where the flowers change, the last place where white yields to red with a billow of that perfect scent. They bring a flush of reflected pink to her chalky white cheeks.

Thyrla's single gray eye glitters, hard and steely.

◆ Chapter 5 ◆

anna

I know what a miracle is, because Sjældent explained it to me as part of the faith these landish people have in a powerful man, a father, who lives above them in the sky. A miracle is a bit of the absent father made visible, to keep the people behaving as they should. It is magic used to their benefit, the same thing witches do when people call them angels.

I may have laughed when Sjældent outlined this landish belief, but now I am quivering. In fear.

As the thorns bite into my flesh and the plant takes hold, I hear the people using that word. It bounces off the rocks and melts into the sea spray, and then it rushes toward me—because *I am the miracle.*

But what's just happened is *not* a miracle. I know this. It has nothing to do with some unseen person but is merely an accident, a misstep from legs not used to land—not used to being legs, for that matter—and the magic I called to my body so I could come here. It is magic of alteration, and it didn't stop working when my own body changed. Or rather, I didn't remember to stop it, to limit it to my body, and so it spilled over into the prickling plant.

At first I can't make this much sense out of what's happening; understanding comes later. When I stumble, it seems the first thorn barely touches my skin before I'm falling deep into branches that have been waiting for me, and then there's the landish smell of earth and urine and meats cooked with fire. I am pinned under the branches but under people as well, all the people who were here before me and who now want to be exactly where I am.

It takes a moment to realize they want to be just here *because* of me. They are touching me, licking me. The branches wind tighter around my body, and my dress and veil tear. I hear a snapping of twig after twig as the landish people rush to pluck the flowers, to chew and swallow as they collect my blood.

They eat magic, I think hazily. *I have to tell Sjældent and Father.*

I hear Sjældent's voice in my head: *To them, eating is magic itself.* And that seems true, too.

There isn't much room for thinking beneath the squirming mass of landish people reaching through and shoving each other away. Not much room for breath, either. And the nauseous smell of them, with the sweet scent of these flowers, makes my final thoughts spin till I could hardly say my name if anyone asked.

28

Just as I am about to drown in this churning tide of landish bodies—hungry as sharks, grasping as octopuses—I feel a jolt. In my arm. A jolt as from one of those eels whose bite carries the same power as a lightning bolt, only this sensation is much sweeter. This feeling mixes pleasure with its pain.

It's a single hand, circling my upper arm, pulling. Somehow this hand has power to make the others fall away, at least after a few heartbeats in which I feel both jolts and smothers. The hand pulls me by the arm, and the thorns rip at my clothes and skin some more as I scrabble to get my feet under myself again.

In no time at all, I am standing, blinking, in the sun and wind. Caressed by sea spray and the scent of a thousand flowers now turned bright red and spicy.

The people have fallen away. They sit on the overturned slabs of wood and shards of dishes, or they hover, hoping to dart back for another touch. My veil is entirely gone, and the silver diadem lies crushed somewhere beneath other feet.

The wind lifts my hair and blows it upward and across my face in a green-yellow swirl, so I have to take all this in during short bursts of clarity. But it's not my hair or the wind that is slowing down the most important observation of all, the one I can barely bring myself to recount. Because the hand that pulled me from the fray is still on my arm, and the face of the person who belongs to the hand is very close to mine, staring through the swirl of my hair with a single silver eye.

I feel a new sort of jolt, a cold shiver. I am Down-Below-Deeply afraid. For a moment I think it would have been better to lie beneath all those landish miracle-criers and hope to sink through the rock than to face this face.

That is because I have now recognized the cause of that first shock and tingle: It came from magic.

The person who grabbed me, the person who still holds my arm, is a person who has magic. And something tells me that she — it is a *she* — is not going to be a friend and teacher to me, at least not at first.

"Who are you," she says in a voice that would freeze a white bear's liver, "and what is your business in my castle?"

Chapter 6

She has always been the Baroness.

Growing into herself in a time when the title of Baroness didn't mean much in these isolated islands, Thyrla learned to be cautious, especially when she felt an itch beneath her eye patch. The eye there is hidden for a particular reason. People may assume this is because the eye is blind or maimed in some way, but they're wrong. It is in fact rather *too* sensitive, and Thyrla keeps its messages to herself. An extra tear or two predict sorrow to come; a dry scrape means hardship. An itch is worst of all. It means the unknown.

She feels that itch today. Just before the stranger comes staggering into the yard and flings herself into the roses, just when Thyrla should be her best and strongest, presiding with her son over the annual feast that keeps the village in thrall to her wishes and needs — at this one moment of equilibrium, when light and dark are in balance and Thyrla can feed on her subjects' greed in the name of the Church — her secret eye begins to twitch.

She tries to ignore the itch and tickle, tries to will it away. She hates to be surprised. The itch is thoroughly maddening, though, and she thinks she probably sounds sharp when she invites her guests to begin eating. She accompanies her invitation with extravagant hand gestures, all so she can let one little finger slip under the patch, just for a heartbeat, to rub the itch.

With that, she only makes the itching worse. And then the eye's omen comes true. The stranger staggers into Thyrla's carefully arranged courtyard and well-planned life—a life in which for decades nothing has changed, not even the lines on her face—and suddenly she loses her people. Loses her white roses, too, though even she can't say what that means as yet.

Roses. Nothing more than a garden flower, growing from a vine so old and gnarled that its roots reach through the castle rock and tickle the dragon sleeping inside. According to the island people.

Superstitious village folk and farmers—Thyrla has counted on their stupidity during the many decades of her reign. She has always been the Baroness, as long as any of them can remember, and her power has grown with each annual feast. Soon, she reckons, she will have enough of both power and treasure to leave these Thirty-Seven Dark Islands and set sail for the world, where she will live on her ship like a queen.

While Thyrla looks into her future, the dragon turns over on its bed of gold and jewels; it heaves a sigh of dream-inducing breath. The sap that springs through the roses is red now, red as blood. The people gathered for Their Lady's feast day have seen it, and seen who started it, and are completely enchanted with her.

Thyrla has no choice but to part the crowd and haul the stranger—a girl, a mere young female—to her feet. Her hand feels a spark where it holds the girl's arm.

"Who are you and what is your business in my castle?" It's easiest to be direct; she might catch the intruder off guard.

The girl makes a sort of purring, hissing sound in her throat, then drops her gaze to the scratches and stabs on her hands. She's a pale, muddy slip of a long-legged creature in a blue dress crackling with salt; green-blond hair tangles far down her back. Beautiful, as young girls always are (but not as beautiful as Thyrla—no one has ever been that). A beauty that might fade—yes, like a flower's—unless something else augments it. Talent. Power. Luck.

Always back to flowers. Thyrla can't imagine how this girl managed the trick. Her skin is as white as the petals used to be; her lips are as shockingly red as the roses are now. And her cheeks are flushed with . . . pride? Yes, she's proud of herself—here in the castle where no one should be prideful but Thyrla.

She dares to ask the Baroness, "Who are *you?*"

• Chapter 7 •

The waterskin singing.

"Have you heard?"

"Is she there?"

"What *can* you hear?"

All Sanna's cousins and all of her aunts, all the boys and men, too, gather on the green-slimed rocks around Sjældent as if the old fright has a special way of knowing. Which, of course, she does—but Sanna is *her* project, and these girls are the ones who usually shun the two of them, make up silly rhymes about what Sanna and Sjældent "really" do while Sjældent teaches her magic.

Especially Addra, that haughty beauty with hair like the sunset and scales to match. Not a good voice, but she's fond of telling others that looks are a talent, too, and it's true— the others fawn on her for no reason other than the flash of her coloring and the chiseling of her cheekbones, and she has no mother to keep her in check. The others let her sling herself languidly in the bottom of the O of Ringstone, that formation that rises midway between the bay town and the castle rock and has made a favorite spot for basking while the *flok* is here.

"Don't be a tease, old hagfish!" Addra calls down from her perch now, and the girls (*and* the boys) giggle at her daring. "Tell us everything you know!"

Addra is combing her hair now with an ivory comb dug out of a shipwreck. For a young girl, there is no pleasure greater than the feel of those tiny teeth scraping her scalp while her hair dries in the sun.

Or almost none greater. Addra feels the joy of admiring attention. Maybe tonight she and another girl will twine their tails together and sleep floating as one on the seaskin.

Now, Sjældent scratches at her own head with nails thick and cracked with time. Sanna used to dig out the barnacles and crabs there, and Sjældent feels the girl's absence very keenly.

"Tell us! Tell us! Tell us!" Addra starts the chant, and the others join in.

Sjældent has had enough of them. "Yer lot are the ones with good hearing," she says, bouncing her words off the water as if she doesn't care. But if she weren't so eager for news of the land, which she hasn't detected yet, she'd let herself sink down to a cozy crag on the seafloor.

She adds, "*Ye* should tell *me* what's what, for ye can ask me three times and the answer'll still be none of yer knowing."

("Old biddy," Addra whispers to the girls who adore her—that silly young Frill and lush, sighing La; even Pippa the Strong, who usually puts up with no nonsense. "What an old, shrieking gull.")

"*That* I can hear," Sjældent calls out.

"I meant you to!" Addra preens herself, getting excited giggles from the others.

"If ye be so daring, why not swim to the land yerself and find out?" Sjældent taunts her.

Which of course is impossible.

Addra ignores Sjældent elaborately and lets cloud-haired Frill climb up and start combing the hair down her back, over the small hole in her neck that expels old air while she inhales new. All the girls behave as if Addra's hair is of utmost importance.

But few are actually thinking of Addra. Everyone from elders to infants is waiting to hear how Sanna is managing her quest. Sjældent, for one, has laid all her hopes on the girl's fragile shoulders. She'd scoff at anyone who said that she, one of the greatest witches of her time or any other, loves Sanna—anyone like Bjarl, the girl's father, who swims up with a gift of the pale pink jellies that she does love—but the girl is more important than the old witch would ever admit.

"Any ideas?" Bjarl asks, as if in exchange for the gift. "Any visions?"

"I'm not a land-witch," Sjældent snaps. "I can't see

everything there." She stuffs an entire jelly into her mouth for a quivering, stinging bite.

Bjarl watches her enjoy her treat. He sighs. "Well, when you do know something . . ."

Sjældent twirls another jelly around a knobby forefinger and eyes him, squinting against the sun. "Wish in one hand," she says, "and piss in the other, and guess where ye'll go swimming first."

After that insult, everyone pretends to be very taken with the sight of a half-dozen dolphins circling the rocks and feeding on fish the girls throw them. The dolphins' happy squeaks and clicks shiver through the *flok's* seavish bones and spread pleasure. There's some speculation as to whether the dolphins will jump through the O, as La swears she saw them do once, and if so whether they'll knock Addra out of it.

But everyone knows what they're really thinking about.

Sanna. And how she is faring in that strange, rocky land from which the smoky smells of roasted meat are wafting even to the lips of the O.

The clan's elders — aunts and warriors and providers — curl into themselves with worry.

Chapter 8

Tainted time.

Who are you? Who is *she?* Someone who asks questions rather than answering them, that's for certain.

Thyrla's fingers clutch the arm hard, and the spark turns to a jolting sensation. *Magic.* "Tell me your name," she orders.

"My—my name is Sanna," the stranger whispers. She's made that hissing, trilling noise again, but this time it is more distinct, as if it might actually be a name or part of one.

Her voice is all but inaudible, yet the people take up the sound, and it echoes around the courtyard: *Sanna Sanna Sanna Sanna . . .* It seems to make the roses contract, then pulse outward with new petals, like so many beating hearts.

Thyrla cuts in: "I am Baroness Thyrla of the Thirty-Seven Dark Islands," she says, as curt as she is grand. "You are intruding on our holy feast. Come with me."

The first thing to do is to get this Sanna person away from the town's eyes.

Thyrla gestures with her free hand, and the castle guards clear a path, though the townspeople cry out in dismay as they see the Baroness and the girl—and Peder, who follows like a brightly clad shadow of his mother, clutching a barely tasted cupful of mead—heading toward an archway that leads from the yard to the castle keep.

The guardsmen may feel every bit as dismayed as the rest to see Sanna go, but they hold the crowd inside the courtyard. And after all there is still food, somewhat crumbled and mixed together, nibbled by animals and stepped on by feet, but still in all likelihood delicious.

The people settle down to enjoy their feast. They bask in the deep red smell of roses, under the pink-cheeked, cockeyed gaze of their beloved Lady of the Sea.

Thyrla propels Sanna to her most private chamber, which she rarely opens to anyone. She needs it now because for her it is a place of strength. They go up several stairs (on which Sanna stumbles as if she's never encountered their like— *Holy oxtails, the girl is clumsy*), through a series of storerooms and sleeping rooms to a place where the walls narrow and one window looks over the courtyard and out to the sea, the other toward the town. Here is a heavy door that's as much strap iron as it is wood, and there are no fewer than seven locks running from floor to ceiling.

"Open it," Thyrla orders Peder. Her hand is still a vise

on the stranger's arm, pain pulsing through from the touch of her. *Magic.*

He sets his cup (now empty) on the floor and unhooks the big iron ring from Thyrla's belt, then tries one key after another till he finds the right fit. He does this with a great show of importance, as if he's already lord of the castle (which he won't be until and unless Thyrla has lived a long, long time beyond this day). And he acts dramatically casual, as if he wants Sanna to think that he's simply opening a door he uses all the time, though in fact his mother rarely lets him visit her here.

As he works the locks, Peder is conscious of the mysterious girl's eyes upon him. She is bound to be impressed (he thinks) by meeting such a boy as he is, around her age and very good-looking, with his bright gold hair and silver eyes and a suit of clothes and jewels to match. Even if she's of high rank wherever she's from, even given her trick with the roses, she must be in awe of what she's found here.

"I'm her son," he introduces himself, feeling very important as he turns the fourth key. "Call me Baron Peder."

"Just Peder," Thyrla says sharply, and although he's not surprised she's putting him in his place, he does think it would be nice if she'd let him keep up appearances around a girl.

As he inserts the fifth key, Peder thinks over the name *Sanna* and starts fitting it into one of the songs he sings to the village girls. He might add new verses especially for her: *Sanna, wanna, shanna* (Will it be clear he means "shall not"? Is "shall not" appropriate for a wooing song?), *canna* (Again, "cannot"), *manna* (from heaven) . . . Imagine, a girl who performs miracles! He will have to be his most creative to compose the right song for her. But in the end, he is almost entirely sure, she will topple into love like any other girl . . .

"Oh, hurry it up, boy," Thyrla says impatiently, as if Peder is one of her servants instead of her son. He applies himself to key the sixth and tries not to think, because when his mother is in such a mood, she can actually hear his thoughts.

With seven, he has the door open, and Thyrla pulls Sanna inside.

"Lock us in," she orders.

She doesn't say whether Peder should enter the room or stay outside, so he steps boldly in and does up the mechanisms, then sits on his mother's green-draped bed, feet dangling. He wants to see what happens.

It's as if he's on a raft at sea, he thinks, as the mattresses cup his bum and the coverlets and bed curtains billow out, then in with his settling. The walls and even the ceiling are draped in green damask, too, so in a way it's more like being *in* the sea, the green part that you see on top when you're in a boat.

And that thought ignites his fear of drowning. Thyrla has warned him many times about the dangers of boats, so he can count on the fingers of one hand how many times he's been in one, though he would dearly love to see more of the world than these thirty-seven islands. Thyrla occasionally speaks of taking a journey . . .

Somewhere Peder hears a kind of knocking, as of small objects afloat; the draperies all around the room billow, though Thyrla has closed the shutters. He shivers. To be honest (as he rarely bothers to be), Mother's room has always made him feel unsettled and small.

By contrast, now that she's here, Thyrla seems to grow larger. She fills the room, in fact; there's hardly space for him or the strange girl or the bed or table or chair and chest where Thyrla does the sums and subtractions that govern her business.

Ignoring Peder, Thyrla grasps the girl by the shoulders and turns her this way and that. The scent of roses intensifies, as if Sanna carried it in with her, as if it's oozing from her pores with her blood.

Thyrla asks of a sudden, so as to catch her prey off guard, "Why are you here?"

The girl says, "I came . . . for you? Or I think I did."

Why does Thyrla get the sense that this is not a complete answer? She detects an accent she's never heard before, not in decades of trade with ships from every country in the known world. The eye she keeps hidden under the patch, the eye that itches when it meets something unknown, plagues her fiercely now.

"For me?" she asks, inviting elaboration, but Sanna doesn't speak.

Thyrla's mind tumbles over itself. It's obvious by now

that the girl has magic. The change in the roses wasn't a fluke; nothing makes a tingle and burn in another witch's flesh like the flow of magic. But does Sanna know how to *use* this power, or is it simply moving through her? And how can Thyrla turn all this magic to her own advantage?

She lets Sanna's arm go. There's nowhere for the girl to scurry to anyway, unless she can sprout wings and fly from three flights up. Thyrla gnaws her lip, thinking, plotting, and tries to shake feeling back into her hand. If she felt Sanna's magic, how much of Thyrla's did Sanna detect?

It's the boy, Peder, who breaks the silence.

"What sort of name is *Sanna?*" he asks. "Do you come from *very* far away?"

Thyrla darts him a look that says to hold his tongue. He's a stupid boy whose name means *rock*, as out of rock he was born and as foolish as a rock he's remained. Which is her doing, but still.

Sanna doesn't answer. Thyrla thinks she's feeling around the room for magic, too, but Peder seems to think she didn't understand him.

"I mean, what *land* are you from?" he clarifies, oblivious to his mother's unspoken command. "Denmark? Sweden? Lithuania? Probably fell off a ship, didn't you?"

The timid idiot is afraid of boats — well, Thyrla made him fear them on purpose, so he never would leave her.

"I was in the sea a long time," Sanna says, almost as if she's confessing a secret.

Caution, Thyrla reminds herself. She'd be a fool to think

Sanna doesn't feel magic coming from her as well. She says nothing for now; silence can be powerful, too.

She touches Sanna's arm again, as if assessing a leg of veal. It is hard and muscled—the arm of a laborer rather than a lady. And yet the girl acts more like a lady than a maid, but not enough like either one to be sure.

Thyrla speaks: "Let's see how worse for wear you are." Both hands numb now from magical sparks, she turns Sanna right, left, forward, back, all under the pretext of examining her wounds. She finds nothing special, other than the drops of blood that glitter as they harden.

And yet the itch in Thyrla's eye is all but unbearable. She wants to scratch and pluck the eye out—but won't, of course. The eye is warning her.

The girl may be special, may be not; it remains to be seen. She might not even know her own strength. She could be under an enchantment. There's no telling what the tides might wash ashore on these islands, or how it can be used.

Around the room, a gentle clatter, as of branches knocking together in winter. Thyrla ignores it.

She says on a note of finality, "My maid will bring some salve for your wounds. And you should have a bath."

Thyrla takes a step back. The girl stands like a pillar of salt. In her once-beautiful blue dress, with her yellow hair almost long enough to sit on and streaked with light green that might even be algae; with her green eyes blinking more than other eyes blink, though the light in the cabinet is dim and the draft almost nothing, thanks to well-fit shutters.

"But before we send you to the bath"—Thyrla changes her mind—"we must have a test. A proving."

"To prove what?" Sanna asks.

Can the girl really be so innocent—so stupid?

Thyrla can't stand the itch any longer. She grabs the ring of keys from her son's limp fingers. She unlocks the chest by the courtyard window, lifts the heavy lid, and takes out a nacreous vial. Breaks the wax seal, then tips the contents over her index finger so a bubble of thick white liquid forms. At last she pulls off the silk patch with the embroidered wink, and with her back to both her son and the stranger, she rubs the unguent on her special eye. It stings, but she'll feel better soon.

She turns around, keeping that eye shut, though it leaks some of the unguent. If she opened the eye, it would pierce Sanna like a pin and hold her bleeding out answers, but there's more to gain by keeping its powers a secret. She slides the patch back down.

"Where do you get your magic?" Thyrla asks abruptly. "Are you a woman of the Church or a witch?"

"The . . . Church?" The girl acts coy, brushing at her hands, shedding those bright bubbles of dried blood. Coy and anxious, or so she seems to want Thyrla to see her. A heartbeat too late, she asks, "Magic?"

Thyrla recognizes a certain knowing behind the

innocence. She begins — almost — to read the stranger's thoughts, and already her eye itches less.

"The roses didn't change on their own," she says, as if it's an established fact. "Not in over a hundred years — not since far, far back in my family's history, that is — have the flowers been any color but white. As far as I know, no other color is possible. *Roses are white.*"

Sanna flushes as red as one of the new blooms, and the air crackles as more magic streams off her. It's as good as a confession.

From the ceiling comes the subtle clatter again, as if the castle itself applauds Thyrla's reasoning.

The Baroness decides to attack. "Do you presume to be both godly and witchly?" she asks. She blinks both eyes fast, trying to reach through the girl's skull and see everything there, though the special eye sees nothing but the darkness of the patch. "Do you make both miracles and dark spells — or rather, do you try? It's never been done. Just ask Father Abel at the village church. He'll dunk you as soon as look at you, if there's even a hint of witchcraft about. Not that dunking would work in your case; you look to have been thoroughly soaked and none the worse for it."

The ceiling knocks once more, louder this time. *Shh, Uncle,* Thyrla thinks with the full force of her personality.

The ceiling quiets down.

Peder sits tense on the edge of the bed, hanging on the girl's next words. He looks to Thyrla like a mooncalf, besotted by something new.

"I already told you I was in the sea a long time," Sanna says.

Thyrla tries another line, hoping to pull this fish in. "Very well. That's answered. But what else can you do? Are you a flower-witch only, or do you know other tricks?"

"Wh-what do you want me to say?" the girl stammers. "What do you need?" Her hands are bleeding again, staining her dress with kisses of blood. She looks like someone who has not planned ahead. She seems *out of her element*, so to speak.

When it comes to witches, as Thyrla knows well, looks are almost always deceiving. It will take a well-devised test to show just what kind of witch she's dealing with.

She decides to be blunt.

"I want you to do a spell," she says lightly, then laughs. Lesser people are always more frightened when threats come with laughter. "*Your* magic, your best magic."

The stranger hesitates. She looks from Thyrla to Peder, the wastrel boy lounging on his mother's bed. Thyrla expects her to lie and say she has no magic, can't do a single trick; the red-rose miracle was an accident. But that is not what she says.

She says, "I'll do magic, on purpose, if you do some first." A half breath, and then she adds, "Please."

anna

It has all gone so wrong, so fast!

Maybe I can forgive myself for being careless with the magic that lingered in my blood (I had no way of knowing about that, and I'll guard against it in future), but how did I let myself be caught—*caught*, as we say in the sea, meaning the worst possible fate—by this woman? I, who have eluded sharks and squid and fishermen's nets since the day I was born, who have sung sailors to their death lest they violate me or a girl of my people: I failed to plan for a danger. A beautiful danger, for the woman and her son are very beautiful; and in the ocean, we learn early that the prettiest and most tempting creatures carry the most lethal poison.

This Baroness Thyrla, as she calls herself, is clearly—

"What kind of witch are you?" I ask her. I'm blunt. "What kind of magic do *you* have?"

As soon as I say the word—*magic*—there comes a hissing sound, a howl, and a series of knocks, though Thyrla doesn't move so much as an eyelash. Then a silence as heavy as stone.

Silver and gold, shining in the half dark, Thyrla glares at me. From all the noises, including the not-noise of her silence, I conclude that she is a witch of the air, as I'm one of water. Which is why she's taken me somewhere so high and windy that the traces of my own element have evaporated.

The boy, Peder, is also staring, though the weight of his gaze feels quite different. Could he be a witch, too, perhaps of a different sort?

Sjældent and Father and all of the aunties told me that in this place, men are superior to women, and women must do as men say, even boys. I wonder if they are mistaken, or if the Baroness is simply an exception. She with her castle and her feast and her rose vine, ordering this boy about—she's no more docile than Sjældent or Addra.

But then, too, there's the strange way Peder looks at me: as if he owns me, the way someone might own a necklace or ring. I think I feel him already deep in my bones, owning me . . . and smiling.

"Careful, Mother," he says in a slow, drawling voice. "Our visitor could be planning a trick."

Thyrla doesn't look away from me. She doesn't even blink.

I don't think Peder means what he says, or else he's decided never to appear sincere for some reason. When I look at him, he winks at me as if we're sharing a joke—or as if he's imitating the silken eye his mother is wearing over her real one.

"Like that trick with the roses," he adds. "It could be no more than any sailor would pick up in a port to the east."

I wouldn't have known a rose to nod at, if I hadn't fallen into them. Now I can't get their scent out of my nose; it's a bright-dark smell of air and sap, as far from salt depths as can be. Completely unexpected.

A test of magic wasn't in my plans, either—and now I've turned it into a *contest,* in which Thyrla and I will battle each other. This is surely not what Sjældent intended when she said I'd find a woman on these shores to help me. No one could possibly know of this Baroness and still expect help, let alone help finding a mother. It's hard enough to believe she's a mother herself, the way she orders Peder around so harshly.

Except now. Now she's guarding her silence and letting him speak.

"Mother," he says, "I think you should go first. Sanna wants to find your weakness."

"Then I'll have to show her my strength." The Baroness, finally speaking, is a little less frightening. Just a little. Her tongue is very sharp, and when she talks I feel that tingle of magic, even without a touch.

She says, "I have just the thing." She goes to the table, picks up a silver jar, and spills sand over the surface. She does this till the table is covered, and then she smooths the sand out; and when *that* is done, she begins to make marks in it. Her finger draws a series of lines that form sixteen squares:

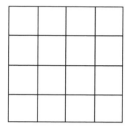

Peder laughs — that sound of landish bells borne through the air — and says, "Oh, Mother."

He says *Mother,* but I get the impression he's speaking to me. Showing off: He knows something that I do not; he knows this magic, too.

"Name a number," Thyrla says to me. "Any number. I will find it for you among others I write in this sand, beginning with one through twelve and conjuring the rest."

My *flok* hasn't much use for written numbers — there is no point in writing on water. But we know about them, as they are often found on things we keep because they're pretty. And of course, we know how to count; we count fish, waves, ships, each other.

"Thirty-seven," I say.

She seems pleased; her eye is bright. "Ah. For the Thirty-Seven Dark Isles. A very nice gesture from a guest. Well, remember your number, and my son will be our witness."

Thyrla bends to the tablet and, pushing her right sleeve

up at the elbow, begins moving the sand around with her smallest finger, making numbers within the squares.

	1		
			2
5		3	
4		6	

It doesn't look like magic to me so far, but I watch. I know the looks of numbers up to a dozen or so; anything beyond that might be pure puzzle.

Thyrla pushes the sand around some more, dotting the squares with more numbers.

	1	12	7
11	8		2
5	10	3	
4		6	9

I think I hear laughter, or something more like teeth rattling against each other. I realize I'm frowning, and I tell my brow to unwrinkle. I wish my landish clothes didn't scratch so much. And that I could guess what Thyrla is doing before she finishes.

"It's very simple," says the Baroness. "These are all the numbers to a dozen, yes? And now we'll find your thirty-seven in every direction."

She fills the other squares with numbers bigger than I'm

used to seeing. I think, *Sjældent never told me about number-witches.*
I know only of elemental witches: sea, land, air, fire, time.

My early self-assurance, whatever there was of it, has
entirely vanished. But that's no magic feat.

"And there we are!" Thyrla steps aside to let me see
even better.

The figure is now complete, with a number for each
square in a seemingly haphazard pattern:

17	I	12	7
11	8	16	2
5	10	3	19
4	18	6	9

No number 37, though. I gaze down and let my face
scowl if it wants to.

The Baroness knows I'm nonplussed. "Now try this,"
she says, with an air of command more than invitation:
"Add them in any direction, up, down, or sideways, and
you'll have thirty-seven each way."

"Diagonally, too," says Peder. He sounds excited. "Start
in any corner and work toward its opposite, and you'll
have . . ."

"Thirty-seven," they say together.

They are very pleased with themselves, mother and son.
I check their sums and see that they are right; the number
adds up in each place they say it will.

As I work the arithmetic, the rattling behind the

tapestries builds, along with the scent of roses still blooming in the courtyard. The smells of the guests, too, and the sound of their jaws grinding away at the food we left behind. I even think I hear my clan, bobbing around the rocks just beyond the bay and talking about me. My senses are overwhelmed.

But . . .

"I don't think that's magic," I say, after careful consideration and a little more addition of my own. "If the first twelve numbers stay in their places, I can use the four spots that are left to create many different numbers. Forty or sixty or eighty-nine. And so can you, and so can anyone who knows arithmetic. And I believe I can make more if I move the digits around."

If I have disappointed them by not being as green a girl as they expected, they don't show it. Their smiles grow wider, and the ceiling sounds like a volcano about to bubble over.

"So you've guessed it's a common dodge," Thyrla says to me. "Aren't you a clever one?"

She doesn't seem to mean it, but she does seem to expect an answer. I think a silence will be more provocative.

And I'm right. "Well," she says, "we've proven we both know some tricks — but as to *magic* . . . What are you really able to do, my dear? Would you like to walk on water, or shall I order some loaves and fishes brought up for you to multiply?"

I'm confused. My mind is tired of clevering, and my body is sore with spells. What could these two expect of me now?

"I'm still waiting for *your* magic," I say.

"And perhaps this as well?" Between her thumb and forefinger, she holds a golden ring with a green stone. My father once gave that to me, saying the stone was the color of my eyes, and I wore it ashore for good luck. I didn't feel her taking it from me.

I make a little lurch to grab it back.

"Now you have it—and now you don't," she says smugly. She slips the ring onto her own little finger and gazes at it with a show of admiration, though when compared to the other stones on her hands, my little emerald is nothing.

"Sleight of hand," I say. "You probably took it when we were climbing those"—I hesitate; for a moment I can't remember the word, and I want to say *snail*—"stairs to get here."

"Hmm." She sniffs at me. She looks very beautiful and very vexed. Then her sniff leads to a cough, and a puff of smoke from each nostril.

Her cough deepens, her body hunches over, and I worry she's having a fit. Maybe I should leap over there and thump her on the back; maybe she needs some healing magic, and if I heal her she'll be kind . . .

Her white skin is going blue; her gray eye is turning

black. I wonder why her own son continues to sit on her bed and doesn't get up to help. He could be just another part of the draperies for all he's doing.

Then Thyrla's lips stretch wide, and out of her mouth pops a lizard.

It lands with a dry skid on the table, blurring the numbers in the sand. Smooth and brown, with slotted yellow eyes rolling this way and that. Its legs are stiff, but its heart beats visibly in its throat.

Thyrla picks it up in a curl of her fingers and holds it toward me, coated with sand, to admire.

"See what a sweet little thing this is," she says raspily, through what must be a very sore throat. "My baby"—with a flick of the gaze to Peder, who laughs uncomfortably while the whole room seems to rattle. "There's magic for you, Sanna! I didn't have *him* inside me a moment ago."

I watch while a tiny tongue of flame blows from each of the lizard's nostrils and then is gone. The lizard's gone, too, as his legs find their strength and he leaps toward a wall.

Peder slaps his hands together. The sound echoes through the room with more of that dizzying clatter. I look around, more confused than ever, wondering where the lizard could have gone. And where he came from, really. I don't have the magic to make a creature out of nothing; I don't think even Sjældent can do that.

"Don't worry a bit," Thyrla says, with one of her easy smiles. "There are a thousand of his kind around the place; he'll find them. Now, Sister Sanna, it's time for you to show me—"

She's cut off when the green cloth behind her catches fire. The little lizard is at the edge of it, coughing flames to make it burn more quickly.

"Oh, bother." Obviously irritated, Thyrla removes her shoe and uses it to smash the lizard to pulp. She moves so fast, it would be easy to miss, except for the mess on the floor.

"Never mind him," she says again, beating the green drape against the wall to extinguish the flame. "Really, this time. A miscalculation on my part. Now, Sanna, you must demonstrate your kind of magic. It's only polite."

Having seen what she does to lizards, I am rightfully afraid of displeasing. And I have learned one important fact: Thyrla can conjure, but she can't always control her conjurings. And the element of fire can hide within her breathy tricks.

She must be a powerful witch, indeed, to command two of the elements (though one rather poorly).

Then my ears fill with that odd knocking sound, and I am overwhelmed enough to swoon.

Chapter 10

The land shakes; the sea remains.

Addra's head swivels, flashing red fire that confuses the dolphins. She beats her coppery tail against Ringstone's bottom.

"Did you hear that?" she calls down to the *flok.*

"You have the best vantage point," says Pippa the Strong, accusingly, for she thinks Addra's selfish.

But Pippa has heard, too, or at least felt the tremble in her bones that is even better than hearing and helps make her a great huntress.

"The islands are shaking," La guesses, round-eyed as a baby seal. "Something has happened."

"I smell smoke," says Ruut, a light-bearded young man; but since he is only a man, they ignore him.

The elders exchange looks that express more than words. Some of them are Sanna's relations by blood or bond—Gurria One Arm, Shusha the Logical, Mar of the

Long Reach—and all of them predict that this venture onto land will have profound consequences for the *flok*, though they are not sure what those consequences will be.

"A *something that happens* can be good," says cloudy-haired Frill. No one pays much attention to her, either.

"Is Sanna safe?" asks her father, Bjarl. "Can anyone tell?"

The entire gathering listens hard. The dolphins chitter to each other and swoop off to sea, without jumping through Ringstone's O. Frill, suddenly hopeless, bursts into tears, though as yet no one knows whether tears are warranted.

At the sound of weeping, Sjældent shudders as if someone has poked her. She comes out of her doze and coughs to clear her throat; then an assortment of wee crabs and worms, which had been settling in comfortably among the gaps in her teeth, goes flying into the waves.

"No telling, no seeing," she says, running her tongue around to feel for more. "Just ye hope our girl keeps some sense about her, and a grip on her magic."

"She'll sing us the story tonight," says Gurria.

"If she's alive," Sjældent agrees.

Bjarl ducks beneath the waves, lest he slap the old witch for leading Sanna into these islands. And for casting the spell that made all of them forget Sanna's mother, his love, in the first place.

anna

I do not swoon, because I must not; I know in my bones that I have to stay wary around Thyrla, even if she is the person Sjældent said would help me. I see now that if I'm going to get anything from her—if I'm even going to ask—I have to know when to hold my tongue. I certainly won't bring up my mother; I won't even think her name (my most treasured secret, or one of them) in the presence of this Baroness.

"Your turn, Sanna," she says again, not minding the lizard's pink and gently smoking carcass behind her. "Show me your own kind of magic. Shall I order up those loaves and fishes? Or perhaps an old man you can raise from the dead?"

I think hard. I can't do anything she's mentioned so far, and I suspect she knows it; she's aiming to embarrass me. Perhaps she guesses my true nature and that's why she keeps offering fishes.

What am I sure I can accomplish to protect myself and keep my place here? I must appear strong but not too strong; I am certain that anyone either too weak or too strong will be crushed, like the lizard, with the wrath of the Baroness.

My eyes fall upon the table, where the sand still bears traces of numbers and of the poor lizard's feet.

Sand.

I know what to do.

I breathe in very gently, very slowly. My eyes flutter; my blood tingles. The sand begins to move.

For as long as I am able to inhale with my shrunken landish lungs, the sand lifts itself upward. The last scratches of numbers and lines are finally erased as the sand becomes first a mist, then a cloud, then a column.

I hold my breath, and the sand continues to move in place. Swirling around the edges and falling into itself, renewing at the bottom and spiraling up again.

A sand-twist is one of the simplest spells; it can be performed on land or in the sea, probably in the midst of a fire. Almost any seavish person, witch or not, can learn to make one, but I believe it's still a marvel to the landish. The twist shimmers in the space between the three of us, in the midst of a pure, surprised silence.

After the initial shock, Thyrla's eye turns from the sand to me to the sand again. Peder's mouth gapes open quite foolishly. I suppose he has none of his mother's gifts.

After a time, my lungs begin to ache, and so does my blood. I can't hold the magic much longer. So I make my lips into a ring and puff out my cheeks, and I blow the sand toward the window, where it knocks open the boards that have kept the light out. It sparkles a moment just beyond the wall and then falls like a whisper over the thick-scented roses and the insects humming among them.

"Holy hops and barley," Peder says, and looks at me with the round eyes of admiration. "You really can do something!"

Thyrla says, brisk and brittle, as if she has to hide some feeling, "Very good, then. Very well."

"Very well what?" I seem to have missed something.

What she says next is the biggest shock of the day:

"You and my son can marry."

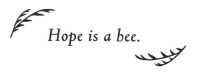

Chapter 12

Hope is a bee.

In the courtyard, the broken feast (as it will come to be called) has been the finest in memory. It is less rushed, less *desperate*, than these meals usually are. Broken food actually tastes better than the elaborate concoctions first served, and with the Baroness busy, the people have all the time in the world to enjoy themselves.

"Flavors taste better blended," pronounces Harald the butcher, who knows more than anyone else about food.

"Hunger's the best sauce," adds his wife, Maria, who is never wrong.

"Nothing tastes as good as hope," says one of many Eriks who go to sea to fish. He is the closest to truth of them all.

The farmers, the fishers, the craftsmen of Dark Moon Harbor—everyone who saw the roses change—is now aware that magic wells up through the unlikeliest of channels. This feast is not just from the Baroness. It is a sign of the promise that the Lord and His representatives on earth offer to even the humblest soul who is capable of trust.

For once, Father Abel leaves the Bible and the dais to sit down among the common people, on benches they've righted and at tables remade. He sits beside Old Olla, Thyrla's beekeeper, and shares her plates of pewter and wood, a trencher of bread, a cup of wine.

Of the tables' abundance, the people eat quietly. Simply, like the butterflies and bees that pleasure themselves in the heady red bowls of the blooms.

All this, too, the people know without discussing. They are sure of it in their souls. Only the tiniest children feel a need to speak, and they just make sounds such as *"Fa"* and *"Foo,"* whatever those syllables mean.

The mothers of the children smile and give them tasty morsels usually reserved for the fathers. The fathers smile, too, and think of the happy futures their offspring will have. The boys will harvest unheard-of numbers of fish; they'll pull astonishing crops from the ground. The girls will marry these prosperous young men and will not die from childbirth or overwork but will raise good families and share in what makes the Dark Islands famous in other lands.

Whatever that is . . .

These children will see those other lands, too. Other castles, some with golden roofs. Barns as big as islands. Churches so grand that they glow with colored glass as with jewels, with figures carved and painted both inside and out to tell happy stories from the Bible and the lives of the saints, rather than cautionary tales. Everything the people have heard about from sailors who stop in the bay for provisions: All this, the children will see for themselves.

The people plan these wonders without pride. Hope is not prideful; hope is trust that all of creation will sort itself out as it should. Hope is (Father Abel thinks it, helping Olla's spotted fingers pull a fish pie apart) a bee — a bee that creates even more goodness than it finds. The future is dripping with liquid-gold sweetness.

Above the feasters' heads, and as if approving of the grand plans and the people themselves, Our Lady of the Sea smiles with her rough pink lips and off-kilter eyes. Is it only in the imagination that her white skin and yellow robe shine brighter now than before? Is it just a fancy that has her cheeks even pinker than when the stranger fell softly into the blossoms?

No, none of this is imagined. It cannot be.

Our Lady's eyes see everything at once. They follow each man, woman, and child in the courtyard, and she beams at seeing how they offer one another bits of pie, slices of beef, morsels of honey-cured fruit.

The scent of red roses soaks the air like a sponge, and Our Lady's wooden arms seem to spread wider, and wider still, welcoming every glad soul into her embrace.

Then, all at once, the bees rise up from the flowers and swarm.

anna

At that word, *marry*, the sand comes flying back in. Or rather, the sand that flew out returns in the form of an insect swarm, thin wings beating furiously and a deafening buzz sucking the air from the room.

They attack the Baroness and her son, stinging, but for the moment they leave me alone. I don't know why this is; I didn't conjure them, and I doubt Sjældent is close enough to have done it.

I'm alarmed to see these two, at first so superior and sneering at me, now running back and forth and beating themselves with their own arms and hands, trying to kill the creatures that still smell of the flowers. Such tiny, loud things — I think their hum is a sort of song like the whales', full of stories and information, only none of us can understand.

The Baroness shrieks, and it's a horrible sound, like a dolphin being devoured by a shark. Small things cause much pain.

Honestly, what did Sjældent have in mind when she sent me here? Had she any idea at all what I'd find? Will Thyrla really help in my quest, or has this been a mistake?

"Marry?" I say, but they're too busy to answer me. "You want me to marry *whom*?"

Chapter 14

Rhyme.

All of you men who ride wooden boats
And cut paths in the sea with cruel purpose:
You're danger, says Mother; you're danger, says Auntie—
You'll tear us apart if you catch us.
So . . . let us sing you away into sleep.
Let us sing you away into Down-Below-Deep.

—*The Mermaids*

anna

"Ever so lucky, to be marrying the young baron, I mean," says the plump maid, Kett, whom the Baroness has assigned as my servant and my jailor. She's bustling around the chamber I've been given, a place too small for us both to move around at once. "There's ever so many girls in love with him. Not that he'd give any of us more than a buss and a tumble, and maybe a bit of a song. He's very musical, you know . . ."

While she prattles and tidies, I curl onto the too-short, too-narrow bed with the rose thorns still in my flesh. The bed is nice and soft, crackling with landish grass that smells of the sun. It makes me realize how very tired I am. Magic is hard work.

". . . I'm sure he'll stop all that now you're betrothed. The singing, I mean. To other girls." Kett positions a flame in a tiny wall niche nearby; it is burning in a dish of oil that smells like fish, which is soothing. "He must have fallen in love right away, thunder and lightning, to arrange a marriage so fast. Now he'll just sing for you."

She sounds wistful. Myself, I am hardly moved by the prospect of listening to the landish boy singing love tunes, but Kett seems to feel she's missed some beautiful opportunity.

On land, girls fall in love with boys, I remember Father and Sjældent telling me. And I remember laughing at it—why, with all I know now of the power of landish men over women, would a girl actually *love* a boy? And who could love Peder? He might be pretty to look at, but I don't see much beyond that.

"Oh, he's lucky, too," Kett says, changing tone, as if she's afraid my silence means I'm annoyed. "Marrying you, I mean. What you did with the roses . . ."

Yes, what I did with the roses.

"There isn't a single girl in these islands who could do the same," Kett concludes—as if (I think) somewhere else a girl is in fact transforming flowers right and left. "Plus which, you will make a very handsome pair."

She says it with a great air of nobility, and of expectation. I satisfy her by saying "Thank you," though of course I have no intention of pairing off with that wastrel.

"Well, then, miss." She smiles sweetly at me in the fluttering light. "Should we begin now?"

I nod.

Kett has been ordered to remove the thorns from my

body. I plan to remove information from her at the same time, for I suspect she is one of those giddy young girls like my cousin Frill, all wide eyes and stories. Kett also has a few of the red spots on her face to which landish young people are unfortunately prone—and which resemble the marks the insects left on Thyrla and Peder, the little dots that made Peder moan almost to weeping.

"Best take your clothes off, if I'm to get all the prickers out," Kett says. "Can you help me, please? Otherwise this candle's sure to douse, with the draft in this little room, and I can't see in the dark." She giggles as if this is very funny or she is very embarrassed.

Sjældent and Bjarl have told me the landish are often shy about being naked; they don't like it, or it makes them feel vulnerable. Completely unlike us in the sea, where we rely on bare skins and scales to propel us swiftly through the water and sense what's happening in it.

Kett begins delicately to lift the blue velvet skirt, which has finally relaxed a bit from its stiffening in salt and blood. I wonder if it frightens her to be touching someone believed to have made a miracle. I used to be afraid to touch Sjældent—but she always was a mean old witch, deliberately menacing to the young with her cackles and the crabs crawling out from her scales at odd moments.

As I struggle out of the clothes into which I first struggled only a morning and a lifetime ago (when they were difficult because they were damp, not stiff) I wonder if this is how all brides are treated here. I wonder if the servants and guests—departed now, back to their own homes in the town that reeks of their lives—I wonder if they think the way the Baroness treats me is strange, or if it all is according to custom.

After the bees left, Thyrla introduced me to the people as her son's bride and said I was sent for from across the seas. I suspect she thinks assigning me this purpose will make the roses' transformation less of a *miracle* and more of a trick. At least, it will give her ownership of the magic.

While she spoke, I gazed down at the tiniest of hurts on the back of my hand, a sting left by a single one of the bees: a prick of white in a circle of red, and an itch and a burn as of magic.

I raised the hand to my mouth and subtly licked the sting. I tasted the salt that is still in my skin, and the death of the insect who hurt me. It ripped out its own belly just to do this.

"Do you want some honey for that?" I remember Peder whispering to me. "There's an old woman here who says the sweetness swallows the sting."

I declined.

However Thyrla explained me to them, the people were delighted to see me once more. They clapped their hands together and blew kisses toward me, and they watched as the old man called Father Abel wrote on a paper with ink that reeked of beetles, with brown-blotched hands that shook and spattered his writing. Then, to this paper, handsome Peder and I signed our names.

At least, Peder signed; I put down an X. Thyrla assured me it was as good as my own name, and Abel said that Jesus's name (whoever Jesus might be; I might ask Kett) begins with X when written in Greek (whatever that language is; again, I'll ask if it seems important).

After that, the Baroness sent the people away and ordered Kett to bring me to this little room. And acted as if she were doing me a grand favor with it.

"A lady can't lie down among the servants in the great hall," she explained, as if I had other expectations (and as if I knew what a great hall is—which I do, but just vaguely, as a place where the landish spend most of the day). "Certainly not if she's betrothed to my son."

She said more, but I recognize a prison when I'm in it. I hope she doesn't realize that I might free myself at any moment I want (or so I believe); I sense the web of magic binding bodies and hearts to the castle, but I think I have the spells to cut myself free. Keeping those spells a secret gives me some power here.

And yet I don't want to escape, not now. I am curious as to what it is like to sleep so far aboveground. This room is a nook, really, like one of the crags in which my people wedge themselves for safety; the little bed nearly fills it, and the candle flame's in danger each time somebody moves.

Then, too, if I stay, I have a much better chance of finding the woman Sjældent has said might lead me to my mother. Whether that helper is Thyrla or—as I speculate now, after meeting the Baroness — some other woman of this place.

I imagine the courtyard with its new red roses, the flowers that fed on my blood. I almost convince myself that I can look through the walls and see the half-made moon behind a tower, slicing into the castle. And all the swaths of stars under which my people love to float this time of year, catching fishes and jellies for a late-night meal.

But it's still too early for all that. If I want moonlight, I'll be waiting a long time.

Instead of my cousins, I have Kett, who (as my eyes adjust to the room) I see again is pretty and kind, with blue eyes and brown hair. She helps me shrug out of the linen shift I've worn next to my skin, and then I'm naked in front of her.

She runs the candle's light up and down my body, then tells me to lie on my belly. "The thorns seem worst in your back, I think. Which is peculiar, since you fell frontwise into the vine. You must've got all tangled up, miss."

I do as she asks. I think it's easier for both of us not to face each other; I just make sure that my hair's bundled over the back of my neck, over the mark left when the magic of remaking stretched a membrane over my breath hole, and then I make myself fit the bed — though I'm taller than it is long, and my feet hang off the end and graze the wall.

"Goodness, miss!" Kett exclaims, and then laughs — I think it is over my size. She sets the candle on its table again and bends over my back, squeezing at the skin to force a

74

thorn out. With the first one, she bursts out with an "Ah!" of satisfaction, and then there's the faintest of taps as she drops it into a small jar.

I decide it's time to make the most of our isolation, or there's no point staying here.

"Who is Jesus?" I ask. I think it's a safe question.

"Jesus!" She pops another thorn free. "Why, he's the son of the Lord and the Virgin Mary! Do you call him something else where you're from?"

Oh no. "I suppose we do," I say cautiously.

Kett bends to her work again. I feel her breath on my lower back.

"You must have traveled from ever so far, miss, if you don't know what Jesus is called."

Her voice holds a kind of wonder mixed with hope. I've often noticed that mixture in the landish people we meet on our migrations; they're bound to the rocks and sand on which they're born and into which they'll die, so they long for travelers' tales. Yet, oddly, not tales of the sea itself— no, they want to hear about other *lands.* As if there's only one true way to live and eat and work and die, and they grub around in the dirt.

"Yes, very far," I say. Then, to be kind, "Have you traveled much yourself?"

"*Me?*" I feel the light from her smile warming the darkness as she plucks another thorn from my back. "Oh, isn't that silly! My father did—that is, did and died. He was a fisher, he was, and one time he went so far to the north that the ice never broke, and he found a white bear and killed and ate it."

"Is that how he died?"

"Nah. Storm at sea, I suppose, the next time he sailed. We never did hear. My brothers, three of 'em, is all fishers, too. They don't go so far—our uncle won't allow it. My two sisters married farmers, and I'm here at the castle."

Now I hear pride in her voice; it drips onto my skin like a balm. It's good to have a certain amount of pride. Not as much as the Baroness, but some. And Kett's pride is in being here.

"I suppose Thyrla has seen the world." I take a guess, hoping to get at what really interests me.

Kett is quiet a moment, squeezing and pulling till she has two or three more thorns in her jar. She dabs at a scratch that I could tell her will heal before morning; I don't tell her, because this talk is as good for me as her nursing.

"I don't know," she says at last, and her voice trembles as if some faith has been shaken—although why this is, I have no inkling. "She's always been here, long as I've known, and my ma and all the old people say so, too. And that she's hardly aged a day in all that time, just added some silver to the gold in her hair. They say Father Abel was a young man when he come here—all the way from Denmark, that's a voyage for you—and look at him now. And her still looking like my ma's younger sister. If my ma were noble, that is."

This gives me a lot to think about. It sounds as if the

Baroness ages as slowly as the women of my clan. Could she be one of us? No, of course not; if she were seavish, even partly so, she'd have recognized me for what I am at once. As I would have recognized her.

"It's the dragon," Kett says surprisingly.

"Dragon?"

"Some people say that's what keeps her young. Living in the rock here, right below the castle. It's his breath making the warm drafts through cracks in the floors, and it keeps us all fresh. So the old people in the town tell us, at least."

"What an interesting story," I say, though it is neither more nor less unusual than some of the things I've seen in my journeys. I imagine the dragon as a sort of longnose fish, a creature we admire because the fathers guard the babies in a pouch of belly skin until the young can swim on their own. Perhaps this dragon of the Dark Islands watches over the people in the same way, with the rock as his pouch.

"Isn't it?" Kett squeezes another thorn. "Well, for myself, I wouldn't mind aging a few years so these spots'd leave my face."

Poor girl. I suppose this is the same on land and sea: None of us ever think ourselves pretty enough, except perhaps Addra in my *flok* and Thyrla in Kett's. And even they probably hide some uncertainties.

"You're pretty, Kett," I say. It's awkward because I'm not used to giving compliments. I've been so determined to find my mother that I haven't spent much time with girls my age, let alone courting them. My cousin La, however, has already chosen a mate—a girl who lives far to the south, where the days and nights last equally long without changing and the beaches belong to what we call the Basking Waters.

"Thanks, miss, but I know how I look. My brothers have told me often enough." She sighs, and her breath (not the dragon's) is intimate over my skin. "And the young baron has shown me by his actions. If I were pretty, he'd have had me on my back even though his mother don't allow it."

I hear a clapping sound and realize she's slapped her hand over her mouth. The candle's flame whooshes up and then nearly out; I let my magic push a little to keep it alight.

Kett says, "Oh, please don't tell anyone I said that!"

By this I know she'd like nothing more than to lie on her back with Peder upon her, which is how I'm told these landish people do it. *Mating,* one on top of the other, rather than coiled together as we do.

I say, "I won't tell. I promise."

She goes back to unthorning me, even more carefully now. "Baron Peder, oh, *he's* traveled, 'least in one sense of the term. You should hear the mistress. He says sometimes he wants to go to sea, wants to visit the places Father Abel's been, but she tells him not to dream of it. She says, 'You've traveled enough, my boy. You've been inside every tavern and every tavern *girl* in town.'"

This might have been meant as a joke, but in Kett's voice, with its odd emphasis, it's plaintive.

"So Peder has had many girls," I conclude for her. This kind of "travel" is unusual among the boys of my people but not too off-putting, as we rarely limit ourselves to one love in a lifetime. We say to our elders when they're nearing the end, *You have lived long, you have seen much, and you will be remembered.* Passion never enters the phrase, though some of them have loved as much as they've seen.

Love. I'm not even going to think about it until I complete my quest. Not now, when I have at least another hundred and twenty summers in which to feel it.

However, there is still the presumption here that I will marry Peder, and I can't see anyone trying to convince me I should want to. I ask, purely from curiosity, "Has he loved all of those girls?"

"Oh, not any of them, miss," she says reassuringly. "Not a single one. And I'm sorry to speak that way of your betrothed, but that's the fact. The girls all like him because he's pretty and rich, and he has a beautiful voice for songs. But I don't believe his own heart's ever been touched. Until today, of course," she adds. "I'm sure he loved you as soon's you walked in. He signed the paper and all."

What I take from this, what I mull over after Kett leaves with her jar of bloodied thorns and her candle, when the door is locked behind her and I'm alone and naked on the bed of crackling straw: *Peder has a beautiful voice for songs.*

That, at least, is something my people understand.

anna

That night, I sing. Or at least I try to.

I promised this to Father and Sjældent: If I didn't return to the *flok* right away, I would sing my farthest-reaching songs to tell them how I fared and what I intended next. I imagine them now waiting out in the calm waters of what the landish know as Dark Moon Bay, floating on their backs and eating the fish we call moon-skippers because they leap from the waters at night. The *flok* waits for my song.

But how will they hear it? There's not a single window in this tiny cell, and the door is guarded by Kett and (I smell them) two landish watchmen. I could work a spell of unmaking and slip out, but I'm not sure I'd be able to return to the castle if I wanted to. I'm tired, and there can't be that much magic left in my blood.

I sniff along the walls, nuzzling like an eel looking for a crack to slide out through. That's what I want—a crack, some little space that will let me send my voice into the world, to tell those who care that I'm still alive and apparently soon to bind my life to a weak landish boy's. A wedding that will never happen . . .

Ah, there it is: the merest trace of a cool draft, a fissure no wider than a hair of my head. Through it, I smell sea air. This is a relief, for although I don't entirely believe what Kett told me about the dragon living under the castle, I also don't want to sing directly into his ear.

With my lips so close to the slit that they brush stone again and again, I begin the song of my first day on land. The pain of the change, the trouble with walking—some of which my people witnessed in earlier stages as I practiced, with girls like Addra envious as I gained passage to a new element, and girls like Pippa curious. And then the things they don't know about because I only learned of them today: the sweet-water springs in the middles of islands, the grasping plants, the strange insects, and the smells of the foods that this landish *flok* eats. My clumsy fall into the roses and its accidental display of magic, which I can't sing of without shame.

And, of course, Baroness Thyrla and her son, and my betrothal to that boy of the earth and the rock, and my confusion as to what it all means.

It is a very long song, and I don't even know if it's reaching my people. The notes could die on the sea air and be crushed in the waves. It's not like singing a song of allure for the landish men in their boats; there's no crash or howl to tell me I've hit my mark.

But as I sing, I feel a change in my skin's punctures and scratches, all the wounds of the rose vine and the one from the bee. They are sealing themselves up. As I tell their story, my magic spreads outward and grows.

I feel my blood getting stronger.

As to whether my clan can hear me—I honestly don't know. The only sound I hear back is a soft rattle and creak in the stone.

Chapter 17

The song's beat is in blood.

Bjarl and Sjældent have been waiting an eternity. In landish time, that is, whereby days are broken into mealtimes and prayer times, hours and even minutes, measured by sand falling through glass; all so the brief landish life can account for itself in the end.

In this sense, Bjarl and Sjældent have become like the landish, counting fractions and degrees as the sun sank toward the seaskin. In seavish time it's been barely the wink of an eye.

"But that eye has a boulder inside," Sjældent says, in her way that is both cryptic and not-cryptic.

During the wait, other members of the seavish clan may have wandered off to eat or rest, but these two have remained steadfast. They waited till the sun dipped far toward the water in the west; now its last curve sails along the waves, while to the east, the blade of the silver half-moon is cutting a pathway toward night. A few stars have also pierced the sheet of sky. And night has brought back some members of the *flok* who are curious to know if their girl—their niece, cousin, friend, rival—has survived as the first of their kind to walk, actually *walk*, among landish people in longer than anyone can recall.

"Next we hear, she'll have grown wings," guesses La, who may be preoccupied with her own love affair in waters to the south but loves Cousin Sanna just the same.

Addra scoffs. *"Wings."* And plucks a fly from the air to crush, just to show what she thinks of Sanna's magic in general and wings—or feet—in particular.

The clan is listening, floating, with long hair tangling together, the flats of their tails keeping them afloat. If a moon-skipper happens to land on a belly, the belly's owner will make sure the fish disappears inside right away; but they are not here for the hunt.

They have come for the song.

"If there is no song . . ." whispers cloud-headed Frill, making a show of her timidity.

"There will be a song," says Pippa the Strong, who has already been sung about herself.

"But if there isn't—"

"There will be." This time it's Addra who insists, stubbornly—Addra the Beautiful, who was never particularly kind to Sanna but will be the first to befriend her if she succeeds in her quest. Addra is hoisting herself back into the O of Ringstone after an evening of hunting and basking. "I'll never forgive Sanna if there isn't one."

Bjarl doesn't join in the speculation. He collects a handful of moon-skippers and brings them to Sjældent, who lies dry on a rock because her floating days are mostly past. When old age finally comes, it weighs heavy.

The witch is facing a long, dark, permanent night; but before she goes, Bjarl is going to make sure she keeps her promise to help Sanna. Which is only right, as Sjældent is the one who cast the spell of forgetting that has kept the entire *flok*, including Sjældent herself, mystified as to the whereabouts of Sanna's mother. Sjældent is the only one among them who can even remember a name, and she sees to it that Bjarl forgets it each time it comes to him.

"*Will* there be a song?" he dares to ask her now. "Do you know what has happened to Sanna?"

Sjældent slides a shiny skipper down her throat, swallowing with a gasp.

"Just ye be patient," she says, and reaches for another fish.

So they wait, till the stars are numbrous and bright, the sun a mere drop puddled upon the water. The seaskin a shimmer as unbroken as land or ice.

Then, at last, Sanna's first words arrive. They are reedy and twining, the whine of a new baby bird; but there is no mistaking the fundamental sweetness of that voice, the one that ice-colored Gurria One Arm, who is not only Sanna's aunt by bond but also an elder, has called the most gifted of all.

For a while it's enough merely to listen to that sweet

sound. But a song should also make sense, and some of the scenes Sanna describes and even the words she uses are mystifying.

"What does she mean, 'miracle'?" Frill asks.

"And is she really going to live with a landish boy?" Pippa sounds outraged. No self-respecting *marreminde* would do such a thing.

La shudders, thinking of her beloved Ishi in the waters to the south—O, to live with one's love! And to do it *now*, not to wait! Love is a rarity in seavish life, but when it's felt, it's felt keenly.

The elders, the aunts, hush the girls.

"Mark this song in your memory," says Shusha the Logical, who is mother of three daughters, including La. "It will be repeated forever."

"Through all the known waters in all the known curves of the great big watery world," adds Mar of the Long Reach, who is something of a singer herself. She pushes back her gray hair and remembers that time when travels were new, when each strange thing that met the eyes was a delight.

"It contains Sanna's life's blood," Bjarl says, so quietly the women don't hear.

Sjældent can't resist speaking up smugly: "She's doing it all just as I and she planned. *And* she'll be back soon with a treasure. Just ye see."

"With her mother?" Bjarl asks, with all the yearning of

a heart starved for love. (What is that love's name? Will Sanna—*L, Li, L . . .*)

Sjældent smacks her barnacled lips together. "There's treasure and then there's treasure," she says, as if there's something profound in the repetition. "When starting a quest, it's better to know what to ask than what to find."

No one can make her say more, even after Bjarl and some others blanket the rock with Sjældent's favorite jellies, including the fragile white ones that regress to polyp form when frightened.

"Everagains," she says, poking at them to watch the change. "Now, there's magic for ye, and they don't need a single word to make them so."

After that, though the song continues, some of the seavish get ready for sleep. They sink to the sandy bottom to wrap their tails around strong rocks and their arms around each other, for a *flok* is nothing if its members don't cling together like limpets.

But for those who stay awake on the shimmering seaskin, there is a much greater reward in listening on.

"Soon we'll know everything about the landish," Addra says languidly, combing her red locks with her fingers.

"We'll know how to defeat them in battle," says Pippa the Strong.

"Girls, girls," Shusha quiets them. "Listen."

Chapter 18

Siren song.

Three hearts, eight arms, one beak for biting—
Would you rather love an octopus or me?
Come deep, come deep.
                                        —The Mermaids

• Chapter 19 •

Not dragons but bones.

What kind of magic do you have?

This the stranger asked, in this very chamber, a few hours ago. The walls echo her question as the Baroness pulls on a series of cords that release the draperies and let the room's splendors *take a breath,* as she calls it, though of course they can't breathe at all. And don't need to.

With the yellow-white knobs and curves laid bare to her single wax candle, Baroness Thyrla has the audience she wants. She lifts a goblet of fragrant mead brewed from the honey of her primeval rose vine — and vents an inelegant snort.

"As if any witch worth the title would give *that* away," she says aloud, ignoring (for now) the lingering itch beneath her eye patch. "Only family should know the nature of a woman's powers. And not even *all* of the family."

She takes a sip and watches the room respond.

The sound of her voice is a key that turns an automaton's works. The walls, ceilings, window shutters—all begin to move and to clatter. That is, the bones mounted there begin making those noises: If they have jaws, they knock; if they have fingers, they snap. Some orphaned fragments simply vibrate, and their small sounds add to a thunder that shakes the room and certain parts of the castle, right down to the waterlogged stem of rock where the legendary dragon sleeps.

Thyrla smiles.

"A witch who lists her powers is either very smug or very foolish," she informs the bones. "Either way, she's set herself up for a downfall."

The bones rattle again.

Thyrla draws the chamber's single chair to the table and sets a steel mirror behind her candle. Light blooms and illuminates the room's smallest pockets: It gleams on bones lacquered dark with age; it catches in the cobwebs between and turns them to clouds. The spiders themselves go scurrying into the deepest corners possible. Even dumb creatures know that no good comes of the Baroness's attention.

It is a room made of bones.

Skulls line the seams of the ceiling's vault; ribs are butterflied upon the walls; vertebrae and finger bones, toe bones and femurs, make complicated whorls around the spaces between, echoing and amplifying the complexities of the human bodies from which they were taken.

Thyrla lifts the golden diadem from her hair and

watches in the mirror as she drags her fingers through the long silver-gold locks. She gazes into the reflection of the most beautiful woman, and the cleverest and most gifted, that she knows. Also the loneliest.

She breathes in the power from this room, where in her youth she began mounting the remains of friends and enemies as signs of her relentless ambition for magic. Each bone represents at least a year harvested from someone weaker than she; and with each bone, Thyrla grew stronger and lived longer.

Soon, soon now—thanks to this stranger, perhaps in the next few days or months at most—she'll have the strength to make a final harvest, extend her own life and secure it so she can climb onto one of the boats that come to her secret harbor, then sail off toward the horizon. See the world by living in it, the most powerful witch of all time.

In good part because of the bones.

They are as close to family as Thyrla wishes to come. Some of them once were in fact inside blood relatives whom she calls Mother and Uncle, even some children (the winter babies) long gone. But most are family only by courtesy and habit, as they've hung so long on her walls, they've as good as grown there. She has discovered in them a strength that can serve her own; put together this way, they make a hive of advisors.

For example (she reflects as she sips at her mead), even the smallest dead skulls are much more useful and far more clever than her living son, Peder. Flesh of her flesh, the boy is a slave to the vices of women and drink. Which, to be fair, she encouraged in him, just as she discouraged any curiosity about history, literature, mathematics, and trade. All so she wouldn't miss him much when they parted—and so, in the end, and up *to* the end, he would truly love and be loyal to no one but her.

"What harvest brings greater yield than the son of a witch?" she asks the bones—especially the winter babies, who were conceived and born so as to be harvested by leaf-spring. They tremble above the bed where their mother sleeps soundly at night, safe in the bosom of the dragon and her own phenomenal powers.

"I'll tell you," she says, propping her head on her fist and sighing into the mirror: "The child of the child of a witch and *another* witch."

"Sigh that hard again and you'll blow us all out to sea," says Uncle, the chattiest member of her ossuary council. He occupies the northwest corner, a dark skull that still keeps most of its teeth and a little of its hair. "Ye might use that wind for straightening out your grammar."

Thyrla makes a face at herself in the mirror. "You know very well what I mean."

"Ye want to breed your son with someone else," Uncle says agreeably enough. "Well, that will make a change, won't it."

The yellow-white ribs known as Mother expand and contract, creaking out a noise that almost makes language.

"I've had to design a certain kind of life for myself,"

Thyrla says, more to her own reflection than to the family. "At least up till now. I think, I *believe*, I may have everything I need at last, once I figure this girl out."

As she says it, Thyrla's heart jumps. She feels she's on the brink of a new life. Her moment has arrived. Maybe.

"Don't you agree, Uncle?" she says.

Uncle gnashes his snaggle teeth. He always agrees, unless he's making mischief; even in what most people would call death, he seems to find pleasure in schemes and politics.

Deciding to take his gnashing as encouragement, Thyrla spreads a square of white silk on the table, over the remnants of the sand through which she and the stranger demonstrated their magic. Then she takes a jar from her pocket: the one that the maid Kett handed over when she left Sanna's chamber, just as the moon had begun to cut a path through the late-summer stars.

The jar makes the tiniest of rattles as Thyrla shakes it, then dumps its contents onto the silk. At the scattering, her wall bones erupt into a joyous bumping that sounds for a moment like birds' wings.

"It's only thorns," Thyrla says sternly, to silence them. And to quiet her own nerves.

These are the thorns taken from Sanna's body. A few are still wet with her blood, which makes the smallest possible stains on the white cloth. The magic in them calls to the magic in Thyrla's own blood, and she takes a deep breath for strength.

She pulls the winking silk patch from her right eye. For the first time today, she sees fully. Sharply and not sharply, for the chamber is a layered palimpsest, with so much information in it that Thyrla needs both eyes to make sense of it all, if sense can be made.

Exposing the eye changes the room's web of energy. Uncle can't contain himself. His teeth bang against each other savagely, and Thyrla doesn't bother to hush him. She needs time to adjust.

Much more than any imaginary dragon or the patterns of trophy bones, certainly more than the riches traded by the ships that come and go in the harbor, this eye is the source of her power. This eye—the midwife warned Thyrla's mother, who warned Thyrla in turn—might be the mark of the Devil or the sign of a genius. Either way, it needs to be covered around pious Christians and fools, and the pain it causes is (almost always) worth the advantage it brings her.

Because this eye is more than an eye. More than one eye, yes, and certainly more powerful. In a single orb, Thyrla has two complete pupils, two irises. The irises are different colors, too. While her ordinary, everyday eye is a piercing pale silver, the irises of her secret eye are pink and purple, the colors of dawn and twilight, studded with wide black pinpricks of pupils that see directly into the past's wintry grave, where the sun never shines and ordinary eyes are driven mad by assorted shades of dark. Also, dimly, into the unknowable future, where vague shapes flutter with cryptic signs.

Tears run down the Baroness's cheek. The right eye is pure pain, doubly sensitive to light, air, everything—and it still itches—so Thyrla dabs at it as she bends over the thorns, straining to see in them some secrets of the stranger she has betrothed to her disposable boy, the one child she raised into near-adulthood.

What kind of witch are you?

Here is the answer to Sanna's question: Thyrla is both a land-witch and, much more rare, a sort of time-witch. There is great advantage to seeing so many moments at once, past, present, and future all in a jumble.

"Bit selfish, isn't she?" asks one of the little skulls.

"Evil, I'd say," offers Mother—or something like it— with ribs beating like an eagle's wings.

Uncle laughs at them. "Nobody who truly is evil," he says, "thinks of herself that way. All evil people have some long and elaborate reason for the things they do. Or else it's a *simple* reason, which is worse."

"What," asks a tiny skull, one who lived barely a week, "is evil?"

"*Shh,*" says Thyrla. "I need to concentrate."

Gazing at the red thorns on their white sheet, she watches again as Sanna stumbles into the courtyard, tripping on her own feet and twisting into the rose vine's embrace. She sees the people rising, the tables crashing, the breaking of platters and pies. The spread of the red through the petals. And then . . . things she doesn't understand.

She's confounded by a distracting noise.

"I mean it — *shh!*" she tells the bone family.

But it isn't the bones that are making the noise. The whine is coming through the castle rock itself. And there's nothing to do about it.

As the sound continues, the pain in Thyrla's special eye grows, and the itch that afflicts her in the presence of something new becomes all but unbearable. The thorns stay put on their white silk, but at last their message shifts — and brings a confusing vision.

Thyrla sees green. A bubble of green, and she is inside. At first she dismisses this as a glimpse of her own chamber with its tapestries, but as she stares longer and the color doesn't resolve itself into anything familiar, she concludes the impression is the result of some warding-off spell cast by Sanna herself, who is clearly capable of much more than making a column of sand that flies out a window and returns as a swarm of bees.

Whatever this green stuff is, it's suffocating Thyrla. So is she looking into the past or the future or both?

A tear escapes her wiping and lands on the thorns: a fat drop that spreads. It melts the blood off a particularly sharp pricker, and the blood finds a pathway in the woven white silk, spiraling down — then spreading into black.

With that, the secret eye, which follows its own rules, suddenly decides to stop seeing. Only the left eye works now, and it perceives nothing but the present. The perplexing, anxious, but ultimately ordinary present.

Half-blind, Thyrla feels her ears overtaking her senses. That sound in the walls . . .

No, it isn't the familiar bones making noises and sharing opinions. It's . . .

A song.

A kind of song, anyway. A thin, high hum that sets her own bones to vibrating.

Then again — and this seems more and more true the longer it lasts — to call the sound a whine or a hum is an injustice. It is the most perfect note, in a pitch so high it reaches the angels (if there are indeed angels). It contains in itself all of creation, all yearning and hope, a vision that is far more than vision or any other commonplace sense. It lifts Thyrla out of herself, almost —

"Maybe ye'd like a chance to make a friend?" Uncle suggests. "Instead of harvesting one, I mean."

For reasons to which she will never admit, Baroness Thyrla bursts into tears. From both of her eyes.

Chapter 20

The shimmer down deep in the stones.

One-day-to-be-baron, sooner-to-be-husband, Peder lies in his chamber with the windows open on the night sky, contemplating his future. With Sanna.

"I think she'll make an admirable wife, don't you, Chicken Legs?" Peder asks, using the hateful nickname he gave his paid companion, Tomas, on the boy's first day at the castle. "The two of us will look very well together."

He rolls over and jabs Tomas hard in the ribs. "Don't you think so?"

For a treat, Tomas has been allowed to share the bed, rather than sleeping on a straw pallet on the floor. The pile of feather mattresses is easy on his spine, and he is grateful in an uncomplicated way for this comfort, even as he is dismayed by what he has to do to earn this soft spot — namely, agreeing to everything Peder says, a task that is particularly onerous tonight.

Peder rarely, if ever, is less than entirely selfish. Tonight he wants to talk, which means Tomas has to listen and respond. That is Tomas's purpose at the castle, after all: to listen to Peder, to fetch what needs fetching, to be sure Peder ends up safe in his bed if he's been down to the taverns to drink and sing and flirt.

"Yes, of course," he mumbles, though his heart aches to say it, "you'll make a handsome couple."

That seems to be enough for a moment. Maybe Peder will fall asleep now.

But no.

"Chicken Legs," says the future baron, "have you ever contemplated taking a wife? No, don't bother to answer — of course you haven't."

Tomas hasn't dared to imagine it, in fact. All he can foresee for himself is this servitude to Peder. Who loves the sound of his own voice, and continues:

"When you need a wife, I'll find you one. When it suits me to have you married — when I want the companionship of another married man, that is — I'll choose just the right girl for you."

Tomas's heart sinks. It would be like Peder to marry him to an old woman or a donkey or some other horror, just for a joke. He comforts himself, as he so often must, by imagining the silver coins he will drop into his mother's hand when his quarterly wages are earned. Those coins keep her and his five siblings — two brothers, three sisters — in relative comfort in town, and Inger doesn't have to work hard. Her body is exhausted with childbirth anyway, both with the children who lived and with the ones who did not. She calls Tomas her wonder, as he was born just after a baby who died at birth; she says no child has ever been more wanted than he. She stayed steadfast through several more failed babies, until he was hired at the castle and the coins he provided bought his parents better food and living children. He has sworn to repay her love in kind. And in money, always more money, which is why he must please the young master.

"Marriage will otherwise be a lonely state for me," Peder goes on, filling his lungs to the bottom and then releasing the breath (scented with roses but also with onions and herring). "To be with one girl forever, even one as sweet and special as Sanna, and to watch her grow old and still be expected to share her bed . . ."

Tomas feels a jolt. Peder has elbowed him again; he must want Tomas to speak.

"You'll have children," Tomas says.

Maybe it's ridiculous for a seventeen-year-old boy to think immediately of becoming a father, but it's all Tomas knows to say. In the town, adults' thoughts are always on children. How to feed them, how to divide among them the chores that will ease the general burden of the day, which of course ends again in how to feed the mouths that huddle together beneath a patchy roof. The farmers and fishers think of little else, and most especially of having sons, because sons can go to sea or plow the land. Or end up as furniture in the bedchamber of another boy, one too rich to know or care how to treat others with kindness.

"Yes, children," says Peder, gazing at the ceiling. "You're right, Chicken Legs. They'll be some company for me, as I am for my mother. Think how lonesome she would feel here with no one else of her rank! Well, now she has Sanna in addition to me."

Tomas thinks that if Sanna does give Peder babies, they might quickly outgrow their father in emotional and mental capacity, for Peder is such a child himself. But that's not a very kind thought.

Truth is, Tomas feels jealous. Not that he believes *he* deserves to be married to Sanna, that wonderful stranger — just that he wishes he had more than this groveling life of servitude, a life he would never think of offering to a wife. Then he feels guilty, because he gets to eat well and work little; he has an easy life compared to almost anyone else in these islands. It's just not really *his* life, and that's what bothers him.

"I could teach them to fight with swords," Peder says, though he doesn't know how to fight himself; he has only heard about fighting, in epic songs performed for entertainment and the rare, enchanting plays put on by men who dock in his mother's hidden port. "They could learn to . . . build things, I suppose."

Tomas realizes that Peder (like the townsmen) is thinking only of sons. He wouldn't know what to do with a daughter any more than he knows what to do with a wife, beyond the basic mechanics of coupling. He is a great seducer because his wealth and beauty are dazzling, but once he has succeeded with a girl, neither he nor she has any notion of what to do next, given that their stations in life are so different; and so they part ways.

Peder turns on his side and props his head on his fist, studying Tomas's face as if seeing him for the first time. "Can you build anything, Chicken Legs?"

Tomas thinks of early years with his father alive, building boats—three of them—and coops for his mother's chickens in winter, while his mother was always pregnant and usually disappointed.

"Not a thing," Tomas lies. "Don't know one end of a hammer from the other."

He is not going to let Peder own that part of him.

Peder sighs and flops onto his back again. "Should've known it," he says cheerfully. He revels in the stupidity of others; it makes him think more highly of himself. "Why my mother ever thought to buy you for me, there's no one can say."

Then the boys are quiet. Tomas pretends to fall asleep as the half-moon lights the sky. Yet he is aware when the castle begins to hum gently with a vibration of sound that is more of a shimmer than an actual noise.

He concentrates on those vibrations. There is a beauty in them—and, no, he doesn't think this is the sound of the dragon's breath; this is something new, something beautiful, full of questions . . .

Peder breaks into Tomas's thoughts. He says, "I'm going to buy a new lute. I have a notion to compose some new songs."

Tomas mumbles, "I'll tell your mother you want one." It also falls to him to ask the questions that might annoy Thyrla.

Peder falls quiet again. Maybe he's listening to the same shimmer that Tomas hears.

Peder says, "I want my new songs to be *good*."

If Tomas weren't so sure he knows Peder as he does, as shallow and slight, he might think the boy has revealed a new depth. He might even think Peder has fallen in love.

anna

While the castle sleeps, while my skin heals from the thorns and Kett's well-meant squeezing and digging, let me swim back against the tide of time. I'll explain how I came to this place and why my quest is so urgent, and the quest will be part of my song.

Growing up in a clan guided by women, there inevitably comes a day when a girl wants to know—*has* to know—everything about her mother. A mother's life can be a good indication of a daughter's; whether a girl makes the same choices or not, she is forever defined by sameness and difference.

I've seen this with my cousin La, who fell in love outside the *flok,* as her mother, Aunt Shusha, did long ago with Aunt Gurria. And Pippa the Strong, who willfully ignores the songs that made her mother's beauty famous: Pippa appears to hate beauty now, even ignores her own and cuts her hair with a knife, and she has trained herself to be our best salvager. Vain, beautiful Addra, whose mother met a terrible death among sharks, won't go near anything bigger than she is. I think she'd be happy to spend her whole life on a single rock, basking in the admiration of others.

So, good or bad, every girl in the clan has decided who she is by looking at her mother's life.

But I never knew mine, or even much about her. As a child, I knew only what she did not do: She didn't die at sea, for example, because then there would have been a song about her — like Frill's mother, whose death is the subject of songs sung just before sleeptime, as the *flok* floats on the seaskin. I knew, also, that my mother didn't join another seavish clan, because then we would have visited her on our migrations.

"Where is she?" I remember asking almost as soon as I could speak; and my father, Bjarl, answered, "Not here."

It was all the answer I'd get for years.

Other girls without mothers stayed around their aunts, but I swam and slept beside Bjarl. In fact, I was the only one who stayed under a father's care rather than a woman's. My aunts are generous, kindhearted people, and they would have taken me; but my earliest years were spent either alone or catching fish and crabs with the boys (almost never the girls) my age.

I noticed that my father was always a little apart from the *flok* as well. Even the men rarely invited him to swap stories or mend nets. He was liked, yes, and tolerated; but he did not entirely belong.

We were different from the rest, though I couldn't say precisely how. And the older I got, the more I saw how apart I was, how unlike other girls.

I was not strong: Even Frill could move more rocks than I could, lift heavier treasures from shipwrecks, wrestle bigger fish to submission.

I was slow: I couldn't swim with the fast ones and was often at the rear of the clowder with the young and old, though I usually didn't need to be towed in a net like the very weakest of us.

I was not especially pretty, though I wasn't ugly, either. Or at least I didn't think so when I looked into another girl's eyes and saw myself reflected there in points of black.

Then there was my tail: It matured to a lovely light green color, the shade of morning sea; but it was not as long as the others', though it shimmered with pinks and yellows and purples perhaps more noticeably than theirs.

My eyes: Like my father's, they are the same green as my tail, but they are too big and too sensitive. When we swam through sandy waters, the grit irritated them until I did have to be towed, eyes shut, until we reached clear water again.

My hair: It never grew past my waist, and its pale gold was often tinged with green, for it grew algae in warm climates. Of the girls my age, only Pippa the Strong had hair any shorter, and that was because she hacked hers off in order to swim fast and accomplish her feats of strength.

In short, I was a mystery to myself and even more so to the other girls. And sometimes (especially to cruel, beautiful Addra, who of all the girls would have had my heart) I was an object of teasing.

Sanna, Sanna, no mother at all, they used to chant — until the aunts made them stop.

After that, the silence around the subject of my mother was almost worse than the teasing. My motherline was a bound secret, and my people don't like secrets at all.

"Why?" I asked my father, sobbing so as to scare the fish fathoms deep. "Why isn't she here? Why won't anyone say?"

"Quiet, Sanna." Bjarl was always kind, though firmer than most men are with their girl children. "You must not speak of her anymore — *must not* — especially to your aunts. And the rest of the elders."

"But the cousins —"

"The cousins don't know anything about it. They were too little when it happened."

And though in time I noticed that he referred to "it" rather than to "she," by then I realized he must have his reasons, and I stopped asking for a while. I thought that she must have committed a horrible crime, one from which the elders were protecting me by shutting her out of our speech.

So I spent most of my very young days by myself, away from Father and the cousins and aunts, the men and the boys and the elders — who now included my aunts Shusha the Logical and Gurria One Arm, mothers to La, and childless

Aunt Mar of the Long Reach. I collected fish and jellies and curious edibles along the shorelines, usually armfuls of fruits fallen from trees that lined the beaches, and delivered them to the elders to divide. They treated me fairly when I presented my gatherings; I was doing my share.

And always, from the very first bite, I loved those landish fruits and other new foods traded from friendly shore-dwelling *flok*, even when the foods tasted strongly of earth. I was constantly in search of novelty, and slow as I was, I enjoyed our travels as much as anyone else.

My people love motion; we love light and cool waters. We hunger for new experiences, for new people and sights and newly made objects in materials we find beautiful. Colorful stones that glow in the light; gold and silver that gleam. Things that surprise us. The encounter of new friends, who might paint their bodies or wear the skins of animals, was always interesting.

Except in the north. We rarely went as far as someplace like these Thirty-Seven Dark Islands. It would be years before I understood why.

So I was happy enough chasing seasons of cool sunshine, passing through warm waters and into new coldness again. Trading with others we met on the way, amassing treasures too precious to part with.

Some of those treasures, of course, came from ships that wrecked when the sailors went mad at the sound of my clanswomen's voices.

"Augh! Augh! Augh!" the landish men cried when they heard us singing. They jumped off their boats to get near us, and so they often drowned, their ships wrecked.

I felt bad for them; they weren't so different from the other landmen with whom we traded, except that they dared to skate into our element on their clumsy, creaking ships. For a long time, I thought that these men had been shunned by their *flok*, as Father and I were, and I pitied them. Sometimes I wept when the other girls picked through wreckage they had caused and held up their trophies in triumph. It seemed even worse to me when the older girls, women really, pressed their lips to those of a dying landman as if to suck away the rest of his life — and mocked the spark in his eyes.

"Save him!" I cried more than once. "Give him your breath!"

Every one of my clanswomen laughed at me.

"At least" — something in me drove me to say it as I watched one man expire in Addra's white arms — "you might lay him upon a rock so he has a chance."

That was the day Aunt Shusha the Logical took me aside to explain things. "These are the same men," she said, "who destroy our girls if they catch them. These men delight when a net comes up with a *marreminde* inside. They stuff her mouth with landish rags and stop sailing or fishing for the day, in order to take their filthy pleasures on the poor thing. A seavish girl is much easier to violate than a landish one, you know. Landish girls carry their parts between their

109

legs and can close up as tight as an oyster, but our parts are in front. The landmen love to rip away a girl's belly fin and don't mind the pain they're causing. They *like* it."

It was a horrible thing Aunt Shusha had told me. Several heartbeats passed before I could say, "I haven't heard of that happening."

"Not in our clan," she replied. "Not lately. In our clan we're careful—and lucky. If we hear of a girl tangled in a net, even if she's from a strange *flok*, we rush to save her. We chew through the nets and leave the landmen with nothing. But we can't save her if they've sunk a spear in her side. We can only sing and hope to distract them. That is what happened to poor Pippa's mother. She was too beautiful for her own good." She paused a moment, thinking, then added, "Though, in fact, beauty is the least of it. We could be ugly to them and they would still behave this way."

I was more frightened and disgusted than ever.

"Maybe it isn't *these* men," I said, looking at bodies strewn across the rocks where their ship had foundered, and drowned bodies floating to sea.

"My dear," Shusha said, "it is *all* men on ships, especially in the north. At least those who don't prefer other men."

So that was what I knew of sea and land until two summers ago, when I reached the age of fourteen and all that came with it. The bleeding, the breasts, and, most of all, the questions I'd hardly dared ask before, now answered by special permission of the council of elders.

Chapter 22

Rocking song.

What are these rocks but a haven?
What are these arms but a cradle?
Swim to me; let me hold you fast.
I'll rock you so gently to sleep.
                  —The Mermaids

anna

Even after all that Aunt Shusha had told me, I didn't sing much to the ships. I tried to avoid those times altogether. The other girls called me Sanna the Fearful and Sanna the Stone, trying out names I might keep all my life. Addra said I must have the singing voice of a gull, shrill and grating, and that was what kept me from joining the others. I tried not to care.

At the same time, I learned not to protest the wreckings. If I ever did, I was punished; there was an exchange of looks and gestures that meant Father and I wouldn't eat as well as the rest that week, or have a share in the gold and jewels recovered from the splintered ships.

"It is the way of the *flok*," Father explained to me.

"Are there other peoples that are different?"

He sighed — thinking of what, I didn't know till much later. He said, "In our world, in some bit of water or land, every kind of people exists."

✵ ✵ ✵

When I had completed fourteen migrations around the known seas, the questions about my origins became too big to swim away from. I was growing impatient.

It got worse one day when I sang to persuade some mackerel to float up from their depths to my hands, using a version of a shipwreck song:

What are these arms but a cradle . . .

I'd thought I was alone. But Aunt Gurria One Arm— the arm lost to a battle with an octopus, the scar worn proudly—was basking in a hollow of rocks just behind. At the sound of my voice, she pushed herself up on her single palm and started seal-walking toward me, ice-colored body dragging over the rocks.

She made me abandon the fish and slung her arm around my neck to swim with me back to the *flok*, who were already feasting on some jellies and crabs and a big *glopfisk* caught by the boy Ruut.

"Sanna is the most gifted of us all!" Gurria declared excitedly—to the other girls' surprise. And jealousy.

She commanded me to sing, and I saw even the hardest of hard-hearted *marreminder* dab at their eyes before I was done.

Then, because I was gifted, I was offered a special treat. "Name it," Auntie Mar of the Long Reach invited me. "Name your heart's desire."

I chose the right to ask questions.

Amid the consternation caused by my choice, Bjarl arranged for me to meet privately with the elders. It happened at midsun, on an island made of a single rock, so no one could hide and overhear. Those assembled included my father, a half-dozen elders, and a witch so old that not even the next oldest among us could remember her being young: Sjældent, the scraggle-haired, barnacle-crusted, tongue-lashing hag who barely did magic anymore, not even to protect the clowder in a storm. At the time, I couldn't imagine why she'd been included, unless it was as keeper of our memories.

I felt the pulse fast in my neck as I asked my first question.

I began with the cousins: "I know I'm not like them, but why?"

"You are as good as they are," Bjarl told me. "You're just as loved — even more so. By me."

Maybe that was true, because without a love of his own, I was my father's whole world. But I wanted to hear what the elders had to say, and I turned to them and posed my question again.

"I'm *different*," I said.

"You are the best singer," Gurria reminded me.

We went back and forth in this way for a while, and none of their answers were ever enough. But I wouldn't give up. In the end, tired of their darting and dodging, I asked the biggest questions of all:

"Where is my mother? *Who* is she?"

There was a long silence, just the *lap-lap* of waves and the shriek and splash as brown birds dived for fish.

"Well," I insisted, *"who?"*

Father sighed and looked around at the women. They looked back at him, steady and stern. He sighed again, then a third time, as if he were trying to become a creature of air rather than water, or as if he were guilty of something he didn't want to admit.

"Your mother," he said, "was landish."

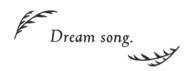 Dream song.

Blood calls to blood; charm calls to charm.
It is the way of the world.
Why should we change?
Come close and tell us your dreams.

—*The Mermaids*

anna

That special sensation that we call Down-Below-Deep is of great importance to all seavish clans. As I have noted, it refers to a real place, or to several real places: parts of the ocean floor where the water presses down heavier than rock and crushes the breath out of anyone unlucky enough to end up there. It is our worst possible misfortune, worse than fishers' nets. It's the punishment with which we threaten the young so they don't wander away and get lost.

"You might end up in the Down-Below-Deep," we say, and the water around their stumpy baby tails grows hot with urine.

In the Down-Below-Deep (so the songs and stories go) we lie utterly overwhelmed, in a darkness so profound, it has surpassed terror. The only creatures who live at that depth are sinewy blindworms grasping for food, and a few fish so misshapen and so frightened (we think) of being there that they bite with long, pointed teeth at anything that moves, even if it's merely a sand-twist.

Sometimes a lost mer-person comes upon such a fish that is equally lost. The frightfish manifests of a sudden when it lights up what looks like a fist growing out of its forehead. Behind the mini-sun of that light, black-moon eyes peer at this thing it has found, this thing into which its fangs are sunk, this thing that is you.

That's how I felt when I learned I'm half-landish.

Everything I had believed about myself was shattered — but everything I'd *suspected* suddenly made sense. Why I wasn't so strong a swimmer as other girls my age, why I liked landish fruits so much. Little things, big things. Why my waist was smaller than my cousins' (though still thicker than a landish girl's) and my spine less flexible. Why even my kindest aunts treated me as something apart from their own daughters, like an otter among seals.

I'd heard plenty of songs about love between land and sea. They were cautionary tales, designed to remind us of dangers; in this, they served much the same purpose as the Down-Below-Deep. In these songs, some girl usually gives up everything special about herself in order to walk on land and be with a man and die young, even when the man is kind, because the earth pulls the flesh toward it.

There is one, not particularly clever, often sung by our children:

> *O, she was a foolhardy maid,*
> *Who made a most foolhardy trade . . .*

Land promised her sweetness and brought her to tears;
To live time divided, in seasons and years . . .

That day with the elders, I found I was weeping. "Why didn't you tell me earlier?" I demanded of my father—of all of them, the elders reclining on their rocks, my aunts and my clanswomen, and the old witch who frightened me. *"Why?"*

Father's light green eyes, so similar to mine, shifted left and right. "I've forgotten why. I forgot about *her* till just now." Then, mysteriously (at the time, so it seemed), his eyes lit on Sjældent, who snored.

Of all possible answers, I hadn't expected that one. How could a man forget the mother of his own child? Especially when he'd devoted himself to that child, as Father did to me? He was a far more attentive parent than any other in our *flok,* and I would have thought he'd remember everything about the woman with whom he made me.

"Really?" I couldn't help asking—accusing, rather. "What about her name?"

He kept his gaze steady on Sjældent. "Really. I can't remember her name."

The blood boiled through my body. I was about to burst with frustration and temper. I was about to say something I'd regret; I was thinking childishly that Bjarl must be very stupid to believe I'd swallow an answer like that—

Then a throat cleared itself: Aunt Shusha the Logical, the kindest of elders and aunties, who gave birth to La, who was exactly my age and the kindest of cousins.

"None of us remember," she said. "Nobody."

At that, the elders shook their heads, eyes and scales glittering, hair waving in the wind. *No one remembered.* And no one said any more about it.

Until the old witch, Sjældent, gave a cough that sounded like death, and she spoke in a voice like wood splintering on rock: "If ye really want an answer, ye'll have to ask *me*," she said.

The elders exclaimed at the sound of her. It had been many suns and moons and migrations since she'd spoken.

And she was telling the truth: She was the only one who knew what I wanted to know.

She coughed again, expelling fronds of sea grass and a baby eel. Then she explained: "When ye were born, I worked a magic of forgetting. It were best for everyone, even ye. Only a dim trace of yer mum remains in some memories, like mine and yer father's, and she don't come back to mind until forced."

"You . . . worked a forgetting magic?" I asked.

"That I did. So well I've forgotten much of that night myself!" She said it proudly, straightening her spine from its usual slouch. "There's not a creature that was on the beach that night, landish or seavish, mussel or crab, that remembers it all. Not yer mother, either."

I felt another pang of loss. So my mother couldn't remember me! Somehow that seemed even worse than the rest of the clan not remembering *her.*

"Can you . . . conjure the memories back?" I asked, hardly daring to hope.

Sjældent shrugged, shedding scales and barnacles in the process. "Might-could. I'd need some help to do it." She pointed her face toward the elders. "Give us permission, then," she said—and cackled for effect, that awful half-laughing, half-coughing sound. "Let Bjarl and me tell the girl what we recall."

The elders turned their backs and debated Sjældent's proposal, in gestures of face and hands we use when we don't want our voices heard.

In the end, Shusha said, using words: "You have our permission to discuss Sanna's mother. But you must make sure the rest of the clan doesn't hear—not even us. And all of you have to swear to keep whatever you divulge a secret."

Sjældent burst into another loud and unnerving cackle-cough.

"Afraid what ye might hear, are ye?" she asked in that splintering voice. "Well, a little knowledge is a dangerous recipe. We'll see if young Sanna is made of stronger stuff."

• Chapter 26 •

Moon song.

Come, lover, and play that I am your moon.
Moon dwells in the sea and is happiest there.
Waves lap her to peace;
Stars fill her hollows with light.
She is sweet to those who treat her in kind.
Yes, let me be your moon.

—*The Mermaids*

anna

So then I knew why *nobody* knew: On the night I was born, Sjældent's magic of forgetting entered each person on the beach. Then it spread from them to the *flok* like a sickness, breath to breath.

"It were a powerful spell," Sjældent allowed with no false modesty.

This forgetting presumably passed from the landish girl to her *flok* as well. Thus (I speculated) my mother and her people don't even know she ever had a child.

I was and am a great gap in her life. *My mother's life.*

But in those first days after the council of elders, I wondered if, sometimes, when the woman who used to be the girl my father loved—my mother—when she scrubbed her family's wash or watched for a sail (perhaps her father's, perhaps a new lover's), she got a feeling in the pit of her belly that meant something was missing, something for which she might look if only she knew . . .

And then, I thought, the sail appeared, or the stain in a shirt was scrubbed out, and she turned back to her own life.

Every person in the world feels something is missing. This is what it means to be human.

So I imagined her thinking. It was the nicest way, really, to imagine her absence from my life, and mine from hers.

That council yielded only a little information. The next step to knowledge was mine to take alone.

As Sjældent herself had said, *We'll see if young Sanna is made of stronger stuff.*

But I wasn't strong, or at least I didn't think so. I was as afraid of the old witch as any other sensible person was; I felt even more so after the council day.

She had always been the most horrible member of our clan, called an *older* rather than an *elder* because she was more ancient than anyone knew and yet so mean that no one would go to her for advice. Plus which, back when she used to speak, she liked being cryptic, so any advice she did give—at councils and shipwrecks, feasts and negoti-ations—came as a puzzle and often stayed that way.

For example, bartering with a landish *flok* who had spread out some favorite objects of beauty: "Gold is where ye find it." So obvious a statement that it either meant noth-ing or had to carry a wealth of hidden meaning.

Watching the rest of us hand-walk and tail-hump

around a beach, picking through the remains of a ship-wreck: "Ever notice how much our girls look like walruses these days?"

Accepting a landish bowl swimming with everagains, the jellies that return to polyps when frightened and are thus born again and again, never quite dying: "Imagine asking to be young and vulnerable over and over." Then holding the bowl to her withered lips and swallowing every last one, which did make them die.

Yes, she was horrible, and I feared her. But I simply had to know about my mother. It took a few alternations of sun and moon, but at last curiosity outfought fear, and one golden morning I forced the courage into myself. I gathered all the gifts I could think of to please her: my favorite comb, which Father himself made from the tusk of a walrus (an animal that did *not* resemble us in any significant way) and carved with a pattern of stars; a golden ring from a landish finger to hang from her nose; a smack of the blue jellies she liked because, she said, their venom was almost the only thing she could taste anymore.

I found Sjældent dozing on a rock, and I woke her up. I said I was ready.

"I'm ready, too," she told me, flexing her knobby old fingers as she reached for my gifts. Her hands were so covered in barnacles, they'd calcified into claws, but I showed her all the deference owed to an elder and to a person in possession of silent truths. I displayed what I'd brought for her.

Sjældent poked at the comb and speared the ring with the tip of a finger. Twirled a jelly's tentacles around one knobby paw and popped it into her mouth.

"Ye're here about yer mother." Still chewing, she squinted at me. "Very well, I can tell ye summat. Not all. What do ye want to know?"

"I would be grateful for anything at all." I thought this was the most courteous way to ask.

Sjældent didn't seem to think so.

"Sanna the Meek," she said, preparing to enjoy another jelly. "Sanna the Herring."

Herring: the most common fish in the north, and the easiest to lure and catch. It was a loathsome nickname.

"Will you help me?" I asked. I was losing my courage. "As you promised?"

She stuffed the jelly in her maw and popped its crown against her palate. Salt water ran down her chin. All the while, she kept staring at me through the clouds over her eyes.

I began to worry we were attracting attention from the rest of the *flok*. It wasn't often that a girl my age — or any person at all, in fact — spent more than a few moments with Sjældent; the other girls were watching us as they lounged on their own rocks, and I thought I heard them giggling. It was becoming clear that Sjældent would hold me as long as she could.

"Ye are pretty," she said suddenly, surprising me with what I thought was an irrelevant subject. "It ben't so obvious on first glance, the way ye carry yerself all hunched and quiet. Yer eyes are a nice pale green, and yer hair's a good color when ye keep the weeds from growing in it."

"Thank you," I said. Snapped, rather—I was losing courage, yes, and patience along with it. "It is always the most beautiful among us who criticize others the most."

At that, she laughed so hard, her withered dugs flapped and scared some tiny crabs out from under. Soon her shoulders were crawling with crabs; she brushed them away and then picked up the comb to scratch under her bosom at the places irritated by their claws.

"Ye have a bit of a sting after all, little herring." Reaching around to her back to scratch there. "Sarcasm—some say it's the last resort of a feeble mind, but I say it's the first tack when ye're testing rough waters."

"Just tell me what I need to know!" I begged. "What was so awful that you had to make everyone forget?"

"'Need.'" She cackled, which ended in a wet cough. (I was to learn, in time, that she viewed laughter as more menacing than a sneer, hence her constant cackling at all of us.) "*Need*, ye say! The spell caught me, too, as it were intended to do. Best nobody remembers the girl's name or where to find her. Best for us *and* for ye."

"I don't agree."

"It ben't ye who decides."

"But we're talking about *my* mother!" I slapped my tail on the seaskin. I was *not* meek; I was not giving up. "Maybe you've forgotten some of it, Sjældent, but I know you remember a lot. You can make yourself do it. So—what can you tell me?"

The witch stopped her scratching. She squinted, taking my full measure.

"There's *can* and there's *will*," she said. "The *can* has its limits, but the *will* begins now."

Then she told me the story.

Chapter 28

Trust guides the way.

You who sail upon the seaskin —
You look to the skies to guide you.
Why up at air and not down to sea?
Trust, we will show you the way.

—*The Mermaids*

anna

Not all at once, though—Sjældent is too cunning for that. She made me perform some favor or task to earn each tidbit of information she could call back to memory.

Scraping the barnacles from her fingers earned me the story of my parents' meeting.

"Washing clothes for her family, yer mum was, where a river ran into the sea," Sjældent said. "Scrubbing and slapping the cloth on the rocks. Meantime yer father was looking along the bank for fruit washed down to the rapids. Bjarl always did have a liking for landish sweets, same as ye. He got curious at the sounds of scraping and slapping, and the girl's weeping—oh, yes, she was mighty delicate, yer mother, and she didn't want to wash for her family. She considered herself far too precious to be scrubbing at landish sweat and dirt."

"I don't suppose I'd like it much, either," I said. The landish people I'd met so far were awfully smelly, and a good bit of the smell was carried in the twists of wool and plant fibers they wore. I didn't see why they wouldn't hop into the sea now and then to clean off, or cleanse their breath with a handful of seavish slipgrass, but this would be one of the questions I'd ask later, over what became the long suns and moons of my time with Sjældent.

The short answer: They fear the water. In part because they fear us.

"So," Sjældent continued, "Bjarl swam over to see what was making that wail, and he looked up through the water-skin as she looked down, and she were so shocked she fell right into his arms and into love."

"Did she?" I paused in my work, and a snail began a trail across my fingers. I shook it off. "She actually *fell* in love?" I'd heard the phrase before, but only in songs. We have a saying, *Falling is easy; swimming takes fins,* and I realized of a sudden that it might be about love.

Sjældent vented one of those sudden, delighted (and off-putting) cackles. "Oh, yes, she fell. Along with all her family's linen. Ye can be sure she was punished for it later!"

And that was all she'd tell me that day.

I had to scrub the green off the witch's tail to get the next part. And it was a very significant part.

I'd wondered how my parents were able to make me, given the differences between seavish and landish anatomies.

Aunt Shusha had told me about the way the landish sailors caught and ravished our girls, but I couldn't imagine how the parts might come together the other way — seavish man, landish girl — and out of affection, not violence.

I'd wanted to ask Father about all this business ever since I'd learned my mother was landish, but I was embarrassed to phrase the questions I'd need to pose, and Father didn't volunteer information. I wondered if Sjældent's magic of forgetting drove that memory from his mind, too.

"How did they make me?" I asked, and grew conscious I was flexing my belly fin tight over my sexual parts.

"They kissed," Sjældent said.

"What's that?"

Cackle. "Ye've seen it with our girls and the corpses. It's what the landmen want from them first of all — a landish practice by which one person presses lips to the lips of another. Sometimes they slide tongues past teeth and rummage around the other's mouth."

"To taste each other?"

"I suppose so, though why they want to taste so much onion and garlic — those're roots that grow in the dirt and taste of it, but worse — is beyond any reason. S'pose it's mostly a sign of trust. Someone could bite off a tongue, but they trust each other not to do it."

The whole process seemed revolting, especially as I was not just scrubbing algae but also pulling worms from between Sjældent's gray scales, and they seemed like tongues to me.

I thought how uncomfortable the old witch must be at every moment of her life, but it didn't make me like her any more than I did, which was barely at all.

"Trust," I said.

"Trust," she said.

"Then what do they do when they've proved it? How do they get to the action that makes the baby?"

She hooted, whether at my question or at the sensation of a particularly long blindworm being pulled from her flesh, I don't know.

"They get to it," she said. "And I know ye're wondering about the mathematics of it, as their men carry their stuff and nonsense in front, as ours do, but their women's stuff is like a wound between those misbegotten legs."

I felt hot with discomfort. But better to hear it from Sjældent than my father. I scrubbed at some scales with a bit of chain mail salvaged from a landish ship, thinking of how the metal links would drape over a man's "stuff and nonsense." They were bringing a nice polish to Sjældent's tail.

"It's a most awkward position and great fun to watch," Sjældent said. "The man stays as he is, but the woman must part her legs to take him in. She hunches around till she's curled like a shrimp in the sun, and she holds on with both arms. Then man and woman rub together till the baby is made—or till the man is satisfied, at least."

I kept scrubbing.

"Oh, yes," Sjældent added as an afterthought. "It's the

men who have the power in the transaction. They have it generally anyway, on land. They decide when to mate, and for how long. They also own land, as they own gold, and the women get the use of it only by permission."

"Well," I said, dazed, "that is different."

"Oh, yes," she said again. "And this'll make ye laugh: The one thing they think they need is *more* men. When a woman's with child, they hope for more boys, boys and boys and boys . . . Why should a woman hope for a son? The landmen take their pleasure without regard for anyone aside from themselves. No doubt that's why yer mother was so glad to have caught a merman."

While Sjældent cackle-chuckled in a rather disgusting way, I moved on to her flukes, which were nibbled away at the ends. I scrubbed.

"One more thing," she said. "In spite of all that I've told ye, when a landish woman's in love, it's 'most always with a man."

She presented this as shocking information, but it was hardly the most astonishing thing I'd heard that day.

Still, I wondered if I could ever love a man in that way, especially such a man as Sjældent had described. I wondered about everything in my life, now that I knew I was mixed in blood. But being in love was still far in my future; there were more fundamental questions first, as I carefully cleaned the last grime from Sjældent's flukes.

I began, "Why did I come out . . ." Then I hesitated,

afraid to face the answer. "Why was I born with a seavish body rather than a landish one?"

She took so long to respond that I thought she must have fallen asleep.

"Sjældent?" I poked the meaty part of her tail.

"It took all my best magic," she said.

Chapter 30

Heart song.

Our hearts are as scaled as our tails.
Only the subtlest eel slides inside.
Shall it be yours?
Are you already mine?
—*The Mermaids*

anna

So not only was I half-landish, I was also the subject of magic. If everything Sjældent said was reliable (which Aunt Shusha would call a very big supposition), I owed the old witch my life. At the very least, my life in this *flok*. Sjældent had cast a net of making and unmaking to create me as seavish and keep me with the clan.

This was an important revelation, and it affected me in both sad and happy ways. It told me that, no matter what else had happened, no matter how much everyone had forgotten, *I had been wanted.* I belonged. I belonged to the *flok* as I belonged to my father; and I belonged, also, to Sjældent.

At the same time, part of me belonged to some other *flok*, people who lived on land and dug a living out of it, who lived quick lives because the land tugged at them as hard as the Down-Below-Deep.

I was a whirl of emotions. I had to know more before I could say whether the good that I knew outweighed what I was missing.

Bit by bit, through suns and moons and seas too many to count, I learned about the land. Meanwhile, I cleaned the old witch's body and kept her healthy, brought her food, and towed her and her treasures in one of the nets used for elders and olders and young. When she fell into a deep doze below the frozen seaskin, which made a slippery kind of land that many of us love to glide upon—when sleeping too long underwater might have killed her—I hauled her to the surface and punched our way through the ice so she could breathe.

Through taking care of Sjældent, I became more noticed in the *flok* and, paradoxically I think, more a part of it. What's more, quite gradually, my cousins and the other girls stopped teasing and started to pay me a sort of respect, or maybe fear, because I was so often with Sjældent.

So it was for many months and migrations. The *flok* had come to rest in the warm waters where the sky is shared evenly between sun and moon—the Basking Waters where La met her Ishi—when, as the ultimate reward for all I'd done and still promised to do, Sjældent finally told me what I'd asked for from the first day: my mother's name.

"When ye give away a name, ye give a power," she said first, with one of those squints that, I'd come to realize, compressed the shape of her eyeballs and helped her to see past the clouds over them.

"I'm ready," I said.

She told me, without further fuss, "Her name was Lisabet."

Lisabet.

I felt curiously disappointed. It was a long name, but it didn't make me think of anything special—not like our seavish names, which capture some sound of the sea or the wind. What could it *mean?* How would a Lisabet look and sound and behave?

That was when I asked Sjældent for something that I'd been, yes, too meek to dream much about before, though I'd been thinking about it since the day of the ice and her near-suffocation.

I asked her to teach me her magic.

"I want to learn making and unmaking," I said, fast and before I could lose courage. "I want to walk on land, and I want to find my mother and meet her. I want to be the magic-keeper of the *flok,* in case . . . or, rather, when . . ." I couldn't quite bring myself to finish; I was predicting her death.

No one could have been more shocked than I was when Sjældent agreed right away. Magic is—well, I've been told the landish people think we mer-people are always magic, but they are wrong. We are just *different* from them, and magic doesn't come naturally to us. Anyone who is to work it (and work it is) must first apprentice to a witch. And Sjældent was the only witch in our *flok,* which meant magic was dying out among us.

"Hasn't been a girl who wanted it in your lifetime,"

Sjældent explained. "Wanted it enough, I mean to say. Your aunt Gurria was curious when she came to us, but she didn't have the courage to stay the course."

"Aunt Gurria One Arm?" She was the ice-colored auntie who'd come from some faraway *flok* to live with us and be Shusha's love; also the one who'd found me singing and declared me gifted, which started this tumble of information about my mother and the land. I'd always considered her brave.

Sjældent shook as a bubble of gas rose from her belly to her lips. "How do ye think the woman lost her arm? It weren't an octopus, though I know she tells it that way — it were a spell gone wrong. Making and unmaking: Not everyone can manage the magic."

I felt a cold nut of fear in my belly, but the rest of me was excited. Learning magic felt like an honor. It felt like something I'd be good at. It felt like my future.

I asked more humbly, "Do you think *I* could manage it? The magic, I mean?"

Sjældent gave one of her cackles, which ended (predictably) in a cough. "Time'll tell. Time is proof. But ye're as brave and smart as any other girl I've known — ye came to me, didn't ye, and never ran away."

For once in my life, I felt different in a good way. And my good feeling must have shown too much, because Sjældent felt the need to take me down.

"It won't be quick," she warned. "And ye won't always like me during it."

She seemed entirely unaware how unnecessary that warning was, how much she was disliked in general; when I told Father about it later, he laughed along with me.

At that moment alone with Sjældent, I made a gesture of thanks with all ten fingertips pressed to my brow and released, fluttering down to my sides.

"Oh"—Sjældent slapped her tail weakly against the stone—"ye should know this at the outset, too: Ye likely won't be able to find the right bit of land for yer mother at first, so get that notion gone. There's no entirely reversing a spell of forgetting, not one so tight as I worked, and there's no accounting for how time might have changed a young girl. Once ye find her, she could be *very* changed. So, now, to be clear—I couldn't tell ye for certain where she is, or who she is, if ye hauled me to shore and flailed me like the landish do to the whales they catch. Ye'll have to find your own way."

The prospect was daunting but still exciting. Feverishly, I agreed to everything Sjældent proposed.

Thereafter, whether the *flok* swam or sheltered, during calm and storm, I was with Sjældent as much as my father. She taught me what I know now, and even promised (or half promised) to teach *everything* she knew. Someday I'll hold all her magic in my blood.

I like to think that, during my apprenticeship, I brought her back into the *flok,* at least a little. She was no longer just the cursing old witch everyone feared; she had formed a friendship of sorts with me and my father and, by extension, our clan. And most important, she was teaching me charms that would help everyone.

"First comes first," she said on (yes) our first day of training. "The most important principle of witchery is that the elements of the world, the parts that make it up, have to remain in balance. That's not just the Overall Elementals, mind ye—water, land, air, fire, time—that's every imaginable piece of our world, down to parts ye can't see. If ye take pain from one, ye must put it into another. Most easily yerself. Do ye understand?"

I understood much more than my answering nod conveyed. Sjældent had said that when I was born, she'd used all her magic to shape me into seavish form, and it must have cost her something. Perhaps she wouldn't be so ugly and gross if she'd left me as whatever I was when I was born.

I would ask her about that later. Meanwhile, I paid for my lessons with gifts of choice: fish, jellies, everagains, and gold. As I called the crackle of magic into my blood, I learned to heal sores and cuts—much worse ones than the wee scratches from Thyrla's rose vine—and to charm a shark or an eel away. I was especially good at healing children who'd succumbed to the temptations of colorful jellies and slugs, only to be stung and filled with poison. I changed venom to giggles and took the poison for myself, to keep the elements of cause and effect in good balance. I grew immune, or mostly so, to seavish toxins, and the young hardly needed to be threatened with the Down-Below-Deep after surviving their first real encounter with pain.

After healing and charming, I learned the more complex magic of making and unmaking. I turned crabs into sucklefish clinging to rocks and then (much more difficult) switched them back to their original shapes. I conjured lava from its restless beds in fissures and cliffs. I sent the lava back again, too, and sealed the rock over it.

Most greatly to my own purposes, I learned to change myself. I practiced unmaking my seavish body and remaking it with legs. I learned that I could endure the agony of my spine splitting in two, and the strange migration of my "stuff and nonsense" from the front of my belly to the hollow between my new legs. I learned to walk by watching how the shorebirds did it.

Before I transformed even once, I learned how to change back to tail and fins again.

"It's the most important of all the magic ye'll have," Sjældent said. "To return things to their balance. To return yerself."

"To have choices," I said.

"To have peace," she said.

Soon after, I asked Sjældent a question that had been in me a long time: "You know all this magic, and it is powerful magic. Why don't you use it on yourself, to walk on land and see the rest of the world?"

"Don't want to," she said. "Won't." And she shut her eyes and mouth and ears tight against me.

That was only the first time I asked. The more I learned and the more I liked magic, the more I wondered why she didn't use this or that spell herself. I couldn't resist asking from time to time.

"Why don't you walk on land?"

"Have you ever tried?"

"Have you ever wanted something so badly in your life?"

"Don't want to. Don't want to. Don't want to," she answered.

After many shifts of moon and sun, she told me, snappishly, "Sanna, ye inquisitive little eel, I do the magic I can and know. I'm not a land-witch or an air-witch or a fire-witch or a time-witch. I'm a *sea-witch*, and that's where my powers work for me. So I might know the right words and tunes, but if I'm not in me own element, they won't work. There's yer answer."

"But they work for me," I protested. I thought she was trying to trick me in some way.

What she said next was truly astonishing.

"Might be ye're a stronger witch than I am."

And while my mouth gaped open in shock, she clamped her lips shut. She stared into the punishing sun for the rest of the day.

• Chapter 32 •

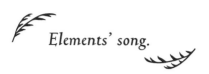 Elements' song.

We are alone, you and I, in the great shell of sky.
You rattle about in your silly small ship,
While I glide and glimmer down deep.
Come, join me in my chamber—
I promise you'll never feel lonely again.

—*The Mermaids*

anna

Father wasn't always happy about my apprenticeship. I'd reached the age at which seavish men must defer to seavish women, but we'd always had a special way of living together, and I let him speak to me about his concerns. I even encouraged it, because without a mother, he was the best counselor I could have.

"I have resented the old witch," he told me one night as we gathered moon-skippers for ourselves and everagains for Sjældent. "And now look at me, taking care of her after she stole your mother from me."

Poor Bjarl, with his sad green eyes and the curly beard that had stopped growing the last time he saw my mother. The night I was born.

I felt an accusation in what he'd said—again, I was at an age when young girls are more sensitive than sucklefish, retreating into themselves at the slightest touch. I thought he resented not just Sjældent but me as well. If I'd never been born, he might still be with his beloved, or he might be more a part of the *flok*, depending on which way his heart went. *And* if I hadn't asked Sjældent to teach me her tricks, he wouldn't have to bother with her sharp tongue and generally prickly demeanor.

"I can look after her by myself," I said, rather snootily. "You don't have to have anything to do with her. Or me."

Father stopped and hovered in the water, body pointing straight down. "Sanna," he said, and I could tell I'd hurt him deeply, "I want to do this. For you, not for old Sjældent — it's what I choose."

Then I was ashamed of myself, getting too prideful with my own father. I touched the five fingers of my right hand to my brow.

"I love you," he said. "You are my clan."

It was both a surprise and a not-surprise, the first time he'd said he loved me and the first time I realized I'd always counted on that love — *klanslovfasthed*, family love — to keep me strong when I lagged behind other swimmers, or when the mer-girls made me feel stupid. He'd been as much a mother to me as he could, within the natural limits of his gender; as a father, he'd been much more than anyone else ever had.

"I love you, Father," I said. And everything I'd learned about him and Lisabet suddenly washed in glittering gold, like the seaskin just after dawn's pink has faded, before the white of day begins.

I thought I was a very lucky person.

anna

Some of Sjældent's most important advice had to do with what the landish call *religion,* which includes miracles and magic. I am grateful to her now for even the little she was able to pass on, since religion immediately affected how the people of these islands see me. It and my magic are the reasons why the Baroness betrothed me to her son.

Sjældent said, "Ye're going amongst people who believe there's someone else controlling their lives. Ye can hear them crying out to this person when they founder on the rocks: 'O God, O God.' Ye've heard it, I know."

"Of course." It made sense; that was what *Augh! Augh! Augh!* must mean. I just never understood *why* they shouted and moaned that way in their distress. "Who is this person? A mother—a queen of some sort?"

Sjældent snorted, and a startled crab came dashing out of her nose. "A *god,*" she said, "is some big man—yes, a *man*—who lives in the sky and tells them all what to do.

Sometimes in just a whisper, so they don't always under-stand. And most of them live all their lives without even a glimpse of him. *Blind faith*, they call it." She plucked a limpet off her elbow and popped it in her mouth to suck on.

I would have laughed at the way she described all this, if we weren't talking about death, or at least the very worst moment these landmen lived through. The death cries were still hard for me to wait out, important as they were to my clan's way of life.

"Why, then?" I asked Sjældent, in one of our very last lessons. "Why do they call to him, if they can't hear or see him? What makes them so sure he notices — or that he will help?"

She cackled again. "They *ben't* sure," she said. "They can't be. But they're so helpless, they don't have a choice. They think he's their father. They call what they do *praying*."

In one of our very last lessons, Sjældent warned me about what might happen if I succeeded in my quest.

"If ye find the girl who birthed ye, chances are ye'll feel yerself being born all over again," she said, gobbling herring in the waters just a few suns south of Thyrla's islands. "Ye won't have my spell to protect ye, and every-thing that we most naturally forget, for our own protection, will come rushing back to ye as if ye were conscious all the while."

"That doesn't seem so bad," I said, trying to sound brave. "I think it would be rather interesting."

Sjældent coughed, and a fat blue slug crawled over her bottom lip. She pulled it off and squinted at it before putting it back and chewing it up.

"Careful what ye wish for," she said. "Think of the everagains. Ye've seen how they grow up and how they shrink back to their polyp selves when afraid."

"That's why you like them," I reminded her. It was almost but not quite a contradiction. Sjældent gobbled up everagain jellies at any stage of their lives; she used to say they aided her magic, but I came to believe that she just liked to thwart the potential magic elsewhere.

She said that day in the foaming waters, "We're all born out of fear and pain, Sanna my girl. Do ye truly want to return to yer birth and reclaim it?"

I took all my hopes in my hands and I said, "I do."

"Ah." Sjældent sighed, and coughed, and looked even older for a moment. "If ye do manage to go back that far, my dear, I'm afraid ye might not be able to go forth with yer life. The stars and fishes know that I coun't do it."

It was the first and only time she called me *dear*. And what she'd just said was the same as a curse.

She finished, "Be grateful for the forgetting. It was my best gift to ye. And if ye *must* go in search of the past—"

I interrupted: "I must."

"Well then, I advise ye to learn how to work the magic of forgetting for yerself. Ye're going to see much that ye won't want to remember."

Now, in this all-but-airless, entirely sea-less cell in Baroness Thyrla's castle, I understand landish religion, at least a little. They call to that unseen power (*Augh! Augh! Augh!*) because it can explain their lives.

We all want some magic when accidents lead us astray.

Trapped by my own foolhardiness, I need that sort of magic, something to make better sense of what's happened than *Sanna wanted to find her mother, and now she is locked in a castle waiting to be bound to a landman.*

I might be tempted to pray now, if their Augh would hear me. I am terribly unsure of what lies ahead. All I know, or at least all I've been told, is that somewhere in these islands I might find a woman to help me, and a treasure so precious I must bring it to Sjældent.

That was her condition for letting me go: I must look for something precious beyond imagination, more wonderful and rare than anything we've ever seen in sea or on land.

"What is it?" I asked when she told me.

"Ye'll know when ye see it." She chewed her own tongue, apparently, for there were no creatures around her to eat.

"What does it do?"

"Ye'll know *that* when ye see it, too."

"I'm more likely to find it if I know what I'm looking for," I had to point out.

She shook her head.

"Just tell me!"

"Can't," she said. "Won't. Ye'll know when ye see it, or else it's no good."

What treasure could possibly lose value through being named? I concluded, and I still believe now, that it must be so special that the old witch fears it—wants it and fears it at once. When she takes it from me, she'll have power; when I bring it to her, I'll have power, too.

Ye'll know that *when ye see it . . .*

I find a surprising comfort in that phrase during the rest of the night.

Ye'll know that *when ye see it. When ye see it, ye'll know. Ye'll know . . .*

I have come here to find—oh, so much.

And yes, I do want to remember.

Chapter 35

To make jealous the mermaids.

On the seaskin, Addra and Pippa, La and Frill: all the girls Sanna's age and near it. They listen as the last note of Sanna's song dissolves trembling among the wavelets' foam.

"You're crying," Addra says to Pippa. It's an accusation.

"*You* are," Pippa accuses right back.

Both of them dip below the surface, so any salt water they've made mingles with the waves.

Dark-haired La sighs. She isn't ashamed of her weeping. "I miss Ishi."

She thinks of Ishi's home many suns to the south, where her clan of aged women and very few men stay put in a lagoon in which there are plenty of fish, with no landish folk to contend with. La will see her on the next migration — as soon as Sanna returns — and then Ishi will decide whether to join La's clan or not.

Sanna's song makes La want her love *now*. No, she is not ashamed of a single tear.

Frill shakes her cloud of white-blond hair. She echoes La's sigh. "I wish I could sing like that. To think we hardly noticed Sanna before!"

"*I* noticed her," says Addra, surfacing just in time to hear.

"Noticed in a nice way, I mean," says Frill, unaware of offending until Addra grabs her by the curls and pulls her under for a long tussle that draws the elders' attention.

"Stop it now, both of you!" Mar of the Long Reach orders them, holding the girls apart, her fingers' webbing over their mouths to keep them silent.

"Mothers," La whispers to Shusha and Gurria, "promise we'll leave as soon as Sanna comes back. The very *moment*, the very *heartbeat*."

Gazing into the seas of each other's eyes — for they think they understand La better than anyone else in the clan — Shusha and Gurria promise this to their daughter, just as they silently promise (again) love to each other.

Chapter 36

Moon song, concluded.

Round-pearly Moon bobs in the waves
Till the Earth cracks her back to a slice.
So it goes and goes, waxes and wanes.
She is never one thing, and neither am I.
Yes, let me be your Moon.

—*The Mermaids*

• Chapter 37 •

Miracles beget miracles.

With morning comes the second miracle.

Father Abel encounters it first, but he doesn't realize. After ringing the bell to wake the town, he shuffles through the church of Our Lady of the Sea, checking that all is as it should be for Sunday Mass — no drunks sleeping in a corner; the statue returned to her pedestal; flowers from her bier now piled on the altar, just slightly wilted, ready to encourage prayer and harvest.

He's glad to find that there are no drunks, no loiterers or malingerers. The day is strong and bright and well-washed. A thin rain last night cleansed the dust off the trees, the offal from the streets.

He will be shocked, later, by what else there is to see.

In the houses, waking up, the people feel exceptionally fine. They'd thought themselves too excited to sleep, but they dropped into slumber as soon as they lay down, then enjoyed sleep of a kind usually described only by residents of the castle — deep, dreamless, restful.

For once, they smile at each other as they greet the day, and they look forward to the week with surety. Fishers are sure that mighty schools of fish are waiting just beyond the rocks that close in the bay. Farmers are sure that when the morning's rain dries, it will bring an exceptionally good harvest. Pregnant women are sure their babies are healthy. And they even dare hope, against all tradition, that they will have girls.

The promise of a good harvest, some already say, has less to do with rain and more with the lovely girl who flung herself into the rose vine and changed the castle (so they speculate) forever.

For this and many other reasons, Sanna is the topic on everyone's lips.

Shyly, blushing, they remember descending upon her — to free her from the clutching vine, they tell themselves — and they remember, too, the taste of her blood on their tongues as they dabbed away at her wounds. Could her blood be what's given this sense of well-being to the day, a spring in the step as if summer's just begun, rather than winding to a close?

Of course it is.

They hunger for more of her, more of Sanna, more of the miracle. Some have a thumb's length of velvet or lace from her clothes, and they work these scraps between their fingers as if conjuring her again.

And why shouldn't she come? No, not by conjuring, but for a proper visit to Dark Moon Harbor. She might as easily walk to see them as she walked into the castle — or they might use the bier reserved for Our Lady of the Sea to fetch her, angelic worker of miracles, from the castle and carry her into this cluster of smoking houses on the lip of the bay.

Talking thus among themselves, the people head to church. They will ask Father Abel to bring Sanna to town for a visit. They'll tell him they should welcome her. She should bless their homes. She should pray in the ship-shaped little church they are entering, the one whose founding stones are jagged boulders rising from the earth in what some believe used to be a pagan shrine. She should hallow the painted walls and the altar, which overflows today with yesterday's limp flowers. She should see Our Lady in her proper place on the pedestal.

They are sure.

And then they see.

It's the girls of the town who actually *see* first, and then only when enough of them are gathered to begin a first prayer. They gaze toward the sanctum's east window, which is streaming gray light, and then . . .

They feel a thrill deep in their bones. The same thrill they felt yesterday, with the change in the roses.

This time, it's not just flowers that have changed, nothing alive or believed to be alive heretofore. It is the statue. Our Lady of the Sea herself.

Her arms, once held wide in benediction and as if to embrace the poor sinners and offer them comfort—her arms are now crossed. Closed. Cradling . . .

"What is it?" asks one of many girls named Maria. This one is a sister of the boy Tomas, who lives in the castle as Peder's companion. She has a certain standing among the girls because of him.

But no one can see just what Our Lady holds. Her cloak and sleeves hide the crook of her arms.

Soon all the girls are asking, "What happened? What's in her arms?" and no amount of shushing from their mothers (even Maria and Tomas's mother, the widowed Inger) can silence the whispers.

Father Abel hears them, and he interrupts his Latin drone to listen. And then to look where the girls are pointing.

"Sweet Mother of God," he says, and his voice echoes through the old church, down to its pagan roots. "It's the second miracle."

Our Lady of the Sea cradles her bundle and smiles. Her off-kilter eyes gaze at the thing in her arms and also into the eyes of each person there, all at one time.

"Somebody must tell the Baroness," says Father Abel.

But no one moves to obey. No one is ready, yet, to let the castle into this miracle. Until . . .

"We have to tell Sanna," a woman suggests. Then all the women are saying it. Some call her a saint; some say an angel. Some say she already knows and quite likely is responsible for changing the statue.

"We need her with us," Inger says firmly.

And like that, so easily, Father Abel is no longer in charge of the town.

Inger's three daughters take off sprinting toward the castle, followed by all others who can run, walk, and stumble in that direction.

anna

In the morning, Kett brings me the linen chemise and the blue dress in which I arrived—cleaner now, and beaten to a softness, but after their rough treatment, more than ever a wreck of the beautiful things they once were. When I'm dressed and my hair's combed (carefully over my neck, hiding the mark in the back where my seavish form exhales), Kett tells me to follow her.

We go down stairs and up them, through rooms decorated with curious things the *flok* would love to collect— any one of which might be the most precious object that Sjældent wants me to bring her. As we push deeper into the castle, I feel the hum of magic increasing. I could find Thyrla even without Kett to guide me.

She is not in the same place as yesterday, however. She's sitting in a room on the other side of the elaborate door to her bedchamber, positioned between two windows—one to the courtyard, one facing toward the town—and is doing something with cloth in her lap. She doesn't look up at us right away, which seems to be normal, because Kett bobs her knees and then leaves us alone.

I use my time to study the place, as I believe Thyrla intends me to do. The door to the bedchamber is locked (I smell the position of the seven irons), and I have the strong sense I won't be invited in there again, unless in case of some dire and as yet unimaginable need.

I think, *The castle is a shell, with many chambers in it.* This might make a line to a song, if my time on land becomes worthy of singing about again. I imagine the Baroness is one of those large snails who spend their lives building one room after another, squeezing themselves through the doors once they've made a bigger chamber in the spiral. The room we're in now is slightly more grand than the one with her bed, and it's not locked away so tight; but it still vibrates with magic and is clearly special to her. Whatever she does in this place is important.

I am seeing how a landish woman lives, I think. I will try to consider this visit a lesson like the ones Sjældent gave me. And to bear in mind that this woman is a land-witch and possibly an air-witch, thus doubly as likely to harm as to help me.

It is a lovely room full of color. The ceiling is made of wood, decorated in bright shades of yellow and green and red paint. Flowers, fish, boats—too many figures to note at a glance. There's green cloth on the walls, a different pattern than in the room with the bed, and two large pictures painted on slabs of wood and framed in gold. But the most remarkable furnishings are the chests and cabinets with lids and doors open, fabrics and threads in every imaginable color, texture, and metal spilling out.

Cloth — it's perhaps the only richness we cannot improve in the sea, as the state of my dress demonstrates now.

I study what the Baroness is doing: She has a light pink-white fabric stretched tight in a wooden hoop, and she's using a fish-bone needle (I've seen landish women do this before) to whip white thread around a silver cord she's laid over it. The fabric covers her lap entirely, looking a bit the color of Aunt Gurria's tail, I think . . .

But I must not think of my clan while I'm here. I don't know the extent of Thyrla's powers, and she might be able to scry everything that runs through my mind and heart. I know some witches have that special magic, one neither Sjældent nor I possess.

I decide I need to engage her in talk, if only to cloud my thoughts from her. It might also lead to some useful information for my quest.

"Thyrla?" I say politely. "Baroness?"

Her only answer is a quiet "Hmmm" and an arc of the needle over the silver worm of thread.

Worm, I think; *Sjældent . . .*

A little desperate to keep my thoughts secret, I step up to study the two pictures. They were made with — I sniff them discreetly—ground-up stones and beetles and bone, mixed with plant oils and smeared onto wood that grows to the south. They depict a woman very like the Baroness, only with both eyes showing and a blue dress like mine flowing from the top of her head to her feet. In one picture she is kneeling at a small table with some papers open upon it, and a golden-haired man with white wings is blowing wind into her ear. In the other picture, the woman is older, still wearing blue, now standing in the cradle of a crescent moon. Other winged people, babies this time, hold her clothes; I believe they are lifting her into the sky.

I don't know what the relationship between the paintings of the woman and the things on the ceiling might be, but I'm intrigued, and I look from one to the other several times.

"The two most important moments in a woman's life." It's Thyrla, still sewing. She has decided to acknowledge me and, I think, hopes to unnerve me by proving she can indeed scry my mind or at least follow my natural curiosity. "Finding out she's going to have a baby—and dying."

I'm no less confused than before, but I sense I should pretend I know what she means, so I nod. This is another way in which landish *flok* are different from seavish ones; we find many other moments in life more important than death.

You have lived long, you have seen much, and you will be remembered . . .

"Please sit if you'd like to," Thyrla says as she pulls a long thread up through the top of the cloth. "How are you healing?"

It takes a heartbeat to realize she's referring to the wee pokes and scratches I got from the rose vine.

"I am well," I say politely. I closed all those little wounds as I sang.

"Your bed is comfortable?"

"The nicest one I've ever used."

Her lone gray eye looks up sharply then, and I remind myself not to make any slying remarks. Even if I think I'm the only one who can appreciate the irony, Thyrla is smart and powerful and will surely guess something's wrong.

I feel a buzz down in my bones. Magic. Anger. Something.

I find one of those hard wooden surfaces on which the landish like to sit, and I sit. Awkwardly.

Immediately there begins what feels like an attack.

Thyrla announces that she intends to contact my family. "They must be so worried about you," she says, poking her needle under the hoop and trusting its point to find the right spot to return to. "And I am worried about *them*."

I take a moment to consider what the Baroness might be planning. Her behavior is careless, which tells me that I must be especially care*ful* now.

The magic thrums hard.

I am half-certain that Thyrla knows I already

communicated with my family. But in case she didn't hear the song or recognize what it was, I ask, wide-eyed, "What news do you want me to give them?"

She smiles. I note that, like Sjældent, she probably finds a smile more threatening than a frown. In Thyrla's case, it's more of a simper or sneer.

Another white thread runs through the cloth, tacking the silver one down.

"Why, that you've been found," she says mildly. "And of course they'll be glad to know you're now betrothed to a very wealthy young man." Another stitch, then a little laugh that holds a note of near-mockery. "You do have family, don't you, Sanna?"

My father, my clan. Sjældent. "Of course."

"Then where should we write to them?"

Naturally I can't tell her that writing's no use; nobody knows letters any better than I do. I also think I shouldn't mention Bjarl or any of the aunts and elders by name, just in case. So I try to distract her.

"Do you know a woman named Lisabet?" I ask.

If I expected something important to happen when I uttered the name, I must be disappointed now. But to me, just *saying* the name out loud, on land, is of dazzling importance itself, and for a moment my head is light with the thrill of it.

Meanwhile, Thyrla lays down her sewing and considers me. The thin white thread and the thick silver one hang toward the floor; I notice she's broken her needle, which could mean she's upset — or that fish bones are too fragile for this landish task.

"Do you mean Lisabet, wife of Valdemar the weaver?" she asks, smoothing some silver hairs away from the eye with the patch. "Or Lisabet who is married to one of the Eriks who work a turnip farm? There's a Lisabet who washes my dishes, but I doubt you mean her. And, I believe, a Mother Lisabet a day's sail away. She's the abbess of a convent specializing in sheep."

I'm bewildered. "So many Lisabets."

Thyrla opens a little gold case in which a dozen or more fish-bone needles are rattling. She selects a new one while that confident smirk lingers in the corners of her mouth.

"Indeed," she says. She slips a white thread through the needle's eye and chooses a new cord, a gold one this time, to lay down as part of the pattern.

Whatever she's sewing has many such bright threads; they gleam in the sun streaming through her windows, the one that faces the yard and the one that looks toward the town.

"I don't think any of those women you mention is the right one," I say, trying to hide my disappointment.

"Perhaps you'd like to tell me about the Lisabet you're looking for," Thyrla suggests.

I hesitate. Of course I don't trust her. I feel like a prisoner, but I don't know why she'd bother to imprison me. I sense danger in explaining why I want to find this Lisabet (perhaps the one with the sheep?), but I'm not sure how I'll be hurt. Whether the woman who will help me is Thyrla herself or some other person to whom she might lead, I don't know. I do know that I have to begin.

"I'm all ears," Thyrla says.

But I cannot begin. Maybe I'll have to make and unmake an escape from the castle after all. I wonder if the Baroness will be disappointed not to have me as a wife for her son . . . If I do leave, I'll be back in a random world, without the least sign pointing toward the Lisabet I seek.

I think what a strange phrase she has used: *I'm all ears.* It makes me notice the sounds around us, the vibrations they make in my bones. There's noise in the yard as Thyrla's workers clean up after the celebration of yesterday, and far away, in the direction of town, I catch a rumble—a rumble of . . . ?

Thyrla is listening, too.

It's the sound of feet. People are rushing toward the castle, bursting from the trees and running down the ridge of the island still pocked with the prints of yesterday.

I hear the word again, in many voices: *Miracle.*

Chapter 39

Why the castle should fear the town.

Tomas is with Peder, sleeping too hot beneath a coverlet of fur, when Thyrla's guards shout: "Attack! They're attacking!"

His first thought is how surprising this is; until now the guards have been mere decoration, like the portcullis and the assommoir down which they might hurl hot oil and broken rocks on invaders. The Islands are far from other castles and kingdoms and have never been attacked. Relations with the town have always been good, too, with the people grateful for any crumb from the Baroness's table. So what would anyone in the castle have to fear?

Tomas pulls a jacket over his shirt and runs out to the rampart, where he sees his sisters: Anna, Maria, and little Inger, named after their mother, carried in fifteen-year-old Anna's arms. They are beaming with joy at the front of the pack, and they run as if their mud-cloddy feet are as light as feathers.

Yes, the people are storming the castle—but not out of menace. They do it with love, as anyone can see who truly looks.

In the castle, doors slam open and shut. The Baroness, with a face written furious, comes to stand by Tomas—then ignores him, instead studying the road from the town and all the pilgrims coming here a second day. Her gold-and-silver hair twists like a thousand ribbons in the wind, and gold and silver threads cling to her white gown.

"What *are* they doing?" she demands of no one in particular.

"Should we stop them, Baroness?" asks the chief of the guards—uneasily, because his family is among the crowd, too, and he doesn't want to hurt them.

"No." She stamps her foot and tries to catch her hair with one hand while scratching under the eye patch with the other. "Let's see what they want."

Down in the courtyard, still littered with broken crockery and bits of food the animals and birds haven't spirited away, plus some last workers cleaning, Tomas and Thyrla are joined by Peder. He has dressed himself once again in the magnificent golden clothes of yesterday, though without his sleeves laced on.

"Hullo, Mother," he says lazily. "Any sign of my bride?"

It's the first time Tomas can remember hearing him ask after one girl in particular. This doesn't make Tomas especially happy; in fact, he has a vision of himself wielding a sword or a pike, mounting Peder's head on top, and carrying it down the broad street of the town.

But he isn't like that. He feels guilty even for thinking it.

Tomas joins the crowd while Thyrla and Peder step onto the dais, in front of the empty niche that Our Lady of the Sea occupied just yesterday. The red roses are blooming even more profusely than last night, and their sweet scent outweighs the odors of ocean and fish.

"Tomas!"

"Tomas!"

"Tomas!"

His eager, skinny sisters address him rather than the lady and her son, and they fling their arms around him as if they've been separated for months, not hours. He is both pleased by and worried over this, as Peder or the Baroness might dismiss him for getting too much attention.

"Tomas, there's been another miracle!" Maria says excitedly. She lost her cap in the race for the castle, and the morning sun picks out a reddish hair here and there.

"Miracle!" echoes the youngest, towheaded Inger Younger. She's pointing at Sanna.

The stranger who turned the white roses red now stands at the top of the courtyard's wooden stair, clutching a handrail as if it might save her life. Tomas thinks she looks scared—but of what?

The people sink to their knees, adoring her.

Tomas wants to run to Sanna and fling his body between her and the crowd, though he knows the town means her no harm. Something in her inspires the wish to protect.

Peder, with a similar impulse, extends one bejeweled hand in her direction.

"My betrothed!" he declaims in a voice louder than the town crier's. "Come, let us greet our people together!"

Thyrla's voice pierces his, deflates it, becomes all the people can hear: "What in Heaven and Hell," she says, "do you all want now?"

• Chapter 40 •

One miracle may hide another.

Not everyone in town can run the miles to the castle. The old and the young and the sick stay behind in the church.

Father Abel stays with them. It's a shepherd's duty to remain with the flock.

At first, he burns a little precious incense, as if to compensate the people for being left behind, and he tries to lead them in Mass. But it's even harder to catch their attention now than on an ordinary day, and Abel's heart isn't in the ritual. He's as curious about the statue as everyone else. In a sinfully short time, he has halted his own Latin and wandered over to Our Lady. At the moment there is no greater service he can do than figuring out how she's changed—how her arms moved and just what they hold concealed within the crook of one yellow elbow. By all Catholic rites it should be her Son and Savior, but Abel wants to be certain.

Our Lady of the Sea is on her pedestal again, and the bundle in her arms is well above the faithfuls' heads. The people follow the priest, but the closer they get, the harder it is to see upward. All Abel can make out is the cracks in the paint of her robe—and these don't even seem to be new cracks. From below, it looks as if the robe has always been carved this way, swathing the Virgin and whatever's in her arms, so that she might embrace her greatest treasure.

He wishes for the ladders that helped move her yesterday. But wish in one hand and spit in the other . . .

"Father, stand on my back."

It's Sven who-used-to-be-blacksmith, an old man of some fifty scorching years, who lost his hands and trade when he fell into the fire while drunk. He has been living on family and church charity ever since, and now he pitches himself down with elbows and knees on the floor, for Abel to climb up.

Carefully, Abel steps on Sven's back. Two men who still have their hands hold him steady.

It isn't enough. He rises only as far as the Lady's knees.

"We need to take her off the pedestal," he says. "We need to bring her to our level."

"Not enough hands," says old Elsa, who used to mend nets before rheumatism turned her fingers to claws.

"Not enough backs," says one of several Knuds who used to go out fishing but have been ordered to stay on land, ever since a song heard at sea made them try drowning themselves each time they came near the water.

"Except to walk on," says Sven, still tabled under the priest's feet.

Everyone joins in the project. Young and old and maimed and mad, they crouch down to make a living ladder for Abel to climb. Two of the strongest women — Gudrun, who once farmed with her husband, and Gunver, who stayed behind because of her twelve young children — give him their hands to stay steady. Their palms are moist and rough against his.

Soon enough, Abel is standing at the top of a human staircase, and he and Our Lady of the Sea are looking each other in the eyes. Her skewed black dots somehow match with his gaze, and for a moment he simply stares, awash in holiness.

This is the reason I'm here, he thinks — *here* meaning the Dark Islands, which until now have felt like exile to a man educated in Rome. *The Miracles of Dark Moon Harbor.*

Below him, someone sneezes. Another one farts.

Abel looks away from the flaking, peeling, beautiful face of the holy statue of the holiest woman ever to live, redeemer of Eve's sins, mother of the One who offers salvation to all. Teetering on tiptoes, he puts one hand on her shoulder and peers into her clasped arms, expecting to meet something wonderful.

He sees nothing. Nothing but her, that is. Her right elbow is raised just high enough, and her mantle falls just low enough, that a flap of yellow wood covers whatever might lie in her embrace.

175

Father Abel gasps, then sobs.

"What is it, Father?" a Knud calls from near the bottom of his ladder. "What do you see?"

Abel leaps off the pile of bodies, landing so hard that one ankle twists beneath him.

It's only wood and paint, he reminds himself. *Only a statue.*

Wood and paint — why does he feel so bereft? Why, in a spiritual system founded on mystery, does he feel such a burning need to know everything about this one event?

The living staircase breaks apart, and the flock soon stampedes the priest. They are worried about his ankle.

They worry even more when they see that he's weeping — not ordinary tears but red ones, the color of new roses.

Chapter 41

What in Heaven and Hell.

The people—the pilgrims—feel foolish. They can't answer Thyrla's simple but rudely put question. What the hell do they expect here?

Harald the butcher, arguably the town's most powerful man, steps forward with his hat in his pink hands. "It's the statue, Baroness. She's changed, and naturally we thought . . ."

Even he can't finish. He trembles on the cold skewer of her silver eye.

"Changed how?" she asks sharply. "Not before she left this castle, she didn't."

A Hans who farms lentils and turnips says, "The coincidence seemed too great to ignore. We thought we should ask Sister Sanna—"

"Sanna!" The Baroness hisses like a cat. "What should she know?"

Indeed, Sanna appears confused, face a beet red (*rose red*) and tongue tied in a knot, one wrist held firm in Peder's grip.

Thyrla asks the town triumphantly: "Came rushing here without all the facts, didn't you? Expect the castle to provide all the answers, don't you?"

The townspeople blush with Sanna. Yes, they were hasty. Yes, they leapt to a conclusion. They wanted to be with Sanna, their living miracle, more than they wanted to investigate the statue.

The Baroness throws her hands up. "Can *anyone* tell us what it means, this statue that shifted overnight? No? Are you all quite sure that you saw it?"

Her son, Peder, steps forward, pulling Sanna with him. He looks disheveled and bleary-eyed but still beautiful — and obviously resentful of his mother.

"Go easy on these good people, Mother," he says. "I'm sure we can clear it all up with a quick trip to town."

"You won't find your answer in the bottom of a beer cup," she says icily.

Now it's not just his eyes that are red; it's his whole face. He's embarrassed in front of the town.

In fact, there's not a single complexion, except Thyrla's, that hasn't taken on the hue of the flowers transformed with Sanna's blood.

So Tomas thinks — Tomas, who would rather die than find out his mother has such a low opinion of him. Which might be the case, since he's usually Peder's companion on those sorties to the taverns, and Tomas always pretends he's drunker than he is in order to make Peder happy.

Tomas's sisters still surround him. He whispers to Maria—second oldest, easiest to speak to since Anna is holding the squirmy Inger Younger—"Where is our mother?"

"Behind with the littles."

His two brothers, twins, born just before their father died of too much pining over voices heard at sea.

Maria is excited; her blue eyes snap as she whispers back, "What's Sanna like? *Really* like, I mean—is she as nice as she seems? Does magic simply ooze from her every moment of the day?"

Tomas hesitates, and not just because the Baroness is shooting daggers at them from her gray eye. The most factual answer he could give his sister would be *I don't know,* but there's another answer brimming at his heart.

"She's wonderful," he says.

Maria claps her hands, squealing, "I knew it!"

And her hand-claps ripple outward, until all the pilgrims are clapping, every last one of them, and the ground trembles beneath their feet.

The roses pulse and push forth new blooms.

With the applause comes a request: "Bless us, Sanna!" calls one voice, and soon the others take up the cry.

"Bless us, Sanna!"

"Bless our homes!"

"Bless our bodies, so we might work to your honor!"

The Baroness is not pleased. She draws herself up to full height—not as tall as Sanna, but impressive—and raises a hand.

The people quiet themselves. Even the sea's waves grow more tranquil, so Thyrla is heard.

"You with your blessings," she says in a voice dripping contempt. "One miracle does not make a saint, you know. And saints are most often martyred before they win the distinction."

Tomas feels sick. He can't bear to think of any of the awful deaths the known saints have met (blinded, beheaded, burned alive; shot with a thousand arrows, eaten by rats, raped)—none of these fates should befall his Sanna.

No, not his. Not Peder's either; just *Sanna.* Nothing bad should happen to her.

As Thyrla's words sink in, the people look stricken. All joy has left, replaced with fear of the Baroness.

Their expressions seem to make Thyrla angrier. She stamps a foot and turns even whiter.

"Go, all of you," she orders. "Sort out this matter of the statue. You go with them"—she turns to Peder. "And you too"—to Sanna. "We'll continue our discussion when you return."

Thyrla may have intended to punish her people by banishing them from the castle, but she's given them just what they wanted. In their relief, cheering bursts out, and with it a wind that lashes the plants in the great bowl of the green sallet island.

Tomas gazes at Sanna, standing tall and pale and tense beside Peder, in her once-grand dress, with her perfect pink skin.

She looks terrified.

Chapter 42

Seaskin.

"What do you make of it?" Bjarl asks Sjældent.

She's come here under protest. To Ringstone, in choppy waters that have wrecked many a small boat and mer-child, just to listen to dim sounds from a barely visible island.

Sjældent cocks her ear and scratches in the lank hair behind it.

"Well, the people are happy," Sjældent says. "They make those noises, slapping their own hands and squalling like children, to show they've got what they wanted."

"Is Sanna in danger?"

She squints at him.

"Should I worry?" he asks, pressing the point.

"Always," she says. And she starts to dream about what Sanna will bring her.

Ye'll know that when ye see it.

anna

My walk is stiff; my heart is weak. All these landish people—have they really formed such a passion for me? Sjældent never warned me this could happen; perhaps she didn't think of it, either. And now I must go with this *flok* to their town, the place where they huddle together with their fires and their smells and their thin-ringing bell.

Peder, Thyrla's son and my betrothed, walks with me, hand under my elbow in a way I would find possessive and infuriating if it didn't help me to keep upright and going forward. My feet and my limbs and my very blood itself ache from yesterday's adventures.

Tomas, Peder's friend, walks just behind us, and with him walk his sisters (now, *there* are meek girls; they haven't said a word since Thyrla banished us); after them— everyone.

We cross the sweet-salt water at the edge of the garden island and enter a forest, where morning mist is still thick in the leaves. And then come other isles, too many to count, as if someone took a handful of pebbles and hurled them into the sea.

Where there are bridges, Peder insists on helping me cross them, and while I still find his possessive manner repugnant, I'm grateful for the steadying hands. He's also there to catch me when it's my turn to hop a stream or a channel with no bridge. I start to see, a little, why the landish girls like him.

He is explaining the place to me, pointing out what's notable in the farms and fields by which we pass: "Niels the plowman still has wheat to bring in," and "That's where Harald fattens the cows he will slaughter."

It is all very interesting, and through him I find the beauty in the land. The leaves, for example, are almost as green as the top layer of the sea, or as green as Thyrla's cloth-covered walls. I wait to hear the name *Lisabet* in his list of citizens, and I plan to remember everything so I can add it to my people's store of knowledge.

At the same time, I'm nervous.

This will be my first time in an actual town, at least as landish people understand a town to be. I've never walked through a collection of buildings where a *flok* eats and sleeps and works to make the things we take from them when they wreck at sea. I can already smell it, the smoke and urine and fleshiness that make towns both repugnant and fascinating to the *marreminder*.

Soon we're coming out of yet another woods, one where

trees grow in lines and smell sweetly of fruits, into the sun and a curious garden of sticks. These sticks grow in rows like other crops, but with other perpendicular sticks lashed on with rope or battened down with nails.

I know what these are—crosses, Sjældent has called them, and she told me they represent both the death and enduring presence of the invisible god of this landish *flok*. They mark their own deaths this way, too.

Where ye see sticks crossed like daggers, she said, *ye can be sure there's sorrow underfoot.*

The island of sorrow rises to the back of a chalky white building with a wooden roof and a tower where the bell hangs. By the bell I know that this is the church. I know also that now we've found the town.

"Dark Moon Harbor," Peder says grandly, halting at the top of the church's small hill. He waves an arm as if to give me all the mean little houses, the smoking chimneys and tethered boats, and the gutters and dogs and piles of excreta—everything that is ugliest about life, heaped together in this one place where the Dark Moon *flok* lives all their days.

"Welcome to our home," says Tomas, behind us.

I do my best to smile.

Chapter 44

She may not always be the Baroness.

Time has sped up for Thyrla. With this second miracle, she feels it spinning away along with her power. All thanks to one stranger, an enemy whom (for now) she is keeping close, in case *her* powers are useful later.

And *later* is going to come sooner than Thyrla ever planned.

This situation can't go on for long, with the town worshipping Sanna and objects being struck with magic right and left. Who's to say Sanna won't magick a person next, sap away some power that rightly belongs to the Baroness? She might steal everything Thyrla has worked to acquire over more decades than she'd ever admit.

Thyrla must educate herself as much as she can, try to deduce Sanna's powers and purpose. Otherwise she, Thyrla, may never leave these islands; she might be stuck here forever, like one of the bones on her walls, nothing more than a baroness who once had a plan.

"Go into town," she tells her servants. "All of you."

The grating sound of chain mail. "Even us guards?"

They're uneasy; they've never been dismissed before, not all at once.

"Every last one of you," she says. She needs the castle to herself.

When they're gone, she wanders from room to room, from the rose-choked courtyard to the great hall where the servants do most of their work; through the guards' hall with its crossed pikes and swords, never used but in training; and from room to glorious room, places for sewing and writing and living, with chests full of treasures and coins, gorgeous clothes in the latest designs, jewels so fabulous she wouldn't believe they existed if she didn't own them herself.

She checks, of course, the room where Sanna slept last night. More of a box, really, sometimes used for storing root vegetables and grain. There's little of Sanna still in it; there hasn't been time to accumulate the scurf of living. Thyrla has to hunt to find a couple strands of pale gold hair and a sliver of something that might be a broken fingernail. She tucks these into an ivory box and grabs a handful of bed straw just in case it's caught something.

She buries her face in the straw and sniffs deep. Nothing, not even a tingle. Of course, the girl isn't that much of a witch, not from what Thyrla's seen so far.

Roses dyeing, sand whirling—neat little tricks, yes, but *little* ones.

Thyrla lets the straw fall. There's nothing more to discover here.

She returns to the bone room that's also her bed's room, with relatives glued to the walls. She pulls back their drapes and gives them some air, considering each skull and knuckle in turn. Every one has contributed something to her magic, and she needs all of them now.

"She looks too innocent," Thyrla says, addressing no one in particular, just seeing how the skulls respond. "She wouldn't take the strength from a fly if it begged her."

The skulls that were Thyrla's babies rattle toothlessly, like little birds learning to use their beaks.

Uncle says, "She's taken the town from you, my girl, that she has. There's your strength gone."

When Thyrla doesn't reply, his teeth grind in mockery. "Thought you'd take all your treasures and live like a queen in the world, didn't you? Never counted on a rival: prettier, smarter, more powerful—"

"We don't know that yet," Thyrla snaps.

"Proud of herself, our girl is," says one woman's skull to another.

"I can hear you!" Thyrla declares, but it doesn't stop anyone.

Two orphaned teeth rub together: "Full of herself!"

"And no better than she should be."

A half-dozen babies rattle and prattle: *"Dja, dja, dja."*

Thyrla interprets even their nonsense (correctly) as ridicule. Somehow the bones know everything that's happened on the islands, and whatever sympathy they once had for her has vanished overnight.

Not that the babies should feel at all kindly toward her. They are the children she bore in winters when her entire staff went to sleep; the children she might have raised if she hadn't needed their lives to feed her youth. Little ones fathered by sailors who came and went in her harbor, babies sacrificed ("Not without tears," Thyrla reminds them) for the greater good of the family. Of, at least, their mother.

Oh, why did this happen *now*, when Thyrla is almost ready, with riches amassed and youth banked, enough beauty remaining to make her (yes) a queen, or something even better: a woman who has no ties, no duties, who gets to pursue her own pleasure and has the money to do it. To see the world and finally *be seen* in it. To enjoy herself. *Why?*

Is Sanna planning to drain the years from these islands and leave Thyrla to starve in old age, alone on a rock?

Trembling, Thyrla pulls herself together. She reminds herself that she has resources. She has the hairs and the fingernail to work with; she *will* make them yield up Sanna's secrets.

"Dja, dja, dja," taunt the babies.

"Shut up," Thyrla says.

anna

I can't say the town is a disappointment, precisely. I can say it is not beautiful; it is not grand. At first it seems far less pleasant than other landish places I've explored. I stand with Peder (and Tomas, and his shy sisters) on the flat place in front of the church, looking down the broad path called a street where the landish live and work and trade the things they make. I see all the way to a tangle of wooden piers and boats with sails down, and beyond them the wide bay glittering blue and silver. Wispy white clouds streak a turquoise sky. And that is the entirety of the world as these people know it.

I wish I could see my own people. I long to break free and swim for the *flok*; but if I do that, I'll forfeit any chance that I will find the help Sjældent promised awaits here. So, instead, I let Peder take my hands and seat me on a hard bench beneath an old tree—where I feel a faint hum of magic. Seated, I get even more tremors from the base of the church nearby, where rocks jut upward like teeth into which someone has stuffed this place of landish worship.

Then I'm surrounded by people and can see nothing but them, one gaunt belly after another at eye level. Just as yesterday, the landish are massing around me, but now they are deferential, kneeling and beseeching. They wouldn't dare steal a scrap of my dress or lick the blood from my wounds now. Overnight, they learned to see me as beyond their touch—except Peder, who stands behind me with hands on my shoulders as if I'm his possession.

This change in the landish attitude toward me has something to do with that statue, which I haven't seen yet . . .

"Sister!" It's the old man's voice, Father Abel's, calling to me as he makes his way across the square, supported by two women.

Sister? I wonder. I'll ask about it later. For now, I wiggle sideways so he can sit by me. I smell pain coming from him.

"My ankle," he says, as if apologizing.

"May it heal quickly," I say—and he exclaims in sudden relief.

He walks straight now. It seems I've just cured him.

At that, the women untie their caps and drag them off; the men remove their hats. They kneel at my feet.

"Bless me, Sanna," begs a woman with a scalp flaky with scabs. "Heal my sore bones."

"Ask the Lord to do it," Father Abel says on a note of reproof.

"Yes, Sanna, ask the Lord."

I am to make many requests of this Lord today. One by one, head by head, I bless the people of Dark Moon Harbor. So many of them that my hands shine with the oil from their scalps, which they seem to expect me to cup in my palms while murmuring some words over them.

"Your touch helped me yesterday, Sister," says a woman who is called, I believe, Birgit or something like it. "Your blood. I'm sure I conceived a daughter last night."

I fumble, touching her again, thinking what the people must have done after departing the castle. With my blood on their lips, they made love and babies, for which they will credit me.

"May the Lord bless you and heal you," I say.

Soon enough, we establish a rhythm to their approach and my response, and they are bobbing up and down like birds on the waves to receive a little heat from my hands and a whispered word of goodwill.

"Thank you, Sister," they say humbly each time.

More often than not, it's Peder who says "You're welcome," though he has nothing to do with the process. Myself, I feel like a sham. Except that I *could* heal these people, at least some of them, if I felt safe enough to use magic on purpose now. Father Abel's ankle seems to be another accident of magic, or perhaps it healed only because he believed it would. I'm in an agony as I debate within myself—should I truly cure all these ills or not?

Best not, at least until I know more about the place and

have taken my quest here as far as it can go. Until I have answers in addition to questions. For now I'll just say the words.

Meanwhile (blessing the head of a Torvald who reeks of sheep), I fear the event of another prominent "miracle." The first made me property of the Baroness and her son, and the second brought me here. The third would surely bind me to the earth.

I concentrate on the blessings. In return for each one, I ask for a name. I get more Marias and Gudruns, Elsas and Birgits and Gerdas. There are a few Lisabets, but none feels right under my hands. None of those heads give me the crackle of recognition I've come to expect.

Recognition. Blood calling to blood. Love lying dormant.

It isn't here—*she* isn't here—so why did Sjældent send me to this place? Simply to minister to these suffering women? Such charity wouldn't be in her nature. Not to mention all the men and boys, who have far more complaints than the women and girls. I hear about pains in the feet and the fingers, rheumy eyes and ears, "manhood" that won't perform. I bless them all, and I do my best to beckon the women forward when the men push too hard.

I'm surprised to recognize some of the workers from the castle, the people who cook the food and who walk back and forth with pikes. Thyrla must have let her clan go for the day. I'm not sure why she would do that, but perhaps it's a landish custom. They come for their blessings the same as the others, though they don't seem to need much. Every last one of them is as healthy as Thyrla and her son—Peder, still standing heavy-handed behind me, as if each blessing must be approved by him.

And Tomas, Peder's friend—he's always there, too, but just to one side, visible in the corner of my eye. He stands among children I think are his brothers and sisters, and a blue-eyed woman I assume is his mother. They seem kind. They ask nothing of me, not even a blessing; they simply beam good wishes in my direction. In that way, they are a source of strength.

"May the Lord bless you and heal you," I say over another bare head, and I push some magic toward Tomas's family.

Chapter 46

The Baroness, once a bride.

It is sometimes hard to believe — as Thyrla pokes the
woodwork of her enormous bed, looking for tools and treasures she's stored there — that she once was married. Bound
to a man, in some part dependent on him.

But it's true, and the evidence is his long, pale, fragile
skull mounted on that selfsame bed. As she works, it oozes
beads of salt water from eye sockets and cheekbones. His
ribs, spread over the head of the bed next to Mother's,
expand and contract in a sigh.

Lot was a sighing sort of man in general, not at all
one with whom Thyrla would imagine spending her hard-
fought eternity. She chose him in part for that quality,
knowing he would pine away in her islands, giving her a
child but no trouble thereafter. He sailed in on a ship from
the Norseland and became known in the town; he was forever wandering down by the bay docks so he could look

to the horizon for a vessel big enough to carry him away. She was as kind to him as it was in her nature to be, but his kindness was for others. He attended Mass at Abel's church and took a listless, dutiful interest in the cloth and baskets and herrings and nets that the people made in a long, dark winter.

Then one day he stopped going to town, and nobody noticed. Certainly nobody came to the castle to ask what had become of him. Snow covered the islands, and ice silenced the waves. In spring, when Thyrla's servants awoke and the priest came to visit, she mentioned casually that Lot had died, and the offhand announcement seemed good enough for any curiosity he'd aroused.

By then her belly was enormous, and she made a very public to-do about becoming a mother. It suited her interests to let this one live, at least until he might be big enough to be of use to her. She named him Peder, meaning *rock*, because the island seemed more of a father to him than the pale man who drifted into her life and onto her wall, giving her only a few good years to add to her balance.

"Planning on another, are you?" Uncle asks now.

Thyrla realizes she's been rubbing her belly. She lets her hands drop.

"A bit old for it now, I'd say," Uncle continues. "'Less you suck the life out of some other poor soul to quicken your womb again."

"Oh, please, let it be Kett!" says the jawless skull. "I like her so much. She can settle in next to me."

"No one is settling," Thyrla says, but absently rather than with her usual sharpness. "Nothing is going to move or change until I want it. For now, I simply need information."

She presses a last peg in the bed frame, and out pops a box full of tricks. Animal bones and bricks and splinters of wood she's gathered over the years, finding a power in their ordinariness and the lives they've touched. She sits at her desk and spreads these things over the surface, tracing her fingers through the piles, rearranging them, waiting to feel the tingle that means her magic is ready for questions.

She feels nothing.

Until she takes Sanna's twin hairs from the box in her pocket. They tingle, yes, as she winds them around the little gold ring she lifted off Sanna's hand when the girl first arrived. And the scrap of something that must be a fingernail—that practically jumps from her palm to the table, and once it is there, it continues to pop and shift, like an ember in a fire.

"There's one bit that'll never stick on your wall."

The bones rattle.

"Quiet, Uncle." Thyrla watches the scrap jump this way and that, making its own kind of path among the litter on the desk. "All of you, quiet down."

The bit of something she thinks is a nail, isn't. The bones are eager to tell her so.

"Didn't come from a finger, oh, no."

"Not from a toe, either."

Thyrla doesn't bother to hush them now. The clean

light of noon is streaming through her windows, and it changes the way she sees the scrap.

It gleams. Pale green, with a nacre of yellow and pink. Like the shimmer inside a new-opened shell or the light on the sea during a good dawn.

The itch in Thyrla's doubled eye becomes unbearable, telling her that she's happened upon an object unlike anything she's known before.

With a deep breath (but not so deep that she inhales the delicate green thing), she pulls the patch away from her special eye. She is going to scry through time again, now with better tools.

anna

By the time I've blessed the heads that Abel thinks I need to bless, the sun has gone golden on the rocks that mark the far end of the bay. I am exhausted.

Father Abel sees me sagging on that very hard seat, weighed down by Peder's hands, which have grown sweaty and slack. I guess Abel is having difficulty deciding what to do, especially since the people already blessed did not go back to their homes and farms but lingered, watching one another, counting out my blessings and (I think) waiting for immediate signs that a touch has had the effect each person desired.

"Lady Sanna," he says, giving me a startling title, "what would you like now?"

What I'd like, really, would be to float on the seaskin with my clan, eating jellies and gazing at the perfect sky. But I have enough control not to answer honestly.

"I'd like to see the statue," I say. I am still curious, and it seems the most polite response.

Peder insists on helping me to my feet, which are both numb and prickling when I stand. I have to lean on him to make my way into the church, where I feel the tingle of magic growing stronger as the prickles in my feet fade.

Interpreting my weight as affection, Peder—a beautiful boy, yes, and temptingly redolent of pleasure and self-indulgence—stretches up to whisper into my ear.

"Until now, I have not kissed your lips," he says as we cross the church threshold. "I plan to do that tonight."

I realize I am to be another of his pleasures. A prize, a treasure looted from a wreck.

Without saying anything, I stiffen and pull away. My shoulder brushes Abel's, and then I stumble into Tomas's family as if they were a protective net: the girls, Anna and Maria and Inger Younger; his mother, Inger Elder, who carries two young boys; and Tomas himself.

I think I have found a clan of sorts. They surround and support me, and together we advance to gaze at this thing made by landish hands and changed by a magic none of us can understand.

"Beautiful, isn't she?" Tomas whispers.

The uneven black eyes somehow meet both of mine as Our Lady clutches her bundle to her breast.

"Yes," I say, for I've caught a bit of landish reverence, which is (I see now) a kind of magic in its own right.

"My mother prayed to her while she was expecting me,"

Tomas says, not taking his eyes off the statue. "She lost her first baby just after the birth, and she wanted more than anything to be a mother."

Lost her first baby . . .

"Our Lady is our family's patron saint," Tomas concludes.

Before I can ask him more about that first child, Peder sidles in between us. "Make room for me here, Chicken Legs."

The spell is broken.

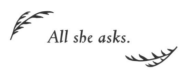

Chapter 48

All she asks.

Thyrla has divined it, the nature of the shiny green fragment that hops and flips as if to escape her triple-timed gaze. It's definitely not a fingernail.

It is a scale. A fish scale. But a scale for only half a fish — for the bit of skin she's licked from one corner is not fishy at all.

Sanna is a *marreminde*, a creature of the sea.

When Thyrla says it aloud, the bones clatter applause. She is once again their darling, the clever girl who solved the puzzle, added two and two and found something more than four. Or so she concludes, because it is how she feels about herself.

But what is Thyrla to do with this knowledge? Turn it to her advantage, of course — how?

She catches the scale in her fist, where it cuts into her skin. She's not going to let it escape, not now that she has recognized it. She'll keep it in a box even more tiny, even more special, within the woodwork of her bed. It will prove useful someday.

Holding the jumpy little thing, Thyrla finds an amber box and closes it with a snap. Once that's done, she becomes all logic, at least for a moment.

"Let us review what we know," she says, as she might have said to her son if she were giving him lessons and stretching his ability to reason.

The bones' crackle now is of tension. They hold themselves still in suspense, like examiners at a university.

"We know that young Sanna's a mermaid," says Thyrla.

A fierce, stabbing pain in her double eye threatens to unfocus her thoughts, take her away from Sanna and into her own body to look into future and past. She will not allow it; she'll continue her lecture.

"And what do we know about mermaids? Nothing, really, since we haven't met one ourselves before now. Isn't that right, Uncle?"

Uncle's teeth chatter *yes*.

"We know only the legends that others pass along," Thyrla notes. "The legends tell us that mermaids wreck ships at sea — which makes Sanna our enemy, because she has probably wrecked some of my own boats and cost me treasure and coins."

The itching in Thyrla's eye is unbearable; she gives in and rubs it, though the action increases the pain and the pull toward multiplied time.

The bones do not move, which means they agree.

"We also know, according to legend, that *marreminder* are drawn to the land. They fall in love with princes and huntsmen, and they transform themselves so as to come ashore and make love to these men."

Still no disagreement. The bones that she dug from the earth seem especially intent; they are the most steeped in land, thus (they hope) the most likely objects of Sanna's affection. Meanwhile, the smell of the red roses grows so strong as to be nauseous. Thyrla's special eye is streaming tears; she goes to the window to close the shutters.

"There are no princes in these Dark Islands," she says, finding her way back to her chair in the half shadows. "And the huntsmen are old and ugly. Therefore there can be only one object of Sanna's interest—"

Yes, yes, the bones wait to hear it . . .

"—and that object's my son, to whom she's already managed to betroth herself." Thyrla rubs her eye again.

"Well," she continues, in something more like her usual tone, "isn't Sanna a cunning slut? She was here barely an hour when I let her convince me to promise her my son."

Uncle vibrates so hard he makes the whole room tremble, or maybe it's the dragon turning over in his sleep. Mother's ribs, and Lot's, open and close slowly, like feeding butterflies.

"A promise doesn't always keep," Thyrla says, looking down at the trash scattered over her desk. "Betrothals break like glass on the rocks. Though there may be some advantage in letting Sanna marry my son . . . and have children . . . and live, at least for a while . . ."

All of a sudden, her right eye sees clearly. Among the pebbles and bones and sticks before her, there is a pattern: Thyrla sees grandchildren, infused with the magic of another element, combining land and sea and time. Tadpoles with fat heads and long tails; herring with tails bent in the shape of an *L.*

How clever the magic has been.

Grandchildren. With powers both inherited and trained—perhaps the most powerful creatures ever born, at least here in the north. What they could do, whether willingly to please their *bedstemor* or unwillingly mounted on her walls . . .

The ribs she calls Mother creak a protest as they expand and contract.

Is Thyrla able to wait so long?

Try as she might, pained as she makes them, Thyrla's eyes can't scry a map to her destiny. Looking into the scraps, she sees only scattered scenes of babies floating in a green that she realizes is water rather than wall hangings, and fish and floating forests that must be boats with clouds snagged on their masts.

When, reluctantly—because she might lose it—she drops the scrap of a scale into the mix, she sees a little more; but it's still confusing and, she believes, jumbled as to time. An iron-haired *marreminde* screams in agony; a girl squats onshore with her skirts hiked around her waist and a fish sliding out from between her legs. A veritable army of mermaids at least Thyrla's age (and she is much, much older than she looks) advances through the waves holding swords in both hands.

The pain grows unbearable. Thyrla blinks, and the patterns fade before she can sort them into a story.

"In the end, there's really just one thing I know," she says, rubbing the doubled right eye. (The pain there is terrible; if she were a true Christian, she might cast the eye out, for it offends her mightily.) "What I know is—is . . . I've stumbled on a source greater than anything I've ever known. Or rather, it stumbled into my castle of its own free will."

The bones seem to echo her: *A source, a source, of what . . .*

"Power," she says, still rubbing that tortured right eye. "Magic. Life."

Uncle is so excited that he can't resist: A sudden *pop!* and one of his yellow teeth flies across the room, to *ping* against Mother's ribs.

"And all she's asking of me," Thyrla concludes slowly as she feels for the discarded silk eye patch, "besides my son, that is"—she finds the patch and slips it over her eye, creating a comforting dark—"is to help her find a woman called Lisabet."

The bones break into a charivari that would wake the dead, if there were any dead so foolish as to sleep in Thyrla's castle.

"The greatest trick will be to make it all seem like her

own choice," Thyrla says, trying (failing) to sound again like a university lecturer. "Magic is strongest when it comes of free will."

The baby skulls make the *dja* sound.

In the end, with her single eye that sees only the present, Thyrla delicately picks the green scale from the rest of the litter on her table. She puts it into the amber box, then the ivory one; then the rest of the things go into *their* box, and clutching both, she staggers to the bed and falls into the softness.

She's asleep before her head lands on the pillows. Whatever else the bare bones might have to tell her is lost.

anna

That night Thyrla is ill, but she has given Kett some orders about me.

"A new chamber for you, miss, with windows to it," she says cheerfully, unlocking a door at the top of the castle keep. "And fresh clothes, too. The Baroness says you two can talk about your family in the morning, begging your pardon for her being indisposed just now."

No pardon is needed; I'm glad to avoid the woman. And to be in this new chamber, bigger and airier (though naturally not as expansive as the depths and breadths of the sea). My heart lifts at the idea of space, air, light—the possibility of joining my clan easily again, if I find myself unable to stick with this visit to the land. Even if I only go away and swim awhile, eat what I like, and return, I will be gladder and stronger for it. And I can sing from this chamber and know I am heard.

One question I'm sure my own clan will want answered (I've already asked it myself several times): Why have I returned to the castle? The only logical reply I can give is that this is the most magic-rich place in the islands, the place I might find the tricks and clues I need to locate Lisabet. It's the place Sjældent told me to begin, after all.

But my true reason is that I feel drawn to the place. I know it has dangers, but I *sense* it's important. So when I was worn out with blessing the heads of Dark Moon Harbor, and marveling at the statue remade overnight, I let Peder and Tomas practically carry me here between them, rather than running away to rejoin my seavish *flok*.

And it seems the Baroness already planned to reward me for the return. Kett shows me more and more comforts: With the new room I get a new bed, which has a feather mattress on top of the straw one. The new clothing is also nice, a linen shift and a linsey-woolsey dress in blue-gray, with red embroidery at the neck. I believe I'm being honored as the future wife of Peder, perhaps even the future baroness. Though it's hard to imagine the woman who coughed up a lizard, and then squashed it, offering me comforts from the goodness of her being.

"Two stairs above the Baroness, you are now," Kett says, flinging the shutters wide and leaning over the courtyard, to fill her lungs with the scent of red roses. "This chamber's as nice as hers, if you ask me. Which no one ever does," she adds honestly.

I hear a wistfulness in her voice and, despite the ache

down deep in my muscles and bones (I am not a walker, not a blesser, not nearly prepared for what it seems I must do while I'm here), I go to stand by her.

The servants have finished cleaning the yard. Nothing's down there now but a single carved chair and the flowers that have spread themselves even farther. The niche where the statue stood yesterday is all but obscured in the blooms, which give the impression of pulsing redder as the light slants toward nightfall.

So what does Kett see to fill her so with longing? It may be the half-moon already rising, slicing the clouds behind the crenellations of a far tower. And the chair, for some unknown reason, at which Kett gazes as if it's a lover.

Curiosity more increased than satisfied, I climb into the bed, despite Kett's protests that I still have my old clothes on. I discover that the feathers add a layer of comfort, but it's not as good as lying buoyed up by the sea. Nothing ever could be. . . . Oh yes, as soon as I'm able, I'll sneak out of the castle and rest in my own element. I'll see Father and Sjældent, the aunts and the elders. I'll get advice. And in the morning, I'll return to my quest with more vigor.

I'm impatient for Kett to be gone, but she shows no inclination to leave. In fact, she settles in more securely, propping one plump thigh on the bare windowsill, leaning her head to one side, and giving the appearance of melting into the stone.

Down in the courtyard, her interest is caught. Down in the courtyard, Peder has made an entrance.

I hear it from my nest in the bed, which I have no desire to quit. His footsteps brushing on the courtyard's bare bedrock, his bum sliding onto the chair seat. His fingers picking up a wooden box strung with animal sinew. A cough clearing his throat.

His fingers pluck the strings. His voice—well, I suppose the landish call it singing.

> So far, my love, from me, my love;
> So far from me you are—
> You might be just the moon above;
> You might just be a star.

I cringe, wishing I still had seavish ears that could close themselves against water and sound.

But in the window, Kett purrs like a porpoise. "Oh, miss," she says, "he's made a new song just for you."

"A new one?" It barely sounded like anything to me; certainly we wouldn't call it a song in the sea.

"One I've never heard before, miss. He does sing to the girls sometimes, you know—or used to do, before you arrived. But this is a new tune, and the words are new words as well."

I listen a moment longer.

> My heart, my love, is yours alone.
> My thoughts are all of you.
> I don't know how to love you more;
> I know just that I do.

Kett sighs. "Isn't it lovely? Come, stand at the window—he's looking for you."

Such a song is hardly worth a murmur, but to please Kett, whom I like far more than Thyrla's son, I do as she says. I cram in beside her and look down into the yard, and there is Peder, golden in moonlight, gazing up at us.

He sings the last bit again:

I don't know how to love you more;
I know just that I do.

It is a ridiculous statement, a very poor tune, a song that would wreck not a single ship. If anything, the sailors would try to go faster, to escape the crumbly landish voice and silly words.

But Kett finds it enchanting.

"Toss him a favor," she whispers. "A bit of cloth or a flower. It's the custom here."

To play along, I reach for a rose —

And that's all: I reach. My hand won't cross the sill, and it won't grasp a single stem. Instead, it tingles; and the harder I try to reach out, the stronger the tingle, until it becomes pain.

"Magic," I mutter, and I fall back.

Thyrla has magicked this room with a warding spell to keep me inside. I underestimated her.

"Oh, yes, miss," says Kett, still dreamy. "When the young master sings, it is always magic."

Peder's last sour note dies, and there's a merciful — or ominous — silence below.

Kett says, "Aren't you going to give him a rose? He's waiting."

"You do it," I say, to see if this new spell works against everyone who occupies this room or just me.

Without trouble, with even a sort of grace, one round arm reaches beyond the sill. Kett lies crosswise, bosoms on stone, till she grasps a thorny stem and plucks a flower.

She turns to me, holding the rose out as if I might want it now.

The strong smell of it makes my head swim. As does the knowledge that I alone am a prisoner. This is no routine magic; it is meant to hold *me*.

"Give it to him," I say, turning away from the window.

Kett lets the rose fly.

• Chapter 50 •

No hearts will wreck.

"It's insulting, really," Addra says. Her curly red locks are dry from another long wait above water, and they blow behind her like angry flames. "It's offensive. That Sanna should go to land and make us listen to *this.*"

"She's not the one singing, my dear," says Aunt Mar, who is not Addra's aunt by blood but knows her faults all the better for having no family interest in the girl.

Addra slaps her tail on the rock of Ringstone, where many of the *flok* have gathered to hear Sanna's news. As the most beautiful among them (and the most selfish), Addra has again draped herself in the grand O, and she does look lovely in it.

Her orange flukes inadvertently slap Pippa the Strong, who slaps them back.

"Do all landish voices sound that way?" Frill asks, in that voice that forever gives the impression her eyes are wide in wonder.

"Sanna's doesn't, and she's half-landish," Pippa observes.

"Shh," admonishes mighty Mar. "Listen. You might learn more about the landish if you open your ears."

So they do—Addra and Pippa, La and Frill, Mar and Shusha and Gurria and Sjældent. And the other girls, and the men, and Bjarl, Sanna's father.

My heart, my love, is yours alone.
My thoughts are all of you.
I don't know how to love you more;
I know just that I do.

"Do you suppose she actually likes it?" Frill wonders. "It's not just that it's a boy singing—the song is horrid."

"Frill said that," Addra notes smugly. "I didn't."

The elders rarely chide Frill for anything; they pity her for being motherless and, it is privately believed, rather stupid. But no one can disagree with her assessment of the young man's performance.

"The words make no sense at all," says Addra, who has been the subject of many songs already—songs that are important and meaningful, because they're about her.

"Love makes no sense, either," La says, "but it is the greatest happiness."

Addra is vexed enough to give La, in turn, a gentle slap of the fluke. "Sorry, I slipped."

"No, you didn't—"

Their squabble is interrupted by a wet cough and a rasp in an ancient throat. Sjældent is going to speak but must rid herself of sand first.

"No hearts are wrecking over that song . . ." she begins at last, between hacking coughs.

"Unless they're dashing themselves to death over the pain in their ears," Addra finds time to insert.

"Hush now, girl!" Sjældent's voice grows stronger. She issues a dire warning: "There's something amiss on the land."

"How can you tell?" asks Frill.

"We're hearing that drivel, aren't we? And Sanna's hearing it, too, and she aren't doing a thing to stop it."

No one can argue with the old witch's logic. Something's gone wrong for Sanna, or else they'd be listening to her song instead of this abomination.

Bjarl's stomach knots with a father's anxiety. And to make matters worse, the boy starts again:

So far, my love, from me, my love;

So far from me you are —

Yes, it is indisputably grating.

But nonetheless, beneath the seaskin, two of the younger maidens twine tails around each other, feeling their hearts quicken for the very first time.

Chapter 51

A voice hoarse from song.

It's not a knock on the door but a rattle of the latch that announces the young master's arrival. This is the right way, he believes, for true lovers to come to each other—impetuously, urgently, bearing lutes and flowers and arms aching for an embrace.

The door does not yield.

"Sanna!" he calls, with a voice hoarse from song. "Undo the locks and let me in!"

No answer, only whispers hard to make out.

". . . my love!" he adds as an afterthought. It's a nice touch, though one usually not necessary with the girls in town. And really, a fellow might expect a betrothed girl to heed her husband-in-future.

Ah, the locks. One set of works after another turns over, reverses, falls into position. And then the latch lifts, and the door opens, and Peder is face-to-face with . . . Kett. The pudgy maidservant whose eyes follow him hungrily wherever he goes.

Peder is adept at looking through and past what he doesn't want to see. So all he really sees is Sanna, standing by the bed and holding to one post, as if she's weak in the knees at the sight of him.

A single stride, and he's with her. The lute drops to the floor and so do the roses. He fills his arms with Sanna, pulling her face down toward his (she is so remarkably tall).

"So close, my love," he says, breath hot on his lips and hers. And then his lips are *on* hers and he's claiming his kiss, the just reward for the song composed and sung, and most of all for his signature on the document that binds the two of them into the future.

The kiss completes a promise. And Sanna is warm, so very warm, in his arms.

Peder thinks, *This is love.*

And is shocked to realize he means it: He, Peder of the Thirty-Seven Dark Islands, has fallen in love.

anna

I'll admit I've wondered if Peder might carry any of his mother's magic. During the day, as we walked over the islands and as he stood behind me at the blessings, I waited to feel that tingle, that hum, that might say I was in the presence of power. I don't even know if landish boys can work magic—it isn't so in the sea, but landish powers are so topsy-turvy that it might be so here. When he kisses me, I wait for the telltale vibrato and buzz.

I don't feel anything.

Or rather, the tingle that I feel is not from magic; it's from the pressure of his lips against mine, my lips against my teeth, my own blood pushed around my face and springing back to where it once was as Peder's lips move back and forth and up and down.

It's the prickling of brute force, animal, with nothing of magic about it. It makes me remember my aunt Shusha's warning: *These northern people have harmed our kind for as long as we've known them.* And landmen especially love to ravish mermaids.

Peder seems harmless now, but he is a landman. And a spoiled boy—I can smell pleasure on him again; it is a very sharp smell—who is used to taking everything he wants.

So I remain stiff in his arms, and cautious, even as I allow this kiss to continue. I consider it part of my landish reconnaissance. A kiss, Sjældent said, began my own parents' making of me. I would not have been born if it weren't for a kiss.

And the kiss—the caress of which landish people make so much—the kiss is . . . landish.

By this I mean that it is strange, and different to me, both natural and unnatural, given my mixed blood. It tastes bitter, like the landish beer and ale Kett has brought me and that I know are favorites of Peder and his kind. It also tastes sweet, like the sauces in which some castle dishes are swimming; and I like things sweet. It (and a certain curiosity) is why I remain standing awhile, letting Peder kiss me.

He sighs out my name—"Sanna"—and his voice sounds much nicer up close than it did in his song. I soften a little toward him.

At the same time, I am very aware of Kett still in the room. She must be watching us. I know she likes Peder, in that inexplicable way that landish girls seem to like him generally, and I think she is probably as jealous as she is curious. She is both living through my lips and resenting them.

But no, Kett doesn't understand the meaning of *envy.* She is a generous soul; if anything, she is blessing this kiss as I blessed the people by the church.

Peder kisses on and on as I think these things through. At some point he decides to put his hands on both sides of my face, holding it still and bent to his level, while he works his mouth against mine.

I wonder, then, what I'm supposed to do with my hands. I believe Peder would like me to embrace him, but I can't bring myself to do it. I don't have that much curiosity in me, or that much strategy. I am beginning to find the kiss tiresome.

But Peder would disagree. He pursues me like a hunter, presses harder against me until my mouth opens. His tongue—a fat, warm little eel—works against my teeth and then slithers between them.

I hear Kett catch her breath, watching us. Mine's already caught, stuck somewhere down in my lungs, where it's able to stay for landish hours if it needs to. Which is good, because Peder has smashed his nose against mine, and I couldn't breathe easily if I wanted to. *Now* I dislike this business of kissing, and I start to pull away.

But . . .

Peder seems to reach a certain goal when his tongue touches mine. For a moment he relaxes, and I do feel a tingle then. Of magic? No, not as I've understood magic to be. This is something different; it is simply the physical sensation brought on by kissing. Or so my logical mind decides.

When he starts to rub my tongue with his, I bite down. What he is doing revolts me.

Peder doesn't seem to mind. Maybe he thinks I am playing—I haven't bitten that hard anyway. As a response, his hands release my face in order to slide down my shoulders and to my waist. He pulls me closer to him, and I feel another eel trying to reach into me: that equipment that all male things have, landish or seavish, carried in the same spot below the belly.

In this I have utterly no interest. I can't stop myself from wrenching out of his grasp and leaping across the room.

Kett, our lovelorn audience, cries out. "Are you all right, miss?" She's all aflutter, all concern, her little hands reaching to catch me as if I am fainting. She guides me toward the bed. The curtains brush my cheeks like wings, but I feel them as a reminder of my imprisonment.

My mouth is sore. I press my hands to it.

"The experience of love is often overwhelming," Peder says, congratulating himself, "for virgins and girls gently born."

I want to snap that this is not love and there was nothing gentle about my birth—Sjældent has made that clear—but, perhaps fortunately, my lips are too swollen and my tongue too raw to manage the words right away. Soon my rational self, well trained by Aunt Shusha the Logical, prevails. There's nothing to gain by antagonizing Thyrla's son. And he didn't go too far, not like the sailors who pull up a *marreminde* in their nets and take cruel pleasure on her.

"Of course, of course!" Kett is agreeing with him and caring for me all at once. She bustles around with pillows and a pitcher of the sour potion called wine, which she pours into a silver cup and holds to my lips, making me drink, even as she eases me down on the soft bed.

As far as I'm concerned, wine is just a variation on the bitterness of beer, and not something I ever need to taste again. Like Peder's tongue — I can't help shuddering, recalling how it felt exploring the corners of my mouth as if it owned them and were planning to set up housekeeping there.

The body, like the castle, is a chambered shell, I think.

I may be a little bit drunk.

"You are exhausted, my love," Peder says grandly. I hear his clothes rustle as he stands tall, puffing out his chest so as to fill this chamber of his mother's castle. He is very proud of having kissed me. "I should allow you to rest."

"Thank you," I murmur, because it's true — there's nothing I'd like better than to be alone. I need solitude in order to figure out how to regain my freedom. And how to report on the day to my people, as promised.

Peder seems to be waiting for something, probably some endearment such as he's used with me. But I can't force myself to call him *my love*, even in the interest of staying on and continuing my quest, so I say — intending nothing beyond a simple courtesy — "It's a shame we must part."

It would be a worse shame to stay together.

"Indeed." He sounds and looks very pleased, pink cheeks dimpling and pride radiating off him.

I realize I've just given him even more pleasure than the kiss, because — like most hunters — he enjoys the hunt. Seeing me as prey, my love still not too easily captured. He hasn't ravished me because he wants me to offer myself up, exhausted, and say that I love him.

"'Indeed'?" I repeat, intending to mock and repel.

"*Indeed*, we must part," he says, and bows to me. "And, *indeed*, it's a pity. Till morning, then, my love."

Ignoring Kett, he struts from the room and closes the door with a *thonk* after himself.

I envy Peder. I'd like to find it so easy to leave, but I'm quite sure that the door is as charmed as the window.

Of course, if I *were* Peder, I'd be a boy and a fool, and I wouldn't want that either.

His footsteps recede through the anteroom and into the winding stairs. I wish I could follow — not to be with him, but to leave. In this moment, I want nothing more than to be among my own clan again. I might even be willing to give up finding Lisabet.

Kett tries to press the cup to my lips again, but I push it away and curl into myself. If I try, I can feel the sea rising in me. I wonder if Thyrla has magicked the place so thoroughly that not even my voice can escape, if I try to sing about the day's adventures.

Want is streaming through the room, desire so strong it

is almost magical. I realize it's coming not just from myself but from Kett as well.

It's not desire for me, of course, or even for Peder. She wants to ask a question.

It might do me good to help Kett. "Is there something you need from me?"

Chapter 53

A simple girl yearns more than simply.

Kett sees how tired Sanna is, lying curled in her bed, curtains open, looking like a child despite the length of her. When she speaks, her voice sounds wet, as if she's been weeping, but she doesn't sniffle or sob.

"Is there something you need from me?"

"Oh, miss, I—" Acting on instinct, Kett places a wrist on Sanna's brow, which is moist with perspiration. "Oh no! You've a fever!"

"I'm not ill," comes that muffled, wet voice. "What is it *you* need?"

Kett hesitates. It isn't like her to ask favors, especially in the Baroness's castle. Today, in the town, she didn't thrust herself forward for Sanna's attention. But there is something she wants *so* much. It won't result in evening serenades and kisses from the handsome baron-to-be, but it will help. And maybe it is a modest request after all.

"The people who touched your blood yesterday . . ." she begins, then pauses.

"Just say it."

It seems Sanna is getting testy. Kett should just go—but that might irritate Sanna further. One thing Kett doesn't want is to try the patience of a saint with her dithering.

"Well, miss, they said it helped them. And then there were the blessings in town today. And I was wondering . . . Well, if you'd be willing, I'd like to be blessed, too. And"— now that she's brought herself to asking, the words come in a tumble—"I was hoping you might bless me in a specific way, to take these spots off my face."

Those horrid spots. Her sisters tease that they come from the food at the castle, the rich sauces and creams as much a curse as they are a luxury. Kett knows it's vanity, but she'd like them to be gone.

She doesn't even mind growing plump on the sauces, for plumpness is a sign of prosperity. She'd just like to be less ugly in the face. She'd like to make her next trip to town with her head held high.

"Ah."

That's all Sanna says, but an odd sensation sweeps over Kett like a breeze, though there's nothing blowing. She gets the feeling Sanna has heard all the thoughts running through her mind, and that Sanna understands.

The girl in the bed (no older than Kett herself, but so very different) uncurls herself and rolls over to peer out.

Her pale green eyes are luminous in the shadow of the hangings. "Lean down."

Kett does more than lean; she kneels. And closes her eyes and whispers a prayer, giving thanks for Sanna and wishing her well. Then she feels the warm hands on her head. They cup it like an egg, only more preciously.

Warmth spreads downward from the hands, through Kett's scalp and face, down her neck to her breasts and belly and all the rest of her. She blushes. She burns.

She thinks, *So this is how it feels to be blessed.*

It feels wonderful. Dizzy-making. And the spots on her face are burning, but in a good way.

Words seem unnecessary, yet Sanna says them as she did today in town: "May the Lord bless you, Kett."

At that, Kett feels her spirit soar out and far above, to fly among the stars and look down at the castle as a tiny, insignificant thing.

Chapter 54

Sea change.

"When will *she* sing?" Frill asks plaintively, her thin voice a whine in the breeze. "The boy finished ages ago. We've been waiting so long, my face has cracked dry."

"She's forgotten us," Addra says with some satisfaction. She flashes her red-brown eyes toward Sjældent, who now floats in Bjarl's arms. "There's your clan loyalty, old witch."

"Shh." Shusha the Logical has pulled the dark hair away from one ear to listen to some stray sound, but no—all she heard was the cry of an albatross.

"Don't call her an old witch," Pippa says sternly. She considers it a violation of the *flok*'s unspoken etiquette that for a second night in a row, Addra has cradled herself in Ringstone's O, displaying her red-and-white flesh in the moonlight as if inviting a lover. Who will not be Pippa; it will never be Pippa.

"Don't call her *her*," says the old witch herself. Sjældent squints at all of them, the girls and their mothers and aunts, elders a century or so younger than herself. "And if yer face is cracked with waiting, me girl, dip it under and get all the song ye need."

The mermaids heave a collective sigh. They don't like Sjældent—no one does—and they hate taking orders from her. Especially cryptic ones. But Bjarl, Sanna's father, obediently dives and stays down long, and nobody, least of all the *flok*'s most glorious girls, can let a mere man show them up.

One by one, they dip down. Addra last, for she's not sure there's anything worth finding in the familiar waters, and she hates to give up her perch.

One by one, again, they surface, Bjarl last. The water around him is warm with excitement.

"Did you taste it?" Frill asks before she's entirely cleared the blowhole at the back of her neck. Water seeps in the wrong way, and she has to cough it out through her mouth.

"I did," says Pippa.

"I did," says La.

"I did," says Addra, "but I don't really care."

Sjældent hoots with laughter. "My, aren't ye the proud one?" she addresses Addra. "Soon enough—sooner than ye think, it's always the way—ye'll look like me, and have the personality to match."

Before Addra can retort and continue a pointless argument, Bjarl speaks up: "I tasted my daughter's tears."

"What do they *mean*?" asks Frill, who is pleasantly

wet now and disposed to curiosity. Floating vertical, like a knifefish, she sticks her tongue in the water. "I taste the current, but I can't understand it."

For once, the elders think she might not be so stupid; her willingness to ask what's on everyone's mind is a point in her favor.

Sjældent, supported again by one of Bjarl's arms, also has a tongue in the sea. "It's not tears," she says, spitting out a mouthful of eelgrass. "She's summoned the waters within the stone and sent them coursing toward us. Very clever, really."

"What is she trying to tell us?" Bjarl asks, his Sanna-green eyes hooded with anxiety.

"She's saying she's captive," Sjældent says.

The girls gasp and squirm in alarm. The elders tense.

"What are we supposed to do about it?" Addra and Pippa ask at the same moment, but in very different tones.

La thinks of Ishi, not a captive but so many suns' swims away. "Will this delay the migration?"

Sjældent, wriggling out of Bjarl's arms, dips fully below the seaskin for a taste, then comes up again to speak.

"It means," she says, "that all's wrong and right at once, and according to plan. *My* plan," she adds, as if there's doubt.

Chapter 55

Friends close, enemies closer.

The walls and the family are covered again, and Baroness Thyrla lies in her bed. Thanking whatever it is that has silenced her rough-throated son.

What a song he has sung; what a dolt he is! She should break his lute in the morning, when she recovers her strength.

Thyrla takes a deep breath and then another. She is not a witch of the air, but every witch needs that element to exist. She is so worn out that her body might forget to breathe; in fact, the fear of forgetting is all that keeps her awake now.

After the day's scrying and spelling, she was too spent to do much more than tug the series of cords that pulled the green damask back over the walls, and to work the magic needed to fix everything in the castle in its place. For now, anyway. She's kept Peder and the bones close, Sanna wrapped like a fly in a web. Keeping them this way is to her benefit, far better than setting them loose in a world where they might be hard to find. The web will hold Sanna snug until, like a spider, Thyrla can consider her prey.

Peder's feet sound in the stairwell, winding upward to the chamber that holds his betrothed. He is following an ancient script of romance. All to the good, all to the good; it is best to know what the young people are doing, and love makes a boy predictable.

While her son rattles his true love's door, sleep tugs at the Baroness like the only lover she knows. She's too tired now for plotting, too tired even for resenting the young and their pursuit of each other.

All I can do is endure, she tells herself. *And pay attention. Stay awake just a moment longer . . .*

From the subtle shifts in her web of magic, Thyrla knows what is happening between Peder and Sanna. She knows about the kiss. She feels it along with her son: the pliant strength of Sanna's lips and the reluctant, salty cavern of her mouth. She knows when Sanna pulls back, and when she sends Peder from the room that Thyrla has sealed with magic.

She even knows when Sanna musters her powers to bless the maidservant Kett. And she is surprised the girl still has powers inside Thyrla's web.

"I'll take care of it in the morning," she says, before Uncle can start chattering to chide her. "I'll give her some poison to cripple her magic. Something that draws on the sea—and more. Everything, everything . . ." She feels herself starting to doze.

A worthy witch works in all the accessible elements (earth, air, fire, water) and in that which lies behind and above them, governing all: time. Until today, tonight, Thyrla was sure she was the strongest witch in existence. At least in the north.

Perhaps she was wrong. But (also perhaps) she can make herself right again.

Two levels above, Sanna's door opens and closes, and dutiful Kett uses her keys to lock it up tight—for Sanna's protection, as the Baroness explained to her earlier. Now Kett will bed down on a pallet of straw laid across Sanna's door, not that the door needs protection. The illusion of need will help Thyrla's cause. The maid won't even get up to pee all night; she'll fall asleep counting Sanna's snores.

Silence.

Thyrla floats for a while, breathing carefully, watching the sparkle of her own magic in the gloaming. She begins to feel safe, lulled, almost ready to surrender to sleep . . .

Then she notices something on the cloth hanging above her. Something new and growing. At first it's the size of a fingertip, quickly becoming a thumb; it spreads in a widening patch, like blood from a wound.

But this is not blood. It is liquid, yes, but not thick. It drips onto her arm and stings.

She puts out her tongue and takes a tentative taste: water. Salt water.

Thyrla's heart leaps. Is the upstart upstairs trying to drown her? Or is the castle itself crying? The legendary dragon . . .

No, it is some version of magic, distilled into liquid but harmless in nature. It soaks the bed hangings and seeps down to the floor, probably below that as well. It damages nothing but Thyrla's tongue.

The taste of that single drop has dulled Thyrla's senses and blunted her strength. She lies still while the cloth on the bed, and the walls, and the ceiling, darkens and clings to what touches it. Sopping. Wet.

She lies while the skulls grind against each other, making a horrid squeal that is the sound of their joy.

For the first time in decades, they have something to drink.

• Chapter 56 •

Basking Bay.

No matter how oddly Sanna sings of Dark Moon Harbor, the people there are not the only strange ones the *marreminde* clan has encountered, at least in La's opinion. For her, in age and singularity and lack of interest in treasure, the seavish *flok* of Basking Bay is among the oddest. They are also the people among whom she found the love that has given meaning to her life.

La thinks Basking *Island* would make a better name. The *flok* who lives there ventures into the water only in short bursts of time for a hunt or a wash; they prefer lying on land and sunning themselves, rubbing one another's scalps with their fingers. They have no other combs; they have no desire to swim forth and explore, either, not even if a little travel promises treasure traded with other peoples and harvested from ships. They are a peaceful *flok* who don't hunger for more than they have, and they are so content that they haven't bothered to reproduce themselves much. Thus they have dwindled to a small clan of only a dozen or so women past childbirthing age and a few men just as old.

But they include that one young, lovely girl: Ishi. Whose dark, angular face springs into La's mind's eye whenever she hears love sung or spoken of.

Now, after the rest of her clan have closed their noses and gone down for a sleep, La heaves herself into the cool O of Ringstone, to sing quietly to herself about Basking Bay and what she found there.

La's song extols Ishi's beauty: her skin as dark as the distant line where sea meets sky, her eyes as deep as the ocean trenches where little's alive but shadow.

In the few days they had together, the two of them slept first holding hands on the seaskin, then below water with their tails entwined, as close—so La thought—as it is possible to be.

La's entire *flok* noticed, especially her mothers, Shusha the Logical and Gurria One Arm.

"You're young to feel it," said Shusha, who despite her moniker is known as one of the age's great lovers, having wooed and won the once-beautiful, now-fierce Gurria from a clan who lives so far north that everything among them is white—white seas, white islands, white bears, white seals and birds. White skin and hair and tail and almost-white eyes Gurria has, making her hard to hide in the green and blue waters the *flok* mostly knows.

"To feel—?" La wanted to hear the word from her own mother's lips.

"*Love.*"

The sound was like a blaze of light, striking La deep in the belly and radiating to her nipples, her fingers, her face, and that most seavish part beneath her belly fin.

"I love Ishi," she said, wonderingly.

"Don't tell me," said Shusha. "Tell her."

So La did. She swam up to the beach and hand-walked, tail-humped to the cozy hollow Ishi had dug for herself, where she was scratching the scalp of a woman so old and wrinkled, she might have been born next to the ancient witch Sjældent.

"I love you," La announced, not even waiting to get Ishi alone. Some part of her thought that time alone would come only after these words.

The old woman to whom Ishi was ministering, as deeply blue-purple as Ishi herself but without the pink shimmer to her tail, smiled toothlessly at them both.

"What do you think I once sat on?" she asked them and no one. "A turtle!"

"That must have been very nice, Auntie," Ishi said kindly.

She and La held their giggles in till they reached the water. There they clasped hands and pushed off with their flukes, riding the waterskin like a pair of dolphins and laughing from pure joy.

"Do you . . . think you could love me, too?" La asked

238

when they collapsed, exhausted, and floated on their backs still holding hands, the sunlight making red lava of their eyelids.

Ishi rolled over and around her, blowing bubbles from beneath. They tickled. La waited in agony for an answer.

Ishi surfaced and said, "I already do."

That night, they were very happy together.

And this is why, out of all the voices in the sea tonight, La is most offended by Peder's poor attempt at a song.

"Come with us," La begged when her people, already bored, decided to push toward cooler seas to the south and west. They'd heard of an island inhabited by enormous people more stone than flesh, people so fond of the land that they sit buried in it to their chins and don't even rise for tempests or invasions.

La had wanted to stay where they were awhile longer. She protested to her mothers that these stone people didn't sound any more lively than the *flok* of Basking Bay, but Shusha remonstrated that sometimes simply looking at something might be as much of an adventure as fighting it.

"You can bring Ishi along if you want to," she said, "but we aren't leaving you behind, even if I have to wrap you in a net and tow you myself."

So La begged her new love to join her.

"Come with us." She got no answer. Soon she was repeating the invitation like a child learning the first words of song: *Come with us, come with us, come with us . . .* "Come with *me*."

Still, Ishi hesitated. She'd heard of the Island of Heads, too, and it held only mild interest for her. What did interest her: La. And her own people.

"I'm the only one young enough to protect them," she protested, demonstrating a loyalty that La found both admirable and frustrating. "They can't hunt big fish, and what if a *flok* arrives here less . . . gently than yours? They might all be killed."

"You don't love me!" La wailed.

"You know that I do. But I wouldn't be worth loving if I didn't look after my clan."

With that, La had to be content — or at least, she had to accept it. And she extracted a promise from Shusha, Gurria, Mar, and the other elders that during the next migration (to begin as soon as Sanna concludes her business on land), they will return to Basking Bay, where La might persuade Ishi to leave. Or Ishi might talk La into staying.

This, La sings, *is love.* This is pain and loyalty and admiration for all the good the beloved might do in the world.

Is Sanna's quest for her mother more important than this?

La sighs, and the name *Ishi* hisses over the waves.

Chapter 57

A miracle is missing.

In the morning, the townspeople sense it: a shift in the wind, the sea, the earth itself. Leaffall is already here.

The farmers rush to finish the harvest. The shepherds count heads, worrying over lost wool. More souls than usual wander toward the church, then into it, asking, *When will Sanna return?*

One blessing is not enough; they want more to carry them into the winter. They want Sanna in their homes. They want her to live among them. They suggest building her a chapel, a house. They bring baskets of food and goods to pile at the feet of the recently transformed statue of Our Lady of the Sea, hoping she'll reveal the contents of her bundle to them. Hoping to lure Sanna to town with the best they have, which they know is not nearly as good as the simplest thing in the castle.

The people have to try. They're hungry: Having tasted one miracle, they want to gorge on miracles and blessings.

They know they are gluttons and they beg for forgiveness. They kneel before Our Lady of the Sea to pray. They ask Father Abel to go to the castle and fetch Sanna for them.

"She was here only yesterday," he protests. He also longs for Sanna, but he has known the Baroness a long time and knows, too, that she will not be pleased at the request.

Nonetheless, as the light sharpens toward noon, and the smell of mown wheat and hay mixes with that of the sea, Abel can wait no longer. He sets off hobbling the miles to the castle, feet still sore from the last journey, intent on finding out how Sanna fares and if, incidentally, the third miracle has already occurred. He knows in his bones there will be one; the only question is time. And then after news is sent to Rome, the islands will become a place of pilgrimage . . .

He's alone on the path, with birds crying above and squirrels clawing up trees in alarm. The only other humans are far away now, bundling the last sheaves of wheat, milking the final cows, spooning up lentils and onions for dinner.

It is here, now, that Abel sees beauty in the Dark Islands. A special beauty that emerges only on a day like this one, when green leaves shake their way toward yellow and the breeze carries more than a mere marine crispness. It's clear that summer has ended, that the rocks and earth are clinging to the last heat they've stored. The birds are whistling about flying south; the squirrels will soon be asleep.

In short, when the foreseeable future is sheer ugliness and hardship, the fields and forests and even the dung heaps have a certain charm. Beauty is most haunting when it begins to fade.

On days like this, naturally, Father Abel misses the minimally warmer land of his birth. And Rome! He spent nearly two years among its seven hills, learning doctrine from the wisest Church fathers. In summer, the days were so hot that labor stopped in the middle and men slept. He loved those times best, when he could sit sweating in his robe, turning the pages of a book with moist fingers and smelling lemons and olives on the still midday air. He was at the beginning of his living and his knowledge of God. He was all hope and possibility.

Sanna gives him a bit of that feeling, too.

And suddenly he realizes he's nearly at the castle.

Greatly to his surprise, when he leaves the woods and crosses the sallet isle, watching the castle grow larger and heavier before him, he finds that the gate is closed. Not just the gate; the drawbridge, too. It's been pulled in for the first time in all the years he's lived in these islands.

Father Abel is nonplussed. Can he really have come so far (his feet swollen up like pink loaves) only to stop at the waters that separate this bountiful garden from the castle rock?

Maybe this is some test devised by the Baroness.

For once, Father Abel is bold. He cups wrinkled hands around his mouth and bellows, "Ho, the castle!"

Nothing. Wind; gulls. Sunset.

He tries again: "Baroness, it is I, Father Abel! I've come to bring you . . ." For a foolish moment, he looks around himself, wishing he'd thought to pack a present. Everything now in sight belongs to Thyrla herself. ". . . news of the town!" he ends lamely. He coughs, already hoarse. "The people have sent me with their warmest regards and thanks! May I come in!"

Shouting makes everything, even a question, seem like an order. And, as if obeying an order, a guardsman's head pops up between the ramparts' crenellations. He's wearing a hood of chain mail. So is the next guard, and the next; soon a half dozen are peering at him while staying mostly hidden among the stonework, as if the tired old priest is a threat.

The first boy (Abel knows his parents, of course; they are fishers) shouts back something Abel can't catch. The wind is against him and carries his words backward toward the orange ball of sun.

Abel cups his hands again. He has to speak briefly now, saving his breath and his throat: "The drawbridge! Lower it! Let me pass!"

The guards all seem to jabber at once, as excited as the squirrels Abel passed on the way. He can't catch a syllable of their talk, but he gets the impression they're saying, *Sanna's not here.* Which would freeze his bones in fear if true.

"Bridge! Bridge!" he calls. But he's flagging; if they

were going to lower the bridge, they'd have done it by now. He has to face the fact that he'll be walking back to Dark Moon Harbor without even a scrap of bacon or bread to sustain him.

This trip, he thinks, has served only to emphasize the distance between town and castle and the fruitlessness of asking for favors. Thyrla does as she pleases, and for now she pleases to keep Sanna to herself. It may be his duty to so inform the townspeople.

Abel gives voice to a groan as loud as any of the words he has called, starting to shuffle his gouty feet eastward and home again. No, he shouldn't say or do anything that might turn the people against their Baroness, who is the only source of good things in a harsh clime. He reminds himself to live like Christ, humble, poor, and—

Just then, a shutter midway down the castle wall flies open. It opens so hard, in fact, that it comes off its hinges entirely and bounces against the wall, then scrapes on the foundation before falling into the rough sea channel.

Thyrla herself, barely visible, speaks from a chamber that must be carved entirely out of the island's bedrock. And by some trick of the wind, Abel can hear every word.

"I'm sending over a boat," she says. "Today you'll eat and sleep under my roof."

anna

It's been a long morning—an *interminable* morning, locked away by myself.

Before I came to these islands, living as an oddity among my own clan, I thought I knew loneliness and had a talent for it; but Thyrla is showing me I had no true understanding of solitude before. She has worked some magic that even muffles sound and smell, such that since I awoke I've been able to learn nothing of what was happening in the castle or out of it—no clanking sounds of work, no chattering human voices, no birds, no smells of bodies circulating or food cooking . . . And the shutters have been magicked tight, so I can't look out, either.

I am *alone.*

I believe Thyrla wants to bore me into submission, and it's working. Seavish girls aren't meant to be locked in airy landish prisons; my very heart is drying up like a nut.

Right now I'd give up everything in order to go free—the Lisabet I seek is not here, and whatever fabulous object Sjældent wants from the place, I'll try to find that same thing elsewhere. If only I can get out.

Just after the sun has passed its midday peak, the locks on the door start working themselves open. Or not precisely that; Kett's little hand holds the keys. I brush the water from my eyes and sit up, excited that I'm able to hear and smell this much. And at the very least, I'll see how my healing spell worked.

Perfectly. The Kett who comes in has a face as clear and creamy as foam in the middle of the widest sea, and a smile as big as the moon.

"Oh, miss," she bursts out, flinging herself to the floor and taking my hands in hers, "thank you! I've wanted to come in for ever so long, but the Baroness—"

The Baroness wouldn't allow it, of course.

Kett doesn't need to finish. Instead she pulls off her cap, brushes her hair back from her face, and turns it upward to me.

"Not so much as a pinprick!" she declares, and it's true.

"You're beautiful," I say, and that's true, too—not because her spots have gone but because she's so *happy* they're gone. Sjældent used to say that happiness, like youth, guarantees beauty.

"Oh, miss." She doesn't believe me. She puts her cap back on and ties the strings under her chin. "You're very kind to say it, I'm sure. Well, now"—getting to her feet again—"the Baroness has sent me to get you ready."

"For what?" The possibilities are alarming.

"She has an errand for you," Kett says, opening the shutters as if there's no magic on them at all. "You're to pay Old Olla a visit."

With the shutters' release, the sounds of the castle and sea come flooding in, and I feel such a relief to be hearing again, to be *feeling* sound in my bones, that I almost forget to ask who Old Olla might be.

Kett shakes out the blue-gray dress from yesterday and drapes it across the table, ready to slide over my head. She opens her drawstring pocket and pulls out a wooden comb, then starts to work on me. Which feels wonderful, almost as good as if I were basking in the sun and tending my locks with the other seavish girls.

"Old Olla's the beekeeper," Kett says, carefully untangling a snarl.

"Beekeeper?" Bees are those small things of the air that hum from flower to flower. They seem to keep themselves.

"An old woman who lives alone and tends to the hives. She harvests the honey and brews the mead."

Ah. I put flowers and honey together and realize: Bees transform the scent into the sticky liquid that I love. I have tasted honey before, when I've been able to trade for it, and my mouth comes alive at the expectation of more sweetness. I remember it hanging heavy in the air when I tripped into the Baroness's feast.

"How will I find this Olla?" I'm already planning to magick myself back to seavish form and swim to the *marreminde* clan. I've had enough of the land.

"The young master will go with you," Kett says, dashing my hopes. "And his companion, Tomas Chicken Legs." She picks up the blue-gray overdress. "Are you ready, miss?"

Silently, with my hair soft around me, I lift up my arms to receive the weight of landish cloth over my body.

I am pleased to be outside in air that seems newer and more tender, with colors more beautiful, than ever before. I'm even glad to be on this errand with the two boys. They've said it's just a few islets away "as the bee flies," but that humans must take a longer route to avoid crumbling banks and dangerous jumps.

I'm looking for a chance to slip away from them on the journey, even though I'm curious about this old woman who lives all by herself, removed from the *flok* and yet part of it. Such an arrangement would never be possible at sea; an old woman would die this way. I'm not sure whether this gives the land a slight advantage over the sea.

Thus far Tomas and Peder have treated me well enough, but I am embarrassed to be near Peder after last night's kiss. And I never can quite forget my aunts' warnings about what landish men do to seavish girls. These two are only boys, but still . . .

"It's this way, Sanna—just do as I do!"

Peder hops over a stream, then turns and reaches a hand

toward me to offer help. Smiling, friendly, with the gleam of a kiss's memory in his eye.

Reluctantly, because it's necessary, I take his hand. Jumping was not in my original practice, and it sends a jolt through my bones.

"*O!*—lla," I say out loud, trying to disguise a cry of pain.

The more I've thought about the woman's name, the more it has sounded seavish, the kind of name we give each other that is a sound made by something in nature. *Olla* would, for us, be the rounding tension of a deep wave and the hollow *boom* it sends through our bones when it folds in on itself.

"Isn't it a funny name?" Peder asks, almost as if he's heard my thoughts. "Sounds like a war cry." He chants, without even the minor music of last night: "*Olla-Olla-Olla-Olla-Olla*—"

"Olla is very nice," Tomas says, interrupting. "And very good with the bees. My sisters love to visit her, when the Baroness allows it." After a dubious moment in which Peder whoops again, Tomas adds, "We've never had a war here."

Peder breaks off. "Careful, Chicken Legs," he teases. "We might marry you off to the old woman if you like her so much. Anyway"—hopping again, this time over a tiny spring that trickles from a rock for a few hand-spans and then melts into the earth—"she'd better not be giving away castle honey to just anyone who visits. That's one reason we need to see the bees. Mother's worried about a change in the honey, now that the roses are different."

I feel warm with embarrassment, or perhaps it's anxiety. *Worried* means the change is bad, and if such is the case, whom would the harsh Baroness blame but the stranger who transformed the flowers themselves? I can't think of anything to say that would make the new color and doubled petals seem less important, so I focus on walking.

And, a little bit, on Tomas. He trails along behind, silent and (I can smell the mood on him) for some reason sad. I turn and try to catch his eye as we step one by one over a saltwater channel that has no bridge, but he's watching his feet.

We pass into a forest and out of it, then over another saltwater channel. Soon enough comes a wisp of smoke over the trees, and a lumpy black chimney poking through. A roof made of grass, a square house made of stones gone green with age and moisture. A dozen coiling yellow domes sitting around it like sleeping snails, and around them the air in a blur. With bees, I think; I feel their hum as a tickle in my bones.

Seeing them, I open my mouth and inhale. I taste sweetness on the breeze, then all around; even my clothes and my skin and the boys walking next to me seem suddenly sweet. I am dizzy, as if it's a tide that can carry me off.

"Olla's islet is our land of milk and honey," Tomas

says, watching the pleasure wash over me from the corner of his eye.

I suspect this is one of those things people say because they can't tolerate a silence, but nonetheless a scene flashes into my mind—of a sea of thin white and thick yellow roiling together—and I have to ask what it means.

"Bounty," Tomas explains. "Endless goodness."

I imagine myself with my lovely green tail, swimming through sticky-sweet *bounty*. But just then my landish toe stubs a rock and I fall.

Quick as a spark, Tomas swoops to catch my elbow and hold me upright. Peder makes a *tcha* sound of annoyance, then rushes the last steps forward to the stone hut. With a brazen air of belonging, he pushes at the door and gestures.

"Sanna first," he says.

We go inside.

The little house is dark, with multi-hued light falling weakly to the floor, where the dirt and clay of ages have made a hard covering over the planks. Smoky, from a fireplace that dominates the east wall. And sweet, so very sweet it might bring on a faint. My senses are overcome.

"What is Olla, really?" I ask. "Is she a—"

Just at that moment, I see her.

She's been here all along, it seems, in a corner where a window is filled with fragments of colored glass and a spinning wheel sits still in the jeweled dark. She is simply . . . sitting, dreaming awake, or under an enchantment that keeps her invisible till her name's called. Once it's been uttered, her body starts to move.

First, the bees that have been resting in the stray white hairs that have come out of their braids: At the sound of her name, those bees wake and start circling her head like a flower.

Then Olla herself stands and shakes out her apron, looking around as if trying to remember some task of which she was in the middle. I see she's perhaps the oldest woman I've met since I arrived in the islands, but otherwise not as expected: still tall for a landish person advanced in age, with none of the hunch that they seem to develop as the years weigh them down. She has brown spots all over her dry-wrinkled hands and her face, but they are not from the bees.

She is old the way Sjældent is old, I think vaguely; and Olla herself is vague. She plucks the gray string on her spinning wheel as if finishing some project, then crosses to the fireplace and throws a handful of wood chips into the low-burning embers—all without appearing to notice us.

The wood gives the fire new life and makes the pull of smoke and sweetness in the place even stronger. I start to feel dizzy.

"Olla!" Peder says loudly, banging his hands together. Then she startles, looks around (it isn't far), and sees the three of us standing just an arm's length away.

"Oh, by Our Lady!" The surprise overtakes her. "It's

you!" And she doesn't mean Tomas or Peder; she's looking at me. "How marvelous!"

She reaches out both hands as if to clasp mine, but I'm too confused to approach, and in a moment she seems to have forgotten her intention. "My girl, you must have a seat." She looks around the little room, eyes lingering on a few barrels in one corner, then spots a chair and drags it toward me.

"It's a real one, with arms and a back," she says rather proudly. "Just the seat's a bit narrow, but you're skinny enough."

"It was destined for a monastery," Peder puts in. "Uncomfortable on purpose, so the monks don't fall asleep in all those hours of praying and singing. Mother gave it to her."

Here's something else I must ask of Kett: the meaning of monasteries. I have some sense they are for men choosing to live together.

"Oh, are you Thyrla's boy?" Olla asks, looking at Peder. Her eyes are brown, like few eyes I've seen here. "How big you are — almost grown up! A special gift, this chair was. It's made of something called bogwood, pulled from the earth in a land to the south. The Baroness let me have it as a favor. The bees like it, you know. They've tried to build a hive in the back, but I won't let them . . ."

While Olla keeps speaking, Peder turns to me. "It's from one of Mother's ships. Made in Denmark, I think, or

Scotland. But what a lot of bother over a chair! Go on and sit down already, since she's offered it to you."

Knees shaking, for I don't like to be ordered about, I sit in the chair, and it is *very* narrow in the seat. I grip the curved arms and smile with what I hope is the serenity of that Lady they all think so well of.

"Nothing for me?" Peder says to Olla. "I've walked a long way, too." So she fetches the little three-legged stool from behind the spinning wheel. When he sits, his knees nearly touch his nose, a pose that looks foolish, though he seems quite unaware of it.

There is no seat for Tomas. Or for Olla, really; Tomas rolls an empty barrel over to her, and they perch together on the round side with their toes on the floor for balance. I think he is holding her up. She thanks him with a smile — though her first interest, as with all the islanders, is in me.

"Have I seen you before, dear?" she asks. The bees buzz obliviously around her head, weaving a net from her silver hair. "I believe I have."

I'm taken aback. She greeted me with such enthusiasm, I was sure she recognized me from the day of the feast.

"Of course you have, Olla," Peder tells her. "She's the stranger who walked into the courtyard and turned the white roses red."

"My name is Sanna," I add; I think it only polite.

Olla gives me such a (yes) *sweet* smile. "Hello, Sanna. Welcome."

"She's been made quite welcome already," Peder says, swatting around himself, though I don't see any bees near him. "She's staying in the castle and is going to be my wife soon — Can you stop those infernal pests?" he interrupts himself.

I suspect he's afraid of being stung again and embarrassing himself with the cavorting dance of pain.

"No one stops the bees," Olla says, gazing around as if counting them. "Except the queen."

"Of what country?" Peder snorts. Then snorts again, as if trying to clear a worm from one nostril.

"Of the hive." Olla draws a hand through the air, and it seems the bees do follow it, or at least they calm down and settle into her hair again rather than bothering poor Peder.

Yes, I do actually pity him in that moment, at least a tiny bit. He is so afraid of being found less than dignified — *poor little man*, as we'd say to one of our seavish babies.

"Do you know," the old woman says in a confiding tone, leaning so far forward that the barrel nearly rolls out from under her and Tomas. Tomas has to throw all his weight into keeping it upright. ". . . how the bees came to be here, on this islet with me?"

Peder shrugs. "Blown by the wind, I suppose."

I don't speak; I can't. My eyes are locked with Olla's, lost in their deep, muddy brown.

"My dear, they followed *me!*" she says. "Or so I thought at first. I had the queen trapped under my cloak, you see, and didn't know it. The others, loyal fellows, followed me because they wanted her. Needed her, rather."

"How did she get trapped?" Peder asks.

"Wh-where did you come from?" I manage to ask at the same time.

"The castle. I think." Olla's eyes leave mine and fall to her hands, which she seems surprised to find folded in her lap. "I remember the white roses — so many roses!— and Baroness Thyrla, who was so kind to me."

Thyrla, *kind*?

"I needed a home and she gave me one. This one." Olla looks around at the rough yellow walls, patterned with colored light from her hodgepodge windows. The fire has burned to embers again, and there's almost nothing left of it but smoke. "I was lost, you see, and she found me."

"Were you in a shipwreck?" I ask, thinking guiltily of the many people my *flok* has left lost or worse.

Olla makes a new gesture, half shrug and half sigh, and smiles at her now empty lap, though it isn't a genuine smile. It's clear she's confused. "So long ago," she murmurs apologetically.

"The Baroness told you to come here." Tomas coaxes her back into her tale. "To this hut in the forest." He's rocking the barrel back and forth a bit now, gently, as we would do with a young one on the waves.

"Oh, yes." Olla brightens. "It was very easy to find. A stone hut in a sunny woods. She said I could stay here if I found something to do."

"And you brought the bees with you."

"And then I had something to do! But they brought me, I think," she says confidingly, folding her hands again. "I think they wanted to come here, and we've been together ever since."

I feel a faint tingle, as of magic, and think I feel a rain falling—or rather, a mist. A light, sticky, sweet mist. I wonder, now, if Thyrla has sent me here partly as a warning: *This is what will become of you if you don't marry my son.* Obviously she doesn't know I can return to the sea.

"Mother wants a jug of new honey," Peder says abruptly, halting any thoughts the rest of us are having. "Harvested since the Assumption Day feast."

"Since the roses changed," Tomas adds, explaining. He's put one hand on Olla's two and is patting them, as if he feels she needs consolation for something, or at the very least human contact.

"She— *We* want to know if it's changed," Peder says, and he's once again his usual imperious self. "Does red-rose honey taste different? Does it carry miraculous properties? What have you noticed, Olla?"

She sighs at her hands, then smiles sweetly at Tomas, then me, then Peder. I'm not entirely sure she remembers who any of us are now.

"It's early yet for a harvest," she says. "I haven't gathered honey since July. The bees haven't had time to make much."

"What do you know from early?" Peder demands. "Go

get us a dipperful now and put it in a jar to take home. Leave the comb in it if you must."

Olla doesn't protest; she must be used to his commands. She rolls off the barrel and stretches to full height—head nearly grazing the rafters, as mine does, and Tomas's and Peder's—and without a word goes out to do as she's told.

The three of us wait in awkward silence. I want to tell Peder he's rude to his elders and that I won't marry him if he continues to behave in this manner; then again, I don't intend to marry him anyway. So I stick to my policy of keeping quiet and observing, trying to see as Sjældent might if she could—and determine what could benefit us here.

With Olla gone, the humming sound recedes; she has brought the bees outside with her. In its place is a very faint, very gentle *hoo-hoo*, and the soft noise of feathers brushing each other as a bird sleeps.

"What bird lives here?" I ask Tomas, but it's Peder who answers.

"An old owl, as white as Olla's hair," he says. "As old as Olla is, too, for all we know. It lives up in the thatching and eats the mice and insects that would steal the honey."

"Not so old as all that," Tomas demurs. "Just last spring, I believe, the owl laid eggs."

"Eggs!" Peder hoots. "Where did you hear that?"

"From my sisters."

"Those silly girls growing fat off your wages? They

wouldn't know an egg if it broke over their heads. No, Olla's owl is like Olla herself—too old to lay eggs, too old to do anything but keep the honey safe."

"Why doesn't it eat the bees?" I ask what I think is a logical question.

"Who knows?" Still folded ridiculously on his little stool, Peder shrugs. "Maybe Olla's a witch and that's her familiar, and it always does as she wants."

My heart nearly stops. Olla—a witch! Could she be the woman Sjældent promised would help me? She doesn't seem self-possessed enough to help anyone . . . but maybe, with the bees and the bird, she might be an air-witch.

"Olla's no witch," comes Tomas's voice. He is standing stiffly at the door, watching her.

I want to join him, but the most I can allow myself is a push out of that uncomfortable chair to peer through the crackled green-white-red-yellow of the window glass. I see Olla with her braids down, calmly digging into one of the golden snail-like swirls, from which she's removed the top. The bees have clouded around her but don't seem to be stinging; they simply roost on her arms and hands and hair as if to share in their own sweetness before she takes it away. Or so everything seems through the wavering glass.

Peder is focused on what's inside the hut, and he has witches on the mind.

"Just look at the size of that cauldron, Sanna!" he says, pointing to the fireplace, where a large iron pot hangs from a pole, the smell of a very old stew sitting heavy around it.

Tomas dares to keep disagreeing. "She's just an old woman, a confused old woman, doing her best to please the people who grant her a living. Don't torment her with rumors."

I feel a pang of disappointment. Of course Olla has no powers to help me. But still, that tingle . . . "Are witches so very bad?" I ask, but Peder is already on to another subject.

He winks at me. "I'd never torment anyone," he says. "Right, Chicken Legs?"

Chapter 59

They think of captivity.

"I don't understand," Frill protests, but no one expects her to understand much, anytime.

Addra, twisting in the water to see the sun gleam on the coppery edges of her scales, reaches lazily out, hooks Frill, and draws her below for a dunking.

When they come back up, Frill ejects air from her blowhole so forcefully that it sprays the other girls: Pippa and La and a dozen or so roughly their age.

"I don't understand, either," La says, bravely risking the others' ridicule. "Why was it good for Sanna to be in prison last night, yet better for her to be out of it today? Sjældent, you are always contradicting yourself."

"The old witch could be wrong, too," Addra says, largely for the benefit of her admirers ranged among the rocks and waves. "*I* certainly don't smell or hear or taste anything different."

Sjældent and Bjarl, the only two on the rocks who have reached and surpassed the age of wisdom, exchange a look. On Bjarl's side, it is questioning; on Sjældent's, it's almost blind. A limpet has attached itself to one eye.

"A prison," says Sjældent, "is a compliment. It means the prisoner is too important to let loose."

A shiver runs through the *marreminder*. They have lived in the fear of being *caught*; now they have to think differently of captivity somehow.

"Then why don't we have prisons?" asks Pippa the Strong.

"Oh, don't we? A prison doesn't need nets or landish walls. We're all prisoners somehow." Sjældent stops speaking to cough. She has been noticeably weaker since Sanna left; she might be talking of the prison of age. "Sanna's a prisoner now as she walks with"—sniffing for dramatic effect—"two landish boys."

The girls remember the times they were unkind to Sanna—and to Sjældent, and to Bjarl—leaving them out of feasts and plunderings.

"A prison can be outside, too," La concludes, with logic that would please her mother. She is thinking of Ishi, who is not exactly in a prison but is not with La now, which is almost (illogically) the same thing.

"Sometimes being disliked is a kind of compliment," Bjarl says.

"Weird people might be the most powerful," adds Sjældent.

Addra laughs at them, exultant in the power of conventional beauty. "Who needs *that* kind of compliment?" she asks, winking at her admirers. "Give me love — and love — and love — all the time!"

Splash! Splash! Splash!

The girls (and a few boys) who have been watching Addra now take the invitation to dive after her. They twine their bodies around hers, spinning in a long wheel of scales and hair and flesh.

Alone on the rock, ignoring the young, Bjarl cups Sjældent's chin in his hand. He turns her face to meet the light, then begins working as delicately as his thick fingernails will allow, coaxing that limpet away.

anna

We're not even halfway back to the castle, and I haven't had time to change form for an escape, when a pair of castle guards present themselves on the path.

"The Baroness says you've been gone too long already," they say, as one voice. "We're to hurry you back immediately."

"Immediately?" Peder asks, mocking them. "Does my loving mother fear we're in danger?"

"She told us to protect Sanna's virtue, my lord," says one of the guards—a boy who looks hardly older than these two, thus no great indication of Thyrla's concern.

"I suppose you mean to protect her from me?" Peder asks, lifting one eyebrow. With a hand on my sleeve, he pulls my body closer to his. "What do you plan to do, murder me?" He pauses, reflecting, then pulls in tight to whisper in my ear: "If I died now, no one would know how much I love you. Just give me time and I'll show everyone."

Behind us, Tomas doubles over, as if in pain.

I tear myself from Peder and fly to him. "Are you ill, my lord?" Putting my hand on his back, where I feel his heart beating like a bird's wings when it's trapped. I wonder if a bee stung him, but we all seem to have left the cottage unharmed.

"I'm perfectly well," he says, "but you shouldn't act as if I'm a lord."

"Tomas is a servant," Peder says with his superior air, "*my* servant."

We may not have servants in the sea, but I understand the hierarchy by now. What strikes me most is that Peder doesn't call Tomas by his humiliating nickname but uses his proper name instead.

"Take your hand off my servant, Sanna," Peder commands me.

I can't stop myself from resisting, stroking Tomas's back as I would an ailing baby's. "A cramp?" I ask softly. "Nausea?"

"All of it," he whispers back. "But not for the reasons you think. You'd better let go of me."

I take my hand away, and Peder's there to catch it in his fist again. "What ho?" he says loudly to the two guards. "There's no danger to her virtue in holding my hand, is there? We've been together all afternoon with no one but Chicken Legs to protect her."

Tomas straightens up, with a sigh of forbearance for the burden of his nickname, and we walk on, all five of us.

After this strange encounter, I think I've found my moment. Out here, in the clean air, with the sea so nearby, I could dash away—could use my powers and change midair, return to the *flok* and the southward migration that will take me far, far away. Sjældent will be angry that I haven't brought the mysterious prize she expects, but Sjældent is always angry about something, and it rarely affects the *flok*.

But I can't do it; I can't make myself. Looking around at the four boys who are to protect me (and more than me, the honey), I smell Thyrla's worry upon them. I decide one last time to go back, if only to see what she wants me for so badly.

The guards ask Peder for the jar of honeycomb. He hands it over, and then they carry it as if the jar is a very precious thing. This allows Peder to keep a hand on my elbow, steering me.

He holds me back slightly so he can stretch up and whisper in my ear. "I'm not afraid of much in this world," he confides. "But I am very afraid of my mother."

My heart skips. Here I am doing all I can to find the mother I think will be a boundless source of comfort—and there's Peder, afraid of nothing but his.

Maybe he's not so awful after all.

I keep thinking so until we cross the so-called sallet island and discover no bridge between us and the castle.

"We have a boat for rowing," says one of the guards, as if issuing an apology.

There is a plank with room enough for three to sit. Peder is first in, and he sprawls himself, leaving Tomas to help me into the boat and no room for Tomas to sit.

We return.

anna

Inside the castle, Kett is waiting. She escorts me to my little chamber at the top of the rock pile, then sits me on a stool—wider than Olla's chair—and sets about combing my hair again, almost as if she understands how important it is to the *marreminder.* And knows that I am one.

"You've been gone ever so long, miss," she frets, scraping my scalp with the wooden teeth. "The Baroness has been quite frantic." Without pausing, and as if this information is equally significant, she adds, "You don't have a single louse, miss—how do you manage that?"

The answer is that I haven't been on land long enough to catch landish insects. But Thyrla? Frantic?

"What did she think would happen to me?" I have to ask.

Before Kett can answer, Thyrla herself bursts into my chamber. I think that she doesn't bother with locks but simply manifests — showing off her magic, I suppose. She's wearing a dress of black velvet shot through with gold thread, and her hair is waving down her back in a silver-gold starfall. She doesn't need two eyes now; just the one carries enough power to frighten the angels of which landish people seem so fond.

So close to her, I feel like a snail kept too long out of water. I leak a few tears in a message that I hope might (*might*) find its way to my father.

"Grow up," she says to me, seeing the tears. She blazes like fire and ice together, filling the chamber. "Grown women do not weep. And girls who weep don't marry my son."

I wipe the wet from my face against the earth-odored blanket that covers my bed. I feel heavy.

On land, water is always heavy; in water, cloth weighs us down. In any case, I should never show weakness to this woman. Even if I do secretly hope she'll stop the wedding herself.

I pick on one little comment Thyrla made. "I haven't been weeping," I protest, though I know I sound like a child.

"It would surprise me if you didn't," Thyrla says. "So far from your family and in a strange place. You must want them at your wedding."

"My wedding?" As if I've never heard of it before.

"Tomorrow," Thyrla says, sleeves swooshing like flukes as she crosses her arms against her bony bosom. She appears very pleased with herself. "Tomorrow we'll have you married. In the courtyard, against the red roses."

I'm stunned, gaping like a *glopfisk.* How foolish I was to return here! I had no idea the wedding would come so soon.

". . . We must take advantage of them," Thyrla continues, speaking of the roses, "before they fade. There's no telling how long they will last, and they will make a beautiful bower for a bride."

She gestures, and I realize the chamber door is open and women are waiting outside. They come in, two of them, flushed with pleasure, carrying a long length of that pale pink silk Thyrla was sewing yesterday.

"Well, hold it up to her," Thyrla snaps. The little room is very crowded now, but Kett pulls me up from the stool and holds me steady. One of the women stands on it and the other on the bed, and they let that pale pink silk run down the front of me like a spring.

"Excellent." Thyrla taps her fingers against her mouth and her foot against the floor. "Or it will be. We'll take it in here," she says, pinching the cloth at my hips, which Kett pins. "And I'll make sleeves to cover the fingertips."

"What is this?" I dare to ask, though I already have a good guess.

"It's your wedding gown, miss," Kett says, barely daring to breathe around the finery. "Isn't it lovely?"

It feels like another web of magic weighing me down. Tingling. Crackling.

I think then to ask Thyrla: "How did the honey taste? Was it changed as you expected? Did you like it?"

Thyrla nods, but it's an ambiguous gesture, and I don't

know what it means for the honey. I do know that she expects many changes—more than I can count—and they involve me. Marrying Peder, who sings those ridiculous songs and is afraid of his mother.

She says, "Father Abel is already in the castle. He will spend the night, so as to be ready for the ceremony. Yes, by midnight tomorrow, you'll be a wife . . . Don't look so surprised," she admonishes mildly. "All that marriage requires in our part of the world is three days of intention and an announcement to the church leader. Your time will be over tomorrow afternoon, and then—family or no family—you can become my son's helpmeet before man and God."

Helpmeet: What does that mean? I hear *meat* in the word and feel afraid.

"Man and God?" I echo, since I feel I must say something—and hearing, in memory, the sailors crying, *Augh! Augh! Augh!*

Thyrla throws back her head and laughs in a practiced way that's meant to unsettle the hearer. (*Goodness,* I think, *how alike she and Sjældent are at the heart.*)

She says, "Man and God and woman and child and—whatever you'd like to believe in," she says. "In any case, I'll welcome you as my very own daughter."

Then, knowing full well that I'm going to weep in earnest now, she twirls on her toes and vanishes, leaving me to fret for the rest of the night.

But—and this is greatly to my surprise—marrying Peder doesn't seem so bad right now, at least in the abstract. I'm sure I'll escape long before this ceremony happens, and even if I don't, a landish wedding won't mean anything in the sea.

So even the prospect of another night of Peder's singing is not too unpleasant. Maybe Tomas will sing with him this time. Maybe Peder's song will explain why he's so afraid of his mother, and I'll learn more about mothers that way.

• Chapter 62 •

The change in the honey.

It's still buried deep in the comb, thick and warm and waxy from the creatures that made it. When she went to fit the pink gown to Sanna, Thyrla left the comb on a silver plate to drain, and when she arrives there is still nothing out.

"Some snakes even a beauty like you can't charm out," Uncle teases. There's a bit of him showing through a gap in the drape, and Thyrla grabs a long stick to push the cloth over.

It's not a snake, anyway; it's just honey, and even honey from an enchanted vine should follow the rules of nature. And if not—more magic.

This she will do alone, seating herself at the little spell-casting table, arranging her black velvet gown to concentrate light and shadow as she wants them. She begins a humming in the throat that is meant to bring hidden things to her reach. It has worked well on gold and jewels in the past.

". . . or a beauty such as you once were." Uncle's voice comes muffled.

"Damn you!" Thyrla slams both fists on the table, making the plate and the honeycomb jump. Uncle has destroyed her concentration.

He's also awakened the other bones. Even behind the green damask draping, she feels them moving—expanding as if for a breath, rattling as if for a dance. She can't concentrate now.

So she takes a sharp little knife from a box never locked, and she slices into the comb as if killing it. Then the hearts of those tiny hexagons spill all they've withheld: amber liquid, thick and slow and sweet.

And spicy. Thyrla licks it off the knife's blade. Red-rose honey is warmer and . . . *darker*; there's no other word for it. And it makes the tongue tingle like spices from the East. Only, Thyrla's quite sure this tingle means magic, not distance. And the magic tastes like . . . years.

She becomes greedy. She licks the knife clean. She licks the plate clean, too, and then picks up the waxy bits of comb and chews and sucks at them, trying to take in all the honey she can.

"Careful, my girl, no one looks pretty when stuffing her cheeks" comes a voice from the walls.

Thyrla thinks it is Mother's.

"Even less pretty when jealous," Thyrla says aloud. "*And when all the flesh has dried from the bones and fallen away.*"

She finds a tiny drop of sweetness hidden deep in a corner. She tells all her senses but one to be still. Only taste. She must taste this.

Chapter 63

He was marvelous himself.

Such a night Father Abel passes in Thyrla's castle! He normally rents a flea-infested room in a crowded weaver's household across the square from the church. Now he is surrounded by luxury: a feather mattress, a pillow, a basin for his waste; hangings on the bed, a carpet on the table, a wax candle, a fire in a brazier; a boy at his beck and call in case he fills the basin or wants wood for the fire.

And if he wants a *book*—the Baroness made this clear as she herself showed him the chamber—all he has to do is ask.

Over the course of the night, he asks three times. For a Bible, which he knows by heart but asks for out of duty; for *The Golden Legend,* which is about saints' lives and deaths; for a book of hours said once to have belonged to a queen of France. He leafs through all of them, too excited to do more than read a line of Latin here or there, indulging his eyes with the rich illuminations of lapis blue, cochineal red, real gold laid on as thin as a whisper but jumping out as both pleasure and assault to eyes so used to duller things.

Not even in Rome did he have access to such treasures. Looking at these beautiful books feels utterly sinful, though they are religious texts and subjects. From time to time he thinks, *There's no one in town to ring the bell and close the day, or to start a new one.* But then he tells himself that studying these precious texts is of far greater value to his flock than the ringing of a bell, given that sunset and sunrise do perfectly well to mark the passage of time.

Around midnight, Thyrla's young servant (a plump, curly-haired boy, very clean, very respectful) offers him a treatise recommended by the Baroness herself: "*De amore,* Father, written by a monk about the nature and practice of romantic love."

That one Abel refuses. He does so by instinct, or so he thinks. If he is to be honest with himself—if, that is, he *were* as honest as the Lord he has sworn to emulate—Abel would admit he refuses *De amore* out of fear.

Surrounded by pleasures of the body and mind, reading about the nature of bodily love, he might succumb to Capellanus's instructions. He might even feel what he has sworn not to feel: vile animal lust disguised as a kind of emotion called love. He might feel it for young Sanna of the Miracles—or, more realistically, for the Baroness herself, as she seems a creature nearer to lust and physical pleasures.

He pushes *De amore* out of his mind. He reads the saints' lives and he eats.

O, such food! Thyrla even has it brought to him here. "So you might enjoy your food while reading, the Baroness told me," says the boy. As if books are common enough to spoil with crumbs and sauce! But it is true that they are doubly good together, as if it is possible to eat and digest the words and images along with the Baroness's eel pie and aniseed cake.

Abel saves the wine to drink, carefully, from a silver cup while looking at the queen's book of hours. He feels full in heart and soul and body at once, until he dozes . . .

. . . and then the servant boy, seeming to anticipate Abel's need, comes in and helps him to bed, blows out the candle, and stacks the books on the table as if they belong to Abel instead of the Baroness.

Sleep descends as both blessing and curse.

Abel sleeps deeply but with the impression of not sleeping at all. He wants to stay awake, because he can't bear to lose a precious hour of the wonderful night.

Happily, the night gives the gift of dreams.

These dreams are dark and light at once. Asleep, he is able to keep eating and drinking as he'd done a short time before; at the same time, he is somehow reading and yet not reading. He sees the pictures in the beautiful books come to life and peel themselves off the pages, enacting their stories and somehow involving Abel in the best parts. Not in the martyrdoms, of course; he is more often the fellow who brings the martyrs' stories to Rome (Ah, those happy months when he lived and studied in the holiest city in Europe!) and presents each case for sainthood before the Pope.

Common gossip in the islands says the castle's dragon is responsible for the exceptionally good sleep enjoyed by anyone who beds down in Thyrla's great hall. Abel has never commented on these stories, dismissing them as the remnants of old gods worshipped before the True Lord's emissaries arrived and made these islands the barely habitable place they are now. When he wakes, however, he could almost believe in such a beast. A Leviathan or a Behemoth. An angel of the Lord.

Thyrla's servants claim they can't remember their dreams, only that the dreams are beautiful. Abel — urinating into the basin, accepting a morning tray of beer and pork pie — is fervently grateful that he can remember his.

In those dreams, he was not just a witness to marvels; he was marvelous himself.

• Chapter 64 •

anna

All I can think of for the rest of that long night is what
Thyrla said when my name was first connected with *saint:*
  Saints are most often martyred before they win the distinction.
  I wonder what she's planning for me.
  Outside, I hear the clank of iron against stone, the
screech of dragged wood, the thick smells of fire and of
flesh cooking on it. Torches and the swelling half-moon
have made nighttime almost as bright as day, for there's
some special building afoot, and I can't read the clues as to
what it is. I know only that it must have something to do
with the wedding.
  I go to the courtyard window to see what I may, but
Thyrla has tightened her net of warding magic. I can't so
much as poke my nose across the sill. It's the same at the
townward window, too, and even trying to push so far as to
get a look toward the trees sets such a crackle in my veins
that I fall back and bang my head on a corner of the bed.

For a moment, I can only lie on the floor and (yes) weep.

While I'm weeping, it seems the castle weeps, too. It shakes: a more or less gentle vibration that carries its own sort of sound as articulate as speech, though the words are creaking, rattling, heavy on consonants, painful to hear.

I imagine it's saying: *But here you are loved! Here you will stay forever!*

The castle is my version of that garden of death behind the white church. But no one will raise a monument over me.

And I'm a fool to think rocks might speak, let alone speak of love. I almost wish, now, that Peder would appear and sing to me; but he is elsewhere, not even (as far as my senses can tell) in the castle.

Chapter 65

He will be a beast of burden.

"She'll be riding me day and night!" Peder declares to the crowded tavern. *"Peder do this* and *Peder do that* — I'll be her ass for certain!"

His audience — a motley assembly of men and boys collected as he and Tomas strode through town, inviting every male thing they met to celebrate Peder's last night as a free man — this audience laughs, with a tinge of unease, and they make themselves busy with drinking.

Peder doesn't understand why his speeches don't get a bigger laugh. It's the kind of thing he's heard other fellows say the night before (or just after, or well into) their marriages, what no one takes seriously because, after all, if a wife displeases, she can be punished or sent away.

"Her beast of burden!" he says, belaboring the point. "Hog-tied and henpecked!"

A weak trickle of laughter follows, and deep draughts from the serving-house cups.

Tonight Peder has decided that it's wonderful to be the lord, yes, but there's also good fun in being a man.

"Tomorrow I'm married!" he cries for the third or fourth time, slamming down an empty wooden cup. He's confused in his verbs but nobody cares; what's chief in their minds is another hour for drunken pleasure with the bill to be paid (it's presumed) by the castle.

"Hear, hear!" cry the guests, and the brewer's wife and daughters run among the trestle tables, filling cups.

The men fling themselves into the spirit of making toasts.

"To your health!"

"To marriage!"

"To my bride!"

But when Peder tries to make them toast Sanna, an uneasy quiet falls. It doesn't seem quite right, congratulating this wastrel boy on lawfully bedding a saint.

"Drink, drink!" Peder urges, but still they are slow. He subsides sulkily into his own cup.

Sanna will soon be his. He consoles himself with this thought, for he really does love her. A beautiful girl better than his dreams, whose kisses fill his mouth and his body with fire in a way no other girl has done before, though he was (he is proud to think it) quite a seducer in his day.

But it isn't seemly for a boy so highly born, lord of the Thirty-Seven Dark Islands, to express excitement over marriage. Instead, he throws back his head and brays like a donkey.

At least, he makes the sound he imagines an ass makes, which is of course not like any that ever walked the Dark Islands' soil. It's curious enough to quiet the crowd and make them all listen, so Peder—enjoying the attention—brays on for a while, careless of looking ridiculous.

The sound draws the attention of the brewer's three daughters, all of them busy at work. All of them, at one time, have also been busy underneath Peder, as *his* beasts, assuring him his kisses were sweet even after so much beer, his caresses welcome whether or not he was the lord.

Not after tomorrow. Everything changes in marriage. In love.

Peder clamps his jaw shut and sips beer through the merest crack in his lips. He doesn't even want a last tumble before Sanna; that's how much he loves her.

Tomas, who has been with Peder for almost a decade and knows how he thinks, watches this idea run through the young lord. It is one more astonishment in three days that have never stopped amazing.

Most amazing: Sanna's touch, rubbing his back, when he doubled over with heartache on the way back from Olla's. It is said that love is like the tiny sting of a bee, so much pain from something so small. Tomas's love is indeed that way; he can feel nothing else but the ache of it. He doesn't drink, because there's no way to slake his thirst; he doesn't eat, because there's no filling the emptiness in his soul.

Peder is marrying Sanna. A girl so wonderful would naturally never belong to Tomas. But still, amid the laughing and gulping and burping, the scrubbing and pouring and singing of the men's celebration, there is a little part of Tomas that asks, *Why not?*

Just then, an elbow jabs his side. It's Peder's, of course.

"Why the long face, Chicken Legs? Have you already forgotten that I'm the ass here?" And Peder sets to braying again, for so long that at last the other men have to laugh, to roar with laughter, because he is so very ludicrous.

"We'll sleep at your mother's house tonight," Peder announces, pausing for breath. "No, don't worry about your sisters—their virtue's as safe from me as Sanna's. We'll sleep there tonight, and in the morning, great things!"

"What things?" Tomas asks, unable to leave misery behind.

"Great things in the morning!" Peder shouts for all to hear.

The men drinking with him cry, "Aye, aye!"

anna

If I don't do something, I'll go mad.

In the little chamber where Thyrla has me trapped, everything sizzles. Any magic I try sparks up with a *pop!* and floats ashily to the floor. Waves of spent energy smash into my head, bouncing off the walls, making me dizzy and angry and sick and sad. I can't sing.

The light never moves. Moonlight, starlight—night. Clouds. Barely any light.

I swear at myself. I wish for my unknown mother and kindhearted father and even for sly old Sjældent.

None of that helps. The waves of my longing bounce against the walls, too, and they return to me a thousand-fold. I'm in prison, no mistake, and something (Thyrla) is even preventing me from crying. No one in my *flok* will know of my distress. Soon they might forget me, as they forgot my landish mother.

I have an idea: Maybe the way out is the way in—into my past. I'll look for an answer or at least the right question. Whatever led me here.

I use the reasoning method of Aunt Shusha the Logical.

Point the first: The reason I transformed myself and came to Thyrla is the same reason I learned magic at all—Lisabet.

Point the second: At one time I may have wondered if Thyrla could be Lisabet under another name—if I might be her daughter. She is the right age. But when I mentioned the name to her, she didn't react, just rattled off that long list of other Lisabets instead.

Conclusion: It is unlikely that Thyrla is my Lisabet, even if Sjældent worked her magic of forgetting here.

What's more, I (gladly) see nothing of myself in Thyrla's body or temperament. She's cold and mean, and small and dainty and silver where I imagine Lisabet to be sturdy and dark.

Third, the magic is too strong in her (or so I believe) to allow her *not* to recognize me as her blood if that were the case.

And last, if she really were my Lisabet and knew it, she would not be proceeding with this wedding. She certainly wouldn't want me to make children with her son.

I return to my mental image of the girl who gave birth to me, the one who supplied the traits that are not like my father's. I make my blood hum—gently, so as to keep the vibrations within me and not strike the walls—and I get a misty picture of pointed nose and sharp chin, long fingers and tiny waist. (All landish girls have small waists compared to ours; they don't have a tail to control with the belly muscles.)

It's not much, and yet gradually I'm able to pull away from the image of Thyrla and back into how I've imagined the mother who was barely older than I am now when she fell into Bjarl's arms.

For the next part, I must use my powers. It's obvious by now that Thyrla is not going to help me, and I haven't guessed which precious object Sjældent wants brought back to her. So being in the castle must mean something else, and to find that meaning I must use my magic.

I take a deep breath and rub my thighs, where the bones have been aching to melt and re-fuse into a tail. I ask the castle rocks—and the dragon, if there is one: *Help me remember Lisabet.*

Immediately a sensation comes to me, a wave of emotion that makes my blood jump. Perhaps this is purely my magic returning; perhaps it is amplified by Thyrla's, or the dragon's, or someone else's.

Whatever the source, it plunges me into a Down-Below-Deep of the mind, a trench where memories press so heavily, they might crush me if I don't fight back.

I am in darkness. And (yes) fighting, by instinct; I'm surrounded by water and also by flesh. It yields, but only a little, as I punch and kick. I feel pain pain pain pain pain, and then a rupturous release. A sudden light, a fall that knocks the wind out of me.

For a moment I'm aware that I'm still lying in Thyrla's straw bed, panting and sweating. I believe I've conjured the night of my birth once again, but this time not from Lisabet's perspective or even Bjarl's—I'm actually recalling my own messy burst into the world.

I close my eyes and feel down along my legs, but I can't return to that instant and sense the baby me. Of course, back then I would have been too weak and confused to check my body—or even to know there might be something to wonder about . . .

But the Down-Below-Deep sensation swells again, and now something new: teeth chewing through the cord that has bound me to the only life I've known. There's pain in that, and itching and yearning. I want to be free of what held me, but now I am drowning where once I felt safe. Then comes a slap on the back that empties my lungs of the sea inside and opens me up to the air.

I scream. I don't know if it's just in memory or in the now as well. But silent or not, the scream ends the magic. It forces me back to my captivity in Thyrla's castle.

I'm surprised that I don't feel any afterburn of magic. Sjældent said she had to use all her powers to shape me into a seavish girl, so my memory of that night should include breaking, making, unmaking.

It occurs to me that rather than the past, I've been

looking into the future, at a baby that I myself might bring into the world . . .

With Peder as the father?

I shudder—not so much because of Peder as because the very idea of birth is now terrifying to me.

And with that, I leave the last ragged bits of the vision and come fully into the bedchamber. Workers are shouting outside in the fragile light of dawn; my wedding day advances as my body shakes back into itself.

For the very first time in my life, I ask what now seems an obvious question:

Is Lisabet even alive?

 *Silly boy.*

There was a silly boy
And he grew into a man —
A man who loved the sea so much he drowned in it.
Now his flesh is eaten and his bones have turned to sand.
Silly, silly boy.
Foolish man.

—The Mermaids

• Chapter 68 •

It looks like time.

Abel's night of wonders is over and a long day has begun. After a little more reading in those marvelous books, he is summoned to Thyrla's neat sewing room.

He finds the Baroness sitting calmly in her lush black gown, despite the bustle that got underway as soon as the sun rose. While workers break rocks and bake bread, she is embroidering threads of gold and silver on a length of cloth that sometimes shines pink, sometimes white.

Silk, Abel thinks; he touched some once in Rome, on a cardinal's robe. It was the softest substance he's ever felt.

Noticing his curiosity, Thyrla holds up her cloth and turns it this way and that in the light. "What do you think, Father?"

Abel studies the needlework politely. This thing is rich and complicated and fine; for a moment he thinks how lovely the statue of Our Lady would look wrapped in it — but no, the Baroness would not send such finery over to town. Anyway, Our Lady must be loved for what she is, a simple figure made and maintained by humble hands in the name of the Lord. And the name of the Virgin.

Of course, Our Lady was worked miraculously into a new pose only two days before, and what is inside her arms? Even after all last night's reading about miracles, Abel still doesn't know.

Now, *that* is art: the divine mystery that lies within all great works.

"What a wonder of feminine crafts you've made," he says, since the Baroness is clearly waiting for a compliment on her work. "And how quickly you've done it!"

Apparently unaware of his condescension, Thyrla returns the silk to her lap and picks up her needle again. "I started the night Sanna arrived. You see, I knew immediately that she and my son —"

Her explanation is interrupted when the son himself bursts in. Young Peder and his companion, Tomas, are back after spending a night in the town. The boys are red-faced and wind-blown, soaked to the knees, having run all the way and tripped into more than one channel in their haste. Peder will brag later that their rowboat nearly capsized between the sallet isle and the castle (his mother still not having seen fit to put down the bridge) — but for now, they have more urgent news.

"We're doing it," Peder blurts out, heedless of the priest. "The most incredible thing. Mother, you can't imagine —"

Tomas demurs, but in such a low voice that perhaps

only Abel hears it: "(I think your mother can imagine almost anything.)"

"—what we are doing to the church!"

"The church?" Abel exclaims. "The *church*?"

His imagination (still fed by last night's reading) pictures all sorts of horrors, from pestilence to vomit to desecration of Our Lady herself. Martyrdoms. And fire—the roof is made of wood.

"I must go!" he declares, but the Baroness stops him.

"Stay where you are, old Father," she says. Her silk work slips like water to the floor and puddles at her feet. "Let the boys explain themselves."

With those words, Abel is frozen, unable to move. His feet (healed from the long walk the day before) feel rooted to the floor.

Yes, he thinks dazedly, *it is best to listen before you go rushing off . . .*

This thought is the thought of a stranger. For a moment, Abel feels—oh, not quite, though he does wish it—that the Lord is speaking directly to him.

Could this be the third miracle? Could Abel have been singled out by the Lord and Savior to receive His word?

The voice told him to listen.

". . . a great hole, Mother, big enough for Tomas and me to walk through together," Abel hears Peder say.

The Baroness's son is positively glowing, and her color matches his as he tells his tale. Those two are mirror images of each other, female and male.

"Big enough to walk side by side," Tomas puts in. "We spent the night with my family. We invited them to the ceremony today, if you approve——"

"Nobody minds your family, Chicken Legs. I can invite who I please," Peder interrupts. "So, Mother, the people have taken it upon themselves to build——just guess!"

"How can I possibly?" the Baroness asks drily.

Father Abel feels panic rising in his gorge. One night at the castle, and the people are tearing down the church—— and adding to it, which could be even worse. He thinks of the awful frescoes they've already made, the Whore of Babylon and the hideous serpent of Eden.

"What are they doing?" he asks, forgetting for a moment that no one (except possibly the Lord) has spoken to him in a long while.

"Building a chapel, Father!" Peder fairly trumpets the news, then laughs. "Don't pull such a face, now——it's not the worst that could happen. I designed it myself, in charcoal on a stone."

"The chapel will be dedicated to the Miracle of the Roses," Tomas explains, as he always fills in what Peder leaves out. "The statue of Our Lady will have her own altar inside, painted with red roses. Or roses as red as the dyers can manage, at least."

That is a relief. And how nice of the boy to acknowledge what Abel considers to be the town's greatest treasure, the statue.

"There will be a big painting of Sanna and me——"

Peder continues, but for once Abel doesn't defer to him.

"Where is Our Lady right now?" he asks anxiously.

"Under cover, Father," Tomas assures him while Peder goes on about the wedding portrait that will cover one wall. "The workers took her down and carried her to Magnus the fuller's house. They laid her in his family's bed."

Peder inserts, "She'll be out of the way as they fling mortar about."

Abel shudders at the thought of the precious statue and her hidden bundle lying in the bug-infested, urine-soaked bed where Magnus and his wife and three children and at least one aged parent sleep.

"At least it *is* a bed," the Baroness says, as if she can hear his thoughts. "And I doubt the family will actually lie with her."

"They're going to sleep on the floor," Tomas says.

Everyone looks to Peder now, for what else he might have to say. But his attention has left the church and moved to the cloth at his mother's feet; the silk, he thinks, lies like a cloud holding dawn inside.

"That's pretty," Peder says, leaning down to grab at it. "That thing you're making. Is it for the wedding? Is it for me?"

Abel cannot let the subject of the chapel go. He's ready to dash off and stop the work if he must — but the voice said to listen. "Who's taking charge of the building? When will it be done? If the winds change and the rains come . . ."

"Oh," Peder says, rubbing the pink silk, "these things don't take long, do they? A few days." He rubs the embroidered part of the cloth against his face, where it leaves threads of silver and gold behind.

"A fortnight," Tomas says, always in that low and humble voice, so he doesn't appear to be correcting his superior. "Magnus says he knows how to do it. And some of the farmers have promised to help when they're done bringing in their crops. They have the knack of building, after all."

"For cows and pigs," Abel says. He regrets his night of indulgence with food and wine and books; he should have been watching his Lady.

"And chickens!" Peder crows in delight, then whips the pink silk into the air and flaps it in Tomas's direction. "Dance, Chicken Legs! Dance for my wedding! We'll build you a chicken coop all to yourself."

From Peder's hands, the fabric unfurls and spreads dawn through the chamber. Against the green tapestries, it looks like the inside of a shell, a shell that might hold a pearl. (And who would be that pearl? No need to ask; they all know.) Only the heavy cords of gold and silver that Thyrla has sewn on weigh it down. They pull it back toward her, and it becomes like a net that has caught a pink jellyfish.

"That's not for you, my boy," says the Baroness.

The wind does change then, and the scent of roses wafts in stronger than ever, as if the beautiful garment is pulling it inside.

"Oh," Peder says, clearly disappointed. "Then it must be for Sanna."

The shutters rattle.

"She is the bride, you know," his mother points out. She's suddenly irritated and pokes a finger beneath the patch embroidered with a sleeping eye. The real eye below (or the wound, or the scar; Peder's never seen it and never dared to ask) must be itching.

Father Abel speaks up again. "The church, Baroness. I must go and see to it. There's no telling what damage the people may inflict—with the best intentions," he adds, remembering Peder is responsible for the design.

"Don't worry, Father," Peder says, making his voice boom above the sound of Thyrla's scratching, even above the workers and waves outside. "The improvements will be finished by the time you return."

"But I must go right away!" Abel wipes his palms on the brown wool of his robe. He'll need to hurry if he's going to town and back in time for the wedding, but he still can't get his feet to move. "I need to be certain—"

"Oh, stop!" Thyrla says sharply, and immediately everything *does* stop—the talk, the sounds outside, the wind, even Abel's heart.

Silence, utter silence. Is there anything more terrifying?

"I need you here, Father," Thyrla says, and it all starts again. "It isn't every day there's a wedding in the family."

In the family—what an odd way for her to put it.

Abel still feels he should leave and tend to the team of

enthusiastic if unskilled builders. But suddenly not only are his feet rooted to the floor, but his bum is attached to a chair for good measure, though he doesn't remember sitting down.

Obviously, he is at the Baroness's beck and call. And feels uneasy about it, truly uneasy, for perhaps the first time in their long acquaintance.

"Don't worry, Father," says Peder, now lounging in the wide seat of the courtyard window and watching the activity below. "You'll like the change. The builders knocked their hole straight through the Whore of Babylon. They took her legs clean off."

Yes, Abel thinks, *that would be better.* And yet not better.

He thinks of building and churches in general and remembers, oddly, what Jesus said to his chief apostle: *You are rock, and on this rock I will build My church.*

Saint Peder. Quite different from this boy, who is delighted by the hole in the Whore's legs and is marrying Saint Sanna (someday she'll be known by that name, Abel is certain) that very night.

You are rock, and on this rock I will build My church.

Abel doesn't realize he's said it aloud until young Peder speaks up.

"Mother named me after the philosopher's stone," he says, with the air of correcting an imbecile. "So that I might turn lead into gold."

"That's pagan magic," Abel says. He feels dazed as well as paralyzed. "Your mother would do no such thing." But at the moment, with Thyrla caressing her embroidery as if it's more alive than the priest himself, Abel isn't so sure.

Peder smiles his golden smile, suggesting that even in his youth he knows much that Abel does not: "The stone grants immortal life."

"What a dreadful thought!" If there is one event to which Abel looks forward, it is his entrance to Heaven. The older he grows, the less he minds aging, for it brings him closer to Paradise.

Suddenly, but with a feeling of *at last*, Abel recalls one of last night's dreams: A very old man was bent over so far that his skull appeared to be growing out of his hip bone, and he was in pain. He'd been hobbling along a road without end, begging at each step for release. And a merciful angel with wings the color of—yes, the color of the silk Thyrla is embellishing for Sanna, shimmering pink and white, with silver and gold spines to the feathers—this angel swooped down and carried the old man away.

"Eternal life while keeping one's youth," Peder says, as if he's had the same dream.

"Well," Abel says, shaken by the memory of a vision that was not so beautiful after all, "that does sound better . . ."

Thyrla, changing needles, laughs. "Listen to you two— professors of Dark Islands University!"

Suddenly (*at last*), Abel knows what the marvelous dress reminds him of.

It looks like time.

anna

There's so much banging and sloshing outside that I can't even hear my own thoughts. I also can't imagine what's causing the noise, and I can't lean out the window to see, either, because of Thyrla's guarding magic. It's all I can do to keep body and spirit together as I lie atop the bed and think of the birthing memory I conjured. For a moment I even wonder if, like an everagain, I am reverting back to infancy . . . if I'll become once more that stumpy creature who burst from her mother's body and (I think now) perhaps killed her in doing it.

No, that can't be right! Lisabet is alive—and I didn't kill her! Otherwise I can't bear to spend another heartbeat in this place.

I'm so agitated that I almost don't hear the keys turning in the locks—one, two, three, four, five—before Kett enters my room with a tray.

"Your breakfast, miss," she says, setting it down on the colorful stretch of tufted wool laid over the table. "The Baroness said to eat a little, but only a *very* little. The wedding feast will be your main meal today."

I think, not for the first time, that the landish are overly concerned with what to eat and when to eat it. I suppose it comes from having so little, and needing to pull what they get from the ground.

Still, it's nice not to be alone with my thoughts anymore. I won't find any magic just wrestling with my own lack of memory.

"Is that what the noise is about?" I ask. "Something for the feast?"

Kett's eyes sparkle and she claps a hand over her mouth, then makes a gesture for turning a key between her lips. "Can't tell you, miss," she says through her fingers. "It's a surprise. But you'll like it, I promise you will!"

I breathe in and breathe out, trying not to feel trapped. The tingle of magic swells into pain, then recedes.

Kett can tell something's wrong.

"Oh, dear, please eat," she says, pushing some dishes around on the tray. "I've already said more than I should. Miss, there is such *news* about you all over!"

She clamps a hand over her mouth again, and this time she seems to mean it, for although her eyes bulge and her newly smooth skin glows with the effort of repressing her secret, she does repress it.

I think how fond I am of Kett, really. More than

perhaps any of my cousins except for La, even though I've been here only a few landish days.

To please Kett, I heave myself up, making the straw crackle beneath the soft feathers. My scalp feels itchy and I know my hair's tangled. By now it may have some landish bugs scurrying around, too.

"What did Thyrla send us to eat?" I ask, mostly because I want to be nice to my friend.

She takes the hand off her mouth. "There are some greens with the last of the summer flowers — or almost the last, as the cooks are saving the rest for tonight. The ones that ben't poison," she adds quickly. "The Baroness's gardeners are very careful, and there's one garden that doesn't even have a bridge, the plants on it are so dangerous. The Baroness has a man row her out when she needs them."

The hand again. I think she might stuff it down her own throat this time. "Forget I said that about gardeners. Just have your breakfast, miss, please!"

I don't know why gardens should be such a secret, but they are a uniquely landish arrangement and one that holds little interest for me. The only seavish parallel is the array of bits of shell and stone that an octopus will make outside its lair, and it's not as if the octopus is trying to grow anything.

"Why don't we look at the tray?" I ask, mostly to please Kett. I doubt I'll be able to eat.

She displays the dishes for me: the promised array of greens with yellow and purple flowers about which I have doubts; then a variety of fishes, some salted and pickled but some raw and cut into strips. I will taste those. And something that smells sweet and grassy —

"Oatcake, miss," Kett says when I ask. "Don't you have it where you're from?"

Her question doesn't need an answer, but I try a bite. Earthy, yes, and flowery, and I do love sweets. So much that for a moment my mood lifts and I feel less desperate. I think of Peder — I hear his voice somewhere in the castle — and I wonder if it will be nice to kiss him again after the sweetness of a feast.

Somehow, though, it's not his lips I imagine against mine. Not even Addra's lips or Pippa's, or anyone I've imagined kissing before —

There's a knock at the door. Kett unbolts and unlatches, turning keys as she must.

"Tomas!" she exclaims. "I thought you'd be the Baroness!"

His face is red, as if he's ashamed of something. "She wouldn't knock," he points out in a mumble. "May I come in?"

Kett stands aside, and the lanky boy, all long neck bones and arms, scuttles in. He closes the door himself. He probably shouldn't be here, according to the rules of the castle; it's the first time I've seen him without Peder, and one rule I have been able to parse is that while Peder may sometimes go places without Tomas, Tomas must always be at Peder's side if he's wanted.

304

"Do you have a message from the young master?" Kett asks.

"Yes," he says, then, "No. I mean to say it's not *from* him but *about* him." He turns in my direction and bows.

I smell that he's been drinking beer, as Peder must have done also while they were gone. And although his clothes are plain, and his feet rather pungent, his hair brown rather than gold, his eyes blue instead of silver—I think that, as boys go, Tomas is not an unappealing one.

I wish Kett could set her heart on him rather than Peder. Tomas is a boy who will try to make a girl happy, and even if he doesn't succeed, she could love him for trying.

I feel my heart swell, as if I have found a member of my own *flok*.

"What is the message?" I ask.

Chapter 70

She doesn't have to do it.

It is agony for Tomas, being this close to Sanna. He feels his entire body blush. He is full of love and longing and, most of all, reverence. Which comes with a fierce desire to protect.

So he's here. Sneaked away, had to come, even if it means losing his post at the castle. He *needs* to help.

"What is the message?" Sanna asks, and he opens his mouth to speak.

"Is it about the chapel?" Kett guesses before Tomas can get a word out.

Although he wasn't thinking of the chapel at all when he came here, he nods. He'll begin with small news, something everyone is allowed to know. Or Kett will; she loves the gossip.

"Tomas and Baron Peder saw it themselves when they were in town today," Kett tells Sanna. She raises a hand as if to slap herself, then drops it and sighs. "Oh, I am terrible. I probably wasn't supposed to say anything about that, either."

Sanna says, "I don't understand."

Tomas is relieved to have a beginning; he will work his way around to the true meaning of his visit.

"The people are building a chapel onto the church," he says, adding an explanation by instinct: "It's a wee chamber to the side of the nave in honor of something special. Baron Peder designed it."

"The something special is you," Kett says, as if Sanna might be confused.

Sanna is, in fact, looking bewildered, her huge green eyes blinking and her brow wrinkling in a way that breaks Tomas's heart but remains beautiful.

"Your miracles," he explains further, wishing he could just tell her absolutely everything that's in his mind and heart. "The roses and the change to Our Lady of the Sea."

Kett exclaims, "Oh, miss! You're looking pale!"

Indeed, if Sanna's skin can have gone whiter, it has. Even her lips are alabaster, not the pink cushions they were when she arrived or when she sang . . .

"I—I—" Sanna sways as if her legs won't hold her any longer. As if hearing that the people love her and honor her miracles has somehow overpowered her.

Kett grabs her left elbow. Tomas feels justified in grabbing the right one, and when he does so, he gasps. With that single touch, a flood of warmth has spread from his hand to his heart and his belly and his everything, even more intensely than when she stroked his back the day before.

They help Sanna to the bed, sit her down, and feel her brow. Both of them do this at once, and their fists knock awkwardly. Tomas doesn't think he feels a fever, but then his own hand is so hot, he might not be able to tell.

How soft her skin is, like a baby's . . .

"I'll get some wine," Kett suggests. She reaches for a silver pitcher that sits with Sanna's breakfast things, then stops with her hand poised midair. "Oh, I hope this won't mean you can't be married tonight!"

At *those* words, Sanna turns so pale she seems to glow in the half shadow of her bed, and she sinks to her side with eyes closed.

Tomas can't contain himself any longer.

"You don't have to get married," he blurts out. "I mean, not to Peder. Not tonight. Not if you don't want to. That paper you signed—it's an agreement *de future*, for the future, not for the now."

Sanna's voice (her clear, high, beautiful voice) comes from the pillow: "But this *is* now."

"The wedding doesn't have to be." Tomas balls his hands into fists. He knows he could be dismissed for saying this, maybe even killed, but Sanna deserves to know. "I checked in the town, and I checked with the priest just now. The Baroness can't force you and Peder to marry if you don't want to."

"Of course she wants to!" exclaims Kett.

Pain stabs Tomas. "Well, if you'd rather wait awhile . . . I just felt I should tell you. The paper isn't magic." He tries to joke but knows he's only displaying his misery. "It can't make you do what you don't want to. Lords and ladies and kings and queens break betrothals all the time."

"Why bother to make an agreement if you won't follow through?" Sanna asks, her voice a ghostly whisper.

Kett stands at the ready with wine, but Sanna presses her lips shut and shakes her head.

"It's just . . . custom," Tomas says. He doesn't have a real answer. "I don't know why. They like to promise each other things. I heard about it from my father, who heard it from a sailor from a ship that sailed up from the south. People say they're going to marry all the time and then don't do it."

"But when they do marry, it's forever," Kett says.

Tomas says, "That's why it's so important that you be sure—"

"She's going to do it!" Kett says, stamping a foot and spilling the wine. "Who wouldn't want to marry Baron Peder and live in the castle and wear pretty clothes and always, *always*, be in love?"

Neither Sanna nor Tomas has a reply for this question. But they look at each other, and he has the loveliest, lovingest sensation of swimming in pale green depths. Though of course he can't swim at all, and if he tried he would drown.

anna

When Tomas visits, I feel a sudden expansion of the elements, as if I'm a crab that's wandered from a small shell into a big one. And when Tomas leaves—abruptly, after suggesting I can make a choice about this wedding—Kett and I gape at each other until Thyrla walks through the door he left open.

"Ah, the bride," Thyrla says.

Kett squeals with joy at the word. I think how pure she is, being able to feel happy that someone else is marrying the boy she clearly loves.

"I've brought something for you, and also some*one*," Thyrla says.

The someone is Father Abel, following close behind with anxiety streaming off him so thickly, I can not only smell it but touch it as well, pluck it like a string. What could have him so upset? It's not as if he's a prisoner here and forced to make promises he shouldn't keep.

"Good day, Sister Sanna," he says, and touches the fingers of his right hand to his forehead, then his breastbone, then both shoulders. He looks at me expectantly, and I bow.

I am curious about Father Abel, who is (as I see it) the only elder of this landish *flok* other than Thyrla, and Thyrla seems to take an interest only in affairs directly concerning the castle. I should know more about Father Abel's specialties: the statue of Their Lady and what the church means to the town—and what I and my "miracles" mean. I wish he had come alone, though Thyrla would have prevented him if he tried. He might even help me find the thing I am to bring back to Sjældent; and if I'm very lucky, he'll help free me from Thyrla's warding spell so I can return to my people.

But I have to wonder why he came this time, since the something that Thyrla promised is a bundle of that white-pink fabric that she shakes out and holds in front of my body.

It seems the dress is all but finished.

"I must see if it's a good fit," she explains, lifting the shoulders of the garment to my shoulders. "Help me, Kett!"

Kett stands on a chair and has me turn around so they can measure the length of the dress against the length of me. The dress requires a lot of struggle, for it's as light as air and as eager to fly off.

Can this be the thing I'm supposed to take back to Sjældent? I wonder. If so, then is Thyrla the woman who is supposed to help me after all? I can't imagine what good this dress might do Sjældent—or what would make Thyrla want to help, since she seems to dislike me even though she's binding me to her son.

It is all so bewildering; I feel I'm in a terrible tangle. And I wonder why the priest is here.

I think of tangles, too, when I turn back around and see Kett still holding up the dress. Thyrla must have worked on it night and day, for it's covered in an intricate pattern of gold and silver, straight lines and curves combined. And yet it's not quite a tangle; it's a *pattern*, and though I can't make sense of it, I know instinctively that it means something.

"What do you think, Father?" Thyrla asks the old man. "Isn't it a fine gown?"

He seems afraid of it somehow; his brown-spotted hands are shaking.

"Or will be, once I finish off the hem and we tie the sleeves on," Thyrla says, still admiring her work.

I feel magic crackling. It may come from the dress or from Thyrla herself, but it's something far beyond the warding spell that keeps me shut in this room. Maybe it has to do with the priest.

"Could I speak to Father Abel?" I ask impulsively. "Alone?"

Thyrla gives me a cold stare from that single living eye.

The one sewn onto the patch looks sinister in its perpetual wink. "Why?" she asks.

"I have questions about marriage as it's practiced here." I do, indeed.

Father Abel clears his throat and speaks nervously: "All young virgins should seek spiritual advice before a wedding."

Thyrla presses her lips into a line and gathers the dress up rather carelessly. "Well," she says. "I suppose that's a good idea. I'll have to start sewing right away, if this dress is to be ready in time."

She's gone almost before she says the last word, leaving the three of us confused.

Why do I have the feeling that, despite how Thyrla just behaved, this is what she wanted all along—for Abel and me to talk?

Chapter 72

It is better to marry than to burn.

With all going just as she might have planned if she'd actually predicted Sanna's arrival, the Baroness takes her sewing to her most private chamber. She will draw on the strength of family to finish making this dress all she needs it to be.

Surrounded by those bones, and more than a little pleased with herself, Thyrla threads a new needle with silk and lays a silver cord at the height of Sanna's ankle. She anchors the thread and begins to stitch—wondering, incidentally, whether the beginning of a foot is at the same place as the beginning of a fluke, or if legs and tails are even more different than she thought.

There's a clatter behind the green damask, but she won't give the bones the satisfaction of daylight. She's here to use them, not to entertain them, and she pulls severely on their magic to keep her needle strong.

"Ouch!" cries Uncle, but he's quickly silenced, and Thyrla goes on with her work.

As she sews, she listens. To the work underway on a nearby rock too small to be counted as an island itself, yet big enough for her needs and close to the castle besides. It is progressing apace.

She listens, also, to conversation within the castle itself. Every sound in the place percolates through the rocks and fissures, vibrates the bones, and comes out through the gap-mouthed skulls in the ceiling.

Thyrla's ears select the voices of Abel and Sanna. They are discussing marriage.

"Is marriage important?" Sanna's voice asks. "Is it . . . necessary?"

Thyrla hears Abel's heart beating; it rattles the former Lot's ribs.

"Marriage is approved by the Church Fathers," Abel says, straining to control a quaver in his voice. "But . . ."

"But?"

"The most desirable state is virginity, as our Lord ordains: 'It is best for a man not to touch a woman.'"

"So much for *your* plans, my girl," Uncle comments from the ceiling.

Thyrla tells him, "Shh," and takes another stitch that shuts his mouth.

Sanna asks Abel, "Then why does the Baroness want Peder to marry me?"

Abel's voice answers, "Our Lord also says that every

315

man hath his proper gift of God, one after this manner, and another after that."

"What do you mean?"

Abel coughs. This is clearly not what he had hoped to discuss with the girl he already refers to as a saint. Down in Thyrla's room, even Mother's ribs are moving now— with laughter over the mortal man and his plight.

The answer comes: "It means that some men don't have the gift for chastity, and they must touch women. For them, it is better to marry than to burn with lust, and so the Lord approves of the practice of marriage, which binds two people together and steers their desire for each other toward procreation in a virtuous manner."

Thyrla has to "*Shh!*" again; the skulls are laughing too hard. "I want to hear what Sanna says," she tells them. "Don't you?"

They quiet.

But Sanna is also silent awhile, until Thyrla fears she's missed what the girl might have replied to the priest. Then again, Sanna is probably trying to parse what Abel has said; it was hard enough for Thyrla to follow, and she understands the ways of the Church.

At last Sanna asks, in a very small voice, "What if the woman does not feel lust for the man?"

A chair squeaks; Abel must be adjusting his skinny arse in excitement. "Then it is far more blessed not to act upon lust at all! If you have the gift of chastity, it is holiness, indeed."

316

"I'm not sure I do have that," Sanna says, and Thyrla wishes she could see the priest's face. (She takes another stitch.) "I want to be in love someday. I just don't feel that way about Peder. Or anyone else," she adds hastily, as if she's afraid she's been rude.

"You don't?" Abel's voice is full of wonder. And this is, in fact, an astonishing admission; most girls, even wealthy ones, even nobles, would fall in love with Thyrla's boy for his beauty alone. "Well, if that is the case, my dear Sister Sanna, you must accept the gift of chastity."

"He might have you there," Uncle says to Thyrla.

Thyrla stitches calmly on. "The girl needs to feel she has a choice."

"Can she choose without knowing her future?"

Thyrla snips off a thread with her teeth. "Most people do."

Above them, Sanna says, "Who is this Lord you keep mentioning? Can I meet him?"

Pandemonium breaks out in Thyrla's chamber. Neither she nor the bones thought the girl would be so stupid as to reveal her ignorance about a basic aspect of daily life.

"I believe that in a sense you have already met Him," Abel says, apparently (blissfully) unperturbed. His calm, Thyrla believes, is a sign of his need to have faith in something, in Sanna—which is what Thyrla needs from him.

She takes another stitch.

Abel says with growing excitement, "At the very least, my dear, you have been blessed by Our Lord, or by Him through the Virgin. It is true that He is a mystery and largely unknown to us here on Earth, though He does reveal Himself on occasion to those who need Him. Thus He is always our fascination as well as our benefactor . . ."

Thyrla (still stitching) recognizes a phrase from the book of hours that Abel borrowed last night. She thinks, *These churchmen are so fond of quoting each other, it's a wonder anyone comes up with a new idea.*

"One truth is certain." Abel concludes his speech. "You could not have worked your miracles without His favor. Two so far, and surely a third will come . . ."

The bones make a creaky sound that's their version of snickering.

Thyrla hears Sanna take a deep breath. "My miracles . . . I don't think I would call them that."

"Of course you wouldn't!" Abel trumpets so loudly that he might be heard in every room of the castle, if it weren't for the work going on outside with hammers on rock. "You are humble. But, my dear Sister Sanna, in time you must realize how special these last days have been. No one, to my knowledge, has seen a red rose before, let alone watched while white turned to red. And have you noticed that not a single petal has dropped, not a single leaf turned yellow, since the transformation? They only grow and bloom more."

"Is that unusual?"

Sanna sounds so innocent that Thyrla wants to carve her up like a dumb fish — and would do it if she didn't have a much better use for the girl. Instead, she sews.

"It is *exceptional*," Abel says. "In an ordinary year, the Feast of the Assumption marks the last day the flowers bloom. By the end of the month, the rose vine is normally bare. But this is clearly not an ordinary year or a normal month, thanks to you. The statue, for another thing—you can be sure her arms have never before moved from the shape in which they were carved decades ago. These are special days. This is a special *time*."

Sanna's next words seem wary, as if she's uneasy with the priest's fervor. "I didn't mean for any of this to happen, you know. And those things—the roses and the statue—you don't know for certain that they happened because of me."

There's a thud and a scrape and a groan in Abel's voice. Thyrla guesses he's flung himself out of his chair and onto the floor, to beseech Sanna like an illustration in a book.

"O holy Sister!" he says. "Consider what these marvelous events mean to the people of this place—what *you* mean to them. To us. You are a sign that we in the Islands have not been forgotten. Your presence shows that Heaven is holding us. That is why the Lord allowed your ship to wreck in our waters—it is all part of His plan."

Thyrla's lips twitch: Part of *a* plan, anyway. Now. She and the bones wait as Sanna makes a tiny sound, as if chewing her lip.

"Abel," Sanna says, "do you know of a woman named Lisabet? Not the wife of a farmer or the widow of a fisher—or maybe, but not only that. Do you know of a Lisabet who had a baby many years ago, before she was married?"

"Out of wedlock?" He sputters; he is, of course, nonplussed. "I assure you, none of our girls have done such a thing."

So they are back to marriage again, and to burning.

There is another long silence. Thyrla sews in a reminder to find out more about this Lisabet and what she means to Sanna. A benefactress of some sort? A rival to Thyrla? Maybe a—

Abel says, suddenly and surprisingly, "It is now clear to me that you must marry young Peder after all."

"Why?" Sanna is clearly very tired.

"You want to lead a good life and then enter Heaven, don't you, Sister?"

Sanna sighs, as if she might blow away—but of course she can't escape; the warding spell on the chamber is too strong, and it's getting stronger with every stitch Thyrla makes. "I suppose I do."

"Then it is far better for you to marry. Marry young Peder and stay in the Islands, where I can serve as your spiritual guide. Don't you agree?"

Thyrla smiles. Her web is spinning without a flaw.

"Sister?" Abel prompts the girl.

"Yes," Sanna says, "I suppose I'll marry him."

Thyrla finishes off a thread, bites it, and fits a new one to her needle.

Chapter 73

The sky and sea so careless.

After leaving Sanna, Tomas isn't ready to take up his duties with Peder immediately. Instead, he goes to the great hall, where he walks past the servants busily polishing silver for the wedding feast. He ignores their greetings and instead crawls out a window, then down the ladder leaning there, to walk the system of planks and stones that make a temporary bridge into the second surprise Thyrla has planned for Sanna and Peder's wedding.

On the far northern side of the castle, on an isolated rock, workmen have been digging and sluicing; heaving a boulder here, chiseling a channel there, arranging precious gravel from all over the world. They are fashioning a garden of a new variety, one made with water rather than earth — a whim of the Baroness, who thinks Sanna will like it.

Seeing him approach, the workers stand aside. They even bow. Tomas came from the town but is not of the town now; being close to Peder, even if only as a servant, has won him some deference he doesn't feel he deserves or wants.

Tomas says hello to some boys he knows and nods to their fathers, who were friends of his father before Tomas Elder vanished at sea. He walks along the steps and the spiraling footpath that Thyrla has designed for Sanna's wedding gift.

He thinks, *A water garden is the sea, only more so.* Like any garden, it is a tamed kind of nature, arranged to a purpose; this one is planned to be the sea at its best, at least at its most pleasing to human eyes. Will it please Sanna? Tomas is not so sure it pleases him, but that isn't for the obvious reasons. The creatures the Baroness has ordered to be placed here — animals more than plants, mostly sea anemones and urchins — look tortured, bruised, unnaturally used. He has a bad feeling about it.

Peder would say (if Peder cared, which he doesn't) that Tomas doesn't like the garden simply because it has to do with the sea.

"You must hate the sea for taking your father," Peder said once, in a rare moment of interest in someone besides himself.

The two boys were down at the docks, and Tomas was holding Peder's shoulders while he vomited into the water, one of his less pleasant duties as Peder's personal servant.

"There's no point in hating it," Tomas said, using his own sleeve to wipe Peder's mouth. "That would be like hating the sky or the air or the land. It's all around us and we make a living from it."

"And a dying," Peder said, groaning dramatically to show he wasn't finished being sick.

"In too many cases, yes. My father was just one such case."

While Peder heaved again, Tomas looked up at the sky and the crescent moon in it, everything there so careless of what happened on land or water.

He thought then, *It would be useless to hate Peder, too.*

Peder was just another element in Tomas's life that had to be endured for the sake of surviving.

That was true until the last few days. Now Tomas thinks that if he is capable of hating anyone, he hates Peder. For being selfish and spoiled and mean, and most especially for thinking he has a right to marry Sanna.

To take his mind away from it all, Tomas inspects this novel thing, the water garden. The men working on it — mostly farmers but also some weavers and a smith — seem to think he's been sent to be sure all will be ready for the bride. They show him buckets of seaweed, starfish sorted by size and color, an enormous tray of tiny crabs. And the places they've hollowed out and filled with water, so that on the mounting path the visitor may walk among a number of little ponds that serve the same purpose as flower beds, to display what looks prettiest.

"Arranged that bit myself," says Rufus the blacksmith, one of Tomas's mother's near neighbors. He points to one where three small green-gray sea anemones are stuck to a rock alongside some mussels and red-brown seaweed. The anemones are no more than blisters collapsed inward, nursing the hurts of being handled; presumably they will open by nighttime. There's a small, ragged blue-white jellyfish that looks half-dead floating on the surface, buffeted gently by the occasional sea spray that surprises the lot of them, and two faded red starfish below. "It's a real treat to be working with water instead of fire."

"It looks good," Tomas lies politely. "But will the animals stay where you put them? Won't the urchin — and the sea stars and jellies, whatever you find — wake up and move around?"

He doubts that undersea animals can be made to please human senses the way a rose vine can, or a fragrant herb garden, or a field of flowers. Some things are not meant to be tamed.

"'Course they will," Rufus says, pulling back from Tomas. "But that's part of the beauty, see, said the Baroness. They'll move and make new arrangements of themselves, because beauty is meant to be fleeting, like youth. They'll be in the same pool forever, though." He ends in a less booming voice, as if there's something about the garden's philosophy that troubles him.

"But won't it freeze over in winter?" Tomas asks.

"Not here." Rufus sounds cheerful again, proud of his work. "There's a warm current spouting in the center, under the spiral, you see. It will keep thawed in all months but the worst."

Tomas is curious about the big pool. "How big?" he asks.

Rufus points upward. "Just take the path and see."

Tomas follows the footholds around and around this rock, and Rufus follows after him, till they reach the top. Here is a big pool, indeed, wider and deeper than seems possible, given the path that leads to it and the size of the rock when viewed from afar. Two grown men could fit inside this pond and swim around comfortably.

"What belongs in here?" Tomas asks. "According to the Baroness's design, I mean."

"All the wonders of the islands!" Rufus says grandly, looking down. There seems to be a sort of tide, or at least a whirlpool, in that water. "Eventually, anyway. We'll have an example of every kind of animal and plant that lives in these seas, and some scraped off foreigners' ships. There's a blue squid waiting in the Baroness's bathtub right now, and Torvald the fisher is looking for a young seal." He thumps his chest with jolly pride.

Tomas shudders. Even as accustomed to farming and hunting, slaughtering and gutting, as one must be in the Dark Islands, what Rufus has described sounds horrible.

"Do ye see it yet?" Rufus asks. "Bend down and look closer."

Tomas does as Rufus says. All he sees is a swirl of

blue-green water flecked with foam, spinning in a direction opposite to the footpath's. It makes him dizzy.

"The center's full of jellyfish!" Rufus crows again with pride. "Immortals. Maybe ye can't see them as yet, as they shrank back to babies as soon as we caught 'em. Young Master Peder and his bride will have the pleasure of watching them grow to adults — then shrinking when they're scared. The Baroness says the sea garden will make our islands famous all over Europe."

That prospect seems doubtful to Tomas, and he gets a sick feeling when he looks back into the water and realizes that what he thought were flecks of foam were in fact these jellyfish. Not that he should care much about the dumb sea creatures — perhaps it's more that they remind him, again, of his own life, caught here in the castle, enjoying its riches but never able to grow up and leave unless it's at someone else's pleasure . . .

That's what this is, he thinks, watching the swirl. *It's a prison.* And somehow he connects the prison to Sanna and her marriage. He swallows an impulse to vomit.

Meanwhile, a woodsman named Knud has made a teetering way up to examine Rufus's pond. "My boys caught an octopus," he announces excitedly. "We're chaining it to the rock by a foot. It can feed itself from fish in the deep channel."

"All we need now is a kraken," says Rufus. "Or summat of similar size."

He probably means it as a joke, but the men grow somber, thinking of monsters. Ambitious.

"How about a unicorn seal?"

"And the Baroness's dragon, to come out of his shell."

But that prospect is too frightening. All the men within earshot turn to gaze at the rock on which the castle sits, fearful that the dragon might break his way out at the mere suggestion.

"Whoa, there, boy!"

Tomas finds Rufus and Knud are holding both of his arms. They've hauled him back from the whirlpool into which, it appears, he was just about to hurl himself.

"Don't ye dare spoil the wedding!" Rufus says, and Tomas has to be content with aiming his head to vomit down the far side of the rock.

Chapter 74

Saying it won't change a thing.

"But I don't understand," Frill protests while the other girls comb their hair. "Why hasn't Sanna sung to us again? And why do we keep coming to listen if she's done?"

"She isn't done," says Sjældent, the one mote of ugliness in the pretty scene of young mermaids basking around Ringstone. "She's *caught*."

"*Caught!*" The girls repeat it — once, then many times:

"*Caught!*"

"*Caught!*"

"*Caught!*"

The word has special meaning, connoting intense peril and torment. They imagine a *marreminde caught* in a net and hauled up to be ravished. This is far worse than merely *imprisoned; caught* is absolute.

"Quiet yerselves. Ye sound like a pack of sea cows," Sjældent says, letting irritation show. "She's *caught*, and saying the word won't change a thing."

The girls obey, chastened, and for a moment there's nothing to hear but gulls and waves.

Soon enough, five heads pop above the seaskin, expelling air from noses and necks: Shusha the Logical, Gurria One Arm, Mar of the Wide Reach, Pippa the Strong, and Bjarl, Sanna's father.

While the other girls chattered, Pippa dived deep to fetch the elders.

"The old witch says Sanna's been *caught*," Addra calls down to them from her perch in the O. "*Caught* and on land!"

The others repeat "*Caught!*" again, until Mar of the Wide Reach raises a long arm.

"We need to hear Sjældent explain it herself," she instructs. "And to the entire *flok*."

More heads are bobbing, more bodies surfacing, all around the rocks. Everyone who could hear or see or sense Pippa's summons below has come for the news.

"Please tell us, Older," Gurria says respectfully, "what is happening to Sanna?"

For once, Sjældent doesn't pause to cackle before she speaks.

"Feet are not a freedom," she says in a tired, small voice. This seems to be one of her cryptic non-pronouncements — everyone has thought of feet as of wings, a new power and mobility—but no, it is a simple statement. "There's no power in leaving your element."

This pronouncement is met with blank silence.

"Really?" La asks, fearful; and

"Really?" Addra adds with scorn.

Sjældent says, "Every new freedom carries a new trap," and clamps her mouth shut.

anna

When Thyrla returns with the dawn-shaded dress, now completed, I feel as if she holds my future in her hands. I have to remind myself that it's a future I can accept or refuse — at least according to Tomas. And to Father Abel, who acknowledged my ability to choose but urged me to accept Peder for reasons I don't fully understand. Something about fire — avoiding a fire-witch . . .

"For you," the Baroness says, and shakes the fabric so it seems to fill the room.

At that, the crackle of magic zags off the rocks. I bang my fists against my skull, not caring who sees me do it. My head feels as stifled as my powers; I can't even form a thought or a deceptive *thank you*. The warding magic now holds me to the center of the chamber and jolts painfully if I try to push against it.

Thyrla knows this, I'm sure—she has to be the one who worked it—but she acts as if all is ordinary and unenchanted as she orders me to take off the blue-gray gown and put on the white-pink one.

"Kett will help you," she says. "And we'll both tie the sleeves on."

I know two things: one, that I don't want to put on this dress; and two, that I must do it. I am powerless now against Thyrla's wishes, and if I'm going to resist her, I need to escape this chamber, which is possible only if I go down to my wedding ceremony. Maybe another part of the castle will allow me more space for my own magic. Or maybe I can simply return to the sea, if I'm able . . .

The dress is beautiful, that's certain; it has the shimmering sort of beauty that we in the ocean recognize as dangerous. It reminds me of why so many of my early magics were about neutralizing the poisons running through a child's body after she played with something she shouldn't have—and yes, the dress seems like a creature to me; it is both created and alive in some way, humming with magic I can't put a name to.

"Go on," Thyrla says. "We don't have all the time in the world, you know."

With a show of obedience, I bend so Kett can pull the old dress over my head and slip the beautiful dress down. I keep the same chemise beneath; none of it will show, Thyrla has so thoroughly worked the fabric. There are laces in the back that Kett pulls to cinch the pink in, and then I'm tied breathless in a gleaming, glittering pattern of silver and gold, laid over silk as soft as the flesh its color imitates. When I bow my head to see it, I look naked. And netted. *Caught.*

"Oh, miss," Kett says, clasping her hands as she looks at me, "with this dress, and with your hair down your back, you're just like a princess! That's even better than a baroness," she adds, unaware that she might offend Thyrla.

"Sleeves," says the Baroness, and each takes one, pulling them up my arms and tying them tight to the shoulders, such that I can barely move them. The sleeves fan out so wide at the bottoms that my fingers tangle in the material and my hands can't find their freedom—also part of Thyrla's design, I am sure.

I must admit that the Baroness looks magnificent herself. She has unbraided her hair, and it waves (now more silver than gold) almost to her knees. She's wearing the cloth-of-gold gown from my first day here, and so many glowing jewels that the chamber feels like one of those warm, shallow seas where everything from rocks to fish is brightly colored and moving fast. Only the patch with the eye embroidered shut could spoil what might otherwise seem like perfection, and on Thyrla it just accentuates her radiant beauty.

She lifts the patch a little in order to rub the space beneath, and the eye embroidered on top truly seems to be winking. There's a message in the gesture, but my clouded head can't understand it.

Meanwhile, Thyrla has been appraising me as well. She

replaces her patch with a curt nod. "Just as I envisioned," she says, and I get a sense that she's holding back some strong emotion such as glee.

It may seem strange for a woman with one eye to speak of her vision, but there it is. Some intention of Thyrla's is becoming real.

I must proceed with caution. As I should have done all along, and *would* have done, if it weren't for that first great accident of bleeding magic into the rose vine.

Far away, I hear the church bell ring, and an idea sparks. "Did Father Abel leave?" I ask in surprise.

"No, he's still with us," Thyrla says. "I sent a boy to ring the bell, since he and the town set such store by the thing. It's tolling for late afternoon, which means time for your guests to assemble."

"*Just* like a princess!" Kett says rapturously. "Married as the half-moon rises behind the castle. It's like something from a story — a *good* story, the kind you want to hear again and again. My mother's come in a boat from the town, and so have some others. My mother came with Old Olla the beekeeper and a jar of new honey."

Ah, sweetness . . . sweet stings, I think. I wonder why Thyrla hasn't put back the bridge that lets people walk into the castle, but I suppose she has her reasons.

"Come along, both of you," says Thyrla, very severe. "Sanna, your husband is waiting."

◆ Chapter 76 ◆

The question.

Nearly the whole *flok* has gathered now, to listen to the elders discuss the problem of Sanna. Shusha, Gurria, Mar, and the others have sent Addra into the water with the rest of the girls, and they hold forth from the cradle of Ringstone's formation.

"If Sjældent says the girl's *caught,* she's *caught,*" Gurria One Arm says by way of beginning.

"The question is what to do about it," says Shusha the Logical.

All eyes turn to Sjældent, who is now ensconced on a rock nearly as tall as the bottom of the O. She is held there by Bjarl, Sanna's father, whose body radiates worry and fear.

But Sjældent, astonishingly, appears to be falling asleep. Her head lolls on its withered stalk, and Bjarl has to shake her to get her to speak.

"What to do about it," she echoes, in so tiny a voice that Bjarl has to amplify it—and he's so loud that the others tell him to hush, lest he bring ships from the land to see what's the matter.

"We're asking you, Sjældent, what we should do," Shusha clarifies. Her voice is not unkind, but it is clear what she thinks of the ancient witch and her selfish behavior. "We need your wisdom."

"How I should know, I don't know," Sjældent mumbles, and Bjarl repeats it for the *flok*. "Never walked on land meself, have I."

Bjarl repeats this as well.

"The only one of us what's been ashore for long," Sjældent says, leaning onto Bjarl, "is this boy, or the boy he once was, when he made the girl on the sand with her landish mother."

This Bjarl does not want to repeat, but when Mar prompts him, he obeys.

"I didn't go *far* ashore," he adds. He's surprised by a sudden gift of memory: "She and I used to meet at the docks, and I took her into the water much farther than I managed on land."

He remembers this with his whole body: holding his beloved in one strong arm, pushing at the water with his tail, cresting the waves and swimming, swimming, swimming with an acre of herring a-glitter in their wake and her head flung back against his shoulder. She was laughing till she cried from sheer delight.

He remembers her chin, the sharpness of it against his

chest. The chin their daughter inherited. His heart breaks once again.

"Bjarl," says his sister Shusha, "tell us about land. What does it mean to be *caught* there?"

"I don't know," he confesses. "The only way I was caught was by love."

He's caught again now, for if someone has taken Sanna from him, his heart is that person's captive.

"Is she even alive?" Addra calls from the water, and the elders pose the question to Sjældent.

The witch's eyes close. Their lids are puckered with baby sea stars. "Alive, yes," she says. "Imperiled, also yes."

"Well, what is happening?" Addra shouts. This time, boys and girls gathered around her slap their fins on the water, fanning her sense of herself as not only beautiful but also wise.

The elders silence the girl with their stares. Her beauty has given her too much power in the clan, or too much cheek; they will need to tame her for the good of the group. But for now, all attention reverts to Sanna, who (they will make this clear to Addra later) is not only Bjarl's daughter but also the heir to Sjældent's magic and destined to be a healer and an elder in the fullness of time, no matter what her age-mates think.

So the attention is, for the moment, really on Sjældent.

"I'm trying to see it," she says, voice almost inaudible. "All I can see is red."

"Stop looking toward the sun!" Addra asserts herself one last time, after Bjarl repeats Sjældent's words.

"What can we do to help?" Bjarl asks, though officially it is not his place to pose questions. "How can we help you to see more?"

Sjældent coughs, then spits a little sand into her fist. "Bring me a bowl of everagains."

"She wants everagains in a landish bowl," Bjarl announces. "Who will go hunting them?"

"Who cares what she wants?" a girl—not Addra, but another as bold as she is and hoping to win her favor— shouts. "We're beyond *want* and into *need*."

"I *need* the everagains," Sjældent croaks.

"This is no time for a meal—" Mar begins, but then they catch a sound from the islands.

The bell at Dark Moon Harbor is ringing. More loudly than they've ever heard it.

"Something's happening," guesses Frill.

The entire clan falls silent, but they know they all feel the same thing without saying a word.

Doom.

"Fetch me that everagain!" Sjældent demands.

A half-dozen boys set off to do it. And only much, much later will anyone remark that Sjældent changed her command to the singular—one everagain, rather than many.

anna

It's only marriage, isn't it, not death? Once the ritual is finished, Thyrla will relax her grip on me, and I'll be able to look for Lisabet once more. *And* I'll punish Sjældent for sending me here with the promise I'd find help. All I've found in three-plus suns is chaos and mistakes, misunderstandings and horrible songs. Of course, a good bit of it was my fault, but for my first significant foray onto land, I might have expected better guidance.

All of this gives me a kick of determination, even as my powers are bound in Thyrla's castle, in the dress she made for me. The distant bell hurts my head and scrambles my thoughts. But I *will* get away, and I *will* see Sjældent and Father and the *flok* again, and then I *will* find Lisabet somewhere along an edge of the great dark seas of this world.

This is how I persuade myself to keep moving, following Thyrla, with Kett behind holding my skirt up, as we wind downward through the castle and toward the rose-ruffled courtyard. Without a touch of rage, I might drop dead of despair.

The roses (which Abel says should have been dying by now) are so thick that they make an unbroken wall of red, and with my sensitive seavish nose, the smell of them could knock me to my knees. There is such a thing as too much sweetness, and I've found it here.

Peder waits in front of the arch that once held the statue of Their Lady of the Sea. Gazing as if he's been searching for me as I've searched for my mother. As if he truly loves me. I am still sufficiently aware of others' emotions to recognize that in him—however shallow I've thought his feelings.

On the dais beside Peder stands the trembling old priest, Father Abel, who thinks that it's better to marry than to burn; with him is Tomas, who thinks I can refuse to be married; and everywhere else there are bodies.

Massed in the courtyard are people who work in the castle and guard it, and people like Kett's mother and Tomas's family, who rowed in boats across the rough channel where there once was a bridge. Olla the beekeeper, whose white hair is studded with clusters of bees that make people keep her at a distance; the fullers who soak wool with their urine to sell. People who are excited, and sweaty, and still not tired of feasting, for I can feel their bellies rumble and their mouths water at the smells coming from the castle kitchens.

340

If only some of that water were salty, I think in a daze, I might make something of it. My own mouth's as dry as midday sand.

"Ooh, miss, everyone's here for you!" Kett coos behind me.

She and Thyrla propel me through the crowd, up two steps, to a place in front of the empty niche. There they arrange my dress and hair until, in all too short a time, Thyrla places my hands (lost within the billowing dress and long sleeves) in Peder's.

My senses are dulled, even outside. I can't so much as guess where the *flok* is, or hear a whale or a dolphin transmitting curiously about us. All I know is that the sun is sinking into pink shades darker than my gown, and the moon is rising silver; a light breeze stirs the roses and carries an impression of some new thing I'm barely able to guess at but believe to have emerged from the sea nearby. Or to have been forced to emerge . . .

"I have a surprise," Peder announces to the crowd, more loudly than necessary, with a grip on my hands firmer than needed as well.

Clouded as my mind may be, I have already guessed the surprise: He wants to sing.

"I've composed a new tune," he says grandly, "with new words, especially in honor of this day."

I hear Thyrla make a *tcha!* of annoyance under her breath, and her silver eye rolls in its socket; but after all, this is Peder's wedding, and she allows him to sing.

Having used my own songs for enchantments, I might normally be wary of one composed just for me. But if this one is anything like the first Peder performed, I see nothing to fear but time wasted.

It begins:

So near, my love, to bliss, my love —
So near are we to bliss —
It shines on us from close above;
We'll reach it with a kiss.

I wait, listening, crushed and strangled in the dress that looks lighter than air but feels heavier than rock. The song goes on and on and is remarkable for its silliness (my mind is not so clouded that I can't recognize nonsense), though not for its innovation. It sounds almost exactly like what Peder sang before, down in the courtyard; despite what he's said, the words have barely changed and the tune not at all.

The time, my love, is swift, my love;
O how the time does fly!
We barely walk the earth before
It's time that we must die.

I'm barely walking the earth as it is. I cast about for ideas. If I could learn to fly . . . Or if I were a time-witch . . .

My eyes happen to meet Thyrla's. She's rubbing beneath the patch again, but the exposed silver eye stares into me, and I can hear her thoughts as plainly as if she's speaking into my ear:

What an imbecile my son is.

I'm shocked. It seems Peder is right to fear her; Thyrla

doesn't like her own child at all. Which raises questions about why we're all here for a wedding, and why she didn't bring him up to be someone she'd both like and love, and whether Peder knows what his mother thinks of him. In this moment, despite his ridiculous song and his vanity, I feel sorry for the boy. In the seavish *flok*, if a parent lacks interest in a child, there is always someone else eager to take care of that child. Girl or boy, plain or pretty, and silly or smart, everyone finds a parent somewhere.

And so, my love, please stay, my love
As long as we do live.
Love will make the time pass swift —

I have perhaps been especially lucky (*blessed*, the landish would say) in my upbringing. I emerged from a landish mother, in a form that no one dares to remember; but Bjarl was glad to have me, and my aunts have always been kind. And then there was Sjældent, who (upset as I am with her, I believe this) probably treated me as well as she would have treated any daughter from her own body.

I continue to pity Peder up to his final sung phrase:

Until we're in the grave.

With those words, I feel landish time swooping down to hold me hard and squeeze the life out. I am, after all, alone and without family here.

Peder's song seems to have impressed the wedding guests, however. The people in the courtyard are weeping, presumably over the beauty and poignancy of it. What I feel most is panic. Landish lives are less than half as long as seavish ones — why must I think already about joining Peder in one of those cross-marked mounds behind the church?

I make a tremendous effort to pull my hands out of his.

He pulls back, grips me harder. Indeed, I have no strength to resist anything that's happening now; Thyrla made sure of that.

"My darling," Peder says, "would you like to sing to me, too?"

Everyone watches; everyone waits. I take a deep breath, which feels as if it may be my last. The bell is still pealing in the distance — and somehow also inside my skull, which vibrates with each knock of sound.

I begin to have an idea.

Gently, answering that vibration, I start to hum.

anna

My song is soft. My song is epic. My song holds all the magic I've learned thus far, and it slips between the threads Thyrla so carefully laid on my gown. It magicks the courtyard and every living thing there.

I find a way to use the stone itself: I make the courtyard a bell, to amplify my magic rather than to contain it in a chamber.

I sing and sing, and though no one understands the sounds, everyone feels their effect.

First, the tears. Salt water springs from landish eyes, rolls down dusty landish cheeks. I can use that.

Then, the love. The people look on each other as if every glance is a declaration, and every heart is enamored. That is my gift to them.

Then, the season.

Abel told me that by now the roses should be shedding their petals and withdrawing into the thorny vine. So, at my wedding to Peder (who sang that he wants to lie with me in an earthen grave), I make them shed.

The red petals quiver at the sound of my voice. They shiver; they give up the last of their scent. Then they begin to pluck themselves, slowly at first and then faster.

I exhale with a *whoosh!* and the petals obey my breath's command: They take to the air and spin, like the sand-twist I first performed when Thyrla demanded magic from me. Only bigger, and redder, and sweeter — whirling petals and pollen and bees together, filling the courtyard as if this is the last magic I will ever work, which it quite possibly is.

At first the people exclaim in delight. Father Abel claps his spotted hands; he believes this is the apparent third miracle, the final sign of saintliness for which he has waited. Peder beams as if it is a great show of my love.

I see Tomas's mother and sisters reach for the petals, laughing for joy when they catch one.

But as more petals detach and take to the air, the cries grow alarmed. Hands begin to swat them away, and children scream as the bees begin to sting. The whole courtyard's a whirl of sweet-scented red and hidden pain. Soon I can't make out any faces. I realize Peder has let go of my hands, and I'm glad; but when I look around, I can't see him, and that worries me.

My magic has turned. It's fighting against me.

I'm exhausted, but I have to wring some last power out of myself. I know Thyrla will do something to stop it, and soon; meanwhile, this is my one chance to escape. I don't have the gifts to make myself fly; I don't even have strength to stop the roses. They have become their own storm in a new element, and I'm not a witch of the air.

A petal blows against my nose and, for the tiniest moment, I can't breathe. I brush it away with the back of my sleeve, then jump into the one place I think will be safe: the empty niche around which the roses bloomed. The inside is bare.

It is like entering a shell. I press myself all the way to the back, and the petal storm doesn't follow me. I hold my breath, hoping these landish lungs are up to the task.

Out on the dais, a bit above the crowd, the petals churn now as thick as water. They don't seem to pose much danger there except to Peder, to whom I addressed my song. Petals cover his nose, his ears, his mouth. He falls to his knees and then all the way down. Tomas tries to climb up to help, but Tomas has to save himself, too.

Then there is Thyrla, bending over her son. The petals fly toward her and veer away; her own magic repels them, so she is untouched. She brushes the soft redness from Peder's face, which (I can barely see) has gone blue and still. She pinches his nose shut and puts her lips to his, to empty her lungs. Giving him air. She does this three times, then four, while I watch from my safe spot in the wall.

She who thinks her son an idiot must care something about him after all.

This is a revelation. I may not be getting married today, but I have learned more about families. Or witches.

On her seventh breath, Thyrla looks up at me. She's known where I am all along, and her eye is as sharp as a sword when she glares. She doesn't have to speak or cast a spell; I know how much she hates me.

She pulls away the white silk patch, and for the first time she shows me the eye she usually hides.

I see a flash of purple piercing the red storm.

And then I see nothing but blackness.

Chapter 79

The young seize the moment.

Sjældent has rejected every one of the jellies the boys bring.

"No," she says, and

"No," and

"No."

"But this is what you said you wanted!" says Mar of the Long Reach, her skin blazing in the sunset. "Our young have brought the best they could find, and still you reject them—what is it you want, really?"

"I want the everagain," the old witch says stubbornly.

She seems very weak, so weak that Bjarl keeps her cradled in his arms. Her mind is unclear. Insects of sea and air crawl over her, and she doesn't even twitch. Her being has dwindled to this one desire—as if when Sanna was *caught,* Sjældent was caught, too.

Shusha fires questions like landish arrows: "Can you help to save Sanna or not? Tell us what has happened to her. Where is she? *What do you need to save her?*"

"I need the everagain."

Meanwhile, Addra, Pippa, La, and Frill have been talking.

"We're going to those islands," Addra declares. Nothing the elders said has damped her spirits; she has ultimate confidence in herself and in her right to speak up and make decisions. She expects to be an elder one day — a beautiful elder, never an older.

"What do you think you'll do there?" asks Mar of the Long Reach. She's always skeptical when it comes to the young.

La is the one who explains: "We're going to sing to the landish people and draw them out of the castle."

Addra says, "Everyone with a beautiful face or voice will go. We'll sing the moon song — that always works on the sailors. We'll lure away that boy who sings the awful songs."

"We'll find Sanna," Frill says, but in a tone more dreamy than it is determined. "We'll save her."

The elders look at one another. Then all the grown people of the sea look, even the men. They exchange signals and agree: No one should approach the castle or even the town on Dark Moon Bay.

Shusha delivers the verdict to her own daughter and all the rest: "We don't need any more of our young held captive on land."

"They'll never catch us," says Pippa the Strong. "We won't be *caught.*"

"I'm sure Sanna thought the same thing," Gurria One Arm replies. "But even with all her magic, she was *caught*. And now"—with a darting glance at Sjældent—"our *flok* might find itself without a witch at all."

Sjældent, with the life obviously ebbing out of her, feels all eyes on her. Her memory drifts back to the time ice-pale Gurria had first come into the *flok* as Shusha's lover, and how eager she was to learn spells for transformation, especially the healing arts that transformed pain into strength. And then the mere matter of an arm lost changed her mind. That and Shusha's first pregnancy.

Sjældent insists one more time: "Bring me the everagain!"

Addra, floating near Ringstone, hears her and issues commands with all beauty's privilege: "Boys, hunt for jellies! Girls, come with me!"

"Don't do this," Shusha warns La.

La looks uncertainly from her mothers to the land and back again. She thinks of her beloved Ishi, waiting in the warm waters of the middle days. Waiting for her.

But Sanna is her cousin, and she's important to the *flok*. It will be a better clan for Ishi to join if Sanna swims with it.

"I'm going," she resolves. It's time for the young to strike out on their own, no matter what the elders say.

The elders can't restrain her and the couple dozen girls who are considered beautiful in face and voice. No one has the physical or magical strength to stop them. Only

Sjældent might manage, and Sjældent is focused on a craving of her own.

"The everagain!" Sjældent shouts with her last drop of strength.

Addra cries, "Girls, follow me!"

Bjarl, trusting, looks La in the eyes and says, "Bring Sanna back. *Please.*"

anna

I wake up to find that I'm burning.

I wake in the dark.

I wake in some moist place that is all hardness unyielding, all heat, no doors or seams or cracks, only a bit bigger than I am when I'm all curled up.

I am *caught* as no one has ever been caught before. In a terrible, sweltering prison.

I'm inside the rock.

For a long time (or perhaps a short one; there's little telling down here), I reel from the thought that I'm trapped. This is the Down-Below-Deep, and I'm in it. Without the least notion as to how I can lift the weight of the place off myself and swim (or walk) free.

But if growing up as a *marreminde* has taught me anything, it's that simply feeling upset and scared won't save me. I have to exert myself and *fix* myself.

First thing when I regain the ability to think, I reach for my hips and downward.

I still have legs.

But the silk dress is sticky and clingy, and the thick metal threads hold like a net. So, yes, I have legs, but they're bound together with cloth, and the cords won't move.

I think, *Thyrla knows everything about me.*

Can that be true?

I try to imagine how I got here, how she used her powers and magicked me off. Then perhaps I'll see a way I might leave. Find some sliver of time to use like a key in the locks on my chamber door . . .

I remember curling up in the statue's empty niche to hide from the rose-petal storm. That was a cowardly act and an unnecessary one. Of everyone assembled in Thyrla's courtyard that day (Today? A moon ago?), I could have held my breath longest and waited for the storm to end. I might even have saved Peder . . .

I killed Peder. Or I think I did, in yet another consequence I never intended. I have to hope that Thyrla has saved him, though it didn't seem likely when I last saw them.

In the very last moment I remember, Thyrla pulled off her eye patch and glared at me. The eye I was accustomed to seeing was still silver and sharp, but the eye she had hidden was worse.

I remember purple and pink. Doubled, like some

magical creature in its own right. That revealed eye was a monster. Its two pupils shot fire at me. Sparks, then flames, the color of bruises and pain.

They sent me here, to a chamber in the rock. A hot, snug, moist, barely aired place in which the usual elements combine into one and I will never, ever escape.

I feel around myself with both hands and feet, as much as I am able to do in the clinging damp of the dress. I'm so perfectly shut in that there are only inches between me and the rock, which is mostly smooth and featureless. *Polished,* I think, as if waves have been scouring it for longer than anyone can imagine. Or as if it's been hewn out and buffed, like the rooms in the castle that are mostly cut from the island's bedrock.

Whatever made this bubble of stone, it is nearly perfect, and nearly enough to smother me. If I don't find a source of air, I will die in very short order, if I'm not already dead and trapped in some afterlife.

This truth strikes me: I'm in a landish grave, albeit without the almost-husband who sang of lying there (here?) with me. Poor Peder, whose mother wants to keep but not to love him—I can't stop thinking of that, as if the lack of a mother's love creates a true bond between us.

With tremendous effort, I pull myself back into myself, memory and mind back into my body. I need all of my strength. My quest made me selfish; now I have to undo my mistakes. Save Peder. Save myself.

I dig deep and sluice up an atom of magic. I send it outward like the flame on the tip of a landish arrow to learn what I can about this place I'm now in.

It's the wrong thing to do. With nowhere to go, the magic reverberates off the walls and back into me with a painful jolt, much worse than anything I felt in the castle.

And it keeps jolting through me and against the rock, over and over, till I lose myself again.

Chapter 81

Waste.

"Me next!"

"Get us away!"

"— can't breathe!"

"I have five — hand over the oars!"

"My wife swallowed a bee!"

"Patience," Tomas says, in what he hopes is a soothing voice. "Everyone will have a turn with the boats."

This isn't immediately true, but he hopes to make it so by appointing himself the steward of rowboats. The red-petal storm is much lighter outside the walls, but this is one miracle that has frightened the Dark Islands, and as night swings into the sky, the general panic only grows, not lessens. Tomas is trying to make sure that no boat heads toward the sallet isle without a full burden of townsfolk, and that a strong man comes back from each trip so that the boat can fill again. Nonetheless, more than a few of the rowboats have been abandoned on the edge of the sallet isle, which means they've drifted off to sea in the choppy currents.

"Such a waste," people mutter, or sometimes they shout it at the retreating backs of their selfish neighbors—who can't hear even a shout, as the ocean roars loud with the tide, and petals still deafen the ears.

Only Old Olla is not trying to escape. She sits on a low rock just this side of the portcullis, weeping. Tomas believes she weeps for her bees, some of which have died in the petal storm and the wild swattings of the wedding guests. But aren't there always more bees?

He has to turn away as a little boat returns, bouncing on the wild tide.

"Here's one for you, Dame Birgit." Tomas keeps hold of the gunwales, letting Kett's mother climb in, and at the same time he tries to prevent Harald the butcher from shoving his way ahead of her. "Bring your family, then send your son back with the boat so Harald can go home, too."

This seems the best system to him, helping the weak to go first—unaccustomed as he is to managing any event, let alone an escape from the castle that people are usually eager to enter. He is doing the best that he can. He bundles Kett inside, next to her mother and brothers—though the girl hangs back and doesn't quite seem to want to go—then gives the boat a good shove into the channel.

"Tomas, thank—!" he hears Kett call; there's more, but her words are lost to the waves.

He feels a tug on the end of his tunic.

"Are we next, brother?" It's his sister Inger Younger, who doesn't understand that in such a situation—not at all a dire one, as Tomas keeps telling the people fighting to leave—being a relative of someone who works directly for the Baroness's son must not mean getting preferential treatment. At least not if the *someone* is honorable.

"You have to wait, pigeon," Tomas says, as cheerfully as he can. "But don't you worry—there's nothing to hurt you here."

It's true; hard as he looks, Tomas sees nothing worse than a few gulls circling overhead, as if making a deliberate decision about loosening their bowels on the heads of the unlucky townsfolk. Very few rose petals flew beyond the castle yard, and though they now lie there knee-deep, it's been easy enough for the wedding guests to wade through them to freedom, carrying children on their shoulders and in their arms. Nothing worse than a bee sting came to any of them—except Peder, and Tomas won't think about *him* now. Can't. Or of Sanna . . .

Inger Younger persists: "Maria said—"

"Maria's wrong. Go back to Mother and wait, little pea."

As another rowboat comes back, Tomas lets Harald the butcher have the oar seat, then turns to the next-most-worthy group, a poor farm family who wheedled their way here in hopes of a feast and now regret it. They want nothing more now than to return to their turnips and beets, their chickens and their single skinny pig, and spend the winter talking about that dreadful red storm that ended a wedding and (possibly) the life of the young baron-to-be.

"Is the master all right?" asks Harald's wife, Maria, once settled into the boat.

"I don't know," Tomas says curtly, helping old Berta the farmwife along. "Any guess is as good as mine. Truly."

He feels a twinge of guilt; he may be neglecting the one charge he's expected to hold above all others — Peder — and the one person he loves above any: Sanna. How is *she*? It's strange that no one is asking. He hopes the town hasn't turned against her.

Everything Tomas does now, he does with her in mind, as if she's the one he is saving. And to save her, he thinks he must first help these good people. When he's alone with just Peder and Sanna and the Baroness, *then* he might do some real good.

Even Father Abel has left the courtyard and waits, trembling, just behind the slot in the wall where the iron portcullis might fall, if Thyrla wished to keep everyone out of (or inside) the castle.

Tomas gestures to him. "The next boat is yours, Father, if you want it."

Abel comes forward, halting with each step, as if he's not sure what he wants.

"The people will need the comfort of the church," he says. "I believe my place is there."

Tomas thinks of two things: the statue that moved in

the night, closing her arms over an unseen bundle, and the hole dashed into the side of the church for a chapel to be built in honor of Sanna and her miracles. Three days — only three days ago she arrived, and now everything in the Thirty-Seven Dark Islands has changed.

"Clear a space for Father Abel!" Tomas shouts, and he makes sure the next boat is properly managed, with a promise extracted to bring it back for more travelers.

Although, he thinks as if he's completing a sentence already begun, *the people still in the castle might need some divine comfort as well.*

Chapter 82

She needs family now.

The girl took the roses but left the thorns. She took the life from Thyrla's beautiful boy and left only a shell.

Peder is dead.

Thyrla has carried him herself—small as she is, woman that she is—all the way to her chamber in the heart of the castle. And dumped him on the table that serves for her magic, let his loose limbs spill over the sides and his head roll against the wall with a *thonk*.

She pants. There he is. Golden hair, alabaster skin. Wasted.

Can he be made otherwise? Can he live again?

Thyrla yanks at the cords that control the drapery, little caring if she rips the hangings to shreds. She needs the whole family now: everyone, every last finger bone and vertebra and all-but-invisible sliver that normally floats in an ear's waxy sea. She will see them with both eyes, in all times, and together they'll find a solution.

She uncovers Mother, and Mother's ribs flutter.

She uncovers the babies, and their neck bones shriek.

She uncovers Uncle, and he starts spouting advice right away.

"Got to bring that boy back to life somehow!" Uncle chides, and Thyrla snaps: "As if I didn't know!"

"*If only* you knew," he corrects her, "your son would still be breathing now. Choked on your sour air, didn't he?"

If Thyrla's breath is sour, it's because her mouth bleeds from trying to blow life into Peder's lungs. She blew and breathed, blew and breathed, until the boy's flesh was cold and his eyes, open in death, stared past her with the expression of astonishment that all corpses, fresh or untended, seem to wear. As if, just before the final twitch of the pulse, they got a look at their Maker and were surprised to find He exists.

If, that is, you believe the kind of claptrap spouted by Abel and his kind.

"Stretch the boy out on the table," suggests a dark amber skull, probably a woman's, whom Thyrla never met in life but found useful in the beginning.

"All of you, shut your jaws!" Thyrla calls angrily. "You're not being any help at all."

"Neither were your grand plans for a garden and a wedding," Uncle points out. "Trapping the girl in a puddle! 'She has to think she has a choice'—as if you've ever given anyone a choice when it comes to your precious hide and your grand scheme to live forever traveling the world!"

"She could live forever," her own babies squeal. "If she sucks up enough years to make herself young and fertile again."

"I'd eat you if I could," Uncle says to the little ones, and they knock together. "What good's one of you been? A year? Two? Ten? Even if you are a witch's spawn. And the boy——"

"The boy would grant two decades," Mother's ribs creak, "*if* he were alive to be harvested."

"And just think of *his* children with *her*," adds Uncle, and everyone knows he means Sanna. "They'd give a lifetime apiece if taken right."

None of the bones remark on the oddity of this conversation, discussing the very reasons and means with which Thyrla harvested *their* lives and added the years *de future* to her own. They don't have many emotions left, only spite, and they love to see her distraught.

"Proud to think of yourself as a time-witch," Uncle observes, "but in the end you've played it too close——*to* the end."

"Tricked me, who tried to teach you," groan Mother's old ribs. "Then undid yerself with your pride."

"*Shut your jawbones!*" Thyrla shouts. "I need to think!"

"Some of us don't have 'em to shut." Auntie waggles her upper teeth, since the lowers were lost years ago along with the mandible.

Thyrla says, "Whatever's left of you, keep it quiet now! This concerns you as well as me, you know. What do you think will happen to you and the castle if I actually grow old and die?"

"Same's as would happen if you left us to travel," Uncle grinds out.

Thyrla pulls a ring from her middle finger and hurls it at his brow. "Quiet!" she roars as brittle chips of Uncle rain down on Peder. "Don't make any more noise unless you have a good idea about what to do next. Or else I'll destroy the whole lot of you."

The bones are so quiet, for a moment, that Thyrla can hear the wedding guests fighting for boats to row across the choppy channel. She hears the sap in the rose vine drying up, the thorns pushing out of the bark and pricking the last bees that still hope for a meal among petals now ground into the stone and bruised from trampling.

No one but her boy was killed. How will the people, her islands' people — parts of whose lives have also been swallowed into her own — remember this day?

Thyrla doesn't realize she's said it aloud till the skulls respond. Then again, she hardly needs to speak to them now; when she's this agitated, her thoughts don't need words.

"You held on to the idea of a miracle too long," Uncle says. "Look at the tinies over your bed." He means the very smallest winter babies.

Thyrla, for once, follows advice. She studies those little skeletons. They are trembling — in fear? Or delight that even the one out of them all that Thyrla chose to raise has now died on his own, without giving her what she wanted? She probably underestimated their capacity for feeling.

"Well," pipes a skull that almost made it to the age of first words. It has its first words now. "No one can ever say you were an exemplary mother."

Fury overtakes the Baroness. She strikes out, yanks off another ring, and hurls it at the skull that spoke. The ring chips a hole in the cheekbone, which isn't good enough to satisfy her, so she picks up a stick and smashes the skull to bits. Then a few of its brothers and sisters for good measure.

That feels good.

Blinking, Thyrla turns back to the child she allowed to live. She wills the special eye to show her the future: Peder's future, what she must do with him now. She can't have kept this boy for seventeen years only to be left with useless flesh.

But looking at him, even with both eyes, she sees . . . nothing. Nothing but what *is*, in this moment. Her beautiful son, dead in a crumpled heap on the table. Painful tears streaming down her face onto her clothes. The air in the chamber already thick with death.

"Peder." She prods him, tries to roll him onto his back. He is a hollow, heavy shell with no life left to suck out and no way inside to breathe life in. She calls his true name into one ear: "Rock."

There's nothing, not even the gentlest shiver of the bones or the castle itself, the plash of blood in the walls of his heart. Only the sounds outside of people rowing and waves striking.

Thyrla's powers have failed her. And for this, she blames Sanna. Long may she rot in her prison.

"Got too greedy, didn't you?" Uncle taunts. "You know the saying: *Eyes were bigger than your stomach.*"

Now Thyrla's eyes see nothing but red. She grabs the stool and hurls it at Uncle, smashing her wisest advisor into thousands of bits. And when she's done with him, she does the same to all of the others, laying about left and right and overhead. It feels like giving a long, satisfying scratch to a wound that has bothered her for years.

She smashes them till her own flesh is bleeding from the fragments of Uncle, Mother, and all the tinies and all the unnamed.

Chapter 83

Truth unsettles.

The last circuit of sun and moon has opened Abel's eyes to sights he doesn't like, truths he wishes were untrue. Is it better to *know* than to labor on oblivious?

One of the truths is this: Abel is a coward.

He sits in a rowboat with a family that reeks of onions and urine (by coincidence, it's the family of that Magnus the fuller who put himself in charge of the church alterations, though Abel pretends he doesn't know this), and he looks back at the great bulk of the castle, rising black against a Virgin-blue sky. He broods.

After the wonderful night with the books and the dreams came those harsh realities of seeing Baroness Thyrla and, worse, Sister Sanna in ways he hadn't seen them before. They are not as holy as he had believed. Sanna might not even qualify for sainthood. The whirling of the petals, the dying of the boy: How is he to make a miracle of this?

Perhaps he isn't sure what a miracle is anymore. Holiness and truth have dislodged from their bedrock and must be . . . reconsidered.

Gripping the little boat's gunwales, Abel can't shake the feeling that he is to blame, that his own words brought on the storm. To everything there is a season, yes, and a time to every purpose under Heaven; but perhaps he should not have said anything about the roses. He tempted the Lord — or Sanna. So Thyrla's vine has now shed its petals and leaves at the appropriate season but not in the appropriate way, all at once and with grave endangerment to the people. Who are now jostling very selfishly, in a very un-Christian manner, for more space, as if the boat is not big enough to hold them all (which it isn't; Tomas misjudged).

"Can you believe . . ." begins more than one utterance. And no, no one can believe, nor wants to.

"Thought the castle were the safest place in the Islands!"

"And so it was, and so it was . . ."

What can Abel tell his parishioners to soothe their concerns? And his own?

He's still trying to come up with the right words when the boat's shallow bottom scrapes against the gravelly mud where the bridge used to sit against the sallet isle. Then, by the force of a crowd united by a single wish to put distance between itself and the castle, Abel is lifted from his seat and onto the land, tripping as he clears the gunwale and ends up with his face pressed into the earth.

Safe, he thinks. *Safe now.*

Whether it's true is anyone's guess.

He grovels in the mud, trying to pray.

"Do you hear that?" It's Maria, wife of Harald the butcher, stopped just beside him. Cocking one ear.

Abel hears. The most marvelous —

"What is it?" Abel asks. His own ears are ringing; his cap has come off, and he feels the breeze in the few hairs left to his pate.

"Singing," says the woman.

"Sound," says Harald.

Abel tilts his head, too. There is something — but he doesn't feel equipped to face anything more than he's done already. He lies, "All I hear is the wind."

What a relief this would be, if it were true.

Temptation is fierce within him.

Chapter 84

Siren song for Lisabet.

*A long time ago, a girl fell in love
and she thought she would die when love left her.
Now she is old
but remembers it well
and she sits by the sea crying,* Take me! Take me, too!
*But the sea remains still.
It promised her nothing.
What do you think happens next?*

—*The Mermaids*

Chapter 85

They are glorious.

Addra and the others—all the young, pretty ones, the ones with beautiful voices and alluring faces—they sing out their hearts to the vanished sun, the rising moon, the land that never moves.

For Sanna, they pledge; *only for her. Rescue! Revenge!*

But there is much, much more in their songs. They sing of love as the landish imagine it; they sing of their own embrace.

These are their subjects, but their meaning lies deeper and is more powerful than any of these. It is a leap of the mind from one thing to another; it is metaphor, in which each element connects to the rest.

They hear the leaping—the humans, like fishes. Like moon-skippers, the landish *flok* rush toward the *marre-minde* songs, and no one is immune. Anyone landish who hears—whether man, woman, or child—runs toward that beautiful noise; anyone who sees, teetering on the edge of an island where green things grow, or the parapet of the castle itself—*anyone*—flings him- or her- or themselves toward Addra and the girls she's collected.

The girls have never felt so powerful, so *necessary*, in their lives.

"It's the greatest miracle of all!" shouts an old landish man adrift on the waves.

While the landish dash toward them and the elders swim, scolding, among the threads of their song, the seavish girls know it:

There is nothing stronger than love.

Even (especially) when the love's only an illusion they've worked with their voices.

anna

This time when I wake, everything in me is aching. Everything feels charred and used, as if there's nothing left from a terrible fire but a scream.

But the point is that I wake. The point of it all is that I do feel, even after the magical spark and the unyielding rocks have done their worst: *I am alive.*

I will keep repeating until I believe it. Until I convince myself to save this life I've been given.

How long have I been *caught* here? Somehow it's important to know that, to have a *number,* a quantity known and counted. This isolation could hold many rotations of the sun. It could already have lasted from full moon to crescent and back. Then again, it might have occupied only the blink of an eye. Time has a way of changing when a person's in danger or a trap, and I'm in the middle of both.

I think of Thyrla's neat little squares in the sand of her table, and how she ordered her numbers to add up the same way every time. When was that? So long ago.

In the darkness, the damp, the heat, there's nothing to carve away at the simple endurance of time. I could be dead for all I know.

Am I dead after all?

Perhaps so, because the question doesn't really frighten me — no more than I'm already afraid.

Is Peder dead? Did I kill him?

How long ago was it?

I have to remind myself, using my aunt Shusha's logic, that time is not what matters now. There's no great difference to me if I've been *caught* for a day or a season. When I am here (wherever here is), I am *not there*, which is another almost-magic truth made by time itself. I can't save Peder. I can't migrate with the *flok* to the Basking Waters and see La reunite with her Ishi. Time is of little use till I restart it by escaping.

But still, I want to know. It is only human, after all, to try to count time — whether to master it or only to know how and why it masters us.

If I do escape, and if I manage to set things to rights with poor Peder, I'll teach myself to understand time-magic.

I will escape.

I am alive.

I start a hum, a bare wisp of a sound, in the back of my throat.

Chapter 87

The people long to be.

Suddenly, what was almost orderly before has become mayhem. None of the boats are coming back now, but that doesn't matter—nobody wants them anymore, not even those who wait in the castle. The boats don't matter except as a way to reach the sweet sound, and swimming seems swifter anyway.

One . . . two . . . a dozen: The people of the Dark Islands jump into the sea, following the sound.

The sound is of voices. Singing. A wonderful chorus, a song with words indistinct. Only one of them—*love*—comes through clearly.

Tomas hears it in his very blood: *love . . . love . . . love . . .*

This music is the third miracle, the greatest one.

Unless, of course, the listener was able to hear Sanna singing her first night here. Not even a choir of angels can compare to her lone voice that night. Which explains,

Tomas reasons, why he alone is immune to the enchantment rolling over the sea toward all the places the people have gathered. He heard her that night. He listened.

What is making that noise? The people cry out the question as they leap into the wet to be one with it.

But most of them don't speak; they simply react. Men and women, children and dogs, they plunge into the waves, trying to reach the source of the ineluctable beauty, the throats and the tones and the magic. Whatever the source, it promises happiness beyond anything ever known before.

It hints—or seems to—that a listener can become music itself. That's surely worth a swim through rough waters.

But Tomas can see that his neighbors have been deceived. The waters are dangerous. Already Harald the butcher flails in the channel to the south. The waves carry him toward the castle as if to dash him against it; then they draw him back out to sea. And his wife and their three young boys. And this is just one family, now out of reach.

No one is unmoved.

Tomas watches, helpless, as even old Father Abel dodders to the edge of the sallet isle and throws himself into the water. His brown robe spreads around him like wide fins, and he lets himself float toward the source.

Tomas catches hold of his mother, his three sisters, his two tiny brothers—taking them in turns, holding on to their clothes, digging his heels into the paving stones, and hooking his ankles around a post. To save them, as he keeps saying.

"There's nothing but death in that song!" he tells them over and over. "This is how our father died!"

But not even Inger Elder cares about his warning. She, who has lived in order to care for her half-orphaned brood, is prepared to leave them motherless as well as fatherless, if only she can reach the music and lose herself in it.

"It is love," she groans, twisting as she tries to free herself from her son's determined clutch.

"It is loss," he says. "Remember Father?" *Remember Sanna.* "Stuff your ears, Mother, and don't look!"

Maria makes a lunge for the water, and Tomas catches the back of her dress in his teeth, biting down as if saving his own life along with hers. She wriggles and screams.

"You're cruel, Tom! I hate you, I hate you, I—"

Her words are quickly lost. Nothing remains but her hunger for music and her own throaty cry.

Chapter 88

The wicked cannot weep.

With her beautiful boy dead on the table and her ossuary family smashed to bits, Thyrla gives in to that which she hates in others.

She weeps. Out of grief.

The tears come from both eyes, the special and the ordinary. Both eyes burn and their pain is equal as each crystal-rough drop wells up, breaks free from its duct, and rolls down a sorrow-lined cheek. She weeps with all her voice, making noise she has never allowed herself—deafening sobs, a wailing that would break the bones if they weren't already destroyed.

There's no Uncle now to mock her, no winter tinies to accuse. All the magic is gone, leaving only Thyrla and the dead and her tears.

So she cries a long time, through the velvet twilight and into the night of a moon just past half.

Here, she thinks. *Here is proof I'm not evil. Wicked people cannot weep.*

Her tears are so shocking, so seismic, that they cause an upheaval in the castle and even the rock from which it was carved. Everything shakes. If the skulls and bones weren't already in shatters, they would be so now. Thyrla hears precious goods breaking—glass, porcelain, majolica—and crumpling: silver and gold candlesticks, goblets, magnificent chests collapsing in on their treasures. And she doesn't care.

Why should she care? Everything she's hoped for is lost. She never got pregnant after Peder; he was her life, her future, and now her future is gone.

In a way, this is a kind of love, though she never would have recognized it as such on those days when, impatient for her own destiny, she considered sucking his years right away and not waiting.

Who would have thought her cruel heart had enough room for affection? She would have torn it from her body if she knew.

She wails, and the castle shudders to the core.

Chapter 89

Every voice is like song.

It is Addra's greatest moment.

Men, boys, women, girls — everyone in the landish *flok* is in love with her. As they flail in the waves, she cannot resist. She shows herself. Beats her tail on the seaskin and rises up like a vision against the night.

The moony landfish swarm to her like sardines, glittering in starlight.

This is the power of the *marreminder*! Take note, Sanna of the magical tricks!

And where is Sanna now? Avoiding Addra, no doubt; jealous of her power.

As are the clan's elders — Shusha and Gurria and Mar and the rest — who are trying to quiet their wayward daughters.

"No more!" says Shusha, swimming among them, grabbing La by the hair. "Not now!"

"Sing the moon song!" Addra insists, and a few faltering voices begin:

Come, play that I am your moon.
Moon dwells in the sea and is happiest there.
Waves lap her with kindness . . .

The last landish folk cannot resist. They paddle like four-legged things toward Addra and her chorus of beautiful voices. They don't seem to understand the song, which promises kindness only for the singers who are playing the moon, not for the people who are sacrificing themselves to it.

"All of you, *stop!*" Gurria orders them.

To the landish, even her voice probably sounds pretty. Instead of *stop*, they hear *dive*, and so they do — into the wildest part of the water, the choppy waves that ring the castle.

Currents pull them down and spit them back up, dead.

"Start a new one!" Addra cries, watching bodies thrash in the water. "Sing the song sung in seashells!"

Her docile friends do as she commands:

We are alone, you and I, in the great shell of sky . . .

But they don't get far before the elders at last manage to silence them. Mar of the Long Reach grabs Addra herself. She yanks on the girl's coppery tail until she can get one arm around her neck, then pulls her deep under the waves, which will *not* lap Addra with kindness.

With Addra gone, the other mer-girls falter and fall

quiet. The soundscape becomes nothing but waves. Waves—
and human cries.

"These people did nothing to you," Shusha declares,
eyes ablaze. "They are women and children and old men."

To those women and children and old men, Shusha is
also beautiful, also a marvel. And any *marreminde's* voice is
like song. They swim toward her now.

"We didn't mean any harm," Frill says in a small
voice. "We only wanted to help Sanna. They're hurting
her—"

"Is that so?" asks Shusha. She has La by one ear and a
different daughter by another. "All these children? These
women?"

La tries: "We thought . . . Addra said . . ."

"Oh, *Addra* said so," Shusha repeats. She gives her
daughters a good shake. "Maybe you just want to enjoy the
sound of your own voices?"

None of the girls will look at the elders. They won't
even look at one another. They are ashamed.

"Even if you killed every landish person in these islands,"
Gurria says, "how would you reach Sanna? A landish house
is twistier than a nautilus shell. Can you imagine yourselves
going up a winding staircase? You'd be stuck and nobody
would be able to get you out."

Of course not. Some of the younger girls start sobbing.

A few landish people are still trying to reach them; others, their fallen fathers and brothers and elderly, are now

floating dead, eyes gazing up into the purpling sky or down into the green depths of the sea.

It has been a terrible mistake. Even Addra must know it, down where Mar is holding her in punishment.

"But still," Frill persists, "somebody has to help Sanna."

Chapter 90

The land lies bare.

The islands around the castle are cleared now. Of people, anyway; the plants and lizards and insects are doing just fine.

Just moments after the frenzy began, bodies are floating facedown. Tomas thinks he recognizes Magnus the fuller, who wanted to build the Chapel of Roses. Rufus the blacksmith, who showed him the spiraling rock of the water garden just this afternoon. And Niels the cobbler, and Lisabet, wife of Ove the farmer. In fact, there's more than one Lisabet in the water, just as there's more than one Tomas and Inger and Maria and Anna. Just not the ones Tomas himself cares about. He will defend his family; he will keep them alive even if it's against their will, until his own dying breath.

They have cried themselves out, his mother and sisters and very young brothers. They lie exhausted, silently mewling, missing the music. Hating him — but that will pass.

Only one voice is left: Old Olla, the beekeeper, who seems to have been immune to the music. When Tomas last looked, she was mourning her bees. Now the survivors have returned to her, and they sit in the curls of her hair as if it's a hive of its own. She is vocalizing to them, gently buzzing, her lids drooping, her expression abstracted, in the silvered light of moon and stars.

"Why, hello!" She notices him watching her. "It's you—how delightful!"

Tomas nods at her, a quick jerk of the chin. She needs looking after. He'll send her home with his mother or keep them all here—he doesn't know yet. He has to find Sanna. And a boat.

He supposes he should worry about Peder and Thyrla; it is his duty to look for them first, to rescue them before anyone else. But duty be damned—Tomas is going to place his heart, that most secret part of it, above his employment.

"Olla!" he calls. "Come sit with my mother. Watch over my family."

"I have honey and nectar and pollen and mead," she says in a singsong. "A little sweetness will take out the sting."

Tomas nods, too tired to respond further. He thinks, *If only there were enough sweetness . . .* He will find his sweetness soon, or die trying.

He walks back toward the castle and under the arch.

anna

My limbs, bent and cramped, need some release.

I hum; it is all I can do. Tunelessly, quietly, so as to disturb as little in my cell as I can.

Somewhere, I hear a bead of water rolling slowly down a wall. It comes to a rough spot and drops through the air to what I think is the floor, into a hollow made by thousands of such beads dripping over more seasons than we have numbers to count.

Drip.

Drip.

And so it will go till I die.

Drip.

It seems an eternity, or only a moment, until the next one:

Drip.

But by the time I hear it, I have my plan.

Chapter 92

A sinner is silenced.

If there has ever been anything saintly in Father Abel, it has vanished. Gone with the voices that spent their last notes on the ocean air and left him floating, one body among many; one of the last few alive.

He is going to die. But somehow, this failure is not upsetting to him; it is simply part of who he is now, in the last moments before death.

Kept afloat by the air inside his robe, rocked on the waves as in a vigorous cradle, Abel reflects on the last few days with Sister Sanna: broken feast to colored roses, altered statue and ultimate beauty of angels singing over the waves.

Abel held out as long as he could, knowing they weren't calling for an old man with freckled skin. But when he felt those voices enfold him as warmly and eagerly as any man might dream of woman, he succumbed. Like so many of his flock, he flung himself into the water, paddling like a dog toward what he hoped would be the source of the song: a grand column of copper, an angel clad like the Magdalene in her own long hair. Beautiful, so beautiful.

And gone. All of them are gone, and the song is over. Nothing left to hear but gulls and waves.

Abel is sinking. Tiny fish nibble at his fingers and heels; he and the ocean are one. He is one with *all* creation. He knows he has experienced something of which men dream all their lives without hope of fulfillment. He also knows that loving that sound so much, and letting it stir his blood in the way that it has, means that every vow he has made in his life as a priest is now broken. He can't be a priest anymore, and if he is not that, what is he?

He is one creature among many in the wide western sea. Drifting into his death, and he doesn't mind a bit.

Is there any chance that Abel might be a martyr, perhaps a saint himself? The answer is simple: *no.*

What's more, he realizes he has misunderstood martyrs all his life. They are creatures of pleasure. They pursue their own desires when they embrace the mortification of flesh, even unto death.

Death (he knows now) is sometimes a gift from the Lord and His angels. Sometimes it is just death.

And so, alone on the sea with his robe heavily wet, Abel allows himself to sink beneath the surface and fall, fall, fall to the place where the angels await.

Chapter 93

Drip.

Seavish blood is as much salt as water, and seavish water creates a change. Waves break ships and stones to splinters; a flood washes over a town and pulls every brick of it into the sea.

Drip.

One tiny, continuous drop can wear away a surface over a thousand suns and moons. And that drop, which is so used to changing what it strikes, can bring about a change in me. It *has* changed me. And will change me again now.

I feel around myself again, careful to make no spark that will send a jolt through me. That small, stubborn drip has probably been going for longer than even a time-witch could calculate—longer, certainly, than the castle has existed. Perhaps longer than the dragon who lives in the rock has been hearing it.

I find it with one fingertip: a hole perfectly shaped for a finger to dip inside. That finger comes up wet. Then it goes down again, and down again, spreading salt water over my legs — at least the parts I can reach.

This will require some time.

After a while I begin a song of making and unmaking. As best as I can, I wet my legs; I rub them hard. I bring on the awful pain of bones and flesh melting, puddling, re-fusing as something else. I bear this pain because I have to. I'd rather be a caught mermaid than a trapped landish girl — this is who I am.

Slowly, scale by scale, my tail re-forms.

This is the eternity, this pain, waiting to take shape.

I am alive.

I will live.

And then — what?

Chapter 94

At the very least, a witness.

Tomas has never thought of himself as a hero, but he's try-ing. Just as he has supported his family with coins from the castle, he'll do what he can to save Sanna.

There must be a reason she vanished. She has to be *somewhere.* And the castle's the first place he'll look.

As he wades through the drift of red rose petals to begin searching in the great hall, Tomas wishes for two things: a friend and a lantern. The half-made moon doesn't shine bright enough for searching inside, for one thing; and for another, it would be so much easier if he had Peder or Kett by his side. Yes, even Peder (whom Tomas will rescue next, if he can) would be a comfort as Tomas embarks on his campaign of heroism. He might have ideas. He might want to help.

Better still, of course, would be Kett, who knows the castle so thoroughly and is such a jolly, kind spirit to be with. But overall, Tomas is glad she's with her mother and brothers and hopes they've gone safely to town. He didn't see her among the bodies in the waves.

The fireplace in the deserted hall is full of embers, and Tomas finds a pewter dish with a few walnuts on a worktable. He dumps the nuts out and scoops up a coal, then adds bits of kindling to make a flame.

"Holy—"

The metal has burned his fingers. He drops it, and then he has to stamp out the ember lest it burn the whole castle down.

A hero doesn't give up. A hero persists. So Tomas kicks over a bench, then kicks and kicks at one leg of it till he has what could be a torch. A bit of linen to wrap the bottom, one end in the fire; Tomas blows and blows till at last he has something to see by.

This is another reason it would be nice to have a companion: Someone should applaud his ingenuity. Then again, it's an obvious solution to an everyday problem, and there's little to congratulate himself on. Yet.

Waving the torch so the light careens over the walls, the tables, the dogs licking out the abandoned dishes, Tomas begins his search.

He will try Thyrla's rooms next. He has a feeling the answer is somewhere in there, though he isn't quite sure of his question just yet. He knows only that he wants to save Sanna—desperately wants to—and if he can't quite manage a rescue, at least he'll be a witness to what's become of her.

anna

My tail is long (though not as long as some others') and strong (though not as strong as some others') and impatient (no one is more impatient than I). As it forms, it fills the last little spaces inside my rock cell, till I'm packed in as tight as a snail in its shell.

My scales flex and shiver. I'm glad that they're back. The pain in my body recedes.

As the pain ebbs away, I wriggle and squeeze, wriggle and squeeze, until most of my tail's wrapped around me. I bend my neck into my chest, I tuck my arms between my breasts, and somehow I find a little extra space near my flukes.

Drip.

Drip.

And *now*, like a heroine in a history song, the kind we sing for ourselves and not for the landmen—*now* I lift my tail about an inch, as high as the Down-Below-Deep will allow me, and I thump it down hard.

The rock shivers. Another water drop lands in its perfect little well, a heartbeat sooner than it might otherwise. Encouraged, I squeeze my body some more, exhale to compress my lungs, and gain a fraction more space.

I thump again. Harder this time.

The rock rumbles.

I hear a crackling somewhere around me — not an ordinary crackling, like the sound of ice breaking in winter, but a *crack!* that sounds like a breath. Another drop falls against the stone.

I realize I am fighting a thing alive. Quite possibly, I'm inside the dragon's belly, and have mistaken the tough sac of the stomach for rock.

Whatever lives protects itself; whatever lives can be changed. This rock will battle me to the death.

So I imagine the mightiest dragon I can: circling me with his jagged teeth, brushing my cheek with his tail. Squeezing me from his belly because I'm an irritation.

I gather up all the strength I have, and all the space I have, and then *up!* go my flukes, and *DOWN*.

This time, the rock cracks apart.

A whirl of water crashes in from above.

I push my way out, and then I'm back in my element — at least till I reach the castle again.

History song.

The sea itself wept.

—The Mermaids

The heart cries with blood.

Thyrla's eyes have cried themselves dry, but her heart is still weeping when the girl comes upon her: Sanna, the witch who cost Thyrla everything. Who killed the boy whom, after all, Thyrla did want—and whom, in his death, she loves.

Sanna comes with the face of vengeance, sizzling with magic, dripping seawater. Still wearing the dress Thyrla sewed, though it has ripped to shreds and barely covers what women hide by instinct. It glitters with green scales—the girl must have transformed herself recently. Rage steams off her, but no matter how she glows, there is always more water, and yet more, streaming from her hair and her clothes, perhaps from her skin itself.

The girl's once-uncertain gait is now strong and forceful, as is her magic. She seems taller. She shrieks and the doors bang open; what remains of the green cloth falls from the walls to the floor and covers the ruined bones, which crunch under her bare feet.

She doesn't stop when she sees Thyrla weeping. She doesn't even pause. She strides straight to the Baroness and grabs her wrists, then swings her upward and over Sanna's own head as if to dash Thyrla against a wall.

"Vicious," she says — panting, wild-haired, reeking of the cell where Thyrla shut her away. "You are worse than no mother at all, and your magic is evil."

Thyrla writhes like a worm. She feels small and helpless and pathetic.

"*You* killed the boy," Thyrla says. If she works up enough anger, she'll be able to fight as she should. "He was mine and I gave him to you, and *you* did it."

At that, surprisingly, Sanna sets Thyrla down. Gently.

"I didn't mean to harm anyone," she says, her green eyes flooding as if rage can switch to grief so quickly. "But *you* meant to harm — oh, Peder, and me, and I'm sure there were plenty of others."

The shards of bone hiss like sand.

Sanna looks up and around the room. Thyrla realizes she can see in the dark every bit as well as Thyrla can, perhaps better. She feels Sanna's eyes fall on the bits of skeleton and skull still attached to the walls.

"What is this place?" Sanna asks.

She sounds stricken, but Thyrla takes no pleasure in her horror.

"This is my family," Thyrla says simply. "This is all of them."

A pause while Sanna stares. A last shard from one of the tinies' skulls *tinks* to the floor.

"Yes, you would have ended up here," Thyrla says. She finds a kind of courage in admitting it — telling someone just how awful she's been. "After I'd sucked the time and the magic out of you and any children you bore."

Thyrla feels a tingle of magic surging again in her veins. *Truth*, she thinks suddenly — *truth is power, too.*

Sanna blinks. She asks, "So you know what I am?"

And Thyrla answers, "I've known all along." Or almost.

Some teeth that she's almost sure once belonged to Uncle gnash at each other now as if to deny it and keep her, at this late moment, honest. But what Thyrla just said is close enough to the truth that Sanna won't catch her lying.

The girl is now bending over Peder, the beautiful corpse on his mother's table. She runs the backs of her fingers down the perfect line of his face, brow to chin. "You never loved him," she accuses — but it comes out more like a question.

"Of course I did!" Thyrla gathers the hard edges of her heart together and tries to seal it shut. "But I'll admit, not the way some people think of love." An artful sigh; perhaps she can regain her powers, re-spin her web. She might almost convince herself once again that she didn't give a snip for the boy. "I *needed* him."

Sanna looks up fast, just in time to see a last fat tear roll from Thyrla's double eye down her withering cheek.

"Trust me," Thyrla says. "Wicked people cannot weep."

It still sounds as if it should be true.

anna

I think it might break me, switching from legs to tail yet again. But my pain is nothing when compared to what Thyrla has done . . . what we *both* did. To Peder.

He lies helpless and empty, like one of the sailors we *marreminder* charm with songs. He was not a great person, but I will be worse if I let him stay dead. He was just starting (so I believe) to be better.

I have to fix it. I have to fix *him.* And there's only one way I know to do it, one person I'm sure can help.

When time is almost all that matters, Thyrla is no longer important—or not very. I can always come back to punish her. For now, I gather Peder in my arms (his limbs stiff, his body already cool) and take a step toward the seaward window.

The floor crunches under my feet. I feel no pain, at least not of a physical kind.

Thyrla screeches. She's guessed what I intend. She's gone utterly mad, and her eyes make sparks that might set fire to the bones and the cloth on the floor. She lunges for me.

I jump to elude her, feel the brush of her fingers in my hair. I manage all of this awkwardly, with the heavy burden of death in my arms.

I run to the window and—still holding tight to Peder—I leap.

I feel Thyrla grabbing at the air behind us. Then she leans out the window and screams. Not words, just rage.

I have less than the span of a heartbeat in which to do all I need. In midair, I sing the words that will restore my tail, and I am seavish again, or almost, by the time we hit the water—just inches from the rock in which she held me captive, the one that's in pieces now.

Down, down, down we go, trailing bubbles from our clothes and hair. There's no risk that Peder's lungs will fill with water; he has of course stopped breathing (though how long ago, I am unsure). We plunge through the seaskin and the churning waves to the relative quiet of the seafloor, where in the darkness I feel my tail finish forming: the relief as the bones fuse, the push of the last scales through my skin, as good as scratching a deep itch.

I was born to be seavish, and seavish I am again.

There's no breath to take down here, but I don't seem

to need it now, either. My flukes push at the water, and with Peder in my arms, I swim.

Sjældent, I think. *Only Sjældent can put this right again.*

I'll return to my teacher for the most important lesson of all.

Chapter 99

Now they watch.

Tomas arrives just in time to see it: Sanna clutching Peder in her arms, standing on the windowsill, jumping. Thyrla diving, trying to catch them.

Instead, Tomas catches Thyrla. He grabs a handful of hair in one hand, keeping the torch in his other, and he hauls her back in. At least he can do that much.

Together, still struggling, Tomas and Thyrla watch Sanna and Peder plunge feet first into the sea. Tomas feels sick.

She never needed him to rescue her.

She is rescuing Peder.

It was a marriage for love after all.

• Chapter 100 •

anna

Funny, odd, strange: to find again how easy it is, how quick the journey between landish castle and seavish crags. I've done a lot of living since I first made it, things I never expected to do. I even allowed the boy now dead in my arms to kiss me, after the landish fashion, and I felt his warmth and tasted his bitterness.

I saw his mother kiss him, too, during the blood-red storm. I'm no longer certain whether she meant to save his life for himself or swallow the last of it up into hers.

Thyrla is a question to be answered later. For now, I dive down to Sjældent's crag.

I find her with my father. They are asleep, and the rest of the *flok*'s somewhere else; perhaps they've already left on migration. I wake Father and gesture to him to bring the witch. Up from the depths we swim side by side, towing our burdens of ancient witch and fresh corpse.

In the air near the Ringstone, Father is not so keen to keep holding Sjældent, but he hangs on to her hair with one hand and embraces me with the other.

"We thought we had lost you," he says. "Your songs . . ."

"I sang when I could," I say. It is a greater relief than I can express, knowing I have a parent who cares whether I live, die, or simply disappear.

He opens his mouth to ask questions, but I have to say, "There's no time. I don't know how long Peder's been dead, and I need Sjældent's help to cure him."

"To cure him from *death?*" Father asks. He shakes his shaggy blond head, and water drops go flying.

(How I've missed the sea and my clan! How glad I am to be out of the castle!)

I nod. "I think it's possible, using not just a curative spell but the magic of making and unmaking. I do know I can't do it by myself. I need Sjældent."

Through all of this, Sjældent has slept as if dead herself. Father hoists her onto the rocks, and together we shake the old witch back to consciousness.

Why out of all creation did ye save this one? I expect her to ask, seeing Peder.

She doesn't ask.

"Ye're here," she croaks instead, squinting at me in the moonlight. "At last."

I almost laugh because it's so *good* to be with her again, irascible as she is.

She turns her head to the side and sees Peder. "And ye brought —"

"He needs your help," I interrupt. "And fast." Seeing Peder so stiff, his colors and his beauty fading, has given me new energy. I must undo the terrible thing I did to him.

"My help, indeed! My help!" She crows like a landish bird. It's a noise beyond her usual cackle — it sounds . . . actually joyful. "When ye've finally brought me the one thing I asked for all along — ye'll get all the help ye need after this! Of course, I expected him in summat better condition."

She reaches for Peder, groping along the rock with gnarled fingers.

I feel my heart sinking through my belly, to a private version of Down-Below-Deep where there's nothing but sorrow and fear.

"All this time," I say, "Peder was the *thing* you wanted me to bring back to you?"

Sjældent's hand reaches his. She says, "He's the everagain."

Clutching Peder's hand, she hisses — and the force of her magic hurls Father and me back into the water.

Chapter 101

You can't blame a shark.

"You can't blame a shark for catching a fish," Addra signs — underwater, on the seabed, where her luminous skin and tail are all the light she needs to make her point. "You can't blame her for eating it, either. That's her nature."

The elders who have gathered the young girls for punishment, under the sea where the last of the landish can't hunt them — they frown as one being, and their arms trace the patterns that make shame and reproof.

A few of the more tender girls, such as Frill, are weeping. They know now that they were wrong to trust Addra.

But how wonderful it felt to follow her, to sing and show themselves to people who would never see them otherwise! To know that their songs could compel not just the men who are forever slaves to their charm, but women and children and all!

Shusha the Logical signs back to Addra, to all of the girls: "It is not our nature to harm the helpless."

With that, all of the culprits, except Addra herself, feel their bones ache.

"Not so helpless," signs Addra, emphatically. Even at this moment, she admires the way her own white flesh moves through the water, the grace of her webbed fingers, the light of her shimmering scales. No one would call her helpless, even if she were *caught* in a net being hauled on deck so the landmen could take their pleasure with her.

She makes this point, rather eloquently in her own opinion: "These northern people have harmed our kind for as long as we've known them. Men don't grow up to attack unless they are taught that they may."

Even Shusha the Logical has to nod at that.

Addra presses her point: "We wouldn't sing come-hithers to the folk who are kind to us. And we wouldn't have gone today if Sanna hadn't needed us."

The girls feel stronger at that, proud of what they did, protecting one of their own. They may have teased and shunned Sanna at one time, but now that she might be lost, she's a friend.

"*Did* you manage to free her?" asks Gurria One Arm. "Did you manage to do anything more than destroy a few dozen innocent people?"

Addra signs indignantly: "*Innocent*—"

And Pippa, who was not part of the *marreminde* chorus,

signs at the same time: "Intentions were good, though the outcome was wrong."

The elders look over their daughters and nieces, searching their faces for contrition. Pippa is rising even further in their esteem; she is practical and smart beyond her years, likely to become an elder herself.

All that the other girls show is their grief—mostly at being taken to task in this way. If no one were scolding, they'd be giddy with triumph.

Addra signs, "Where are Bjarl and Sjældent? If we ask them, they'll surely agree we were right to try to save Sanna."

This idea sinks in most painfully, especially since the elders are aware that those two haven't always been treated as well as they deserve.

Dizzy Frill follows up: "Shouldn't they be with us now? Maybe they should choose our punishment."

The elders hold still for a moment, perplexed.

Addra is sure that she's won the quarrel. She throws her head back and exhales: a thousand bubbles dancing up to the seaskin.

anna

How foolish have I been, to have fallen into the schemes of not just one but two witches?

I may have been leery of Thyrla, but I actually trusted Sjældent because I so longed to learn the magic I needed. I never suspected her magic would make me harm the one thing, the one *person*, she wanted me to bring her from the land . . .

But I can't waste any more time being mad at myself. I have to pull together everything I know; I'll need every last scrap of magic, every bit of understanding of a world both seavish and landish, if I'm going to undo the harm I've done.

I don't even know the half of that harm yet—it will come later.

After the first moment of horror, I take a deep breath for strength. As deep as I can manage, anyway; something is squeezing my lungs. I think that it's Sjældent's magic. I feel the telltale crackle as she gropes her way over Peder's body, hoisting herself atop him as if to entwine in the act of mating. Somehow the fact that he's dead doesn't bother her at all; she must have some powerful magic that can exploit him even in this condition.

Father and I aren't (of course) helping her now, but she has a power that comes from madness, or else from being at the very end of life and unwilling to let go.

I use my breath to say, "Sjældent, he's not for you to take!"

I try to pull her off him. She shivers, and I'm flung into the water.

Father, meanwhile, is frozen still. Truly frozen—the water radiating from him is cold, and crystals of ice glitter in his hair and his beard. Ice is forming, too, in the water around his skin.

"Sjældent, is this why you taught me your magic?" I call from the water, approaching the rock again. "So I would help you to kill others?" My strength of moments ago is now almost gone. Sjældent has hexed me—*me*, the girl as close to a daughter as she's ever come.

"Were you *ever* going to help me find Lisabet?" I manage to reach far above my head and grab hold of a jutting rock. I think I might be able to distract her by talking about things other than Peder and what she plans to do to him.

But Sjældent is too clever to be tricked. She keeps busy with Peder's corpse, arranging it in some way known only to her (and perhaps Thyrla). She strokes his hair and licks his ears, all the while worming her tail around his feet, then his calves, and up to his —

The cool light of the half-moon silvers us all, but Peder's skin glows an unnatural white, as if he's made of the stones found to the south of here from which the landish like to carve statues and bowls.

"Sjældent!" I cry. Breath is coming hard. "Did you ever care about me?"

At that, she stops. I expect a squint and a cackle, but I get neither one.

"'Course I did," she says. "Ye were always the one who'd help me live another round. I knew it from the moment I pulled ye from your mother."

The rock breaks off in my hand, and I sink. *She has been planning this since I was born. She always expected that somehow I'd give her the everagain she wanted. And it turns out to be Peder, whom Thyrla raised for this very purpose: giving more life.*

In fact, for a moment, I think I feel Sjældent's hands around both the me who is being born and the me who imagines herself as Lisabet. Those crooked fingers are grasping and pulling, ripping the baby (me) out of the mother I imagine.

But I can't let the old witch distract me, either, not if Peder is going to have any chance of living. I drag myself back into my body and swim for the rock, where I swing a little and manage to find another handhold. I drag myself up another inch, scraping breasts and belly as I go.

I try to shame her. "But the *flok* —"

"Never did me a single kindness, 'cept ye and yer father." I can't see her now, but I hear her ripping Peder's clothes. "And those ye two did out of yer own self-interest."

"That isn't true!" I exclaim—but is it?

Again, I have to pull myself back *into* myself. I say, "You have lived long, you have seen much, and you will be—"

"Oh, spare me that pap from the death rattle. I've lived longer than any of yer like can reckon, and I don't care much for what I've seen."

"Then why"—I have to ask it—"do you want to live longer?"

Now I get the cackle. It helps to cover the noise of my skin and scales scraping as I pull farther onto the rocks.

Sjældent says, "Well, it's all there is *to* want, isn't it? Life. We get plenty of time to find out what it is to be dead. There's not so much time to feel what it's like to be alive, and I haven't found the pleasure in it as of yet. Which I won't do at all, 'less I live another life through."

There. I'm on the rock now, and I can move toward her. Softly, like a snake.

"Then why Peder?" I ask, trying to throw my voice to the waves (using a trick she herself taught me) so she won't know I'm nearly upon her. "How did you know to send me for him?"

She coughs, then turns it into another one of those cackles. "Pleasure," she says, "and magic. I need a creature with both in its veins. Ye're fine on the magic, but ye aren't much of a one for pleasure. And I might ask ye the very same question: Why, out of all the lives ye and the others have seen taken through song — which include a couple-score lives tonight — do ye choose this one to save?"

I don't have an answer. Why Peder, indeed? I don't think much of him as a person, and I don't believe he loved me as I'd want to be loved. But he did show me some kind of affection. There was that kiss after the first song he sang for me . . . In a motherless way, he's my brother. He's one of my kind.

"I didn't want to hurt him," I say, softly, sliding forward with my tail. "I didn't want to hurt anyone. I want to find my mother, and not to taint the quest by harming someone else."

It's as close to the entire truth as I can sort out in the moment.

I see Sjældent and Peder clearly now. She's stripped him nearly naked, so he's clothed only on the arms and from the middle thigh down. His clothes look almost like a merman's tail, peeled away and shoved down as they are.

Sjældent is licking her fingers and making marks on Peder's naked skin — his forehead, chest, shoulders, hips. At first her movements look like the gesture the landish make for holiness (brow, chest, shoulder, shoulder), but there's nothing holy in what she is doing. I watch, gathering strength — and memorizing her gestures, because I am still her apprentice. I still believe I can come out of this situation and do something good for the people.

My people. The seavish *and* the landish.

I'm struck with a sudden realization, something I hadn't noticed before. "You mentioned a couple-score lives. What happened?"

But now she's too wrapped up in her work, or rapturous, to answer. Perhaps she doesn't even hear me. She has pulled herself completely onto Peder's body and lies chest to chest with him, her lips just over his lips. Her parts on his parts, as if she expects to make a baby.

The baby (if there is a baby) will be Sjældent, as she steals what life and magic are left inside Peder and makes herself into an everagain.

I grab another handhold and slither an inch or two closer. I could almost reach them now . . .

It hurts — not just the scraping along the rock, but the pressure against Sjældent's magic. I'm running into a bubble of deathly interdiction that she's cast over herself and Peder. The closer I come, the more it stings. It attacks everything in me, till almost all I can think is *pain pain pain pain pain.*

And yet, a tiny part of my mind speculates: *Sjældent must be a stronger witch than Thyrla. Thyrla couldn't do anything with Peder's body dead, but Sjældent thinks she can use it.*

And: *Sjældent said once that I might have magic stronger than her own.*

That memory gives me all I need. I ram against the bubble of magic, and I force my way in till it bursts.

Chapter 103

What lies beyond memory.

It is a marvel to Bjarl, what his daughter is doing. (It's also a marvel that he can even see and hear it, given that the old witch froze him to the marrow.) Sanna, the girl her cousins called Lonely and Meek, is beguiling the great Sjældent herself. And she's as strong of body as she is of mind, slinking along the rock to save that landish boy whose life, to most of their kind, would not seem worth keeping. After all they have lived, and all that Sjældent made them forget, Sanna's strength remains.

Why not give Peder to the witch and see what else Sanna might learn from her? The idea never seems to occur to Sanna.

Bjarl can't help but wonder (as his brain and heart slowly turn icy themselves) whether he could have saved his beloved. Who isn't dead, as far as he knows—but who never was given the option of changing to seavish form and living with him and their daughter.

Her name, he remembers, was Lisabet.

He remembers, also, some parts of that night long forgotten. How happy he was, how proud, to hold baby Sanna in his arms, with her wee mouth screaming, fists flying, tail beating the air.

"Hungry, she is," Sjældent said, and of course Lisabet must have reached for her daughter.

But there was Shusha, Bjarl's sister, who was already nursing a baby called La and whose breast was ready for another. There seemed never to be a question of giving Sanna to Lisabet to nurse; her bright, pale head fit neatly next to La's dark one, and the milk (Bjarl supposes) helped keep her seavish.

Empty-armed, Bjarl embraced Lisabet once more while the old witch worked between the girl's legs.

"No one in your *flok* will know about tonight," he whispered into Lisabet's hair, damp with sweat.

"They'll know I had a baby," she said, weak from the work of birthing his child. "They've known for months it would happen."

Bjarl didn't know what to do about that. "Sjældent?" he asked.

Still working on Lisabet's wound, grunting out the magic that would seal her flesh tight, Sjældent said, "I'll make 'em forget, same as our people. Yer landish family will never think to ask—ye'll be a virgin again." She paused to rub her nose with the back of one hand. "Ye'll think yerself virgin as well, after the magic I work on us all."

418

Lisabet stiffened in Bjarl's embrace. "I don't want that! I don't want to forget anything!"

Already Bjarl's body ached with the loss. He begged Sjældent, "Don't take all our memories, please . . ."

"Ye, my boy"—Sjældent squinted at him—"ye lost the right to choose memories when ye made a baby with this one." She slapped Lisabet's thigh for emphasis.

Bjarl begged, "Let us remember *something*—"

"Not yer choice," Sjældent said. Then, without warning, she leaned back on her tail and spoke the magic that would cause forgetting to ripple over land and sea alike.

It was such a strong spell that even now, as his heart and mind give a last throb before freezing entirely, Bjarl can't remember Lisabet's face, or imagine how she made it—virgin again—back to her family. All he remembers is sorrow (over her) and joy (over Sanna). And he's grateful to have even a little bit of the past that he couldn't recall before.

He has lost so much that was precious. But he has retained what matters most: the girl who just might be about to best the old witch, or be killed by her, while Bjarl looks helplessly on. His daughter; his and Lisabet's.

anna

My father is a plank of floating ice when I attack the old witch. He might die, too, if I don't manage to work wonders now.

After I break through the bubble of magic that's meant to keep me out, I fling myself across Peder's body — which means shoving Sjældent off it. She rolls over the rocks with a wail and ends up facedown, her neck hole exposed and crusted with barnacles no one has scraped. The bottom of her tail still has hold of Peder's ankles; it's all that's keeping her above water.

She looks pitiful, and small, and tender. I feel my insides melt in pity. I'm tempted to show her mercy — take Peder from her, yes, and swim him back to the land and the castle, but leave Sjældent alone for nature to take its course. There's a dignity to death when it comes of old age.

She won't let me give her that. She intends to fight till there's nothing left of her or Peder or me, if she can't get what she wants. With a horrible shriek, she rises up on her tail, still attached to Peder. Her skin sparks and the shriek becomes fire.

She blows her flames at me, as if to burn away all the magic she's taught me.

And I can't let her do that. I rise up, too (Peder's ribs cracking under my weight), and I summon the magic of the elements.

I echo her shriek. I turn her flames back on herself.

In the end, I've chosen well. Sjældent is old, and her body is dry. In the wink of an eye, it's blazing brighter than any fire I've seen before. Its light turns the moon orange.

Sjældent shrugs off the first flames, but there are too many, and they are too strong. She breathed spite at me, and spite hurtles back many times more intense, and it burns brighter the longer it lasts.

The element of time—most powerful of all—is fighting for me. Every way I add up the elements, I get the same sum: Myself. And Peder. And Father.

For a moment, Sjældent is a pillar of fire that pierces Ringstone and bolts it to the moon. And then she is . . .

Nothing.

Or *almost* nothing. Just a speck of light that wavers in a nimbus of luminous air; and then the softest wisp of ash, which lands on the seaskin and glitters a half breath before sinking down to join with the sand.

And then quiet. And dark.

anna

It isn't easy to decide what comes next. For a moment, Father and I gaze at each other through the empty space that used to be Sjældent.

As her last magic fades, Father unfreezes, with a soft *ptink!* sound as each ice crystal bursts and becomes water again.

So Father will survive Sjældent. What of Peder? Can he survive me? Can I heal even death?

I start with some questions. "How long was I gone?"

Father's beard crackles, but only with ice and not magic, when he speaks. "Four suns, three moons."

Four suns. That means my time inside the rock can't have lasted long at all. Which means, in turn, that Peder has been dead much less than a day.

This gives me hope; I think that maybe I can bring him back to his element and his life after all. Self-serving as she was, Sjældent taught me well, and surely there's something I know that can work. If the old witch could suck the life out of a dead boy, then I must be able to figure how to put more life back in.

Or so I tell myself.

As I did earlier in the evening, I lay the backs of my fingers (webbing translucent in moonlight) against Peder's cheek. Now that I know he's been dead such a short while, I think I feel a little purr of life deep inside. Maybe Sjældent coaxed it back to him. Maybe that's all I need.

Bjarl pulls himself onto the rock, still so cold that his joints pop as he moves.

I embrace him, my living father instead of my dead betrothed. I rub his back and arms to help his blood heat itself again. I am exhausted. But I cannot stop now.

"What's happened since I left?" I ask. "Where is the rest of the clan?"

Chapter 106

The sweetness swallows the sting.

By the now-quiet waters of high tide, still sprinkled with corpses, Inger Elder and her children doze in exhaustion. Gray clouds wisp over the sky; the ground beneath them rumbles. A storm is coming, but Inger is too tired to move.

Until the two little boys, barely out of diapers, begin fussing. It's been too long since they've eaten, too long since they saw Tomas. Inger's heart prickles with worry.

"I don't know what to do," she murmurs, more to herself than to any of them.

To her surprise, there's an answer.

"Oh, it's you!" Old Olla is cooing to the boys. "And you! How nice!"

Inger had all but forgotten her — but she is their salvation. She has a jar of new honey in her drawstring pocket, and she is already dipping her fingers in the stuff, then dabbing the little boys' mouths.

They feed hungrily. "Baby beelings," Olla says indulgently.

When she sees Inger watching her, Olla dips back into the jar and brings up a small honeycomb. "Yours."

Inger puts it on her tongue, licking her fingers, and lets it dissolve. It is the purest, sweetest mouthful she's ever had. It sticks her soul back together like a most delicious glue.

"A little sweet takes out the sting," Olla observes.

The bees in her hair buzz.

anna

Father has explained everything. The songs, Addra's display of herself, the frenzy for boats and for diving toward the music even when it was impossible to reach. In short, the worst that I've seen between *marreminder* and landmen, this time with women and children as well.

The story sickens me. "All those people who came to the wedding died?"

"I don't think anyone meant it to happen," he says. "Not even Addra. They set out to rescue you, not to hurt the landish."

I shudder. Addra. So beautiful, so selfish. I doubt she had any scruples where the people were concerned. She has always loved the sound of her own voice and the sight of her own face.

I say as much to Father, and he looks sad. "Maybe," he admits. "But your cousins and other age-mates, they went to the castle for you. They did what our people always do. They sang till the landish destroyed themselves."

"Did *everyone* die?" I ask again. "Everyone from the town?"

"I believe," he says cautiously, "that everyone near the castle did follow the song. But there were people left back in town—their families and such—who didn't hear it. And probably some who got home before the songs started."

I think of Tomas. Kett. Their families. And so many others, dead (ultimately) because I was doom-bent on finding my mother.

I touch Peder's face again and see in him all the faces of all Dark Moon Harbor's dead. Those who drowned will be puffy and swollen, and all of them must wear the dead look of surprise. Absolutely no one expects death to be what it is.

I breathe in deep and feel a thousand hearts broken on land.

I say, "I have to go back."

Father's confused. "To save this boy?"

"At the very least."

The wind shifts, and I hear a distant whistle as it blows into the church bell. I am beginning to get an idea.

"Come with me?" I ask Father.

We take hold of Peder's arms, and we dive in to swim for the town.

anna

A long time ago, when Sjældent was training me in curative magic, she said, "Each one of us is ruled by an element, and we can be healed by that element, too."

For example, a *marreminde* who cuts her hand can be mended with seawater, sea leaves, perhaps the ink of a squid. Peder is a landish boy, and he was hurt by seavish magic working through a landish vine.

Where in these islands will we find the *most* landish place in which to magick him back to life? There is a place, and it is not the castle where his mother raised him like a goose with its feet nailed to the floor. No, the greatest concentration of landishness is in wood and stone and urine and faith: the church, which is also the center of landish magic, and of the faith in that invisible father who looks over them all.

The trouble is that *my* father cannot go there with me.

He and I work together, beating tails against the seaskin, to hoist Peder onto a dock between jostling herring boats. Then, as we rest floating on our backs, I tell him my plan.

"You mean the place at the top of the hill?" He's understandably uneasy. The moon has swung past its midpoint and Peder's body is stiff as ice. He's a lot for one tired girl to manage.

"It's not a steep hill," I say, trying to stir courage into myself. "These islands are flat." I am grateful for that; in my life I've seen hills that rise straight from the ocean floor — hills Sjældent ordered me to climb as part of my training with legs.

Sjældent. I feel a pang, missing her. Or rather, I miss what I thought she was. And I hate that (however inadvertently, however much she deserved it) I had to kill her.

Gamely, Father pulls himself onto the dock and sits dripping over its splinters. I'm still in the water, and I force my arms and tail to lift me as well.

"Can you change me when you change yourself?" Father asks, his voice so soft I can barely hear him. "I can't manage a hill with a tail, but with legs . . ."

I suspect he's thinking of Lisabet and wishing he'd had the magic to make himself a body like hers back when they were lovers.

"Father, no." I touch my brow with my fingers in our silent language for thanks. "You are very dear — *very dear* — to think of going with me, but I can't let you. It takes a long time to learn to walk, and I'm not even sure I

have the magic to give legs to you. I might turn you into"—
I shudder—"some kind of quarter-creature, who's neither
landish nor seavish and entirely unable to move."

I think, for example, of the little lizard that Thyrla conjured on my first day in the islands—and then how she
crushed him and left his pink innards gaping for the flies.

Father says, "I'll risk it. For you."

I draw a deep breath. I have to acknowledge the worst,
what he's trying to protect me from. I begin, "If the
townspeople see us, if they know what we are . . ."

I don't need to finish, but he does it for me: ". . . they
will kill us because our kind has killed some of theirs."

"Exactly." I look away from the town, toward the bay
and the open sea. My people will be leaving on their migration today; of that I am sure. The elders must be arranging
it now—who will tow the nets of treasure, who will look
after the old and the young.

He says, "Without you, I don't want—"

I stop him before he can finish. "Father, you have to go
back to the clan. They need you; they can't lose both of us.
Go with them when they leave. Don't wait for me."

"I'm coming," he insists. "Somehow."

This is the very first time I defy him entirely, the first
time I take my place as a woman and head of the family:
"You can't do that without my magic, and I won't work it
for you. Tell the others what happened to Sjældent. Tell
them what I'm doing. Ask them to help, or try to."

I've never felt so set apart as in this moment, when I ask

Father to explain to my clan and my *flok* that I'm risking my life to save a landish boy.

"We need you," he says.

"I know. I'm the only witch left."

"Not just for your magic. *We love you.*"

Hearing this, my heart both swells and aches. This time it's Father's brow I touch, and when I release, I shake my fingers like a school of fish until they rest on Peder's chest.

"You are a wonderful father," I say. "If I'm able to return, I'll never ask to seek Lisabet again."

"But you must seek her!" His voice and his body radiate heat. "It's the quest—the *question*—that gives you such powerful gifts. Sjældent told me so."

Sjældent again. We always return to her, or always for now, at least. She did live long, and she did see much, and she will certainly be remembered. But in time that memory will become the tiniest atom of light, as she herself became in the end, and hers will be a benevolent name invoked in the songs of our *flok*.

Powerful gifts.

The wind shivers through the bell in the church tower.

I have another idea.

"Father," I say excitedly, "please tell the elders—and Addra, and everyone else who sang—to find the dead and bring their bodies to town and lay them here." I pat the plank of the dock. "Landish people set great store by returning each other to the earth. We can at least offer that much to them."

Maybe more — but I'm only beginning to imagine what that might be.

"Ah." I can almost hear Father's thoughts, which are of Lisabet lying in the ground. But now that I've given him a task beyond a goodbye, he is ready to act.

"I'll tell them to do it fast," he says. "Before the sun rises."

"Yes, do that."

Before I begin the magic, yet again, to switch my body to another element, I watch him swim away.

Maybe I never really needed a mother, I think. *I always had Bjarl.*

• Chapter 109 •

He wants to feed her soup.

That night, anyone who's still awake — keeping watch for a loved one who vanished, awaiting the inevitable news — all of Dark Moon Harbor, in fact, is listening for the tread of a return. And watching through cracks in the shutters. And praying to the Lord, the Virgin, the Son, and the Spirit that the lost ones will be brought home.

As a reward, they see something remarkable, something they never even dreamed of.

It's Sanna. The young holy woman with the face of an angel and the flesh of a —

Yes, flesh. They see it: Head to toe, naked. Walking up the broad street in the moonlight with the Baroness's son in her arms. Stars sparking in her hair, pale eyes beaming green light before them, marking a path that goes all the way to Our Lady of the Sea.

The people know they should turn away. They aren't supposed to see this; even married couples hardly look at each other naked in this cold, shame-riddled town. But the sight is too marvelous to ignore.

It seems, also, to be an invitation. Sanna's nudity summons them to leave their homes and follow her. But who would actually dare to do it? She is so far removed from their dull little lives, it would take enormous courage to follow her. They are clearly different people, or at least *she* is different, from the day on which they scurried from their corners to ask her blessing. She is not only holy now; she is also terrifying.

The street clicks with the sounds of latches being raised and bolts unshot. A few heads dare to poke out from the windows, where the air is abuzz and dizzy-making.

Does Sanna hear them? Does she know they are there?

Those are Tomas's greatest questions as he opens the window for his mother and sisters and brothers and Old Olla. He left Thyrla in the castle and brought his family here to keep them safe, to make sure they don't throw themselves into the sea; now he might need to keep them from following Sanna someplace too rare for them. *Does she know we are here?*

Of course, he's grateful she's alive when so many have died. Including Peder.

Watching her, Tomas feels an intense desire, but not one he's ever felt before. He wants to rush forward with a blanket and cover her nakedness, take her home and feed her . . . feed her . . . soup? Something warm and hearty.

Ridiculous.

It's impossible to imagine what Tomas might do with Sanna if he saved her, because he doesn't need to save her. So he doesn't try. He simply tells his mother to stay home. He is the only one of the townspeople who dares to follow Sanna wherever it is she's going.

He hears the townsfolk sighing as he steps into the street.

"Ah, there's Tomas. There's our lad."

"He'll make sure it all turns out in the end."

"For both himself and the girl."

"And for the Baroness's boy."

Tomas doesn't know where this confidence in him and his abilities comes, unless it is the product of simple accumulation: his years in the castle, where he was nothing but a lackey called Chicken Legs.

Nonetheless, carrying the hopes of his family and neighbors on his skinny shoulders, he turns uphill toward the church. Sanna's steps leave a pale green shimmer with each strike of her foot against the earth; Tomas places his feet exactly where hers have been, and he climbs the hill after her.

That's our lad!

anna

That boy is following me. Tomas, who seemed so kind during my time in the castle. And so devoted to Peder . . . He must be following to make sure I don't hurt Thyrla's son.

His presence makes me anxious. And also, somehow, comforted; I am not going through all this alone. He has no magic to offer, but he does understand the land and the faith here. He will help me.

The moon slants in such a way as to make the church glow blue-white as we approach. A storm is coming. The wind keeps up and gets stronger, until I have to shut my ears as much as I can to the high whistle of the hanging bell, a sound that might drive dolphins mad with its pitch.

Perhaps it's a message from the element of air itself? *Stay away, stay away* . . .

If that's the case, I'm not going to heed it. I *will* save Peder; I will not be the murderer of an innocent boy. In a way—I realize it to my surprise—I do love him, even if only because his mother does not. Pity might be a kind of love.

The church's wide front doors are locked. Of course. They buzz when I touch them, though it's impossible for me to tell whether it's with Thyrla's magic or someone else's. Anyway, it's easier to look for a weaker spot through which to enter. And I find it on the northern side, where (as Peder and Tomas described it) the people zealously pounded a hole into the wall in order to build something else on.

A chapel, I remember. *A place to honor the Miracle of the Roses.*

How much has changed since I arrived! I wonder if even Father Abel still thinks of what happened as a miracle. He who told me it is better to marry than to burn—I hope he's not among the landish dead, but it seems unlikely that even he could resist the lust my sweet-throated cousins are used to stirring in landish men's loins.

So thinking, I step over a toothlike bit of rock that has remained from the demolition—and from much further back in time than that, I believe; it vibrates with a very old magic. And then Peder and I are inside the church, where the light comes only from that hole through which we just stepped. I can see that the place is totally empty, nothing but the stone altar too heavy to move and the paintings on the walls, which twist eerily in the dark.

There's no sign of the statue.

I didn't realize until this moment that I was counting on Their Lady to help me. I know she's as wooden as the roof beams, painted with chalk and egg and oil and urine, but she is one of those objects so dear to landish people that they soak up a kind of magic from the reverence. I suppose I thought I could lay Peder at her feet and (silly as it sounds when I describe it) ask her for help and even get it. But she's not a witch. She's not even a person.

A gentle sound in the space reserved for the chapel: Tomas is stepping over the rock tooth in exactly the place I crossed.

I turn to him, my arms still full of Peder. I feel tears swelling in my eyes, and I blink them away as fast as I can.

"He's dead," I say. My voice sounds strange, echoing in this empty shell of a church. "I didn't intend it."

"Of course you didn't," Tomas says.

His voice is so kind, so understanding, so full of faith in me, that I sink to the floor sobbing. I lay Peder down as carefully as I can, though he's long past the need for a delicate hand.

"I'm going to try to fix him," I say. "I *want* to fix him."

"I know you do."

I hear Tomas coming close. I expect him to take Peder from me, claim him for the Baroness — with the best and most innocent intentions; I don't think he knows (who would guess it?) what Thyrla had planned for her son.

Thyrla. I'll have to do something about her . . .

Tomas surprises me. He crouches down and puts his arms around me, hugs me to his chest. My shoulder against his heart, which is thudding so strong.

He smells of earth and sweat and onions, the usual landish smells, but something else as well. Sweetness. Is it possible that good intentions have an odor on land? If so, that's what I'm picking up from Tomas. Along with a spreading warmth and a kind of tingle that is almost, but not quite, the tingle of magic.

I realize suddenly that I'm naked beneath my long hair; the last shred of the dress Thyrla sewed for me fell away long ago. But I'm not embarrassed and neither is Tomas.

I lean forward into his arms. My tears fall on him and on Peder, also on myself.

For a moment, we are perfect together, though it is a perfection of sorrow rather than joy.

Chapter 111

A change in the bed of Magnus the fuller.

Our Lady of the Sea smiles at the ceiling, swathed as it is in spiders' webs and an owl's messy nest. Her eyes don't blink and they don't see, or else they see everything, uneven as they are.

No one in the family knows it, not right away, but Our Lady is vibrating deep inside. And the bundle in her arms starts forming itself into something new.

anna

When a people makes its home in the sea, it has little choice as to how to preserve its past. We have spoken words — songs, expressions, incantations. One of these is a common saying: *Fire leaves no history; air ever forgets; water washes away; land holds on too long.*

This is a statement about time. It means that whatever happened today, or in suns and moons past, is somehow preserved in the land. And more than that: Whatever has happened in the church, perhaps over hundreds of years, is lingering in the paint, the plaster, the stones on which it was founded.

After a long moment in which I allow myself to be comforted in Tomas's arms, my heart fortified by his compassion, I ask, "What is this place?"

He sounds genuinely surprised. "It's the Church of Our Lady of the Sea." As if I might have forgotten.

"I mean, what was it before?" I touch the floor, worn slick from so many feet walking and standing on it, as regularly as the tides that govern the ocean.

Tomas's hand follows mine and rests palm-down on the floor, just inches away from Peder's lifeless body. "I think it was some kind of pagan place of worship," he says slowly. "A long time ago. My father told me once. He pointed at the rocks that run along the soil level and showed me that they're in the shape of a boat. He said the people who were here before us used to worship many gods, instead of just the one, and that their churches were laid out like ships that would bring them to their Heaven at the end of time. There's another place like this on one of the forest islands. Some rocks in the shape of a ship, I mean—there's no other church with walls and all."

I consider this history. I put both palms flat on the rock, and I think I feel a pulse, a skipping in the ground below the present church.

Land holds on too long.

Perhaps just long enough for what I need.

"This floor is new." I voice my thoughts as a kind of encouragement to myself. It helps the process of logic that I learned from Aunt Shusha. "New within a few life spans, at least. Before that, it was earth. Strawberries and daisies."

"Is that going to help Peder?" Tomas asks.

I frown, though he can't see it. "Maybe . . . I think the floor can be a sort of conduit between the old stones. Like blood, or sap in a tree. There's magic in several layers here. Some of it goes very far back."

Tomas doesn't seem to think this idea so strange, though even my clanswomen—so much more accustomed to magic that they don't think it comes from a single entity—might mock me for what I'm saying.

"Will it help?" he asks again. Like all landish people, he likes his answers plain.

"I think so."

I leave the comfort of Tomas's arms and lie down next to Peder with my body spread like a star, arms and legs directed at the wide points in the building, my head to the west and the graveyard.

I remember that Peder's name means *rock*. I can call on the rock for help—yes, the same rock on which the castle was founded, the same rock that held me caught. Rock has no feelings, no intentions; it is there to be used.

I hum a little, down in my throat. I ask the place to show me its magic, and it does.

The walls melt away, and there I am in a wild midnight, with wind ruffling the trees, and those toothlike rocks (much sharper than they are now) piercing the stars. Far back in time.

I switch to a tune of making and unmaking, promising the land it will prosper if it grants me a favor. If it lets me borrow a little element of time.

The stone floor responds: It warms under me and begins to go soft.

"What's happening?" Tomas exclaims, as fearful as the landish are always said to be.

So he feels the change.

"Shh," I tell him. "Trust."

He still sits tense, radiating doubt. I think he could easily whisk Peder away and bring the wrath of the Baroness and the townspeople upon me. Or not so easily; I'd fight him if I had to.

Even without a confrontation, he poses a danger. His fear starts to drain the magic, and the floor grows a little cooler, a little harder.

"Maybe you should pray," I tell him. Let him call on the magic he knows.

Wonder of wonders, Tomas does trust me. He puts his hands together and points his face at the ceiling, where a couple of early morning doves are beating their wings and cooing softly to each other.

"O Father," he says, "who art in Heaven . . ."

While Tomas prays, I call on magic much older than his, from a time when the elements weren't so separate as they are now—a time when everything both *was* time and *was not,* because it lies beyond memory and forgetting.

Together, we bring Peder back.

Chapter 113

Life is pain.

It is a slow awakening, as from being deeply drunk. Or frozen, like the bodies of missing fishers and farmers sometimes found when the ice and snow begin to melt.

First, the prickling. Or rather, the pain—frozen fingers and toes thawing.

That pain is followed by others, worse ones, throughout Peder's body. Especially his heart. Something is squeezing his heart so it can't beat; something else is squeezing in order to force it to beat. He can't tell what these two somethings are, only that they might kill him. Again. If he isn't still (already?) dead, which he might be . . .

The pain. He cannot breathe for the pain. He sweats from it, and yet he's still very cold. Now it is worst in his head, behind his eyes, as if his brow is going to burst like an overripe peach and send his eyes flying like two pips. He can't see. He can't hear or smell. He tastes metal, which means he's tasting his own blood. Other than that, all he has is the pain, the intolerable ache that somehow he is tolerating.

Life, he thinks; *life is pain.*

Someone tried to tell him that once (an old man in a brown robe?), but Peder had no idea what it might mean until now, when pain is all he has and pain means he is alive and not dead.

Sometime in the future, if he has a future, he will think back on this moment and try to catalogue the pain: what part's a tingle, what part's a burn, and what's a dagger driving into his organs and stirring them as if he's a stew pot. He won't be able to describe this pain without comparing it to other things, and yet it is like nothing he's ever felt or imagined before. It's the great mystery at the center of life. It is life itself, which is pain.

So Peder circles the question of what's happening to his body. This is how his mind awakens from death, and how — questioning — he moves into the future.

After an eon of pain, Peder's eyelids flutter. He realizes his eyes have been open all this time. They're dry and they need his tears. He weeps; it is his first act in this second life.

Now he finds himself staring into the dark oaken underbelly of the church roof. The first thing he sees is a white dove in the rafters, tilting its head to gaze at him with one beady black eye. Then another alights beside that one, and the two doves study him. Then three.

His limbs are too heavy to move. His eyes, though, can roll from side to side. To the left, he sees Tomas praying, skin sallow in the faint light of dawn, mouse-brown hair falling on his neck as he raises his face Heavenward. He is praying for Peder with the words *salvation* and *Father* and *bless*.

Peder remembers calling this boy Chicken Legs — a lifetime (or a deathtime) ago.

And on Peder's right, there is the girl who was meant to be his wife. She seems to radiate a light of her own, with the skin of a pearl, eyes of pale emerald, hair the shade of a new sun after long winter.

Peder realizes she's naked. And beautiful. And singing. Her song is the source of his pain, but it also brings him pleasure. His newborn (that's how it feels, entirely new) sense of hearing takes pleasure in the voice that makes him tingle all over, though not in a way he's ever felt before. He wants to join in that song.

His throat makes a guttural noise, a grunt.

The singing stops and so does the prayer. Suddenly Tomas and Sanna — that's her name, a beautiful name — are leaning over him, their faces so close to his that he feels their breath stir his eyelashes.

"He's alive," Sanna says, and she sounds truly happy. Peder's heart aches again as it warms even more.

Tomas (*not* Chicken Legs; Peder will never use that name again) lays his head on Peder's chest. "Beating," he says, obviously struggling to stay calm. "Slow, but beating. He's really going to live!"

Peder wants to speak. He wants it very badly. But his lips won't move, and all that comes from his throat is another of those grunts.

"Shh." Sanna has her head on his chest now, listening for herself. "Don't try to speak. Save your breath."

Life is pain and breath is precious.

These seem like simple observations, but to Peder they are profound. When he has the strength, he will tell everyone.

anna

No one is more astonished than I: Peder is back from the dead.

I realize what a great gift this is, and what an achievement. It means I have real magic that can do good in the world.

For a long time, it's all I can do to gaze into Tomas's eyes, across Peder's sleeping, strengthening body, and be grateful.

A while later, it occurs to me that Sjældent was right: Peder is an everagain, who died from a fright and was reborn. Though not into polyp form, and not without help from the rest of us.

I am frightened, thinking of the power I seem now to possess.

Sanna the Meek.

I am exhausted.

Later (How much later? The idea of measuring time still means nothing), it's as if I awake from a dream. I remember Thyrla, who—unlike Sjældent—was alive when I left her. If she knows her son is also alive now, she'll surely come after him. We have to protect Peder.

Nonetheless, I can't take my eyes away from Tomas's. I see in his a reflection of myself, but it is a reflection amplified and enhanced.

I see trust. And faith. And I realize I couldn't have saved Peder by myself. Tomas has a kind of magic, too.

Looking at him, I tingle.

Time does not stay still for us, though I could not say or even guess how much of it goes by before I think of the others. The landish people and the seavish *flok*—the rest of the dead and the ones who lured them to death.

"We have to go," I say, breaking the spell that has held Tomas and me rapt.

"Why?" he asks, and there is a world of questions in that single word.

"We might be able to help others."

I think I can hear the *marreminder* delivering bodies to the docks as I asked them to do. I know I hear (and smell) the landish *flok* opening their doors to start the day.

"Ah." Tomas looks away from me and down at Peder. "What should we do about him?"

450

"I think he should come with us."

I don't tell Tomas that this is more for Peder's protection than for any help he might be; realistically, Peder will offer no help at all. He'll be physically weak and mentally—well, I don't know how death has affected him, but he wasn't very smart before he died. Still, as one who died and then returned, he may be of some inspiration to families who lost loved ones.

Tomas seems to understand. He puts his hands on Peder's shoulders and shakes him.

Peder's head lolls like a baby's, but he wakes. He opens his mouth to speak, or so I expect. Nothing but a grunt, then another, and then a harsh sound like a landish animal's bleat.

Tomas and I look at each other. Silently, we agree to go on—maybe Peder will speak with more time to recover. Again we are grateful, so very grateful and relieved, that our two magics succeeded.

Since we're to go out into the town, I look for something to put over myself and hide my nakedness from people who might find it shocking. I find a cloth on the altar; it makes enough of a dress to be decent and carries some landish magic, too.

Tomas and I sling Peder's arms around our necks. We stand him up, straighten his clothes, and walk him out the hole that's been cut for a chapel, into the fragile light of dawn.

Chapter 115

The sun rises over landish dead.

When the sun starts its daily climb into the sky, Dark Moon Harbor begins its morning as usual. Grieving the people may be, but there are animals to feed and milk, nets to mend, food to put away for winter, night soil to carry outside and dispose of in gutters and kitchen gardens.

This is how they discover it, a sight that to some is even more shocking than the transformation of the roses or the shift in Our Lady's pose: They see bodies, dozens of them, lined up neatly on the docks and drying in a cool breeze, under a pastel sky, by smooth bay waters without so much as a ripple on the glassy surface.

The people drop their pots, splashing their feet with their own waste. They run for the docks to see who is there.

News of this sort travels fast, even to the shops and farms out of view. Soon the broad street is clogged with people eager to find a loved one or simply curious about the Dark Islands' strangest event yet.

They fall upon the corpses—husbands, daughters, sons, sweethearts—and weep.

"If only I'd been there to stop it!" so many accuse themselves. But they weren't there when their precious ones died; they have just the report from Tomas and his family to go on. No words can express the allure of the ocean's song, the ache it created along with the conviction that the fire inside could be satisfied only by a cold plunge into the sea and a union with the singers.

The great wonder is how these bodies were recovered and laid out here to find—but it is better to have a body to part with than it is to have questions, so for a moment the people take the chance to say goodbye. Still, of course, angry over the means of their parting: the treachery of the sea, the seduction of its creatures.

The docks quake and splinter under the weight of bodies living and dead. The wood itself groans as if mourning the losses.

Then the crowd in the broad street parts, and Sanna appears.

Hearts leap; blood quickens. The people call her name. If anyone can comfort them, she is the one.

"Sanna!"

"Sister!"

"Sanna!"

Wrapped in linen embroidered by townswomen long

since passed, hair flying, eyes glowing like the green lights that streak the sky in winter, she is an angel in the thinnest of robes, with the fiercest of hearts. She looks like a somewhat different person, or *personage*, than she was just yesterday. She looks like a savior.

No one now remembers seeing Sanna walk naked through town — or if someone does recall it, that person is sure it's an unholy dream and keeps the memory to himself.

Later, there will be some who swear they hear the great Sanna's heart beat as she passes. There are others who report seeing her squint as she looks out to sea, as if she finds some message there, in the element that robbed these people of their lives.

Another fact will surprise them: Very few notice Peder beside her. Only later will they realize that he's there, and not acting as his usual self. He is quiet and not nearly as golden as he's seemed in the past. Much later, they'll realize he was recently as dead as these bloated bodies on the docks, and that his resurrection is Sanna's third miracle.

Absolutely no one, not even Tomas's family, sees that boy formerly called Chicken Legs on Peder's other side. Sanna's brilliance outshines both boys — for now. Later they'll learn what a part Tomas has played in the third miracle, and they'll love him all the more for it. He's one of them, but he has done wonders.

When Sanna first appears, the people don't dare to hope there can be any change in the corpses' condition, other than perhaps a safe passage from this world to the next, with a good word put in by Sanna to the One who will judge them. They stand mutely behind the bodies, pleading with their eyes, asking her to bless their dead.

When she reaches the first corpses (an Erik and a Hans, both fishermen), Sanna hesitates. Perhaps she's waiting for an invitation that doesn't come — that *cannot* come, because no one dares to voice or even think it. Without Father Abel, there is no one who has the authority to request a miracle.

This is when a few townsfolk do notice Peder and the fact that he is atypically silent and dull-looking. As Sanna bends down to examine Erik and Hans, Peder's weight transfers to Tomas's shoulders, making Tomas visible, too. But Peder's expression — one of astonishment combined with fatigue — does not change.

Sanna squats, then kneels, between Erik and Hans. She bites her lower lip, draws a breath, and puts her hands on Erik's head the way she did when blessing people in the town two days ago. She says the same words, too: "May the Lord bless thee."

She waits.

The people wait.

Nothing happens; Erik is dead.

Sanna moves on to Hans, who was so good at mending nets. She positions her hands as before, says the same words as before. And, as before, there is no change.

The onlookers feel their hearts sink.

Sanna crawls to the next body, which has a mostly dry

apron draped over the face. She pulls away the apron and sees Kett.

Blue lips, blue eyes staring up at the nothing-sky.

Sanna's breath catches in her throat and her fingers fly to her own lips. Her brow ripples with wrinkles, and she looks again like a different girl—a different angel, one of the wrathful, avenging sort, perhaps.

Kett's mother, Birgit, weeps helplessly.

"Never so beautiful as she was these last days," she says. "Coming into her own, was my girl." She looks up at Sanna and begs, "Please bless her. Or if you can—If you can—"

It's clear what she wishes, though she doesn't dare to ask outright.

Sanna understands. She says, "I can try." She hitches up the altar cloth, which is slipping from her shoulders and breasts, and leans over her friend. She takes Kett's head in her long fingers. This time, she speaks different words.

"May you be blessed," she says. Then adds, "May you be as alive as you wish to be in this one moment."

There is a pause. Everyone watches, from the townspeople to the *marreminder* at sea—though they haven't been spotted as yet.

Again, nothing. Sanna might have no powers at all, or this might not be her miracle to perform.

Suddenly, and on impulse, Sanna swoops down like a bird. She presses her lips to Kett's brow in a kiss.

Then patience is rewarded. When Sanna sits back on her heels, Kett coughs, and sputters, and heaves a full stomach's worth of seawater onto the dock. Sanna makes no comment but turns Kett's head lest the girl drown herself again.

Kett's mother, however, flings herself down among the corpses and kisses the hem of Sanna's garment, which is also the hem of the altar cloth (which will seem odd only when people talk of it later).

"Bless you, Sister!" she cries, before shifting to gather Kett in her arms and dot her face with maternal kisses. "Bless you, Sanna!"

The town is too excited to cheer, but the pounding of their hearts makes a noise nearly as loud.

This becomes the way Sanna works with the dead; these are the words she says over and over. She goes from one body to the next, drags the hair from a sufferer's face, and cups the head in her hands, saying —

"May you be blessed." With a kiss for the cold brow.

And: "May you be as alive as you wish to be in this one moment."

It is a strange sort of speech, but it makes miracles. Over and over again.

Her two helpers, Tomas and Peder (still uncharacteristically silent), help those who awake to sit up, vomit, expel the water from their lungs, and ease back into the pain of living.

The reborn people blink and cough and rasp and stretch. They cannot believe they've survived the pain of dying, or that the pain of being resuscitated is so great. At first, life seems a curse, and more than one of them wishes to die again, to escape the pain. But then pain fades, and they see the pink-and-gray sky, feel the brisk air and light rain on their cheeks, feel themselves lifted into the arms of the people they love. After that, not one of them would trade life for death.

And yet they have made a trade of sorts. Peder is not the only one to have left something on the other side of death's curtain. Each person who comes back is missing some ability that was once taken for granted.

Some, like Peder, no longer speak, though they understand when spoken to. Some cannot see, though they have words to describe their blindness. Kett is one of these; she'll never be able to admire her own complexion again. Some can't feel heat or cold or even the prick of a thorn, and it will be days or weeks before they understand that this is not a blessing but a burden.

Every person who's revived has also gained something, other than simply life. As they mourn what they've lost and rejoice at living again, they find they're much more kindly disposed to one another. A blind man helps a crippled one stand, and a deaf child leads them down a path to their home.

In death they have found each other.

To the town's surprise, there are some souls who do not awake. These Sanna might kiss twice rather than once (as she does with Erik and Hans), but when offered the choice to live or remain dead, they choose death. Nonetheless, they undergo a change of their own; their faces re-form into smiles.

Sanna pulls the lids over these persons' eyes and leaves them apparently blissful in Heaven. Their families fall upon Sanna and kiss her dress, her feet, her hands, every bit as grateful (almost) as the families of those who awake.

Neither Peder nor Tomas seems surprised at any revival. Sanna, however, gasps each time a chest fills with air and blue skin turns to living pink. Such is her modesty, and the people love her even more for it.

Among the bodies on the docks, there are two notables missing: Baroness Thyrla and Father Abel. No one but Tomas and his family and Old Olla can describe exactly what caused the rest of the wedding visitors to fling themselves into the sea, and they are close-lipped about it. But the awakened dead remember the voices, and they describe that beautiful sound as soon as they have air enough for speech.

"Sirens," they say. "Mermaids."

At last, there it is: the dreaded word, for all people of Dark Moon Harbor fear mermaids as much as they lust for them.

Though the families accept this cause of death, what they don't understand is how the bodies of nearly all the victims ended up here, on the docks — or why. They agree it must have something to do with Sanna, as all good things must; but there are some phenomena that surpass all sorts of faith, and this is one of them.

The mermaids killed; Sanna heals.

Everyone — *everyone* — thinks, though only a few voice it: "If only Father Abel were here." He would know how to interpret the day.

They look for him on the docks; they look for him in the crowd. But it seems the priest is gone for good.

"To a better place," they say, as he's said each time one of them lost someone dear.

"The Lord's plan."

"But wouldn't he have loved to see . . ."

Of course he would. And since he can't, they watch with extra-sharp eyes (those who can see), and they listen with keener ears (those who can hear), and they savor every smell and taste and touch. Pleasure in small things once again mingles with the obvious pain of this life.

It is eventually presumed that Abel and Thyrla also fell victim to the mermaids' song. And perhaps their bodies, more precious than others, stayed with the mermaids.

It's almost midday before a few children spot heads bobbing in the bay, at just the distance for watching what's happening in the town. By then most of the drowning victims have been moved to their homes, to rest up after the toll that death and rebirth have taken.

The men and women who remain dismiss what the children see. "Only seals," they say. "Mermaids don't return their prey, and they don't watch to see what happens next."

No matter who or what is out in the bay, on shore there

are some easily recognized truths, and they need neither Abel nor Thyrla to confirm.

For one, this is clearly the third miracle, and the greatest of all: It will make Sanna a saint.

For two, within the town and all over the islands, for as long as she is remembered, Sanna will be much more than a saint. She is an angel, and she has done an angel's work.

And for three, Dark Moon Harbor will never again be what it was, a handful of pebbles thrown into the sea to try men's souls.

It is now a town of love.

anna

When it's all finished and each body has been declared officially alive or dead and walked or carried away, I sit with Tomas and Peder on the splintering edge of a dock. Our feet dangle over the water, and we lean into each other, looking out over the seaskin, which appears impenetrable as it reflects the blue of the midsun sky.

Appears impenetrable, that is. I know my *flok* is out there, Father and Addra and all. They are waiting for me to go away with them.

Peder is the first to speak. Or to do what must now be called speaking for him, a series of grunts that ends with a sob, as he's frustrated by having lost articulate speech. He's not likely to sing again, for example, and it might be said that there are some people who are glad.

Tomas, somehow, is able to translate those grunts. "He says we need to go to the castle and look for his mother."

I turn to Peder, the boy who was supposed to become my husband. "Don't you know what she planned to do to you? Or to our children, if she thought they could give her something more than you could?"

He grunts again, then shrugs, then shakes himself in frustration.

Tomas translates: "He says we need to be sure the islands are safe for everyone. He can't do it alone."

I feel a rush of affection for Peder. He is a better person than I thought he was, certainly far less selfish. Maybe it's a result of having died and come back; he left some of his vanity behind.

"He's right," Tomas says. "I don't know what the Baroness was doing in that room, but I know it was evil. I know she wanted to kill you, Sanna." He pauses, damp-faced, chewing his lip. Then admits, "I had a chance to kill her and I didn't. A chance to let her die—but I didn't. I spared her."

My bones ache. Even my blood aches. "I don't think I have any magic left," I confess.

Then comes one of those coincidences that almost make me believe as the landish do, that there is a single author of our lives who arranges events for convenience.

We hear the sound of feet on earth, staggering under a weight, and we turn.

Coming down the broad street, retrieved from the house that was keeping her safe, we see Our Lady of the Sea. She is riding on a platform held by six strong men singing a landish church song. The whole town seems to be with her, a mass of brown clothes and beaming faces beneath and behind that bright yellow robe, that bubbly face, those off-kilter eyes that seem to look everywhere and nowhere at once. I recognize Tomas's family and Old Olla the bee-keeper. Kett and her mother.

Her mother — oh, Lisabet!

How am I ever to find Lisabet now? I don't think I should try. Alone in this great world without a teacher . . .

Not alone. I have friends: Tomas stands, then helps me and Peder.

"The people love you," he says. And as if to prove it, Kett comes running blindly into my arms, gushing, "Oh, miss! Oh, Sanna!" And it is everything.

In her embrace, I feel the altar cloth slipping off me. I wrap it a little tighter around. I find myself moved to tears.

Peder makes some noise, and Tomas translates: "I won-der if we'll finally see what Our Lady has in her arms."

Chapter 117

The puzzle of it.

This is the puzzle of it: No one can agree as to what Our Lady of the Sea is holding.

Some say it's a baby. The Christ, the baby that most Our Ladies were created to hold. But this is the most obvious interpretation, and one at which others will scoff. *You see only what you were trained to see*, they say. And maybe that's true.

There are some from the town who see not a baby but—improbably—a fish. Yes, they say Our Lady of the Sea is cuddling a salmon, looking lovingly down into its round wooden eye. These people are the fishers and net-makers, those for whom everything eventually becomes fishy—as their detractors will point out.

To some with far-seeing eyes and adventurous spirits, what the Lady holds is a ship. Its stern points upward and its sails fold into her robe.

There are a few, a very few — and Sanna and Tomas are among them — who see none of these things. They don't even see yellow or white or gray, the colors in which Our Lady has traditionally been painted.

They see red.

They see a heart.

It is a human heart, the size of a fist and knobbly with veins. So small, really. But it is beating: *Thump. Thump. Thump.*

How many miracles does that make for our town? ask the people who love numbers and facts.

No one can count; numbers don't matter. What matters is this: the day, the wonder, the grace God has granted through the hands and blood and work of the girl who walked out of the sea, when the moon was half-made — a form that from now on will be called *mermaid moon.*

• Chapter 118 •

anna

These past days have been a tumble of magic and curses and luck, culminating with this red heart held by the woman Sjældent promised would help.

Of course I know Our Lady of the Sea isn't alive; she can't have intentions of helping or harming, the way Thyrla and Sjældent could. But someday *none* of us will be alive anymore, and what will remain but what we have wished?

The heart is the world, and it is home. It tells me what I must do.

I say my goodbyes to Dark Moon Harbor. Not in such a way as to make it clear that I am in fact leaving, but in a way the people will understand later. And I do my best to help the landish *flok* recover from the upheavals of these last few days.

I go with them to the castle. We search the rooms for Thyrla and don't find her. We count the boats in her private harbor. No one can agree how many are normally present and whether there's a change in the number now, but everyone agrees she has fled — perhaps following the siren songs, her body unrecovered; perhaps escaped with a crew that moved on after the rose-petal storm and before the deathly singing.

Myself, I'm convinced she is dead. I can picture her jumping after Peder and me; the slap of the seaskin would break all her bones, but still she would try to follow. I imagine burying her in the cell where she kept me, inside the rock watched over by her dragon. But I also know that where she ends up doesn't matter; what matters is how the people who relied on her (in a way) manage to live with her gone.

Peder is now Baron of the Thirty-Seven Dark Islands.

He isn't ready. He's too young, he can't speak, and he knows nothing but how to take silly pleasure in the world.

But to his credit, even he knows he can't manage the place alone. So he asks Tomas to be his steward.

Tomas shocks everyone, including me. He declines. "I don't know any more than you do," he tells Peder. "You should take advice from your mother's men, the ones who have been working for you all along."

Peder agrees. At least, we think that's what he means when he grunts.

"The first thing you must do," I say, "is to wall off your mother's chamber with mortar and rock. Don't go inside — just close it off and forget it ever was made." It's best that no one, especially Peder, sees that place.

So that's where the workers go first.

As I listen to the scrapes of their trowels, spreading mortar over rock three feet thick, I know I'll be leaving the castle and the town with the best possible future. The remains of Thyrla's malicious craft will be locked away, not to be found until, perhaps, the castle sinks into the sea, sometime far in the future.

But I know, too, that malice has a way of resurging, no matter how it's sealed.

Chapter 119

The marreminder *know.*

Addra and Shusha, La and Mar, Gurria and Frill and Pippa and all the rest: While Sanna works her magic of making and unmaking on the docks, they watch the ship that departs from the castle's hidden harbor.

It is a small ship, barely more than a boat, and it flies the flag of a land far to the south. There is only one sailor: a very old woman who can hardly guide the rudder, let alone trim the sails by herself.

"Should we go?" asks Frill, now known as the Tender of Heart. "Should we help her?"

It's perhaps only natural to offer, after seeing Sanna heal so many of the landish dead.

But: "No," say the elders, as the boat zigzags sluggishly to sea. "Let this one go. Let her find her own way."

"She'll be dead when the first big wave hits her!"

"Then," Bjarl says, uncharacteristically grim, "that is her way."

They don't have to wait long. The little boat is still in sight when (for no reason anyone can see or make sense of) it rolls onto its side like a seal.

The old woman who was trying to sail it—for a moment she's a bright spot on the seaskin, and then a current pulls her under. It is one of the so-called trade currents that run to the south and east.

At last, with dead eyes silver and purple and pink staring round, Baroness Thyrla is going to see the world. She simply won't be alive when she does it.

anna

Now it's a matter of moments till I'm seavish again for good. I yearn for the open water, new lands, the experiences of a wider life. I look forward to seeing La reunite with her Ishi, and to looking for Lisabet again. And honing my magic for the good of the *flok* that waits out in the bay.

There is one important goodbye before I go, one friend who has helped me in every way possible on this last, very long day.

Tomas and I meet in the five-sided courtyard. The rose vine is now naked and dry; the sap has retreated deep into the branches for winter, and the petals have all blown away. It looks as if nothing special ever happened here.

The place seems very small, too small to once have held so many townspeople and so much magic. It may have been the wrong place to begin my landish quest, but it's the right place to end for now. Father is waiting in the waters just beyond; it's time for my *flok* to swim south. La's quest.

I begin my leave-taking.

"Tomas—"

He interrupts: "Can I come with you?"

So he's already guessed that I'm going. But he hasn't guessed everything.

"You don't know what you're asking," I tell him.

"I think I do."

"Tomas, I didn't come here in a boat . . ."

"You're a mermaid," he says. "I can see it now—I don't know why it never occurred to any of us. A mermaid's much more likely to come aground here than one of Abel's Catholic saints."

For a moment I'm afraid. I know what happened to his father, and the long history of conflict between our peoples.

"I may be a mermaid," I say cautiously, "but I never meant to hurt anyone. My clan is not naturally hostile."

Despite what Shusha explained to me about why *marreminder* sing against sailors who might rape us, I think I see good in both landish and seavish generally—with a few obvious exceptions.

The rose vine creaks as if to agree with me, but of course it's just shrinking into itself for the season. It holds the heart of the castle, setting the rhythm to which the island *flok* live.

"I know that," Tomas says. His blue eyes are trusting; I think how strange it is that I didn't notice him much before.

"And I know you're a witch of some kind, too. You obviously have a way of changing yourself. Can you change me?"

"I think so," I say, still cautious. "If I can turn a person from dead to living, I can probably change a landman to a seavish one." I have more confidence now than when Bjarl asked me to transform him; I'd never changed anyone but myself then, but now . . .

Tomas breaks into my thoughts. "You say you believe you can," he says, "but *will* you? Change me?"

I hesitate, looking into his eyes and seeing his history there, along with his future—not just the father lost at sea but also a hunger for the great world, so similar to my own. And his hunger for me.

He doesn't have to say it, but he does anyway: "Sanna, I love you."

At that, my heart leaps like a moon-skipper. Another world is opening up, into an element even more expansive than time. And I don't believe I used a single jolt of magic to make it happen.

He's looking at me, I think, the way Father looked at Lisabet, and she at him. But I can't look back the same way, not yet.

"Tomas—" I begin (for the second time).

He hears *no* in my voice and won't let me finish. "I suppose you'd rather take Peder," he says, not bitterly or sadly, just stating a fact. "He loves you, too, you know. He can't say it now, but he loved you from the moment you arrived.

I suppose he'd make a rather good husband after all that's happened."

The specialness of the moment seeps away with each word, finally vanishing with *husband*.

"I don't love Peder," I say. "I might love you—but I don't think you should come with me now."

Tomas's face brightens, then falls. "Why not?"

How can I explain? There is so much left for me to do, and I could be an entirely different person by the time the moon is halved again. Time is moving faster than I ever thought possible, and I'm only starting to get the knack of it.

"Stay here for now," I say. "With your family. Peder can use help from all of you, and from Kett."

"Kett?"

"I have a feeling about those two," I say, and I hope I'm right.

"But," Tomas insists, "what do you feel about *me*?"

There will always be that question between land and sea. We don't experience emotions the same way, or at least when we do it is rare. Like my parents, whose love will be one for the songs and the books, if only it can be remembered.

I tell Tomas, "I'll come back. We can decide then."

With that, he has to be satisfied.

Well, with that and one more thing: I press my lips to his.

Now, I actually enjoy the landish custom of kissing.

anna

This would be a fine way to leave, a most excellent goodbye. But it is not, after all, my last moment in the Dark Islands.

Tomas and I aren't the only people who care about the courtyard and the rose vine. Old Olla, the beekeeper—she cares just as much. And here she comes, with one arm crooked in Peder's and the other in Kett's, to tuck the vine in for the winter. As she explains.

"My bees will go to sleep," she says. "And so will I—you know how it is for old people." She touches the vine as if taking its pulse, then straightens a bit, looks at me, and cries, "Oh, it's you! How wonderful!"

I'm used to her by now. I smile gently and take her bony hand in mine. She is another castaway on these shores; as she said in her cottage, Baroness Thyrla—acting with kindness for perhaps the only time in her life—took her in, fixed her up, and gave her the cottage and bees.

Except that Thyrla is never, ever kind, unless she wants to take something—magic, years, *time*—from someone.

My heart leaps like a fish. I have to swallow hard before I can speak.

"Olla," I ask, "exactly how long have you lived here?"

"Oh." Her head wobbles vaguely, and the last bees in her hair shake loose, fly about, then settle again. She repeats herself: "You know how it is for old people. I can't remember. I can't remember where I was yesterday, either." She touches the rose vine again.

I turn to Tomas. "Do you recall a time when Olla didn't live here?"

He frowns. I think he doesn't like how crowded the yard has become, though Peder and Kett have wandered off to sit in the niche of the dais. I believe I was right about them . . .

"I don't remember," he says. "But I'm only seventeen."

Land holds on too long.

I was so certain. But it was too much to hope.

Sadly, I, too, touch the rose vine—still holding Olla's hand—and I feel a jolt. Along with the vine, Olla has magic. Or she has been magicked.

Now I'm sure. I run. Pulling Olla along with me, out through the gate to the water, where Father waits.

"Bjarl!" I call his name. "Bjarl!"

Once ye find her, ye may find her changed, Sjældent warned me. She can't have been lying about everything.

Father's head pops above the seaskin. Tomas, who has followed us, gasps.

"Father, do you know this woman?" I ask.

His brow is furrowed; his lips make a frown. "Sanna, it's time to go," he says. "The *flok* is waiting."

"Do you know her?"

Olla laughs suddenly. She's confused; laughing is her way of shedding some sorrow. I wait for her usual exclamation — *Oh, it's you!* — but it doesn't come, even though she gazes at Father a long time.

Maybe it's only the curiosity of landish toward seavish. Unless . . .

It flashes into my mind, the right question. I ask: *"Have you forgotten each other?"*

And then there we are.

"Lisabet," says my father.

"Mother," I say.

"Oh," she says, blinking, "it's *you*."

Epilogue

This time, too, shall pass.

Deep in the rock under the castle, the dragon yawns. She feels a pain in her side like the pangs of her youth, when she was no bigger than a lizard and boys used to stab her with pins. It starts her calcified heart beating.

They learned their lesson soon enough.

The dragon breathes in, breathes out, sees the fire from her nostrils gleam over heaps of gold and precious stones. She counts it all: Nothing is gone.

The pain's not so bad after all, only what every aging creature should expect. And as long as she's awake, she can give herself a good scratch. Old scales fly off to make space for the new. They *plink* on the walls and make a softer bed for her bones.

It is then that she notices a crack in one wall. Has there been an intruder? Or just the settling of time?

Someday she might learn the reasons. For now, yawning again, she blows flames over the crack, melting it into a seam and then to a spot so smooth that it blends with the rest of her perfectly ordered lair.

She lays her head on a foreleg.

This time, too, shall pass, till even the songs are forgotten and there's no creature left except her.

Her heart slows again, and she sleeps.

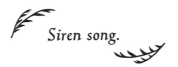 Siren song.

This is just a children's tale; would you wreck
    your ship for it?
Would you drown for a mere mother's story?
It's only blood that calls to blood.
Our voices are foam on the sea!
                                    —The Mermaids

I really do know the gender of worker bees. They're female, just like the queen — but for centuries they were thought to be male, just as the people of Dark Moon Harbor believe their legendary dragon to be masculine. In the Western Middle Ages, it was impossible to think the workers and dragons could *not* be male.

The legends we think we know are the dreams of dragons within the rock. Every old story is syncretic, meaning each person who tells it builds on the foundations of even older tales. And we've reached an epoch in which, perhaps more than at any past time, we're reconstructing our storyscape: Our heroes, like our dragons, are turning out to be something other than what we were told they would be.

I think there's a special potential in the old siren stories. Yes, mermaids are beautiful, but if you look beneath the poems and songs about their seduction (being both seductive themselves and highly seducible by men), they are much more than that.

Mermaids have been with us for millennia — sometimes beneath the seaskin of our culture, sometimes bursting through to the sun. They're in folktales from virtually every people who live near an ocean, lake, or river, and those stories stretch back further than we can trace. They appear in the "high literature" of Homer and Hans Christian Andersen, the lush paintings of John William Waterhouse and Knut Ekwall, and the decals we stick onto our windows or backpacks. They swim into ancient maps and last week's movies.

They started for me with my mother, who was proud of being named after a Danish *havfrue* and who told me to make sure she became foam on the sea when she died, like the mermaid in Andersen's story (which, incidentally, I wouldn't allow myself to read while I was writing this one). And I did make sure a spoonful of my mother's ashes is now scoured into the sand below Copenhagen's Little Mermaid statue, where the lore of Hanne Agnethe Rasmussen Cokal mingles with that of Andersen's forlorn siren. I like to think my mum loves having her picture taken thousands of times every day.

No matter how many mermaid tales I read in my childhood, something always bothered me: These legendary creatures have the power to sing humans out of their minds, to wreck ships, to circle the globe — that is, the mer-*maids* have that power — but still, the old stories put men at the center of seavish culture. In the imagination of past centuries, seavish civilization was ruled by kings; when mermaids came to land, it was usually because they'd fallen in love with some landish man.

I'm all for love and good government, but why should the most powerful creatures in the stories, the ones who can ruin or save you — *and* the ones who can change their bodies to walk on land if they choose — still be a subject class? Why don't they run the show?

It seems to me that *marreminder* must always have been a female-centric group, matriarchal and matrilocal and matrilineal (to use anthropological terms). If you can summon so much magic, if you can be at home both at sea and on land, I think you want to do more than tie yourself to some landlocked prince or farmer. Or, at least, you want to see a bit of the world before making the choice to stay with your true love, whoever she, he, or they might be. So my *marreminder* are a nomadic clowder in which women wield most of the power and (for one girl, at least) the form a body takes is a matter of individual choice. It seems an adjustment to legend befitting our era.

These mermaids don't settle in one place. They don't have calendars or clocks. Their history melts away in the waves, preserved only in song. So how is it possible to imagine a historical tale for them?

When I was first thinking about Sanna and where she might go if she came to land, one of the images that came to my mind was the church that stands at the top of Dark Moon Harbor's broad street. I saw the jagged rocks at the base and the more evenly cut stone blocks fitted into them and rising into a simple nave and bell tower—meaning I saw a Viking shrine or burial place with a Christian church built on top of it. And who knows what might have been there before the Vikings? I have a few ideas . . .

What I do know is that the magic—or faith, religion, spirit, however you think of it—in that place endures for the people who know it, and the spells and miracles worked in the spot grow stronger with years of accumulated faith. That is, faith is constantly reinvented on a single foundation, whatever trappings of story are built above it. Many of the holiest places today are connected with ancient religions that have left little or no trace.

Everyone knows that we build new civilizations on the

ashes of the old. A new sovereign—or emperor, or dictator, or president—moves into the castle of the one defeated. Or a warlord or -lady builds a fortress over a dragon's lair; then someone else comes along, storms the fortress, and adds on to it, making a castle or palace.

This process, known as syncretism, is especially common with religious sites. When a conquering horde arrives, they find the old sacred spots, tear down the shrines that stand there, and put up new ones for their own gods. The people who have lived there long and the ones who have newly moved in keep the habit of visiting that spot, though they worship differently now. Paradoxically, it's a way of including all beliefs and building on them, while still making sure that the conqueror gets final say.

So it happened, for example, with Istanbul's Hagia Sophia. The church turned mosque turned museum has been one of the world's most visited and admired works of architecture for about fourteen hundred years; in remnants and relics, it shows the changing ideas and ideals of the people who live around and go inside it. If you visit, you'll see marble carvings that date to the 400s, Byzantine mosaics depicting Christian tales, enormous tiled domes and minarets in the Ottoman style, and informative placards written up by archaeologists and curators to explain it all for the modern tourist. The place is a model mixture of faiths and ideas by which one culture seems to dominate while drawing in believers who have gone before.

The church in Dark Moon Harbor, with its jagged rocks from the Viking age, is my personal Hagia Sophia. I also imagine Thyrla's castle existing long before the Christians arrived in the Islands. The story of the dragon, like the stories of *marre-minder*, must reach far, far back in time — even further than the Vikings — to as long as people have lived in that bleak north.

Syncretism depends on a certain idea of time, an orderly progression forward and a chain of substitutions linked by causality. But I am no longer certain that time works in that linear way. I wrote this book while sick for what a conventional sense of time would measure in years. My body felt stuck in a Down-Below-Deep in which time was both suspended and jumbled: I couldn't feel it marching forward as we're taught to believe it does. Instead, I felt all times of my life swirling together. I still feel that. Moments from my childhood seem as real and recent as something that happened only a week ago — more real, in fact, and more recent, because I can recall them better. What matters most now is the intensity of emotion associated with each event, not the order in which those events occurred. While each memory does have a certain chain of causes that might move forward for a few minutes, overall it's like looking at a rolled-up Turkish carpet in which the patterns are touching each other and connected more by color and outline than by a traditional structure.

That's how I've come to think of time and memory and stories in general: The important ones stick with us and keep surfacing throughout our lives. Like the mermaids.

I am grateful to the *flok* who have pulled up the good memories and kept me swimming. Thanks to Marjorie, Gigi, Henry, Emily, Steve, and Mindy for the story-specific statuettes and trinkets that hung around my bookshelves for inspiration.

Siren songs to Danny, Michele, Sarah, Gunver, Sue, Lynne, al, Andrea, Josie, and Sachi for not forgetting, and to Clara for being the next-generation mermaid. Starry appreciation to Julie Anderson, who is the thoughtful early reader everybody hopes to have. Greg Weatherford is everything good and especially my husband, who puts the world into order and helps me find the *becauses.*

From the deepest of depths, I thank the Candlewick cohort, starting with the incomparable Liz Bicknell, who was my friend before she became my editor (the very best order for such matters); and Miriam Newman, Sherry Fatla, Pam Consolazio, Jackie Houton, and Erin DeWitt, who scarcely miss a scale. And also my agent, Stephen Barbara, who wheels and deals in gentlemanly fashion.

There is no friend like the one you meet when young and who stays with you through the decades. If you haven't found that friend yet, keep the faith; they come along when you least expect. I was lucky to meet Leslie Hayes when I was an extremely shy and nerdy fourteen, and to learn that she has a remarkable talent for liking people, including (miraculously) me.

Sea or land, forever my clan: This story is for you.